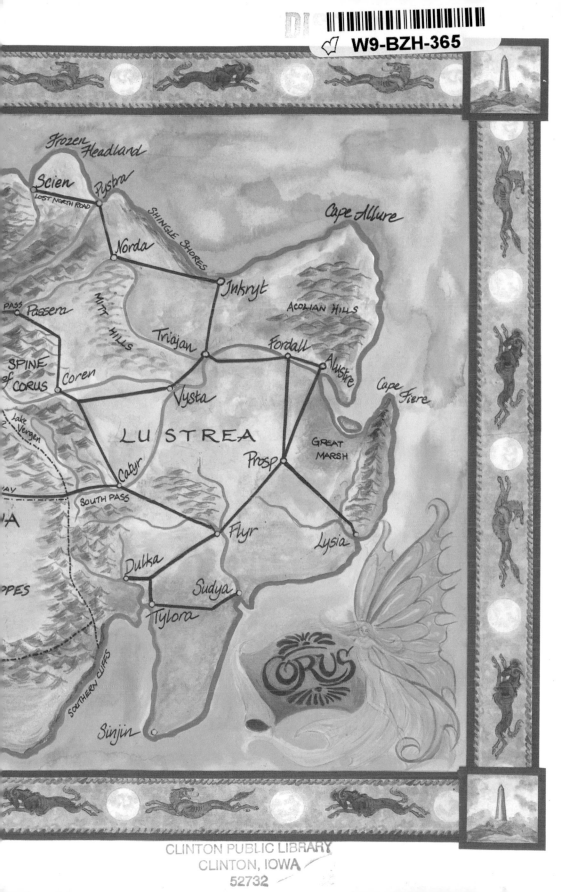

THE LORD-PROTECTOR'S
⊁DAUGHTER⊰

TOR BOOKS BY L. E. MODESITT, JR.

THE COREAN CHRONICLES
Legacies
Darknesses
Scepters
Alector's Choice
Cadmian's Choice
Soarer's Choice
The Lord-Protector's Daughter

THE SAGA OF RECLUCE
The Magic of Recluce
The Towers of the Sunset
The Magic Engineer
The Order War
The Death of Chaos
Scion of Cyador
Fall of Angels
The Chaos Balance
The White Order
Colors of Chaos
Magi'i of Cyador
Wellspring of Chaos
Ordermaster
Natural Ordermage
Mage-Guard of Hamor

THE SPELLSONG CYCLE
The Soprano Sorceress
The Spellsong War
Darksong Rising
The Shadow Sorceress
Shadowsinger

THE IMAGER PORT
Imager*

THE ECOLITAN MATTER
Empire & Ecolitan
(comprising The Ecolitan
Operation and The Ecologic
Secession)

Ecolitan Prime
(comprising The Ecologic Envoy
and The Ecolitan Engima)
The Forever Hero
(comprising Dawn for a Distant
Earth, The Silent Warrior, and
In Endless Twilight)

Timegod's World
(comprising Timediver's Dawn
and The Timegod)

THE GHOST BOOKS
Of Tangible Ghosts
The Ghost of the Revelator
Ghost of the White Nights
Ghost of Columbia
(comprising Of Tangible Ghosts
and The Ghost of the Revelator)

The Hammer of Darkness
The Green Progression
The Parafaith War
Adiamante
Gravity Dreams
Octagonal Raven
Archform: Beauty
The Ethos Effect
Flash
The Eternity Artifact
The Elysium Commission

*Forthcoming

L. E. MODESITT, JR.

THE LORD-PROTECTOR'S
❋DAUGHTER❋

The Seventh Book of the Corean Chronicles

 A Tom Doherty Associates Book
New York

THE LORD-PROTECTOR'S DAUGHTER: THE SEVENTH BOOK OF THE COREAN CHRONICLES

Copyright © 2008 by L. E. Modesitt, Jr.

Parts of this book appeared in the August 2007 issue of *Jim Baen's Universe,* also under the title of "The Lord-Protector's Daughter."

A Tor Book
Published by Tom Doherty Associates, LLC
175 Fifth Avenue
New York, NY 10010

www.tor-forge.com

Tor® is a registered trademark of Tom Doherty Associates, LLC.

Library of Congress Cataloging-in-Publication Data

Modesitt, L. E.
    The lord-protector's daughter / L.E. Modesitt, Jr.—1st ed.
        p.   cm.—(Book 7 of the Corean chronicles)
    "A Tom Doherty Associates book."
    ISBN-13: 978-0-7653-2163-3
    ISBN-10: 0-7653-2163-7
    1. Corus (Imaginary place)—Fiction. I. Title. II. Series: Modesitt, L. E. Corean chronicles. 7th.
    PS3563.O264L67 2008
    813'.54—dc22   2008035104

First Edition: November 2008

Printed in the United States of America

0 9 8 7 6 5 4 3 2 1

For Eric Flint, without whom this book would not exist.

The river boiled, and blood turned to ice,
And Alectors fell to the soarers' device,
Yet deep in the void, they lurk in the dark
Awaiting the time to return to their mark.

Who will protect those who remain;
Whose Talent will our lives sustain?
Lord-Protector, daughter or son,
In whose blood will Talent so run?

THE LORD-PROTECTOR'S
DAUGHTER

1

In the late afternoon of Octdi, Mykella dismounted at the base of the ramp leading to the north end of the Great Piers of Tempre. The top of the ramp ended some twenty yards short of the squarish one-story stone structure that held the portmaster and his clerks. Immediately to the north of the portmaster's building stood the shimmering green tower that dominated the northern end of the Great Piers of Tempre.

Behind Mykella, her younger and taller sister Rachylana also dismounted, if reluctantly, as did two of the four Southern Guards, in their uniforms of spotless dark blue, assigned to guard them, for none of the three daughters of the Lord-Protector of Lanachrona went anywhere outside the palace without an escort.

Mykella hurried up the ramp, and Rachylana followed, the two guards bringing up the rear. At the top of the ramp, Mykella slowed and glanced back at her sister. "Do you want to come in?"

"Why would I want to do that?"

Instead of snapping that Rachylana might learn something, Mykella forced a smile. "I won't be long."

"Not more than a glass, I'd imagine. I'll wait out here." Rachylana walked farther west, her flamelike mahogany hair barely kept in place by a dark maroon headband against the west wind coming off the water of the wide River Vedra. The wind was chill enough that the slightly acrid odor of the waters around the Great Piers was almost un-noticeable, and since the wind was directly from the west, it didn't pick up the far more odoriferous scents from the pens to the southwest where the towing oxen were kept when they were not hauling barges upstream or riding them downstream to begin the process all over again.

Two of the guards waited with Rachylana, as the other two followed Mykella.

The Great Piers were composed of the long base, an expanse of unchanging gray eternastone that stretched nearly a vingt from north to south along the east side of the river, and the more than fifteen stubby river wharves, eternastone fingers some thirty yards in length jutting out into the river. At the far south end of the Great Piers stood a second green tower, identical to the first, each soaring more than sixty yards into the silver-green sky. The towers were hollow shells, each with a single door at the base, but without stairs or any sign within that there had ever been any way to reach the top. Nor were there any windows or signs of any rooms in the tops of the towers, or in the others—identical—scattered across all of Corus.

More than half the piers had either sailing craft or barges moored to them. Carts and wagons were scattered across the short piers, some being loaded, but the majority being unloaded. Seemingly ignoring the chaos on the piers, Mykella walked briskly to the portmaster's door that faced the river and opened it. Two guards followed her step for step as she entered.

Inside, a squat white-haired man immediately rose and hurried to the long counter that separated the waiting area from the three clerks who appeared to be checking invoices for the purpose of levying the proper tariffs. One had only begun that process when he had seen Mykella, she noted.

"Portmaster Chaenkel," Mykella said pleasantly.

"Mistress Mykella, let me bring you the summary ledgers."

"Thank you."

At the left end of the counter, a grizzled bargemaster glanced toward Mykella and the pair of guards behind her, then looked quickly away and back at the clerk who stood waiting for him to finish declaring his cargo so that the form could be completed and the proper tariff levied—after inspection.

Chaenkel set the ledger before Mykella.

She began to study the entries for the week, of the sailing traders and the numbers of barges that had ported and departed, both those towed laboriously upstream, and those headed downstream with the current and guided by long sweeps. Most of those headed downstream were departing lighter than they had arrived, since, as the capital of

Lanachrona, Tempre was generally a destination port, although wines from the Vyanhills and glassware from Krost were sought throughout the entire west of Corus, from frigid Northport to Southgate.

The total number of barges and other vessels was only three less than the total for the previous week, and the total of tariffs levied was close to the same. Mykella nodded and straightened.

"Thank you, Portmaster. How do you think the trading and traffic have been?"

Chaenkel furrowed his brow, then tilted his head. "It'd be hard to say, Mistress. Not all that different from last week. It seems about the same as it should be for this time of year." He smiled, ruefully. "When you get to be my age, the years blur, but I'd know if things were greatly different." He nodded. "That I would."

"Are we getting much trade from the east?"

"Not any more than one would expect now that we're into winter. No less, either, from what I've seen. A bit more iron from the Iron Valleys. Nightsilk—who can say? That comes overland and under guard."

Mykella nodded to that. "Thank you."

"My pleasure, Mistress."

Mykella turned. As she walked from the building, followed by the two Southern Guards, behind her Mykella heard the bargemaster.

"... is she? Not seen her before ..."

"Lord-Protector's eldest . . . checks on tariffs . . . since midsummer . . ."

Had it been for less than two seasons? It seemed longer than that to Mykella.

Once back out on the Great Piers, Mykella continued to where Rachylana was standing. Just short of her sister, she paused to watch as a trading vessel eased out into the current and spread its sails, struggling upriver against the current. Was the trader bound for Borlan or farther east, perhaps to Salaan, the easternmost river port in Lanachrona before the Vedra became unnavigable?

"What was it like, I wonder, when people could travel upstream without sails or oars?" she asked.

"Do you really believe those absurd tales about the Alectors? How could anyone?" Rachylana sniffed. "I mean . . . flying on creatures with wings as wide as sails, and on ships that had no sails or oars at all, and the River Vedra boiling over when it all came to an end in the Great Cataclysm. And soarers—little winged women who floated in midair, yet destroyed giant Alectors. In hundreds of years, no one has ever found the remains of anything like that. Really, I could write a better story myself."

"Perhaps you should," Mykella said blandly, knowing patience to write anything of length was hardly one of her sister's strengths.

"Why bother? Anyone with any sense thinks they're just stories for children."

"Then who built the eternastone highways, and why are the old buildings built so large?" asked Mykella. "We've both seen chairs in the storerooms that are too large for the largest man to sit in them, and the steps in the palace are all too high to be comfortable climbing them."

"It's all nonsense," rejoined Rachylana. "They're just ceremonial chairs built for past Lords-Protector who wanted to seem larger, and the stairs are to make anyone who enters uncomfortable in the presence of the Lord-Protector."

Mykella refrained from pointing out that an overlarge throne or chair only made a large man seem smaller, and a man of average size seem insignificant. Rachylana wasn't about to listen to anything that reasonable.

"You're done, now, aren't you?" Rachylana snapped, rebuttoning the top flap of her dark maroon jacket. "I'm freezing. It is winter, you know?"

"Barely," replied Mykella. Octdi was the eighth day of the week, the last full working day before the end-days of Novdi and Decdi, and this particular Octdi was the second of the winter. Besides, Tempre never got as cold as the Iron Valleys did, the forbidding lands that stretched northward from the far side of the Vedra, reaching almost to the Ice Sands that bordered the Aerlal Plateau.

"I still don't see why you need to come here every Octdi—"

"I'm checking with the portmaster to see how many traders ported this week, compared to the week before. The tariff ledgers in the palace just show the totals collected. It's not the same."

"I don't see why you spend so much time checking on river

traders and talking to people like the portmaster . . . or those barge-masters." Rachylana offered her most serious frown. "You're the Lord-Protector's daughter, not a clerk like Kiedryn."

"If Father's brother can be Finance Minister, I can certainly supervise the accounting," Mykella replied. In any instance, doing that was far less boring than speculating about which son of which ruler in what adjoining land might decide to make an offer for her hand. Mykella preferred to avoid thinking about that eventuality at all.

"It's hardly supervising. Father's just letting you do it so that . . ." Rachylana's voice trailed off.

"So that what?"

"So that you'll know more about accounts when you get consorted, I suppose."

Mykella knew very well that what Rachylana had said was not what she'd started to say, but let it pass.

"Can we go now that you're done with whatever it was?" added Rachylana.

"You didn't have to come," Mykella pointed out. "Or did you think that Berenyt might want to escort us?"

"I thought it might be more interesting than helping Nealia or Auralya plan the dinner menus for next week." Rachylana's tone suggested that she would rather have planned menus, at least if her cousin Berenyt didn't happen to take charge of their guard detail. That was highly unlikely, because Berenyt was a captain in the Southern Guards in charge of a whole company, and captains didn't do escort duties, except on ceremonial occasions.

Rather than say more, Mykella strode away from her sister toward the mounts and the two guards who had remained at the foot of the piers with the mounts. She skipped to her left to avoid a porter guiding a loading barrow stacked with kegs of something, then hurried down the long eternastone ramp, whose surface had remained smooth and hard against any kind of abuse for generations, possibly thousands of years if the old tales that Rachylana dismissed were in fact correct. The two guards trailed the two sisters.

Beyond the base of the ramp waited the remaining guards and the horses. Mykella mounted the gray gelding, hating the fact that she was so short that mounting was always an acrobatic exercise whenever she wasn't near a mounting block. But she refused to have anyone give her a leg up. At least, with practice, she'd turned it into a graceful acrobatic maneuver. It helped that she usually wore trousers and boots, much to the dismay of her father.

Although she was half a head taller than Mykella, Rachylana accepted the aid offered by one of the Southern Guards, even though she was wearing split riding skirts—maroon to match her riding jacket—and could have mounted unaided.

Mykella eased the gelding around and flicked the reins to direct her mount along the stone-paved road that led eastward to the Lord-Protector's Palace—hardly more than a vingt east of the north end of the Great Piers.

"You always do that, you know?" Rachylana said, drawing her mount alongside Mykella.

"Do what?" replied Mykella.

"Walk away when you don't want to talk about something." Rachylana leaned sideways in the saddle and lowered her voice. "At least Berenyt jokes about things, and he's good to look at."

"He is very good-looking." Mykella offered a smile, one she didn't feel, even though she knew her sister would see through her facade. "He can be very humorous and charming. I'd hoped Jeraxylt might have been able to escort us." She knew that was unlikely, because their brother, younger than Mykella herself but older than Rachylana, was still in training, although he was officially a junior officer in the Southern Guards.

"He's escorting a visiting Seltyr from Southgate, Salyna said," Rachylana said, her voice still low. "He might be an envoy from one of the Twelve."

Mykella concealed a wince. There was only one reason a Seltyr from one of the Twelve who jointly ruled the trading city-state of Southgate would be in Tempre, and that was to look for a bride for either a widowed Seltyr or his son. Not the only reason, Mykella corrected herself, but one of the few. From everything she had heard about Southgate, she had no desire to go there, not where women were virtual prisoners and where even the winter was unbearably warm.

She glanced to her right. On the south side of the road, for the half vingt east and west of the palace, were the gardens planted by her grandfather. Even though the trees that were not evergreens were bare, she still enjoyed looking at the stone walks and hedges and banked flower beds, and the bridges over the stone-walled small streams. For the moment, both riding and the view took her mind off her growing concerns.

Mykella couldn't help but worry. Chaenkel's ledgers showed a very normal flow of trade, both of barges and free-sailing traders, but the master finance ledgers showed a decline in tariff revenues. She had her suspicions, but, at the moment, that was all that they were, and there was little enough that she could say, because her father only allowed her to monitor the finance accounts as a favor—until a suitable match for her was available.

"What are you going to wear to the ball?" asked Rachylana.

"The ball? That's weeks away. I hadn't even thought about it."

"I suppose you haven't. You should have, especially if there's going to be an envoy there. You need to plan ahead if you want a dress made."

"I have plenty of dresses." More than she would really ever need, if she had her way.

"People have seen you in every one."

"I'll think about it," Mykella conceded. She was far more worried about the golds missing from the tariff accounts.

2

Novdi afternoon found Mykella more than slightly restless. Her brother and father had gone hunting in the Lord-Protector's Preserve—the hilly woods that extended a good five vingts to the northeast of the palace, a stretch between where the river turned back to the east and the eternastone highway that stretched eastward as straight as a crossbow quarrel for hundreds of vingts until it finally climbed and split the Upper Spine Mountains before descending and reaching Dereka, the capital and home of the Landarch of Deforya—whose sons had been mentioned more than once as possible matches for Mykella and her sisters.

Mykella did not even have the distraction of studying the account ledgers. While she had keys to most of the doors in the palace, since as the eldest daughter of a widowed Lord-Protector she functioned as consort at times, she was so closely watched that everyone always knew where she was. At the moment, she scarcely wanted everyone to know of her suspicions, and going into the Finance study on an end-day would certainly cause tongues to wag.

In the end, by early afternoon, she left the family parlor, although it was officially a sitting room, and started down the main staircase—not that there was any real option, except for the tiny circular service staircases in the four corners of the palace. She had not taken three steps past the pair of guards stationed at the top of the steps when Rachylana appeared, hurrying past the two to join Mykella.

"Where are you going?" asked Rachylana.

"Out to the gardens," Mykella replied.

"Don't you think it will be too cold?"

"There's no wind, and I'm tired of reading." She paused. "Where's Salyna?"

"She said she was going to spend time with Chatelaine Auralya," Rachylana replied. "She says she wants to learn more about how to supervise the kitchens."

Mykella had her doubts about the depth of Salyna's interest, but didn't feel like saying so. While Salyna might be the youngest of the Lord-Protector's children and the youngest daughter, despite her beauty, Salyna was more interested in hunting and arms than in kitchens.

"Would you mind if I joined you?" Rachylana asked, keeping pace, as Mykella hurried down the steps.

"Not at all." Her sister's company would be welcome. At least, Mykella hoped so. Once they were on the main level of the palace, mostly comprising studies where various functionaries conducted the business of government during the week, Mykella turned to her right and followed the corridor west, and then north, to the northwest door, the one that led out to the private walled gardens off the northwest corner of the palace, far more secluded than the public gardens to the south of the palace. Besides, they didn't need escorts for their own gardens.

Mykella opened the door, nodding to the guard stationed there, and stepped out and down the short set of stone stairs to the stone walkway. She preferred this section of the gardens the farthest from the palace, where the outer walls had been sculpted to resemble a section of an ancient wall—or perhaps the builders had actually taken stones from such a wall and mortared them in place. The path leading there wound through boxwood hedges that had shed their leaves weeks earlier, but the remaining branches and twigs were still thick enough to block her vision of what lay on the other side of the hedges, which were just over two yards in height.

With the walls to block any breeze and afternoon sunlight seeping through the hazy silver sky, Mykella was comfortable, even without a jacket. But then, she should have been, wearing as she was black nightsilk trousers and tunic over the full-shouldered black nightsilk camisole and the matching underdrawers, with polished black boots. Her father insisted on those undergarments whenever they were to leave the palace, and it was simpler to wear them all the time. It seemed almost a pity that few ever saw them, and most of those who did would not have recognized them for what they were, since they cost more than a season's earnings for a crafter. Soft and smooth as they were to the touch, they could stop any blade or even a bullet, although a bullet impact would leave a widely bruised area of flesh beneath, not that many could afford hand-tooled rifles.

More than a few had tried and failed to learn the herders' secrets, and now few tried, especially since the Iron Valleys were so cold and forbidding and their militia-men were vicious fighters. What was the point of fighting and losing golds and men when the only thing of value was nightsilk that was cheaper to buy than to fight battles over?

Mykella glanced up into the silvery green winter sky where, a third of the way to the west from the zenith, she could see Selena, the larger moon. Although Selena was full, the light that shone so pearly white in the night sky was more like an off-white beige in the day. The green-tinged Asterta hung just above the west wall of the garden, almost lost in the white glare of the afternoon winter sun.

"Do you think that an envoy from Southgate is coming?" Rachylana asked, as if to break the silence.

"When Salyna asked him, Father didn't say anything about the envoy from Southgate," Mykella replied carefully. "He just said that he hadn't seen anyone from the south in more than a season and that their Seltyrs visit ours occasionally for reasons of trade."

"That doesn't mean that he won't be seeing one," Rachylana pointed out.

"Even if one is coming, it might be about trade or borders."

"More tiresome talks about the land east of Zalt? I hope not. The land's worthless, Jeraxylt says."

Mykella doubted that any land was totally worthless. While the hills and low rolling plains of the southwest might not be all that fertile, they would provide a buffer in case the Seltyrs of Southgate, supported by the Seltyrs of the Isle of Dramur, decided to expand their foothold on Corus. Situated as it was in the midlands of Corus, Lanachrona was surrounded by other lands on all sides, and linked to them by the great indestructible highways of the past. While key passes on the highways could be fortified and blocked, that was practicable only in the east where the rugged heights and cliffs of the Upper and Lower Spine Mountains provided some geographic protection, and to a lesser degree along the River Vedra in the north. But the Coast Range to the west was so gentle that anyone could march an army through it and around any fortifications along the highways.

Southgate was the greater challenge, although the Prince of Midcoast had finally unified the scattered kingdoms of the middle coast some fifteen years ago. The Prince of Northcoast was no real threat, not with the raids the Northcoast towns suffered from the Squawts and Reillies, and the herders of the Iron Valleys just wanted to be left alone.

"Mykella?"

"What?"

"You've got that look again."

"What look?" Mykella asked innocently.

"The one you get when you're listening to Father and you don't agree with what he's saying and you don't really want to disagree."

"You haven't said anything I disagree with," Mykella said.

"Then why did you have that look?"

"I was thinking." Mykella took the left branch of the hedge maze path.

"About what?"

"About us. About Lanachrona. About how all Corus is split up and someone is always fighting."

"Oh," replied Rachylana, almost dismissively, "you're always thinking about that. You'd think that you were going to be Lord Protector of Lanachrona instead of Jeraxylt. You'd be better to consider how you'll deal with whatever match Father can make for you—and how not to get rejected."

When Rachylana talked that way, Mykella almost wished she were a son, rather than a daughter. But she was what she was, and wishing wouldn't change anything. Instead, she kept walking until she reached the northwest corner—and the ancient wall.

"It's colder out here," Rachylana said as she came to a stop in the open quarter circle around the wall.

The two of them stood slightly to the right of the small fountain, still flowing, as it did through most of the winter, except on the coldest of days, when it grew into an icy cone that concealed the statue of the fantastic creature—said to be a sandox—from the top of which issued the water.

A greenish haze caught Mykella's eye, and she glanced toward the corner where the two sections of the ancient walls met. There, hovering in midair, was the figure of a winged woman, no larger than a small girl, but seemingly full-figured behind the gauzy green haze that concealed the precise details of her apparently nude body. For a moment, Mykella just gaped. Could the woman be a soarer?

"Look! Over in the corner," she finally said.

Rachylana turned, then frowned. "What? I don't see anything."

Mykella kept looking at the winged figure and the faint greenish haze that surrounded her. How could she direct Rachylana to the soarer? "There . . . to the right of the horse with the broken tail."

"Is that what you want me to see? That tail's been broken off since before we were born. All that green moss around it shows how long ago that happened."

As Mykella watched, the soarer dimmed, then drifted into the stone . . . and vanished, as if she had never been there at all.

"Mykella?" A tone of exasperation colored Rachylana's single word.

"There was a . . . bright green bird there," Mykella said, after a long pause. "I've never seen one like it."

"Likely story. You're seeing things. Keep it up, and you'll be as bad as Paertaxyl."

"Who?"

"He's the guard who kept claiming he saw a purple glow in the lower chambers. No one else saw anything. Berenyt said that they finally had to send him to duty down in Soupat, fighting the nomad raiders."

"Berenyt would know." Mykella tried to keep the sarcasm out of her voice.

"He knows more than you think. . . ."

As Rachylana began to explain just what their cousin did know and how he knew it, Mykella donned a pleasant smile and prepared to listen, even as she kept wondering about the winged woman in the green haze. Had she been an Ancient? How could she have been? None had been seen in hundreds of years. Most people just thought they were a myth from the days before the Great Cataclysm.

But . . . Mykella had seen her.

Why had she been in the garden? And why hadn't Rachylana seen her? Or had Mykella just imagined seeing the soarer?

3

The moaning of the wind on Londi morning woke Mykella, but she remained in her bed under the blue and cream comforter, thinking about the strange dream that she'd had. She had been walking down a stone-walled corridor through a purple haze that burned, and then a green haze that cooled, while words pounded at her from an upright stone larger than a man and swathed in purple. Yet she could not understand the words, for all that she felt she should have.

All too soon, Uleana rapped gently on the door, and Mykella slipped to her feet and made her way to the window. As she pulled back the hangings and stood there looking out on the grayness before sunrise, her bare feet chilled by the cold stone, she noted the frost on the ancient glass.

Rachylana was definitely wrong, Mykella decided once again as she looked out the window and realized, not for the first time, that the lower sill came almost to the bottom of her ribcage. While she was not the tallest of women, unlike her statuesque sisters, she was certainly far from the smallest.

After a moment, she pulled on a robe and slipped out of her chamber and across to the bathing chamber she had to share with her sisters. Neither was there, and she washed quickly before returning to her own room and dressing in her usual working attire—black tunic and trousers, with black boots. Then she made her way to the breakfast room of the family quarters, entering through the service pantry.

Her father was already seated at the head of the table. "Good morning, Mykella." Feranyt's smile was warm, as it always was. His black hair had only a few traces of gray in it, mainly at his temples, and his clean-shaven face held few lines, except those radiating from the corners of his deep green eyes.

"Good morning, Father." Mykella took her seat, to his right, the spot that had once been her mother's.

As soon as she sat, Akilsa—one of the serving girls—filled
Mykella's mug with tea, hot but not steaming. If Mykella had been
earlier, it might have been steaming. Tea cooled so quickly within the
stone walls of the palace.

To Feranyt's right sat Jeraxylt. He nodded across the table at his
older sister. He was already wearing his dark blue uniform—that of a
Southern Guards officer. Rachylana sat beside Jeraxylt, while, as the
youngest, Salyna was already seated to Mykella's right. Even at breakfast, the green-eyed and blond Salyna looked striking, although she
was wearing a worn and scuffed leather vest that was more suitable
to an apprentice guard than a Lord-Protector's daughter.

Mykella took two slices of ham and two pieces of egg toast, then
poured berry syrup over both, but only a little because the syrup was
cold, and would cool the toast even more. Salyna took three slices of
ham and three of the egg toast, and poured far more syrup over her
breakfast.

Mykella glanced across at Rachylana's plate, with but a single slice
of ham and what remained of a single piece of egg toast—without
syrup.

"Father . . . some of the Seltyrs' daughters have said that . . ." ventured Rachylana.

"Not that matching and marriage talk again," groaned Feranyt.
He shook his head. "No . . . there is no envoy coming from Southgate." He grinned at Rachylana. "Do you want me to send for one?
To tell them that I have a daughter I want to get off my hands? One
that so cannot stand to be around me that she will take any match?"

"Father . . ." protested the redhead.

"Or should I send a messenger to Dereka?"

Rachylana winced. "Dereka's cold, and the air's thin."

"That's what they say," Jeraxylt added blandly. "They claim it was
once a city of the Ancients, too. If there ever were any Ancients."

"There were soarers once. There were," insisted Salyna.

"Thousands and thousands of years ago." Jeraxylt's words were
dismissive. "No one has seen one since."

Mykella sipped her tea, not willing to admit she'd seen one on
Novdi. Or had she just imagined she'd seen one?

"That's not quite true," Feranyt said. "There are a number of witnessed accounts of a soarer appearing to Mykel the Great, far too many for that appearance to be disregarded."

"That was hundreds of years ago, sir."

"But not thousands," Salyna said smugly.

"Enough," said Feranyt firmly, but cheerfully. "Nothing out of the ordinary is happening. You shouldn't want anything out of the ordinary to happen. When such things occur, they're seldom good. Now . . . enjoy your breakfast before it gets cold."

"Colder," murmured Salyna under her breath.

Mykella managed not to grin.

"Salyna," said Feranyt sternly. "All too many in Tempre would prefer your breakfast to what they have. And there's not a Reillie or a Squawt that wouldn't trade their poor food for yours. Be grateful."

"Yes, Father."

Feranyt turned to his redheaded middle daughter. "You aren't eating much, Rachylana. A shrewt couldn't live on what you consume."

"If I ate what Salyna does, Father, there wouldn't be enough golds in the storerooms to buy me a match."

"You could eat a bit more."

"Yes, Father." With a wince, Rachylana eased the smallest slice of ham off the serving platter.

Mykella knew it would remain on her sister's plate, uneaten, after their father left to go to his formal study to receive the morning reports.

Once Feranyt had finished his breakfast and left the table, Mykella rose and hurried back to the bathing chamber to wash her hands before making her way to the Finance chambers on the east end of the palace—still on the upper level, if on the opposite end from the Lord-Protector's personal apartments.

Kiedryn—the chief clerk—was already at his table-desk in the outer chamber, and the door to the smaller study that belonged to Joramyl, as Finance Minister, was closed, not that Mykella expected her uncle to appear anytime soon, especially on a Londi morning.

Mykella settled into her place at the smaller writing table, where

Kiedryn had placed the master ledger. As she opened it, she heard a cough, and she looked up. "Yes?"

"It's updated through the Octdi before last, Mistress Mykella. All of the fall entries have been made." The white-haired clerk smiled at her.

"Thank you."

Now all she had to do was check to see how the tariff collections matched those of the previous seasons . . . and, if need be, those of previous years. That was in addition to checking outlays. She had the feeling that the problem was not in the ledgers, but she needed to start there, because both her father and Joramyl believed that ledgers that balanced were accurate ledgers.

4

Duadi was not that much better than Londi, because, try as she might, Mykella had been unable to discover any reason within the Finance ledgers why tariff revenues were declining. She had hoped that the decline had been the result of poor accounting, but that hope had vanished by the time she had closed the last ledger that afternoon. With what she had learned from the portmaster, revenues should have been higher.

Dinner was quiet, and in the family quarters, because her father and her uncle had been to a banquet held by the Seltyrs and High Factors to celebrate the end of a successful fall trading season. Mykella had read in the family sitting room until her eyes tired in the poor light cast by the oil lamps, and she had retired to her own chambers—where sleep had been a long time coming.

From somewhere, the faintest of greenish lights suffused the dark of Mykella's chamber, rousing her from an uneasy slumber. Green? She squinted, but discovered she was looking away from the window and toward her wardrobe. She turned over, keeping the comforter tight around her, conscious of just how chill the air was even inside the palace. The green illumination was not coming from the window, but from the gauzy-winged and shimmering small woman who hovered above the foot of her bed.

Mykella just stared at the soarer, then slowly sat up, gathering the comforter around her. "You can't be real," she murmured in a voice so low that no one could have heard her words.

The soarer eased toward her, then bent forward, a graceful arm reaching out toward Mykella.

Mykella was half-frightened, but also so bemused and intrigued that she did not move, not until the fingertip of a small hand brushed Mykella's forehead. At that moment, a tingle ran through her body.

If you would save your land and your world, go to the Table and find your Talent.

There was no sound at all in the room, yet the soarer's words were as clear as if she had spoken them loudly and distinctly. Then, the soarer floated toward the outside wall . . . and was gone, as if she had never been there.

If you would save your land and your world, go to the Table and find your talent. What had the soarer meant? What table? Certainly not a banquet table. . . .

Abruptly, Mykella shuddered. The Table beneath the palace. It had to be the stone table in the chamber in the lowest level of the palace, and there was little doubt that the small winged woman was a soarer—one of the Ancients featured in so many folktales.

Rumors and tales, tales and rumors. Still, she could not deny that she had seen and heard a soarer—twice now—and some tales even held that the legendary Mykel, the first Lord-Protector, had been directed to Tempre by a soarer after the Great Cataclysm. Now . . . she had been directed to go to the Table. Could she do any less than her ancestor?

She sat huddled in her comforter for several moments longer. Then she threw it off and padded to the armoire, pulling out garments until she had a tunic, trousers, and boots, all of which she donned hurriedly in the darkness. Was she being foolish? She shook her head, knowing she was trying to convince herself.

Then she slipped out of her chamber and out of the family quarters.

The guards patrolling the corridor outside looked at her as she neared, once, then twice.

"I'm going down to the lower level," was all she said.

Neither guard said a word, whatever they might have thought, since, as the Lord-Protector's daughter who also fulfilled some of the functions of his consort, she had the keys to all the locks and access to any place in the palace.

In the dimness, she hurried down the central staircase to the ground level, then down the west corridor. She did not go so far as the rear door to the gardens, but stopped in front of another locked door—one that looked more like a closet or storeroom door. It wasn't either, but the door to another staircase, the one that led down to the lowest levels of the palace. During the day, it was guarded, but at night, when the palace was locked, the guard was shifted to the garden door, since he could watch both doors easily.

From the door to the garden, the guard inquired, "Mistress Mykella?"

"It's me, Noult. I shouldn't be long." Mykella finished unlocking the door and opened it. Should she lock it behind her? She decided against that and merely closed it.

Her bootsteps echoed dully in the narrow stairwell as she descended the stone staircase to the lowest level of the Lord-Protector's Palace. When she reached the small foyer at the bottom, she paused and glanced around. The ancient light-torch in its bronze wall bracket illuminated the precisely cut stones of the wall and floor with the same tired amber light as it always had—ever since she could remember. Seeing it brought to mind, once again, the thought that it was indeed a miracle that so many of the ancient devices still functioned.

Why was she down in the seldom-visited depths? Had it just been a dream? Had she actually seen the soarer?

She looked through the archway separating the staircase foyer from the long subterranean hallway that extended the entire length of the palace. The dimly lit passageway was empty, as it should have been.

She'd never quite figured out the reason for the boxlike design of the Lord-Protector's Palace, with all the rooms set along the corridors that formed an interior rectangle on each level. The upper level remained reserved for the family and the official studies of the highest ministers of Lanachrona, but there was only one main staircase, of gray stone, and certainly undeserving of the appellation of "grand staircase," only one modest great dining chamber, and but a single long and narrow ballroom, not that she cared that much for dancing. More intriguing were the facts that the stones of the outer walls looked as if they had been cut and quarried but a few years earlier and that there were no chambers truly befitting the ruler of Lanachrona.

Mykella walked briskly down the underground corridor toward the door set in the middle of the wall closest to the outside foundation on the north side of the palace. Once there, she stopped and studied it, as if for the first time. The door itself was of ancient oak, with an antique lever handle. Yet that lever, old as it had to be, seemed newer than the hinges. The stones of the doorjamb were also of a shade just slightly darker than the stones of the corridor wall. Several of the stones bordering the jamb were also darker, almost as if they and the jamb had been partly replaced in the past.

After a moment, Mykella tossed her head impatiently, hardly disarranging her short-cut black locks, then reached out and depressed the lever. The hinges creaked slightly as she pushed the door open, and she made a mental note to tell the steward. Doors in the Lord-Protector's Palace should *not* squeak. That was unacceptable.

She stepped into the Table chamber, closed the door behind her, and paused. At first glance, it looked as it always had, a windowless stone-walled space some five yards by seven, without furnishings except for a single black wooden chest and the Table itself—a block of blackish stone set into the floor whose flat and mirrored surface was level with her waist—or perhaps slightly higher, she had to admit, if only to herself. She was the shortest of the Lord-Protector's offspring, even if she did happen to be the eldest. But she was a daughter, who would be married off to some heir or another, most probably the Landarch-heir of Deforya, a cold and dark land, she'd heard, scoured by chill winds sweeping down from the Aerlal Plateau. She had seen the Plateau once, from more than thirty vingts away, while accompanying her father on an inspection trip to the upper reaches of the River

Vedra. Yet even from that distance, the Plateau's sheer stone sides had towered into the clouds that enshrouded its seldom-glimpsed top.

Her thoughts of the Plateau and Deforya dropped away as she realized that there was another source of illumination in the chamber besides the dim glow of the ancient light-torches. From the Table itself oozed a faint purplish hue.

Mykella blinked.

The massive stone block returned to the lifeless darkness she'd always seen before on the infrequent occasions when she had accompanied her father and her brother, Jeraxylt, to see the Table.

"Because it is part of our heritage," had invariably been what her father had said when she had asked the purpose of beholding a block of stone that had done nothing but squat in the dimness for generations.

Jeraxylt had been more forthright. "I'm going to be the one who masters the Table. That's what you have to do if you want to be a real Lord-Protector." Needless to say, Jeraxylt hadn't said those words anywhere near their father, not when no Lord-Protector in generations had been able to fathom the Table.

Mykella doubted that anyone had done so since the Cataclysm, even the great Mykel, but she wasn't about to say so. Before the Cataclysm, the Alectors and even the great Mykel had been reputed to be able to travel from Table to Table. Another wishful folktale, thought Mykella. No one could travel instantly from one place to another. Yet all of Corus had been ruled from the vanished cities of Elcien and Ludar, and there were the eternal and indestructible highways, and the Great Piers, and the green towers.

She shook her head. So much had been lost. Could the Tables once truly have transported Alectors? How was that possible?

Yet . . . once more, the Table glowed purple, and she stared at it. But when she did, the glow vanished. She looked away, and then back. There was no glow . . . or was there?

She studied the Table once more, but her eyes saw only dark stone. Yet she could feel or sense purple. Abruptly, she realized that the purplish light was strangely like the soarer's words, perceived inside her head in some fashion, rather than through her eyes.

She shivered, then drew herself up, concentrating on the Table. What did it mean? How could sensing a purple light that wasn't there be a talent? And why had the soarer appeared to Mykella, and not to her father or to Jeraxylt? And what was threatening her land? Or her world? And what exactly did the Table have to do with it all? The questions raised by the appearance of the soarer and her simple sentence seemed endless.

Slowly, Mykella walked around the Table, looking at it intently, yet also trying to feel or sense what might be there, all too conscious that she was in the lowest level of the palace in the middle of the night— and alone.

At the western end of the Table, she could feel *something*, but it was as though what she sensed lay within the stone of the Table. She stopped, turned, and extended her fingers, too short and stubby for a Lord-Protector's daughter, to touch the stone. Was it warmer? She walked to the wall and touched it, then nodded.

After a moment, she moved back to the Table, where she peered at the mirrorlike black surface, trying to feel or sense more of what might lie beneath. For a moment, all she saw in the dimness was her own image—black hair, broad forehead, green eyes, straight nose, shoulders too broad for a woman her size. At least, she had fair clear skin.

Even as she watched, her reflection faded, and the silvery black gave way to swirling silvery white mists. Then, an image appeared in the center of the mists—that of a man, except no man she had ever seen. He had skin as white as the infrequent snows that fell on Tempre, eyes of brilliant and piercing violet, and short-cut jet-black hair.

He looked up from the Table at Mykella as though she were the lowest of the palace drudges. He spoke, if words in her mind were speech. She understood not a single word or phrase, yet she felt that she should, as though he were speaking words she knew in an unfamiliar cadence and with an accent she did not recognize. He paused, and a cruel smile crossed his narrow lips. She did understand the last words he uttered before the swirling mists replaced his image.

. . . *useless except as cattle to build lifeforce.*

Cattle? He was calling her a cow? Mykella seethed, and the Table mists swirled more violently.

The Table could allow people to talk across distances? Why had no one mentioned that? There was nothing of that in the archives. But then, the archives did not mention anything about the Table except for its existence. Could it be that no one knew? If they did, wouldn't her father have known? And where was the strange-looking man? Certainly not within the sunken ruins of Elcien. Could he be in far Alustre, so far to the east that even with the eternal ancient roads of Corus few traders made that journey and fewer still returned?

Alustre? What was Alustre like?

The swirling mists subsided into a moving border around a circular image—that of a city of white buildings, viewed from a height. Mykella swallowed, and the scene vanished. After a moment, so did the mists.

The strange man—could he have been an Alector? Hadn't they all perished in the Cataclysm? Mykella didn't know what to think. Still . . . she had thought of Alustre and something had appeared. Could she view people?

She concentrated her thoughts on her father. The mirror surface turned into a swirl of mists, revealing in the center Lord Feranyt lying on the wide bed of the Lord-Protector, looking upward, his eyes open. Beside him, asleep, lay Eranya, his dark-haired mistress. After the death of Mykella's mother, her father had refused to marry again, claiming that to do so would merely cause more problems. Mykella had never questioned that, but seeing Eranya beside her father, she wondered what kind of problems he had meant. As she thought about that, Mykella felt strange looking at her father, clearly visible in the darkness.

Quickly, she turned her thoughts to Jeraxylt. Her brother was in his own chamber, but he was far from asleep, nor was he alone. Flushing in the darkness, and yet somehow both irritated and disgusted, Mykella quickly thought about their summer villa in the hills to the northeast of Tempre.

The mists swirled, and then an image of white columns appeared, barely visible in the dark above the low walls that enclosed the front garden.

Next she tried calling up an image of the Great Piers, and those appeared in the mirrorlike surface of the Table, dark, but clearer than they would have appeared to her eyes had she actually been standing on the eternastone surface and looking west at the short river wharves and the dark water beyond.

After that, she tried to call up the barracks of the Southern Guards, located a vingt east of the palace. The large square structure appeared before her. In turn, she tried calling up images of other places in Tempre—the market square, the public gardens, and the front of Lord Joramyl's mansion, to the southeast of the Southern Guards, situated on a low rise. All appeared clearer in the mirrored surface of the Table than they would have to her eyes—yet they were clearly showing things as they were in the night.

What about Dereka?

An image appeared, and she looked down on a city where dark eternastone and gold glimmering stone mixed, where faint lines of green appeared as well, and where a massive aqueduct split the city.

She'd been to Vyan, and she thought of it. Obligingly, the city square appeared, as did the square in Krost, but even the mists vanished when she tried to see Soupat or Lyterna. Finally, she stepped back from the Table. It still glowed with the unworldly purple sheen, but she could now distinguish between what she saw with her eyes and what she sensed.

She shivered. Telling herself that it was merely the chill from the cold stone of the lower levels, she eased back out of the Table chamber, carefully glancing around before closing the door behind her. Once she had climbed the two flights of stairs and returned to her own simple room, Mykella sat on the edge of the bed.

What had really happened?

5

Mykella hadn't thought she would get back to sleep, not with all the questions running through her head, but she had. With all the confused dreams, she almost wished she hadn't, because she slept through Uleana's first knock on her door and overslept. So she had to hurry in getting washed up on Tridi morning.

Dressing wasn't a problem for her, not the way it was for her two younger sisters, particularly Rachylana. As almost always, Mykella just wore black nightsilk trousers and tunic over the full-shouldered black nightsilk camisole and the matching underdrawers, with polished black boots.

Mykella smoothed the black tunic into place, then hurried down the corridor and tried to ease into the breakfast room of the family quarters through the service pantry.

Feranyt looked up from the head of the table, dark polished oak that had endured many Lords-Protector and their families. "Mykella . . . I had wondered when you might join us, especially when I heard you had gone prowling through the lower levels of the palace late last night."

Mykella managed a rueful smile as she took her place on the left side of the table. "I couldn't sleep. I knew I could walk around down there safely—and quietly—without the guards saying, 'Mistress Mykella' every few moments, or just looking." She looked directly across the table at Jeraxylt, seated to her father's right. "It's not as though it was all that quiet here, either. There were others who weren't exactly sleeping, either."

Jeraxylt smiled lazily, even white teeth standing out against his tanned face and the dark blue uniform of the Southern Guards, then shrugged. "I was in bed early, and I got a very good night's sleep."

Mykella lifted the mug of already-cooled tea. Jeraxylt wasn't about to admit anything, and her father certainly wouldn't press his son, not when they'd both been engaged in a similar fashion. She took a slow sip of the cool tea and waited to be served, since the serving platters had already been removed from the table.

"You look good in that uniform." Salyna smiled at her older brother. "The Seltyrs' daughters and the High Factors' daughters think so, too."

"How would you know, little vixen?" Jeraxylt grinned at his youngest sister.

"I'm a woman, silly brother. I know, and I'm not little or a vixen."

Rachylana raised her left eyebrow. In addition to studying with the most skilled seamstresses in Tempre, Rachylana had pursued the skill of lifting a single eyebrow, as if such unusual talents were required of a middle daughter.

Jeraxylt ignored the gesture.

"What are you doing today?" Mykella asked her brother. "Playing Cadmian again?"

"I'm not playing. You know that. Training isn't play, especially for a Southern Guard."

"It's very hard," Rachylana interjected. "Berenyt says so, and he should know, because he's already been through it."

"You can't serve, not in a combat position, anyway." Mykella eased her head sideways to let the serving girl—Muergya on this morning—set down before her a platter with an omelet and ham strips, along with candied prickle.

"The training is valuable in itself," Feranyt said firmly. "You might recall, Mykella, that I'm allowing you to train in a fashion in working with the Lord-Protector's accounts."

"Yes, sir." When her father spoke in that tone, Mykella knew there was little point in objecting to the falsity of the arguments. As the only direct heir, Jeraxylt would never be allowed anywhere close to anything involving combat or use of arms.

"Besides," Jeraxylt said smoothly, "Lords-Protector don't serve. They command."

"Didn't Mykel the Great serve?" Mykella asked innocently.

"That was different. He didn't fight after he became Lord-Protector."

"That's not what the archives say," Mykella countered.

"They're not clear. Besides, he probably just had the scriveners write the history that way," replied Jeraxylt.

"They're clear enough." Mykella had spent more time in the dusty archives beneath the palace than had her brother, because he'd spent none at all.

"Be careful how you speak of history, Jeraxylt," cautioned the Lord-Protector. "You are the heir and will be Lord-Protector because of that history. Disparage it, and you disparage your own future."

"Lord-Protector . . ." Rachylana looked to her father. "Why don't you just call yourself Landarch or prince? That's what you are, Father, aren't you?"

Feranyt offered his middle daughter a patronizing smile. "Rachylana . . . names and titles carry meaning. The words 'Lord-Protector' tell our people that our duty is to protect them. A Landarch or a prince rules first and protects second, if at all."

Mykella caught the hint of a frown that crossed Jeraxylt's brow. The fleeting expression bothered her, as did a feeling, one that was not hers, yet that she had felt. That feeling had combined pride, arrogance, and a certain disdain. But how had she sensed that feeling?

"Anyway," added Salyna, "every nomad raider in the grasslands west of the Lower Spine Mountains calls himself a prince. There's only one Lord-Protector in all of Corus, and he's the most important ruler in the world."

"Daughter . . ." Feranyt said, "that's not quite true. The Landarch is also quite powerful, and the Praetor of Lustrea rules a land three times the size of Lanachrona."

"He's so far to the east that he really doesn't count, does he?" asked Salyna.

"Actually," Feranyt replied slowly, "he does count. We really should be trying to trade with Lustrea more." He paused. "The rulers of the east believe in some ways as we do. The word 'praetor' comes from an old word meaning 'guard.'"

"So the two most powerful rulers in Corus guard and protect their people," Mykella said, looking at Rachylana. "That doesn't sound like coincidence."

Feranyt chuckled. "It more likely means that the first Lord-Protector and the first Praetor were very shrewd men." He eased back his chair and stood. "I will see you all later."

"Good day, Father," the daughters chorused.

Jeraxylt merely nodded.

After hurriedly finishing the undercooked omelet and greasy ham, and gulping down the candied prickle because she knew she needed to, Mykella only stayed at the breakfast table until the last morsels were gone. Then she departed, washing up slightly before making her way to the Finance chambers on the east end of the palace—still on the upper level.

When she slipped into the outer study, Kiedryn was already at his table-desk in the outer chamber. As usual, Joramyl's door was closed and locked because he had not yet arrived.

Mykella glanced at the white-haired chief clerk. If anyone would know what the soarer had meant when she had used the word "Talent," Kiedryn might. He'd claimed to have read every page in the archives.

"Do you know if Mykel the Great had a special talent?" she finally asked, standing beside the smaller table that was hers. "Do the archives say anything about that?"

"He had many," replied Kiedryn. "He could kill men without touching them or using any weapon. He could walk on water and even on the air itself. He could disappear from sight whenever he wished. He brought an army through the steam and heat when the River Vedra boiled out of its banks during the Great Cataclysm. He was called 'the Dagger of the Ancients' because he cut anyone or anything that stood in his way. He married Rachyla because she was the only one who could stand up to him." He smiled warmly. "There are reasons why you and your sister are named after them, you know."

Much good being named after the first Lord-Protector did her as a woman, Mykella thought. "Do you believe all that?"

"Mostly," replied the chief clerk. "No one with less ability could have created Lanachrona out of the chaos that followed the Cataclysm. The western lands are still mired in chaos, with all their barely consolidated lands and the Seltyrs of Southgate playing them off against one another, and the situation with the nomads to the south-east is even worse . . . and always has been."

"But you didn't say he had a talent, one talent."

Kiedryn laughed sardonically. "You didn't ask it that way. Talent—that's what they say that the nightsheep herders have up in the Iron Valleys. Supposedly, the Ancients—the soarers—and the Alectors all had it. Maybe Mykel had it, and maybe he didn't. The archives don't say. There are hints that both he and Rachyla had something, but they're only hints." He shook his head, almost mournfully. "I'd say that some of the nightsheep herders have it. You'd have to have something like that to handle those beasts. They're nearly as big as horses, and their horns are like razors."

"Why don't the archives say more?" Mykella pressed.

Kiedryn shrugged. "Not many people ever had Talent, except for Alectors, and they weren't people like us. Maybe Mykel didn't want to be remembered for his Talent. Or maybe whoever wrote the Archives didn't believe he had it or didn't want to remind people that he did, because that would make us less."

Because someone had a great Talent or ability, that made everyone else feel they were less? Why were people so stupid? Mykella didn't say that. She would have liked to, but she knew that would have upset Kiedryn. The white-haired bookkeeping clerk always wanted to see the best in people.

After a moment, she finally spoke. "That's sad."

"Only if you look at it that way, Mistress. We all need to feel that we have worth, and we do. Sometimes, it's best not to remind folk that there are those who are far better in ability and insight. Those who have such insight usually are smart enough to hide it."

Hide it? What good did that do, especially if you were a woman, and most men didn't think you thought much anyway?

Mykella decided against saying more and finally settled herself at her table and began to look over the latest entries in the master ledger. When she reached the end of the third page, she frowned. She was seeing the same patterns, except more obviously, that she had been tracking when she'd looked over the final accounts for the harvest season.

She stood and walked to the rows of individual account ledgers set on the dark wooden shelves built into the inner wall, picking out one and taking it back to her table-desk. After studying the second ledger for a time, she turned to the chief clerk.

"Kiedryn? The barge tariffs on shipments from the upper Vedra were down for the harvest season, and even lower for the fall. Both are lower than those for the spring, and spring tariffs are always the lowest."

"Mistress Mykella," replied the chief finance clerk with a shrug, "I cannot say. We did send patrollers to visit all the factors and barge-masters."

"And?"

"They all claimed that they had paid their tariffs, and most of them more than last year. Almost all still had their sealed receipts."

Mykella stiffened. "What did Lord Joramyl say?"

"He claims that some of them must be lying, or that some of the tariff collectors had pocketed receipts. He told your father this last week."

What Kiedryn was not saying was that no one except the Lord-Protector was likely to contradict Joramyl, since he was not only the Finance Minister of Lanachrona, but the only brother of the Lord-Protector as well.

But why had her father said nothing?

Mykella went to the cabinet at the end of those set beyond Kiedryn's table-desk and opened it, leafing through the folders there until she found the list of factors. She carried the list back to her table and began to copy names, although she was already familiar if only by name with most of those on the list.

6

By mid-morning on Quinti, Mykella was close to determining, at least to her own satisfaction, just how much lower tariff collections were than she thought they should have been. She had studied the collection ledgers and accounts for the past three years, and based on the revenues exacted in the past and the amount per landed barge and trading sailing vessel, she estimated that at least two thousand golds had been siphoned out of the Treasury over the past two seasons, just from the seasonal tariffs on the bargemasters and the Seltyrs and High Factors. More accurately, those golds had never been put into the Treasury after having been collected. But her calculations were only estimates based on past years' collections and various ratios between barge landings and other records—and she might be wrong. Nonetheless, she would have wagered almost anything that more than a few golds that should not have now rested in other hands, possibly even in Joramyl's strongboxes in his easthill mansion, with its high walls and guarded gates.

At that moment, the door to the Finance study opened, and Lord Joramyl stepped inside. His blond hair held traces of silver, and his fair complexion was emphasized by his smooth-shaven face and the dark blue tunic with silver piping. His eyes were pale green and large, under bushy blond and silver eyebrows.

"Good day, Kiedryn." Joramyl smiled at the white-haired clerk.

Even though her uncle said nothing and continued to smile, Mykella could sense, somehow, a certain contempt as Joramyl looked at Kiedryn. Then Joramyl's eyes turned to Mykella.

"Always hard at work, I see. You're so diligent in checking the accounts that I suspect I wouldn't even have to do a thing." His grin was patronizing. "You'll make a great consort for some lucky lordling."

"I'm more interested in serving my father right now, sir," Mykella replied politely.

"That's loyalty, girl. That's another trait any man would be fortunate to find in a wife, and more fortunate for a ruler who needs a wife-consort."

"I appreciate your kindness, Uncle, but I fear it will be a time before a match is made." Mykella didn't think Joramyl's words were meant as a kindness, but it was far better to acknowledge them as such.

"Not so long as you think, Mykella. You're pleasant-looking, shapely, and intelligent. You're the Lord-Protector's daughter, and you're of the right age." He laughed, then turned, and unlocked the door to his study. He glanced at the clerk. "Bring me the master ledger, Kiedryn."

"Yes, Lord Joramyl."

Once Kiedryn had taken the master ledger into Joramyl's private study and then returned to the ledger he was working on—the one for roads, culverts, and bridges, Mykella thought—she turned her attention back to completing the list of traders and bargemasters who paid tariffs regularly.

She still had one large problem. For all of her calculations, there was not a shred of hard proof. While she had been careful to be polite to Joramyl, she didn't much care for dissembling, necessary as she had found it to be, both as a young woman and as the Lord-Protector's daughter. She'd been careful as well in not letting Kiedryn know what she had been doing, other than her normal supervision and questioning. The last thing she needed was for the clerk to mention anything to Joramyl.

How could she discover proof? Could the Table show her anything?

It was certainly worth a try.

Late that afternoon, just before the palace guards were relieved by those on evening duty, Mykella carried a stack of ledgers down from the Finance chambers to the door to the lower levels. She could feel the eyes of one of the patrolling guards on her from a good ten yards away. She maintained a resigned expression as she neared the door to the staircase leading down to the lowest level of the palace.

As she stopped short of the door, the guard looked at her directly, and she could sense a feeling of curiosity, a question why the Lord-Protector's daughter was lugging around ledgers by herself.

"These are the personal accounts of the Lord-Protector, but they're several years old. They aren't needed often, but they need to be kept in a safe place, and the older records are stored on the lower level," she explained. "I'll be there a bit because they have to be put in order." She tried to press the need for safety toward the guard.

Abruptly, the man nodded and stepped forward. "Do you need help, Mistress Mykella?"

"If you'd hold these while I unlock the door, I'd appreciate it. These records are only for the Lord-Protector, the Finance Minister, and the head clerk. They'd prefer to keep it that way." She offered a pleasant smile.

She could sense his feelings after she took the ledgers and then closed and locked the door behind her—*too handsome for a Lord-Protector's daughter.*

Handsome? That was a word for men, not women. Yet Mykella knew she didn't possess the ravishing blond beauty of Salyna or the exotic looks of Rachylana. She was moderately good-looking, if less than imposing in stature, but she could think . . . and liked thinking—unlike some women in her family and all too many in Tempre, where a woman's duty was always to her husband and her sons.

She pushed those thoughts out of her mind and made her way down the stone steps and then along the stone-walled corridor to the locked records storeroom door—the second one on the inside wall. Once she was inside, it took Mykella only a few moments to add the ledgers to those in the Finance storeroom. She was about to leave and lock the chamber when she realized that she sensed something. She whirled toward the door to the corridor, but no one had entered, and she heard nothing except the sound of her own breathing. Her eyes traversed the rows of simple wooden shelves that held the older ledgers, covered in a fine layer of dust. The shelves had been built against the stone walls, and there was nowhere to hide.

She frowned. It felt as though someone had been in the chamber, but how could she sense that? She looked at the ledgers to the left of those she had added. The dust was gone from one of the ledgers—and she realized that one volume was missing. Since the black leather binding and spine did not reveal the contents, she had to look through three others before she determined that the missing volume held, not surprisingly, the details of the tariffs collected at the Great Piers from the previous two years. The volume that had been without dust held the same records for the times three and four years previous.

A chill ran down her spine. Yet . . . the use of old tariff collection records proved nothing at all—except that someone had been studying them. But why had someone been studying them? And who had been interested? The only ones with keys to the storeroom were her father, her uncle, Kiedryn, and herself. She couldn't imagine Kiedryn or her father taking out old records. Her father didn't even like looking at the accounts and tended to trust Joramyl. Kiedryn was too honest . . . wasn't he?

She shook her head, then stepped back and left the chamber, locking it carefully behind her. She crossed the corridor and walked back toward the Table chamber, where she entered cautiously, although she felt that no one was around. As always, the chamber was empty, and the Table looked the same as ever—dull dark stone with a mirrored surface—but she could sense more easily the purplish glow. This time, though, the purple felt unclean, repulsive in a way. She also could sense, somewhere beneath and below that purple, a far stronger and deeper shade, what she could only have called a blackish green.

Were the two linked? How? She tried to see or sense more, but could discern only the two separate shades—one superficial and linked to the Table and the other deeper and somehow beneath it, trailing off into the earth.

She paused. Was she just imagining what she sensed? How could she sense purple light that wasn't light, and blackish green illumination that lay beneath the stone under her feet? Yet she'd seen the soarer vanish into stone twice, and she had to trust what she'd seen . . . or sensed.

She finally stepped up to the Table and slipped a sheet of paper out from her tunic, concentrating on the first name on her list—Seltyr and High Factor Almardyn. As hard and as much as she thought about the

Seltyr, all that the Table showed were swirling mists. The same thing happened when she tried Barsytan, only a High Factor, and then Burclytt. Had she just imagined that she had been able to see people in its mirrored surface?

After a moment, she concentrated on seeing Rachylana.

The mists barely appeared and swirled before dissipating to reveal Rachylana. She sat on a stone bench in the solarium on the upper southeastern corner of the palace. Beside her, with his arm around her, was blond-haired Berenyt—Joramyl's only surviving offspring— for now, at least.

Mykella shook her head. Cousin or not, Berenyt would flirt with anyone, even one of the Lord-Protector's daughters, and he could be most charming. Given what Mykella suspected, she had to question whether Berenyt's flirtation with Rachylana was merely his nature . . . or part of something else. Yet Rachylana knew nothing about finances, and cared about the workings of the Lord-Protector's government even less.

After a moment, Mykella let the image lapse. She tried the name of another factor, but the Table only showed the mists. She glanced down the list until she found a name she recognized—that of Hasenyt. This time, the Table displayed an image of the sharp-featured and graying factor standing at the barge docks just north of the Great Piers. Hasenyt gestured to a man in a dark gray vest—a bargemaster, from his garb.

In the end, the Table proved useless for what Mykella had in mind because it would only show what people were doing at the moment when she was looking, and it would only display images of those whom she knew. In addition, except for a handful of the oldest cities on Corus, the Table would not show her anyplace where she had not already been.

That meant she would have to find a way to visit the factors on her list, and that required help, preferably from someone who would not immediately report what she was doing. She hated to ask anyone for assistance, but there was no other way, not in Tempre, where a woman, especially a Lord-Protector's daughter, never appeared in public unescorted.

As she left the Table chamber, she paused. Could Kiedryn have missed something in the archives, something that might shed some light on Mykel's abilities?

With a wry smile, she crossed the corridor, making her way down to the third door on the inside wall—the chamber that held the oldest archives. Once she unlocked the door and slipped inside, she closed the door. The ancient light-torch—one of the few remaining—offered enough illumination for her to drag the old wooden steps to the far left end of the chamber.

She carefully climbed up to the top of the steps and, stretching as far as she could, strained to reach the topmost box and ease it out. Then she began to flip through the documents, quickly trying to find something, anything, that might offer some information.

More than a glass later, filled with too many sneezes from the dust and with her nightsilks covered with it as well, she heaved the last box she had looked at back into place. There was nothing at all about Talent in what she had scanned, and most of the papers had been dull. The accounts had been better kept, she noted. And there had been one interesting reference to a proclamation making Rachyla Mykel's successor in the event of his death, but she'd found no sign of the proclamation itself.

7

That night, Mykella lay in her bed with all the lamps snuffed, looking up through the darkness at her unadorned plaster ceiling, thinking. What was the greenish blackness below and beneath the purple glow of the Table? Why hadn't she seen it earlier? Why did the purple feel so unclean and repulsive?

Question after question swirled through her mind. Was Joramyl the one diverting tariff golds? If so, why? Just to line his pockets and pay for his extravagances? Or was he plotting more? And if he were not the one, who could be? Why would Kiedryn do it? Could Berenyt be somehow involved? Or one of the tariff collectors? That might be the most likely possibility, but if that were so, then why hadn't Joramyl pursued it beyond mentioning it to her father?

The only certainty she had was that it could not be her father. Much as she hated to admit it, he had neither the interest nor the skill with figures, and he never spent enough time with the ledgers to do something like that. Nor was he involved personally with collecting the tariffs.

Mykella felt hemmed in at every turn. She didn't dare discuss the problem with Joramyl, and she couldn't bring it before her father without some sort of proof. Everything would be so much easier if she had the powers that Kiedryn had claimed for Mykel the Great. Even being able to move around unseen would be helpful. Yet, if he had possessed such powers, and Rachyla had been so strong, why didn't any of his descendants have those powers? Or had the early Lords-Protector had them, and the abilities had faded over the generations? And why was the proclamation naming Rachyla as a successor missing? Or had she just missed it in her hurry?

From her bed, she absently scanned the wall-shelf to the right of her small dressing table, taking in the carved onyx box that had been her mother's and the pair of silver candlesticks, the base of each a miniature replica of the eternal green stone towers that flanked the Great Piers. At that moment, she realized that the room was pitch dark, with the window hangings closed and not a single lamp lit, yet she could discern the shape of every object in her chambers.

Could she? She slipped from under the coverlet and walked to the wall-shelf. The onyx box was there, and the candlesticks, but was there more light than she had thought? How could she tell? Abruptly, she closed her eyes, trying to "see" without them.

Slowly, using her senses that were not sight, she reached out for the candlesticks, lifting the one on the left easily, without fumbling, then set it down. She moved sideways to the dressing table, her eyes still closed, and picked up the silver-handled hairbrush that had also been her mother's. Then she lifted the powder box and set it down. Her hand was trembling.

She *knew* she'd never been able to do that. It had to be something awakened by the soarer's touch. But why her? She had no real power in Lanachrona. She didn't even have any appreciable influence over her father or her brother.

She shook her head, then smiled wryly in the darkness. Too bad the palace corridors weren't kept that dark. Then she could just walk wherever she wanted, seeing where to go while others saw nothing.

8

Mykella was up early on Sexdi and one of the first in the family at breakfast, although Salyna was already there. Feranyt followed, and then Rachylana, who wore a clinging green dress that was almost more suited to a ballroom than to the daily routine of a Lord-Protector's daughter.

Mykella wore one of her usual black tunics and trousers. She forced herself to wait to ask what she wanted to know until her father had finished eating and was taking a second mug of spiced tea.

"What was Lord Joramyl like when you were growing up, Father?" Mykella inquired casually, taking a sip of the plain strong tea she preferred to the cider most women drank or the spiced tea her father liked. "He seems so proud and distant now." Arrogant, self-serving, and aloof were what she really thought, but saying so would only have angered her father.

"He's always been proud, but he was always kind to Mother and your Aunt Lalyna. He'd bring them both special gifts from all the places he served in the Southern Guards. Your aunt's favorites were the perfumes he brought back from Southgate when he was your grandfather's envoy there. She even took the empty bottles when she left for Soupat." Feranyt shook his head. "I knew she'd have trouble with the heat there, but Father insisted on it."

Mykella couldn't help but notice that her father did not mention how Joramyl and her mother had gotten along. "He's rather formal with us. Was he always that way with most others in the family?" That was as close as she dared get to what she really wanted to know.

"He's always been hard to get close to," Feranyt replied, with a slight frown.

"Did you play games together?" Mykella pursued, deciding that she'd best change her line of inquiry.

Feranyt chuckled. "Joramyl was never one for games. Except for leschec. He got to be so good at it that he beat old Arms-Commander Paetryl. We didn't play it together, not after we were very young. He was too serious about it for me."

Mykella could sense that even thinking about Joramyl and leschec bothered her father. "Did you spar with weapons?"

"Father forbid it after I broke Joramyl's wrist. If I hadn't, that fight would have ended up with one of us badly hurt. I was better, but Joramyl wouldn't ever quit."

The more her father said, the more concerned Mykella became, especially with what she had discovered about the missing tariff golds. Perhaps her father had mentioned what he was saying before, but she'd never paid that much attention, and now her own concerns gave a new meaning to her father's childhood memories. "Do you think that he feels he'd be a better Lord-Protector than you?"

"Mykella! How could you ask that?" murmured Rachylana, leaning close to her sister.

"Father?" Mykella kept her voice soft, curious, hard as it was for her.

"I'm sure he does." Feranyt laughed. "Each of us thinks we can do a better job than anyone else, but things turn out the way they do, and usually for good reason."

With her worries about what she had discovered, Mykella couldn't believe what she sensed from her father—a total lack of concern and a dismissal of Joramyl's ambitions.

"Joramyl's passion for detail serves us well, dear, as does yours. I'd like to think that my devotion to doing what is right should be the prime goal of a Lord-Protector. If one does what is right, then one doesn't have to worry about plots and schemes nearly so much." Feranyt smiled broadly. "Besides, you can't please everyone. Joramyl only thinks you can, that ruling is like finance and numbers, that there is but one correct way to approach it. If he were ever Lord-Protector, he'd quickly discover that's not the way it is."

"If anything happened . . . do you think he'd be a good Lord-Protector? As good as you are?" Mykella pressed.

"Probably not, but he'd be far better than anyone else in Tempre, except for Jeraxylt, of course." Feranyt inclined his head toward his son. "But enough of such morbid speculations." He rose. "I need to get ready for a meeting with an envoy from the Iron Valleys. Their council is worried about Reillie incursions from the northern moors and the eastern slopes of the north Coastal Range."

"What does that have to do with us?" asked Jeraxylt.

"I'm certain I'll find out in great detail," replied the Lord-Protector. "They're claiming that the Reillies have been armed with weapons having a Borlan arms mark."

"We sell to whoever pays," Jeraxylt said. "Are they going to demand that we stop selling goods because they can't defend their own borders?"

"I doubt that they will express matters . . . quite so directly, Jeraxylt. Nor should you, outside of the family quarters. There is also the question of iron and nightsilk. It would be far more costly to obtain iron from anywhere else, and no one else has nightsilk. So we will talk, as you should do when your time comes. Talk costs little, and often solves much." Feranyt smiled, then turned and walked from the breakfast room.

Rachylana quickly followed, as did Jeraxylt.

Salyna looked to Mykella. "You know Rachylana will tell Berenyt everything you said this morning about his father? She's probably already trying to find him."

"I hope she has better sense than that." Despite what she said, Mykella knew that Salyna was right. She rose and offered her younger sister a smile. "What are you doing today?"

"Watching Chatelaine Auralya supervise the kitchens. I'm learning from her. It's more interesting than adding up numbers in ledgers. For me, that is. I don't have your talents, and Father won't let me spend all my time practicing arms."

"We all have different talents," replied Mykella. What else could she say?

"You ride well," Salyna pointed out.

"So do you, better than I, better than most men."

"I'm not bad with a blade, Jeraxylt says." There was a shyness and diffidence in Salyna's words, but pride beneath them.

"You've been using a real saber?"

"A blunted one, like all the Southern Guards do when they practice," Salyna admitted. "It's fun, and I can hold my own against some of the younger guards. I can see why Jeraxylt likes being in the Guards."

Mykella couldn't imagine sparring with blades as being fun. "I don't think there have been any women in the Southern Guards."

"There were women Myrmidons," Salyna said.

Mykella frowned. "They were Alectors, though."

"The Alectors ruled before the Great Cataclysm, for thousands of years, and women had power. So did Rachyla, and she and Mykel created Lanachrona."

"Where did you hear that?"

"I read it in some of the old journals in Father's study, before he knew I was interested. He moved them after he found out I'd been reading them." Salyna smiled. "I'd already finished them by then."

"Did he say anything . . . about your reading them?"

"He just told me he was removing them so I didn't get any wrong ideas. He said I had to live in the world as it was now, not as it had been."

Mykella sighed. That sounded so like her father.

"Father has trouble seeing beyond what is," Salyna said. "Mother told me that . . . just . . . before . . . before she died."

Why had Aelya told Salyna and not Mykella? Because Salyna was the tallest and strongest and most beautiful?

"She didn't say anything to me."

"You were always the practical one. She probably didn't think you needed that advice."

Truthful as Salyna's response sounded, Mykella could also sense that her younger sister felt that way as well. She paused. In the past tenday, she'd begun to know what people felt. Was that because of the soarer? Or was she just imagining she knew what they felt?

"Mykella . . . why are you looking at me like that?"

"I'm sorry. I was just thinking that you really think I'm that practical."

"I do. Aren't you?" Salyna's words came out with a wry tone.

Mykella managed to laugh. "I'd like to think so. Sometimes I wonder." As she did at the moment, when she was basing her actions on suspicions without hard proof, and feelings she could sense and had never been able to sense before.

"That's something you don't have to wonder about."

"If I'm going to be practical, I need to get to the Finance study," Mykella said.

"See?" Salyna grinned.

After leaving Salyna and washing up, Mykella walked slowly toward the Finance chambers.

Kiedryn was already at work, and Mykella settled herself at her own table, where she began to check the individual current account ledgers. There were no new entries of tariff collections from the bargemasters or the other rivermen. She didn't expect any, since all the accounts were current, and the next collections would not be posted for several weeks at the earliest. So she walked to the shelves and took down the ledger that held the current accounts of the Southern Guards.

The accounts there showed a surplus. Mykella frowned. The Guards had not used what had been set aside. In fact, the expenditures were almost one part in ten lower than at the same time in the previous year, and that was with barely more than half of winter left to run in the year.

At that moment, she heard a hearty voice in the corridor outside the Finance chambers—Berenyt's booming bass.

"Just heading in to see my sire—if he's there. If not, I'll harass old Kiedryn." Berenyt was two years older than Mykella, despite the fact that his father, Joramyl, was younger than his brother, the Lord-Protector. Berenyt had taken a commission as a captain in the Southern Guards and ended up in command of Second Company, one of the two charged with guarding the palace and the Lord-Protector, and one of the three stationed directly in Tempre.

Mykella couldn't make out to whom Berenyt was speaking, but she could sense that the other was male, and vaguely amused. She was not. After what she'd seen in the Table and what she'd discovered, she didn't want to see him anytime soon, much less talk to him.

That hope was dashed as the tall and blond Berenyt pushed his way into the Finance study and planted himself before Kiedryn.

"Is Father in?"

"No, sir," replied Kiedryn. "I haven't seen him yet this morning."

Mykella could easily sense what the chief clerk had not said—*I've never seen him this early*. She tried to visualize herself with the shelves of ledgers between her and Kiedryn . . . and Berenyt.

Berenyt turned in her direction, frowning, and blinking. "Oh . . . there you are, Mykella. For a moment . . ." He shook his head. "You haven't seen Father this morning?"

"We seldom see him in the morning," Mykella replied. "I've always assumed that he had other duties."

"He does indeed."

Behind the words Mykella detected a sense of *more than you could possibly understand*, mixed with condescension and amusement. She managed a simpering smile, although she felt like gagging, and replied, "He offers much to Lanachrona."

"As does your father." Berenyt's words were polite enough and sounded warm enough, but the feeling behind them was cool and a touch scornful. He turned from Mykella back to face Kiedryn. "I hope to find him somewhere, but if I don't, please tell him I was here."

"Yes, sir."

Mykella merely nodded, if courteously.

Berenyt ignored her and stepped out of the chamber, closing the door firmly enough that it shook in its frame.

For the slightest instant, a look of disapproval crossed Kiedryn's face, then vanished.

Mykella just sat at her table for several moments, not really looking at the open ledger. For an instant when he had first looked in her direction, she thought, Berenyt had not really seen her. Had that been her doing? Or his abstraction and interest in other matters? How could she tell?

She really wanted to work more with the Table, but she dared not go down into the depths of the palace too often because, sooner or later, the guards would reveal how often she was going there, and either Jeraxylt or her father would discover her destination. That would lead to even more questions, and those were questions she dared not answer truthfully—and she detested lying, even though she knew that sometimes it was unavoidable, especially for a woman in Tempre.

The soarer's words kept coming back to her, although she had not seen or sensed the winged Ancient except the two times. Was using the Table her Talent? Just to be able to see what was happening elsewhere? And what about her growing ability to sense what others were feeling? Or the ability to see without sight in the darkness?

Did her suspicions about the missing tariff funds have anything at all to do with saving her land? What, really, could she do? And how?

9

That evening after dinner, Mykella sat in the family parlor, a history of Lanachrona in her lap. Across from her, Salyna was seated at one end of the green velvet settee closest to the low fire in the hearth, working on a needlepoint crest. Mykella couldn't help but contrast that domesticity to the focused ferocity within Salyna that doubtless surfaced when she had a saber in her hand. Yet Mykella could understand and accept that duality in Salyna—and in herself, although she had no desire to wield a blade. What she could not understand was Rachylana's acceptance and willing subordination to men, especially to someone like Berenyt.

While Mykella finally succeeded in losing herself in reading the history, in time she looked up, half-bemused, half-irritated. She'd read the parts about Mykel, about how he'd been a Cadmian majer in command of an entire battalion, how he had routed all the forces of the Reillies and Squawts just before the Great Cataclysm, and how he had followed a soarer's instructions to cross the boiling Vedra to Tempre to protect the city. Chapter after chapter had followed, telling of all the battles he had fought and won over the years in establishing and expanding safe boundaries for Lanachrona and in vanquishing invaders and brigands alike.

What intrigued and annoyed Mykella was that there was nothing about *how* Mykel the Great had accomplished anything. There was but a single paragraph dismissing the legend that he had been a Dagger of the Ancients, and that didn't even explain what a Dagger of the Ancients was supposed to have been. Mykella suspected that dismissal was proof that he had been just that, but what a Dagger of the Ancients was remained undescribed. Kiedryn's explanation had conveyed nothing, and her own brief searches of the archives had revealed nothing she did not already know, except that mention of the proclamation that Mykel had signed making Rachyla his immediate heir, which had come to nothing since she had died first.

Mykella tightened her lips as she looked around the parlor with its green upholstered armchairs and settees, the dark oak side tables, and the green and blue heavy, if slightly worn, carpet with the Lord-Protector's crest in the middle. Rachylana had not joined her sisters after dinner. She had eaten little at table, claiming she felt unwell. Mykella had sensed her physical discomfort. Jeraxylt and her father rarely joined them in the evenings, not with their other evening interests. So the youngest and eldest daughters had the parlor to themselves.

The book still in her lap, Mykella stared at the darkness beyond the window, a darkness broken only by the scattered lights of Tempre, those that could be seen from the second level of the palace. She knew that unseen danger surrounded them all, especially her father and brother, not only from the warning of the Ancient, but from what she had begun to sense. Yet no one else seemed to feel the slightest sense of danger or unease. Was she imagining it all? But if she weren't, why didn't her father or her sisters see anything at all, especially her father?

After each of the times she had visited the Table, Mykella had felt that she had gained something in what she could feel or sense. Yet . . . how could merely sensing or feeling more than others save her land? She thought about Berenyt's momentary reaction once more.

Finally, she spoke. "Salyna . . . I need your help."

"I'd be happy to, but . . ." Her younger sister's forehead wrinkled up into a puzzled expression. ". . . just what do you want me to do?"

"I just want you to look out the window for a little while, and then look back at me. Take your time looking out the window."

"Look out the window and back at you? That's all?"

"Please . . . just do it."

"I can do that." Salyna's tone expressed puzzlement, but she stared out the window.

Mykella concentrated on trying to create an image of the armchair in which she sat—vacant, without her in it, the lace doily just slightly disarrayed . . .

"Don't do that!" Salyna's words were low, but intense.

"What did I do?" asked Mykella, releasing the image of the empty chair.

"It . . . it was awful. You weren't there. I knew you had to be . . . but you weren't."

Mykella almost wished she hadn't tried the shield. "I hid. I did it to see if I could move so quietly that you couldn't see me. What else could I have done?" She could sense Salyna's confusion, as well as her sister's feeling that Mykella *couldn't* have gone anywhere else.

For a time, Salyna looked at Mykella. Finally, she asked, "What's happened to you?"

"Nothing," Mykella replied.

"Don't tell me that. You haven't been the same for the last week. You look at Jeraxylt—when he's not looking—as if he were roasting baby hares alive. You aren't pleased with Rachylana, and you've asked Father more questions this week than in the last year. Now, you're practicing hiding, and hiding from me."

"I'm worried," Mykella confessed. "I feel that something's not right, that there might be some danger out there, but I can't even say what that might be." That was certainly true, if not quite in the way

Salyna would take it. "I'm worried about the way Rachylana carries on about and with Berenyt. It's not proper, and it's not a good idea."

"She'll get over it."

Mykella had strong doubts about that, and even stronger doubts about how well Berenyt would treat Rachylana.

"Are they talking about marrying you off to that autarch-heir in Dereka?" asked Salyna.

"Landarch-heir," Mykella replied. "Not in my hearing, and you've heard Father. He says that there aren't any envoys coming to talk of marriage."

"There will be. We can't stay here, Mykella." Salyna straightened herself on the settee. "What would we do? Who would dare marry us? Father wouldn't let anyone of any status do so, because any sons would have a claim on being Lord-Protector, and he wouldn't accept anyone who didn't have position. None of us have any choice. Not even Rachylana." Salyna shook her head. "I feel sorry for her. She doesn't want to see what must be."

Mykella almost said, "That's her problem, if she wants to be so stupid." Instead, she went on, "We'll have to see what happens. Has Father said anything to you?"

"He's said that one of the Seltyrs in Southgate has a son close to my age."

Mykella couldn't help but wince. Southgate was far worse than Tempre for women. It was said to be even worse than Fola or being a Squawt bride.

"They say he's nice." Salyna's voice was level.

Mykella could sense fear, not just concern, from her sister. "I do hope so."

Salyna rolled up her needlework. "I can only do this so long before my eyes cross. Handling a saber is easier." She yawned, then stood. "I'll see you in the morning."

"Good night." Mykella closed the history and set the volume on the side table, watching as Salyna left the parlor. Her sister was disturbed and frightened of going to Southgate. Because their aunt had died there?

Mykella needed to discover more, but, except for functions like the upcoming season-turn celebration and parade and ball, or the High Factors' ball, or riding with escorts, she was expected to remain within the palace, and wherever she went, someone was watching. When she was out, she was never alone.

She had to find a way to get to the Table unseen. Could she test her "disappearing" skill when she took the inside main corridor back to her chambers? Getting past the guards at night should be easier because their post was in the main corridor, well back from the corner of the palace that held the family quarters, and they walked a post between the main staircase and the quarters rather than standing in one place in front of a single door or archway.

Mykella stood and walked to the doorway. How could she do what she had in mind? Sitting in a chair was one thing, but she needed to move. She couldn't keep creating a new image of the hallway without her in it with every step. Could she just create the feel of everything flowing around her as if she were not there?

She moistened her lips and eased the parlor door to the main corridor open. Then, she tried to visualize the light from the parlor flowing around her, as if the door had swung open without anyone there. Her vision seemed to dim, but she could sense the door frame and the open door when she stepped out into the main corridor. One of the guards turned.

She had no idea if he saw her or if the light from the open door had attracted him. She closed the door, and it creaked as she shut it. After a moment, the guard turned away. She moved as quietly as she could, putting down one boot carefully, and then the next, walking not toward her chambers, but toward the guards.

"The door opened . . . thought I saw someone there . . . woman . . ."

The other guard turned in Mykella's direction, but did not seem to be looking at her. "It's closed now. There's no one out here. Who would be up except for his regal heirness, strutting around in a tailored uniform that would never do in combat, panting after another pretty ass?"

Mykella stopped, hoping the guard would say more.

"He looks good in uniform . . . have to say that."

". . . jealous?"

"Wouldn't you be?"

The other guard snorted. "Just walk the post."

Mykella neared the two, but neither even looked at her, and they turned away. So did she, but by the time she stepped into her chambers, Mykella was breathing heavily. She was so light-headed that she felt as though she had raced up and down the main staircase of the palace a score of times.

But . . . the guards had not seen her. She smiled broadly as she sat on the edge of her bed and caught her breath.

Her smile faded as she thought about Salyna's words.

10

The gray light of a winter Septi morning seeped around the edges of the heavy dark blue window hangings. Mykella sat up in her bed, the comforter around her shoulders. Her chamber, while not excessively chill, was far from comfortable, which was not unexpected, since it had neither stove nor hearth.

Thrap.

"Yes?"

"It's Zestela, Mistress."

Mykella wanted to tell the head dresser to go away, but that would only postpone matters. Besides, she'd told Zestela to come before breakfast so that she didn't have to interrupt her day in the Finance study.

She smiled. Perhaps she could test her skills and give the dresser a bit of a shock as well. She slipped from under the covers and took three steps so that she stood against the wall beside the large armoire that held her everyday garments. She shivered at the feel of the cold stone tiles on her bare feet. Even the flannel nightdress didn't help.

Still, when Zestela stepped into the chamber, she would not be able to see Mykella at first.

Mykella then *twisted* the light—that was the only way she could explain it—and called, "You can come in."

"Yes, Mistress."

The door opened, and Zestela bustled in, cradling a long formal gown in her arms and glancing around, seeking Mykella. She frowned as she stepped toward the foot of the bed, then looked back toward the armoire. "Mistress?"

Mykella waited until the dresser looked back toward the door before releasing the light-shield . . . if that happened to be what it was. "I'm here."

Zestela jumped. "Oh! I didn't see you."

"Sometimes I feel like no one does," replied Mykella dryly.

Rachylana entered the chamber. "No one overlooks you, Mykella."

Mykella ignored her sister's words and turned to the dresser. "What do you have there?" The gown didn't look like anything she'd have worn or asked for.

"Lady Cheleyza sent this gown. She thought you might find it suitable for the reviewing stand during the season-turn celebration."

Mykella glanced at the drab beige fabric with the pale green lace. She shook her head. "I'd look like a flour sack in that. A very faded one. I'll wear the blue one I wore at the last turn parade."

"But . . ." stuttered the dresser.

Rachylana frowned. "Cheleyza is only being kind, and you *have* worn the blue before . . . several times."

"People will have seen me in it before. Is that so bad?"

Rachylana and Zestela exchanged glances.

"You can't keep wearing the same blue dress," Rachylana finally said. "Not as a daughter of the Lord-Protector."

"Then," Mykella said, "have the dressmakers make me one just like the blue, except in green, brilliant green—and make it with a high neck. The next time, I'll have something else to wear that looks good on me."

"Yes, Mistress." Zestela bowed and turned to leave.

"*Brilliant* green," Mykella emphasized.

Rachylana stared down at her older sister. "You're being difficult. Salyna said you were in a terrible mood last night. I can see that hasn't changed."

"Because I don't want to look drab in public? Perhaps you'd do anything for dear Berenyt and his stepmother, but I do draw the line in some places. I'd rather represent Father, in wearing something that looks good and doesn't cost more golds."

"You'll cost him more than that, dear sister, with your willfulness." Rachylana's words were cold, but behind them was pure fury. "You'd think you were the eldest son. You're not. You're a daughter, just like the rest of us, and it might be a good idea if you occasionally remembered that." Then she turned and left.

With Rachylana's anger still filling her chamber, or so it seemed, Mykella knew she should have managed something far less rude, and only indirectly cutting, but she'd never been that good at fighting with innuendoes, subtle edges to her words, and expressions that conveyed emotion in a way that could not be faulted, no matter how deadly.

With a deep breath, Mykella turned to the armoire and pulled out another black outfit. That was one of the good things about nightsilk. Besides providing protection against knives or bullets, it scarcely ever wore out, and it washed up nicely without fading. The downside was that tailoring it took special cutting tools and three times as long. She left the clothes on the bed and went to wash up.

Once she returned and dressed, she hurried to breakfast. Although conversation at breakfast was more than a little cool because her sisters avoided speaking to her, neither Feranyt nor Jeraxylt seemed to notice.

After eating, Mykella hurried to the Finance chambers and continued her quiet efforts to recheck all the receipts that had been recorded in the past few seasons. This time, she tried to determine whether the tariffs paid by just certain factors and traders were lower, but from what she could tell, almost everyone's reported tariffs were slightly lower, and none of them were greatly out of line with their own past payments.

That took until midafternoon. By then, she had decided that she had to visit the Table chamber again, if only to see if she could learn more about how it worked, but that would have to wait until evening, well after dinner, when she could plead tiredness and retreat to her chambers.

The day dragged, but she finally reached her chambers after leaving dinner early, claiming she felt unwell. After the morning's incident with Rachylana, her sisters might well believe that. Even so, it felt like torture to sit and wait, but she knew that Salyna or Rachylana would come by and ask how she was, if only to see if she happened to be in her room.

Salyna did, announcing her presence with the lightest of knocks. "Mykella?"

"Yes?"

"Are you all right?"

"I'll be fine. I just need to be alone . . . and get some sleep."

"You don't want company? Sometimes that helps."

"Thank you, Salyna. I appreciate it, but I need to think some things out."

"You're sure you're all right?"

"I'm sure." Mykella couldn't help smiling fondly at her sister's good-hearted concern. "I know where to find you if I need to talk."

"I'll hold you to it. Good night."

Mykella waited longer, a good glass, or so she thought, before she snuffed the wall lamp, not that she needed it much anymore at night, except to read, and moved to the door. She could not sense anyone nearby, and she drew her sight-shield around her and eased the door open and then closed behind her. The guards didn't even look as she slipped along the side of the corridor and down the main staircase, and along the west corridor toward the rear of the palace.

The staircase guard at the rear of the main level posed another problem because he was stationed almost directly before the door she needed to unlock. That had to be her father's doing, and that meant he'd questioned the guards closely. She shook her head. She'd been right about suspecting that he wouldn't want her roaming the palace at night.

She thought for a moment, then moved to one of the study doors along the inside wall of the corridor—a door directly in the guard's line of sight. Using one of her master keys, she unlocked the door, then depressed the lever and gave it a gentle push, moving away and hugging the side of the wide hallway. She stopped a good two yards short of the guard and flattened herself against the wall, waiting.

Several moments passed before the guard saw the open door.

"Who goes there?" He took several steps forward, peering through the dimness only faintly illuminated by the light-torches in their bronze wall brackets, not that all of them worked.

The corridor remained silent. Unseen behind her sight-shield, Mykella eased toward the stairwell door. Behind her, the guard advanced on the open door. Mykella slipped the key into the lock, then opened the staircase door, slipped through it and closed it, quietly locking it behind her.

She took a long and slow breath before she started down the stone steps. At the bottom, she looked around, but the long corridor that led past the Table chamber was empty, as it should have been. She moved quietly forward.

When she entered the Table chamber, she had the feeling that something had changed, although at first glance, everything seemed as it had. There was the faint purple glow of the Table, as well as the blackish green that lay beneath the stone floor.

As she stepped toward the square stone that rose out of the stone floor, a purplish mist seemed to rise from the mirrored surface of the Table. Slowly, the air began to feel heavy and slimy. She wanted to turn and run. She didn't, but instead kept moving toward the Table.

Before she could even think about what she might wish to see, the swirling mists appeared, followed by the visage of the same Alector she had seen before.

You have returned. Excellent. The violet eyes fixed on her.

"Where are you? In Alustre?" She avoided looking directly at the Alector, sensing that was what he wanted.

Alustre? That would be most unlikely at present. But you are in Tempre, are you not?

"Where else would I be?" Mykella tried to feel what was happening with the Table.

You could use the Table to see all of Corus, and with my help, you could rule it all.

Mykella distrusted those words, even as the wonder of the possibility that mastery of the Table could create that kind of power washed over her.

You could rule like no other.

She glanced up, only to see a pair of misty arms rising from out of the Table itself, arms and hands that began to extend themselves toward her, arms that exuded a cold and purple chill. With absolute certainty, she understood that if those arms ever touched her, she would be dead. Her body might live, but what was Mykella would be dead.

She stepped back, but the arms kept moving toward her. She created a sight-shield between her and the arms. The arms pressed against the shield, pushing it back and forcing Mykella to retreat from the Table as more purpleness flowed from it into those icy extensions that threatened her.

What could she do? Frantically, she tried to add another layer of sight-shields, trying to make them stronger, welding them together.

She could feel herself being squeezed, pressed against the stone wall, but she could not give in. She had to hold on. Abruptly, the flailing of the arms against the barrier of her shields lessened. Then the arms themselves began to dissipate, fading and collapsing into the Table.

Were it not for the distance, steer, you would be mine.

Yet the unspoken words contained a note of triumph, as if the distant Alector had discovered something. The purplish mist slowly dissipated, and the purplish glow of the Table subsided, dropping until it almost vanished, as if the struggle between the distant Alector and her had exhausted it.

Mykella uttered a single sigh, almost a sob, shuddering as she stood there in the dimness of the Table chamber. She had to get out. She had to leave. She forced herself to stand there, breathing deeply, waiting until she was no longer shaking or shuddering.

She looked at the Table, then willed her legs to carry her back toward it, until she could see the mirrored surface. She would not be driven from the Table that was her birthright, for it had to be *her* birthright, since no one else in the Lord-Protector's family seemed able to use the Table.

Slowly, she willed the Table to show her Salyna. The swirling mists appeared, then vanished, showing her younger sister sleeping, her comforter thrown back to her waist.

Mykella smiled. Only Salyna would find the chill of the palace too warm.

Mykella shivered, almost uncontrollably, and she found her legs shaking. Much as she would have liked to use the Table or try to learn more about it, she was too exhausted to do more, and that thought generated anger at the distant Alector, who had made her waste the evening.

Reluctantly, she left the chamber, making sure that the door was firmly closed behind her before she made her way to the staircase up to the main level. Once she reached the landing, she paused. She sensed that the guard was back in position, standing less than a yard from the door.

As quietly as she could, she unlocked the door, then, holding the key in her hand, slowly depressed the lever and eased the door ajar, gathering her sight-shield around her. She could squeeze out, but barely, so long as the guard did not turn. Even if he did, he would not see her, but she wanted no attention paid to the lower level and the Table chamber.

She managed to get the door closed, but not locked, before the guard whirled. Mykella froze, standing unseen beside the door.

The guard stared at the closed door. "Not again."

Mykella eased a coin from her wallet and threw it down the corridor. It clinked loudly.

The guard turned, then stepped forward as he caught the glint of silver.

Mykella locked the door and then eased along the side of the hallway. She was even more exhausted and trembling once again by the time she reached her chamber, where, after sliding the door bolt she seldom used into place, she just sat dumbly on the edge of her bed.

As she sat there, still shaking, a greenish-golden radiance suffused the room, and in its center hovered the Ancient, a winged and perfect version of a feminine figure, if less than the size of a six-year-old girl.

You have done well, child.

Mykella wasn't certain what to say to the Ancient . . . or if she could. She had so many questions, but she knew she could not delay. "Was that an Alector?"

Rather an Ifrit from the latest world they are bleeding of life. You must watch the Table to see that they do not try again, and you must become stronger. You will not take them by surprise again.

"I hardly know what I'm doing," Mykella protested.

You must learn to use your Talent.

"How can I learn with all the plotting and scheming going on here?"

If you learn, then the plotters can do little to you. If you do not, it matters little whether the plotters succeed or fail.

"Give me some useful advice." *Not all these general platitudes.*

Seek and master the darkness beneath the Table. With that, the Ancient faded and vanished.

Seek and master the darkness beneath the Table? What did that mean? How?

Mykella sank onto her bed, then turned convulsively and buried her face in her pillow, trying to stifle the sound of her sobs and frustration.

11

Octdi morning was warmer, and a good breakfast left Mykella feeling less shaky than she had been when she woke, although she still felt tired when she reached the Finance chambers.

"Good morning, Mistress Mykella," offered Kiedryn cheerfully, "even if it is a shade on the chilly side."

"Good morning." She settled into the high-backed stool that she had found most comfortable for dealing with the large and heavy ledgers and opened the master ledger that Kiedryn had obviously placed there for her.

After leafing through to the last page and checking the handful of entries, she looked up. "You were a clerk for my grandfather, weren't you?"

"Lord-Protector Dainyl? Aye . . . I was. A junior clerk, down in the ledger entry section."

"What was he like?"

"I didn't see him often, Mistress Mykella. He was dark-haired, like your father, but stern like Lord Joramyl. Everyone said he was hard, but fair. Like his namesake."

"Who was his namesake?"

"According to the archives, and some writings of Lady Rachyla, Dainyl was the last High Alector of Justice and the last surviving Duarch. He was the only one she considered fair and just, but the name wasn't passed on until one of Mykel's great-grandsons received it."

"My grandfather was named after an Alector?" Mykella found that hard to believe.

"He was named after his forebears," Kiedryn said with a smile. "There have been three Dainyls."

"How many Mykels?"

"None. No one wanted to saddle a youth with living up to the name."

"I suppose I'm the first Mykella?"

"The first I know of, Mistress, but the archives aren't nearly so clear when it comes to daughters."

That scarcely surprised Mykella. "Where does Father's name come from?"

"Feran was the first arms-commander of Lanachrona. He came with Mykel. He was almost as fierce as Mykel, and one of his grand-daughters married Mykel's eldest grandson and heir."

At that moment, the corridor door opened, and one of the junior clerks from the bookkeeping rooms on the lower level appeared, carrying several ledgers. He inclined his head to Mykella and then to Kiedryn. "Mistress, sir . . . these be the ledgers with the latest entries for supplies for the Lord-Protector's palace accounts."

"Thank you, Shenyl." Kiedryn took the ledgers.

Mykella went back to going over the latest entries in the master ledger, but there wasn't anything there that looked obviously out of line.

A half glass or so later, once Kiedryn had reviewed the palace ledgers, Mykella began to study the entries there. She couldn't help but wince when she saw the charges for seamstresses. Most of the charges were accrued by Rachylana and her father. Her father? He seldom wore anything that new. After a moment, she nodded. Those charges were for Eranya's garments, one form of payment for her "services," Mykella suspected.

But if Eranya kept her father happy . . . Mykella certainly wasn't going to begrudge him that set of pleasures. Rachylana, on the other hand . . . The only ones she was dressing for seemed to be herself . . . and Berenyt.

By late afternoon, Mykella had the feeling that she had truly determined everything that she could from the various ledgers. She looked over the ledgers piled around her, and then at her personal ledger, which held the notes she had taken about the irregularities in all the official account ledgers. Despite all those irregularities, and what they suggested, they were not proof of what she *knew* had been happening.

In the end, there was no help for it. She'd have to find a way to visit the High Factors, bargemasters, and Seltyrs personally, and arrange it so that she finished those meetings before either Joramyl or her father knew what she was doing.

In the meantime, for the remaining time in the afternoon before she made her weekly trip to the Great Piers, she decided to look into the financial records of the Southern Guards.

Another half glass passed before one entry amid those made near the end of the fall accountings piqued her interest. Fifty golds for tack, paid to one Berjor, with the notation, "leatherworks, per Commander Demyl." She paged back through the ledger until she found a similar entry at the end of the harvest postings. More searching found another at the end of summer, and yet another at the end of spring. Each was for fifty golds. There was no similar entry for the end of winter, nor for the end of fall or harvest in the previous year.

To check farther back would require digging out the older ledgers from the Finance records storeroom, but Mykella knew she would not find any other references to a leatherworker or leatherworks named Berjor. Saelukyl was supposedly the best saddlemaker in Tempre, and she'd heard of others like Hemylcor and Essiant. She'd never heard of Berjor. By itself, that didn't mean anything, but two hundred golds for tack was a great deal, especially when all other outlays for the Southern Guards were steady or decreasing, and she hadn't found much in the way of entries marked for purchasing mounts. Also, Demyl was the second in command of the Southern Guards, just under Arms-Commander Nephryt, and why would it require the commander's approval for tack—except for the amount, which was far higher than it should have been, especially since the Guard wasn't expanding?

She rubbed her forehead, feeling overwhelmed.

Should she return to the Table chamber after dinner?

No. She could feel that she was still shaky, and if she had to deal with the distant Alector or Ifrit or whatever he might be, she wanted to be in complete control of herself, and she still had to ride to see the portmaster.

At half past third glass, she left the study and made her way to the stables, where she quickly saddled her gray gelding. The ride was uneventful, and she discovered nothing new from Chaenkel. She returned to the palace as the bells announcing the fifth glass of the afternoon chimed.

Still, she reflected, as she made her way back toward the family quarters, once she did discover something, she could tell her father that she was not just looking at figures in ledgers. When she reached the family quarters, she washed up and walked to the family parlor. It was empty. She eased up to the north-facing window and looked out at the gardens below, and then at the wooded slopes that formed the southwesternmost part of the Lord-Protector's Preserve.

She couldn't discover anything more until Londi, and she needed to do something to get her thoughts off the discrepancies in the Lord-Protector's accounts. If the weather held, perhaps she could persuade Salyna to accompany her on a ride through the Preserve. Some of the duty Southern Guards would have to accompany them, but on end-days the duty guards didn't mind at all, finding it preferable to standing by in the cramped duty building just to the east of the palace.

Sensing someone nearing, Mykella turned toward the parlor door. She felt as though it had to be Salyna. At that, she froze. How could she know that?

Yet the door opened, and Salyna stepped inside.

"What's the matter?" asked Salyna. "You look upset."

Mykella shook her head. "I was just thinking. I just *have* to get out of the palace. Would you like to take a ride with me in the Preserve tomorrow? If it doesn't rain, that is?"

Salyna smiled. "That would be lovely. Since it's in the Preserve, I can even bring my new saber. It's a fighting saber, and I even got Moraduk to let me sharpen it on the grindstone."

"Would you really want to be a Southern Guard, even if they took women?"

"No," admitted Salyna, "but it's the only way I can learn about weapons, and since I'll likely be matched to some younger son somewhere, I want to be able to protect myself. I had to prove to Undercommander Areyst that I could use a dagger before he'd let me pick up a saber."

Areyst? Mykella had seen the man on more than one occasion, but all she could recall was a vague impression of a blond officer who'd seemed muscular and competent.

"Does Father know?"

Salyna laughed. "I've never told him, but he has to know. Where we're concerned everyone tells him everything. I'm sure he thinks that I'll grow out of it, that, once I'm matched and dispatched from Tempre, weapons and the like will be a thing of the past."

Despite her sister's light tone, Mykella could feel the determination behind those words, a determination that concerned her, although she could not have said why.

"The seamstresses are already working on a green gown for you," Salyna ventured. "It won't be suitable for the season-turn parade, but it will be ready for the ball."

"I didn't ask—"

"Zestela said that you commanded it."

Mykella sighed. Once again, there would be stories about how difficult she was, when all she'd wanted was not to look like she'd been stuffed into a flour sack.

Neither Rachylana nor Jeraxylt joined them, not surprisingly, since Rachylana had been avoiding Mykella, and slightly before sixth glass, Mykella and Salyna stepped from the parlor.

The two walked along the main corridor and then into the family dining room, an oblong chamber on the west side of the upper level of the palace—on the south side of the serving staircase that led up to the pantry. The breakfast room was on the north side of the pantry. The serving staircase, which had obviously been added to the palace building later, led down to an archway through the original wall. On the other side of the wall were the kitchens. Even at an early age, Mykella had been able to see that the stonework of the one-story kitchens did not compare to that of the original structure, and over time, the stone floors of the kitchens had sloped slightly downhill to the west. Unlike the main part of the building, there were no lower levels, and storerooms for provisions had been added to the north and west. In the angle between the storerooms and the kitchens was a walled courtyard for receiving livestock and other supplies.

Mykella stood behind her chair, waiting for the others. At the evening meal, she did not sit to the left of her father at the long cherry table. Rather, she sat to the right of Eranya, who was always seated at Feranyt's right. Mykella had never quite understood why her father felt it proper for Eranya to be served as if she were his wife and consort at dinner, but why Eranya never ate breakfast with the family. Did Eranya just prefer to sleep late, or was there some elaborately rationalized reason for the difference?

Jeraxylt hurried in, wearing his Southern Guard uniform, and took his place to the left of where his father would sit, and then Rachylana followed, taking her place beside her older brother. Salyna stood behind her chair to the right of Mykella.

Within moments, Feranyt and Eranya appeared. The Lord-Protector's mistress was only five, possibly six years older than Mykella, with dark brown wavy hair and a heart-shaped face. She was tall and well-endowed, and every movement was graceful. Her brown eyes were kind. Because of that kindness, Mykella did her best to be polite and charming, difficult as that often was when she considered that Eranya was replacing her mother in her father's affections.

"Go ahead. Be seated," Feranyt said.

No one actually did get around to seating themselves until he was settled into his place at the head of the table.

"An excellent day," Feranyt stated, if to no one in particular, before looking to Jeraxylt. "How was your day?"

"We practiced mounted attacks with sabers." Jeraxylt smiled. "It's harder than it looks to strike down from the saddle without injuring yourself or your mount or those around you."

"That's why you practice, isn't it?" said Salyna lightly. "It looks interesting."

"You were watching?"

"For a time. I'd like to try it."

"Using weapons from the saddle takes skill," Jeraxylt replied.

"I can loose three shafts in a row from my bow at a gallop and hit the targets."

"That would be fine if you were a grassland nomad," her brother pointed out. "The Guard uses rifles."

"They won't let me use one. That's why I use the bow," Salyna pointed out.

"Rifles are not ladylike, are they?" asked Eranya.

"They both kill people," Salyna began, "and—"

"Enough," said Feranyt. "We can talk of better things than killing over dinner, can we not?" He smiled fondly at Eranya. "I daresay that with the grace and beauty at the table, that might be possible." He paused briefly, then looked down at the platter that had been placed before him. "Domestic fowl. More tender than quail or bush fowl, but not nearly so tasty. Not nearly."

Eranya smiled her agreement, politely, not quite timidly.

Mykella didn't agree. To her, bush fowl tasted gamy, almost rancid at times, and unless it was well seasoned and prepared, venison was equally distasteful, but no one wanted to hear her opinion, especially Rachylana.

"Oh . . ." Feranyt cleared his throat. "I do have an announcement of some import. You might like to know that there will be envoys from Southgate and Dereka here for the season-turn ball. Their sovereigns requested—quite politely—that their envoys be allowed to attend and to make your acquaintance."

"How droll," said Rachylana.

"They'll report on how we look and whether we look like good broodmares," added Salyna.

Mykella managed not to wince at her younger sister's words. While Mykella felt that way, she'd never voiced such words.

"Salyna . . ." Feranyt's use of his daughter's name was a clear reprimand. "Before long, I'll have to send envoys elsewhere to find a match for Jeraxylt. I would not wish to have them encounter such an unhelpful attitude. Such an attitude will not be in your best interests, either, I might add."

Salyna stiffened. After a moment, she replied, "I watched the envoys who came to the spring ball last year. They looked at Rachylana like she was a filly for breeding. I know matches must be made, but manners and consideration would be nice."

"I thought they were rather well-mannered, according to what your father said," offered Eranya. "Did they not all ask whether you would be happy in their lands?"

The smile that followed Eranya's words was not totally sympathetic, Mykella thought, but she thought she understood how her father's mistress felt. Eranya was bartering herself to better her future, with no guarantees at all for how long Feranyt's favor would last, while Mykella and her sisters would be granted far more in comfort and favor merely by the fact of their birth.

"I had not heard that," Mykella found herself saying, "but I am glad that they considered our happiness in a distant and strange land. We are fortunate in Tempre, and I would that more men considered the happiness of women."

The slightest hint of a frown crossed Eranya's forehead, then vanished. "We are indeed fortunate here, and beholden, especially to your father."

This time, the momentary stiffness of disapproval belonged to Rachylana.

Feranyt laughed, but Mykella could sense his uneasiness.

"We're all agreed then," the Lord-Protector said. "We're most fortunate here." He gestured for one of the serving girls to refill his wine goblet.

Until that moment, Mykella hadn't realized that he'd downed a full goblet during the interplay among the women. Had he been that uneasy in announcing the foreign envoys? Were they more important than she and her sisters thought?

"We are indeed," added Eranya.

Fortunate? By comparison to what? Mykella shivered. Even wearing nightsilk, she was a trace cold, but then the palace was always cold in winter.

After eating several bites of the already cool fowl, she stifled a yawn. All she really wanted was to finish dinner so that she could go to bed and get a good night's sleep.

12

Mykella slept dreamlessly and woke not that long after dawn. She knew she wouldn't get back to sleep. Unless she was exceedingly tired, once she woke in the morning, she was awake for the day. Even as a small child, she'd been told, she'd seldom taken naps.

She walked to the window and pulled back the hangings, then looked to the west. There, just above the horizon, was the three-quarter green-tinged disk of Asterta—the moon of the Ancients. Asterta had always intrigued her, although she could never have said why. Because she couldn't, she'd never told anyone. Salyna preferred the pearly light of Selena, and Rachylana didn't seem to notice either moon much at all.

With a half-smile, Mykella turned from the window and began her preparations for the day, heading to the washroom, washing up, and then returning to her chamber to don riding gear before making her way to the family breakfast room. Since Novdi was an end-day, Mykella and her sisters could eat breakfast anytime that they pleased.

Mykella had barely seated herself in the breakfast room when Salyna appeared. Muergya poured plain strong tea into Mykella's mug, then looked to Salyna.

"Tea is fine for me," said the younger woman.

"We just have egg toast and ham and syrup. That's all that's hot," offered the serving girl.

Both sisters nodded.

Mykella cupped her hands around the mug. The breakfast room was cold, even colder than her bedchamber, and she was glad to be wearing a wool sweater—also black—over her nightsilks.

"I hadn't heard anything about envoys for matches until Father mentioned it last night," Salyna said, once Muergya had hurried away. "Had you?"

"No," replied Mykella. "The other morning he even denied that there were any coming. I have to wonder what changed that."

"He said that they requested . . ." Salyna let the words trail off.

"Someone had to let them know that there was a possibility . . ." Mykella stopped. "Do you think . . . Rachylana?"

"She'd have to have gone through someone else."

"She wouldn't have gone through Berenyt . . ." Mykella stopped. "Unless . . ."

"Unless she was pretending that we were the ones interested," Salyna said, her voice low. Abruptly, she shook her head. "I can't believe she'd do that. Even Rachylana . . ."

"Someone did, unless it's a coincidence," Mykella pointed out. "I don't believe in coincidences like that."

"What about Cheleyza?"

Their uncle's young wife? That was a definite possibility, Mykella thought. "She'd have reason. Is she expecting?"

Salyna shrugged. "If she is, she's not showing."

"How do she and Berenyt get along?"

"How would any of us know?"

"Rachylana might," mused Mykella. "Could you bring it up with her? I've already said too much about Berenyt."

"I imagine so." Salyna smiled wryly. "I'll have to wait for the right time."

That might be a while, reflected Mykella.

Muergya returned with platters for each of them, and they ate with relatively innocuous conversation, conscious of the serving girl standing and waiting in the pantry.

Before all that long they had finished, then gathered their riding jackets and gloves, and made their way down to the main level and along the wide corridors to the east door.

Once she was outside, Mykella's breath steamed in the cold morning air, under the bright silver-green sky, as she and Salyna crossed the east courtyard to the stables. Mykella preferred to saddle her own mount—the sturdy gray gelding—as much to prove that she could, as to be certain that everything was as it should be.

In less than half a glass, she led the gelding out of the stables and mounted. Salyna was already waiting. Mykella noted that there were six Southern Guards in the courtyard, mounted and waiting. Usually, there were only two guards for each of them—unless they were headed into the city or farther away from Tempre. She turned to Salyna. "Six?"

"I mentioned we were taking a ride to Rachylana, but . . . she said she wasn't sure she wanted to come with us."

At that moment, Rachylana walked sedately across the courtyard, wearing a deep green and form-fitting leather riding jacket that set off her hair and her figure. She glanced toward her sisters. "I'll only be a moment. Ostryl should have the mare saddled and ready for me."

Mykella wasn't certain whether she felt more like sighing or laughing. Trust Rachylana to make an entrance—even if only Southern Guards could appreciate it. Then, that was also another dig at Mykella, without saying a word. Mykella glanced toward Salyna.

Her younger sister just offered the tiniest headshake.

Rachylana was as good as her word, leading the mare out and mounting quickly within moments. She then rode over and reined up beside Salyna.

"Shall we go?" asked Mykella, easing her gelding forward.

One of the guards rode ahead and opened the iron-grilled gate at the northeast end of the courtyard. Beyond the gate lay the Preserve, its ancient and high oaks and maples bare in the winter, with only a scattering of pines and firs to provide a touch of green.

The path immediately north of the gate was packed clay, wide enough for three riders, but Mykella found herself riding with one of the Southern Guards, her sisters behind her. Within moments two more guards eased past her and took the lead.

Mykella forced herself to smile. Although she would have much preferred to have ridden in the lead, the Southern Guards had their orders, and arguing would just have been futile. It also would have resulted in displeasing her father, as well as possibly limiting her freedom even more. So she watched everything, from the men riding in front of her to signs of game well away from the main path, which had turned eastward, paralleling the River Vedra, although the wooded hills to the north blocked any possible sight of the river from the main riding path. Still, if she could persuade her sisters to ride for a time, they would come to the path that led through a low point between the hills to the river. As they left the palace behind, and Tempre itself, the wind picked up, coming out of the north-northeast and carrying a hint of the chill and ice of the Aerlal Plateau.

They'd ridden a little more than a vingt when Mykella heard Salyna, not all that far behind her, change the nature of her casual conversation with Rachylana.

"I was thinking about what Father said at dinner last night," Salyna began.

"Oh . . . he says many things." Rachylana's voice conveyed uninterest, almost boredom.

Mykella forced herself not to look back, but to look to the path ahead.

"About envoys seeking matches," Salyna prompted. "Just last week Father said he hadn't sent out any messages or feelers. Even if he had sent a messenger the day after he told us, there wouldn't have been time for any responses. It's a good week by fast post-rider to Southgate, and that's the closest capital."

"It has to be a coincidence. We *are* among the few daughters of rulers. Of a marriageable age, that is," replied Rachylana.

"You didn't happen to indicate that to someone, in passing, per-haps?" asked Salyna.

"Why would I do that? I'm certainly not in any hurry at all to be married off to some outlander in a near-barbaric place like Fola, or a land like Deforya where it's winter two-thirds of the year." She paused. "I can see why you'd think it puzzling, but I don't want a match like that, certainly not badly enough to send out hints to anyone."

"Do you think Lady Cheleyza might? She's always trying to be helpful. She did send a dress to Mykella."

"She did. That's what she's like. She wouldn't do something be-hind anyone's back. She'd either ask if one of us wanted help, or she'd tell Uncle Joramyl that he should do something to help us."

Mykella frowned. She didn't believe Cheleyza was anywhere near that forthright, and she couldn't believe Rachylana thought so, either, but she had gotten the feeling that Rachylana believed what she had said about not wanting to be married off, and yet . . .

"Ladies . . . there's someone coming. They're riding up from the south."

The three guards rode forward to form a line, reining up and drawing their sabers. Mykella reined up and waited calmly, glancing back at her sisters. Salyna fingered the saber at her waist.

"It's Berenyt," Rachylana declared with a smile.

"Berenyt?" questioned Salyna.

"I told him we'd be taking a ride. He said he might join us. He's coming from the south, because that's where Lord Joramyl's estate adjoins the Preserve."

In fact, very shortly Berenyt appeared, letting his mount carry him toward Mykella's party at a measured walk. Berenyt wore a dark blue heavy-weather Guard riding jacket over his Guard uniform. After he reined up, he bowed in the saddle to the three young women. "Ladies . . . you set a quick pace."

"Mykella always does," replied Rachylana.

Berenyt turned his eyes on Mykella. "Perhaps a match to one of the wealthy nightsheep herders might better suit your temperament, Mistress Mykella."

Mykella knew she flushed at the insult, but she could hope that her reaction was concealed by the ruddiness caused by the wind and the ride. "My temperament perhaps, cousin, but certainly not my taste . . . just as you might be suited by temperament to a passionate Hafin courtesan."

Berenyt stiffened in the saddle.

"Mykella . . ." murmured Rachylana from where she had reined up her mare behind her older sister.

"Definitely a northern temper you have, cousin," Berenyt said, almost languidly.

Mykella could sense the anger beneath the slow and casual cadence of his words. She shouldn't have reacted so directly, but for more reasons than she could count, she disliked and distrusted her handsome blond and green-eyed cousin. "I've been known to be intemperate, cousin, but let us lay that aside and ride. I had thought we might take the river trail, and then come back along the west wall path of the Preserve."

"A healthy ride on a brisk day," agreed Berenyt.

Mykella nodded to the Southern Guards. "We'd best be going, then, if we wish to be back while it's still light."

The three van-guards eased their mounts ahead.

Mykella let them move away before she urged the gelding forward. She disliked being hemmed in, either while riding or in any other fashion.

Salyna eased her mount up beside her older sister, while Berenyt guided his mount around Salyna and swung in beside Rachylana.

Mykella did not look back as Rachylana began to speak to Berenyt. "Where did you find your mount? He's magnificent."

"He's been bred out of the best of the Ongelyan stock that Great-grandfather procured as a settlement when he turned back the nomad invasion. He can run forever. . . ."

"You trained him, didn't you?"

Salyna glanced at Mykella, then let her eyes drift back before shaking her head so slightly that neither Rachylana nor Berenyt were likely to see the movement from behind, even had they been watching Salyna.

Mykella concentrated on riding and taking in the Preserve for the rest of the ride, that and ignoring the low intermittent conversation between Rachylana and Berenyt.

Once they returned to the palace in late afternoon, although she didn't much feel like it, Mykella unsaddled the gelding and began the tedious but necessary grooming and rubdown. She was about half through when Salyna appeared by the stall wall.

"You don't have to do that," observed Salyna.

"No, but I should."

"Only sons who will be Lords-Protector should," countered Salyna.

"Has Rachylana left?" asked Mykella.

"She and Berenyt went to the solarium."

"Leaving others to take care of their mounts, and at her suggestion, I'd wager."

"I didn't see him protesting."

"I heard you asking her about the envoys," Mykella said, returning to currying the gelding.

"She denied that she had anything to do with it," Salyna said.

"No . . . that's not quite what she said. She said she certainly wasn't interested in a match with any outlander."

"Do you think . . . ?"

"I don't know what to think," replied Mykella firmly. Except she did. Rachylana was scheming to get Mykella and Salyna married off and out of Tempre so that she could marry Berenyt. While marriages to cousins were frowned upon, they weren't forbidden and occasionally occurred, usually when they involved land, holdings, or the family of the Lord-Protector.

13

On Decdi morning, the true end-day of the week, the Lord-Protector's family had a late morning brunch, rather than breakfast. When Mykella reached the table, just behind Salyna, it was not because she had risen later, but because she had been thinking, not only about the question of envoys for matching, but also about the irregularities in the Lord-Protector's accounts. The problem with the accounts remained that she was likely to be the only one to claim that there were discrepancies, and she still had nothing her father would accept as proof.

As Mykella seated herself, she noted that both her father and Jeraxylt wore the leather vests they used for hunting. Salyna wore a similar vest, except hers was more scuffed and well-worn.

"I hear you all had a long ride yesterday," Feranyt said cheerfully.

"I didn't," said Jeraxylt.

"Your sisters did. So did your cousin Berenyt." Feranyt turned to Mykella. "How was it?"

"I always enjoy the river trail the most, especially on an end-day. Sometimes, you can feel as though the trees had been there forever. The Preserve is special."

"It is," agreed Feranyt. "Some of the Seltyrs are claiming it shouldn't belong to the Lord-Protector."

"That's stupid," snorted Jeraxylt. "Who else's would it be?"

Mykella took a sip of the tea that Akilsa had poured. It was tolerably warm and strong enough. She immediately took two slices of the sweet cheese bread from the platter in the middle of the table.

"That's not the question," Feranyt replied. "First, those who want something try to get everyone to believe that it's not yours . . . or shouldn't be. Then they start suggesting that it would be better handled by someone else, usually themselves, on behalf of someone else who does indeed appear truly deserving. Of course, if they persuade everyone to let them administer it, somehow, in time, it ends up as theirs . . . or they make a healthy amount of gold in transferring it to yet another party."

"For the Preserve?" asked Rachylana. "It's just woodland."

"It's very lovely woodland on high ground where a great number of High Factors or Seltyrs would love to place an estate, and it's close to Tempre."

"They wouldn't do that, would they? Really?" pressed Rachylana.

"I'm not about to let them, but they would if they could. Most people would take what they could if they could get away with it," said Feranyt.

Mykella nodded, but she wondered why her father did not see that his words might well apply to his own brother.

After several moments of silence, Salyna spoke. "You're going hunting today, aren't you?"

Jeraxylt ignored her words and instead cut a section of egg toast and stuffed it into his mouth.

"Why, yes," answered Feranyt. "At least, we'd thought to."

"Might I also go with you?"

Feranyt frowned slightly, tilting his head to the left, as if considering the matter.

"You've never been hunting," mumbled Jeraxylt.

Mykella concealed a smile. Her father was not quite so circumspect, and the corners of his mouth quirked upward.

"I'm almost as tall as you are and just as good as you are with a blade," Salyna said.

"You're better than some," Jeraxylt conceded.

"If I'm better than some, and you're that good, and I'm with you, then you don't have to worry about me, do you?" Salyna said.

Feranyt laughed. "You can come."

Jeraxylt smiled, reluctantly. "You can see how it's done."

"That would be good," Salyna agreed.

Mykella had to admire Salyna for her adroitness and timing. A year earlier, she would have pressed the issue directly.

Once everyone had eaten and the hunters had departed, Mykella made her way to the library adjoining her father's official study—as opposed to the small private study off his quarters. She wasn't in the mood to read, but she knew that Rachylana wouldn't follow her there. She did spend a little time looking through the shelves, until she found an old leather-bound volume entitled *History of Lanachrona*.

Although she had not seen the book before and leafed through it eagerly, she found very little on Mykel the Great, just a short chapter at the beginning. The opening words clearly foreshadowed what followed:

> The history of Lanachrona as an independent land began immediately after the Great Cataclysm with the arrival in Tempre of a Cadmian Majer who commanded a battalion of Mounted Rifles. Through some means unknown and unrecorded he persuaded the Seltyrs and High Factors to accept him as Lord-Protector of Tempre. Shortly thereafter, he married Rachyla, the aunt of one Seltyr and the cousin of another. No direct records of the time before his arrival remain, and few enough of that time except the words of the oath that Mykel himself wrote and spoke in becoming Lord-Protector.
>
> > I swear and affirm that I will protect and preserve the lives and liberties of all citizens of Tempre and Lanachrona, and that I will employ all Talent and skills necessary to do so, at all times, and in all places, so that peace and prosperity may govern this land and her people.

Mykella read the oath three times before she realized what was different. The oath she had heard her father take was the same, word for word—except two words had been missing. They were "Talent and."

Why had the original oath been changed to eliminate those words? Because Mykel had in fact possessed Talent and expected subsequent Lords-Protector to have it? But if she had such Talent, how much value lay in the ability to move undetected and to sense at times what others felt? Or was there more to her Talent? How much more?

She closed the book and slipped it back into its place on the shelf, then moved to the library door that opened out onto the main corridor. She concentrated on creating the impression of a closed door, even while she opened it and stepped out into the corridor. The guard near the top of the main staircase did not even look in her direction.

While she dreaded descending to the Table chamber, it was more than clear that she needed to learn more. It was already nearly three days after her last and nearly deadly encounter with the Alector—or Ifrit—and she dared not postpone that learning any longer. Continuing her critical review of the ledgers holding the Lord-Protector's accounts had been slow, and less than encouraging, because she saw the same patterns everywhere. There were revenues missing from almost all the accounts, she thought, but any given amount was comparatively small, although the totals were probably not. Again, she had no real proof, only calculations and estimates and comparisons. That lack of real evidence was yet another reason why she had to revisit the Table, although she was dreading doing so. But the Ancient had been quite definite, and Mykella had the feeling that matters were not about to improve by themselves. Greater control of the Table seemed to be the only possible way she could help her father against what appeared to be her uncle's machinations.

Because it was light, the only guards on the main level were posted in the rotunda of the main entrance, although, since it was an end-day, they took turns walking the halls. With her sight-shield, that arrangement was much easier to avoid, and she managed to reach and unlock the door to the lower staircase undetected, as well as lock it behind her. The staircase and the lower corridor were empty, but as quiet as she tried to be, her boots still echoed faintly in the silence as she walked toward the Table chamber.

Mykella pressed the door lever, then entered the Table chamber with trepidation. The Table itself continued to hold a diminished purplish glow, and she released a long sigh as she approached it. Once there, she tried to sense more than the vague impression of what the Ancient had called the darkness beneath. For a time, all she could feel was the slime-like purpleness, faint as it was.

Then, she gained a stronger feeling of the blackness below, deeper and darker and far more extensive than she had sensed before, yet carrying a shade of green much like that of the soarer herself. From somewhere, she recalled that to use some properties of the Table, one had to stand on it. Did she dare?

She laughed softly. How could anything more happen if she stood on the block of solid stone? Still . . .

After a time, she climbed onto the Table and looked down at the mirrored surface beneath her. It reflected everything, and she was more than glad, absently, that she was wearing her usual nightsilk trousers. From where she stood, she tried once more to feel, to connect to the dark greenish black well beneath the Table itself. She pushed away the thought that there couldn't be anything but more rock beneath the stone of the Table, immersing herself in the feeling of that darkness, a darkness that somehow seemed warmer than the purple, though both were chill.

She began to feel pathways—greenish black—extending into the distance in all directions. Was that how Mykel had traveled? She *reached* for the pathways, feeling herself sinking through the Table, even below it, with chill purpleness and golden-greenish-black all around her.

Surrounded by solid stone! Cold solid stone . . .

She had to get out. She had to! Mykella forced calm upon herself and concentrated on feeling herself rise upward until she was certain her boots were clear of the Table. Only then did she look down—to discover that her boots were a good third of a yard above the surface of the Table.

That couldn't be!

The sudden drop onto the hard mirrored surface of the Table convinced her that it could be—and had been. She tottered there for a moment, then straightened. Had that been how Mykel had walked on air and water? By reaching out to the darkness beneath the ground?

She almost wanted to scream. She kept learning things, but what she learned—except for being able to conceal herself—didn't seem to provide the sort of skills she needed.

Mykella eased herself off the Table and studied it, just trying to sense everything around it. As she did, she gradually became aware that there were unseen webs or lines everywhere. Ugly pinkish purple lines ran from the Table to the south, to the southwest, and to the northeast, but those lines did not touch the far more prevalent blackish green lines that were deeper and broader—stronger, in a sense. When she looked down, she was surprised to sense a greenish black line running from herself into the depths and connecting to the stronger web.

She shook her head. Somehow she was connected to the world, but everyone was, and she couldn't see how that could help—except that she might be able to travel that web, if that had been how Mykel had traveled, if indeed the old tales about him were right. But she wasn't ready to run away. Besides, what good would that do, except land her someplace else, where she'd be penniless and totally friendless? As a woman of position in Tempre, she was powerless enough, if comfortable, and anywhere else would likely be far worse . . . and far, far less hospitable. And, if she were honest with herself, she wasn't certain she wanted to feel herself sinking through and surrounded by solid stone as chill as ice.

She straightened and looked directly at the Table. At least, she ought to be able to see what Joramyl was doing.

When the swirling mists cleared, she saw Joramyl with three other men in a paneled study. The four, seated around a conference table, were Joramyl, Berenyt, Arms-Commander Nephryt, and Commander Demyl. Whatever they were discussing was serious enough that there were frowns on most faces. Then Joramyl said something, and both Demyl and Nephryt laughed. After the briefest moment, so did Berenyt.

Try as she might, and as long as she watched, Mykella could not hear their words nor discover more. After a time, as her head began to ache, she stepped back from the Table.

She still felt like screaming in frustration, but she was too tired . . . and too worried. Instead, she rubbed her forehead and then slipped out of the Table chamber and, using her Talent for concealment, made her way back to her chamber. There, for a time, she sat on the edge of her bed, closed her eyes, and thought.

She was angry with herself. Why had she gotten so upset when all the stone had been around her? She'd seen the Ancient appear and travel through the stone. Why had she panicked? Because she hated being closed in?

She couldn't let her fears keep her from learning. She just couldn't.

Finally, she stood, steeling herself to head back down to the Table and try again.

Thrap.

Instantly, Mykella knew that it was Salyna. She could sense her sister, and she hurried to the door and opened it.

Salyna stood there with a slightly bemused expression. Beneath the bemusement was irritation, if not anger.

"Come in." Mykella closed the door behind Salyna before she asked, "What happened?"

"Father said I didn't know enough about hunting etiquette to use a rifle. So I brought my bow. The horn bow I bought last year . . . you know the one?"

Mykella did. It was the kind of bow that the grassland nomads used. Mykella had had trouble even drawing it, but Salyna had practiced for seasons until she could use it from the saddle. "What happened? You brought down a stag?"

Salyna shook her head. "Just a young boar that charged Jeraxylt. He missed, even with the rifle. I managed two shafts. The second one was lucky, but it brought him down."

"He and Father insisted I dress out the boar. Jeraxylt tried to tell me what to do." Salyna laughed. "Chatelaine Auralya already taught me how to butcher and clean—time after time. There's not that much difference between a hog and a boar. None, really. That didn't make him happy, either."

Mykella shook her head. "They won't take you again."

Salyna drew herself up. "They can't say I can't take care of myself."

"They won't say anything," Mykella replied. "They just won't tell you when they plan to go."

Salyna looked defiant for a moment before she frowned. "How . . . how can they do that?"

"Because they can."

"That's not what I meant. How can they . . . just . . . forget that I'm as good as Jeraxylt is?"

"It's easier to ignore than to accept," Mykella replied, "especially for men."

Salyna looked hard at her sister. Then she laughed, if ruefully. "Oh . . . Mykella . . ."

Mykella understood.

14

On Londi morning, Mykella was awake early and the first in the washroom before breakfast, but the water in the pitchers was still barely lukewarm. She washed up quickly and had just pulled her robe around her when Salyna appeared.

"You didn't use all the warm water, did you?" Salyna's blond hair barely looked disarrayed, for all that she'd clearly just left her bed.

Mykella knew that, had she not already dampened and smoothed her own heavy black hair, half would have been standing on end, and the other half twisted into unruly shapes that neither comb nor brush would have turned into anything presentable.

"Just my pitcher. It's not all that warm, though." Mykella tried not to stare at Salyna as she realized that she could see the faintest of darkish brown lines running from Salyna slightly to the west and downward.

"What is it?" asked Salyna.

"Nothing." Mykella shook her head. "I was thinking of something else." She offered a crooked smile as she left and returned to her chamber to dress in her nightsilk garments.

Once she was alone in her chamber, she tried to sense her own line . . . or thread, whatever it was. Salyna's had been a dark brown, but it had held no black or green. Somehow, she could sense that the threads connected people to the world. But . . . how . . . and of what use was sensing such a link? Or did the colors mean something that could tell her about people?

She took a deep breath. As if she didn't have enough to worry about.

After dressing, she brushed her hair until it was smooth and at least presentable. She paused to study herself in the dressing mirror. Comparatively short as it was, her hair was getting longer than she liked. Sometime in the next few days . . .

She shook her head. That could wait.

She was looking forward to seeing Jeraxylt, if only to ask him about the hunting, but when she walked into the breakfast room, his place was empty. She seated herself and waited, while Muergya poured her tea.

Salyna appeared, wearing her scuffed and scraped leather arms vest over her tunic and trousers, attired for working with weapons. Behind her came Rachylana, in a dress clearly thrown on for breakfast, because it was beige, older, and loose-fitting, and Rachylana never appeared in public in anything that did not show her at her best. Mykella noted that Rachylana's thread was a light, almost golden brown.

Jeraxylt did not follow his sisters, and Mykella wondered why he was so late in getting to the table, since he was usually ravenous in the morning.

Feranyt appeared within moments, settling into his place at the head of the table. "Good morning, daughters."

"Good morning," Mykella replied, studying her father's thread, a darker brown, like Salyna's. Did it have a hint of black? She wasn't certain.

Rachylana's greeting was more mumbled and trailed Mykella's. Salyna's mouth was full, and she nodded.

After Feranyt had taken several swallows of his spiced tea, Mykella looked at the empty place across from her. "Father . . . have you seen Jeraxylt?"

"Oh . . . I sent him off on maneuvers with Second Company. They left well before dawn. I thought he needed to get away from Tempre for a time."

"And from his sisters?" Mykella kept her tone light.

"Hardly. He can keep away from you through his own initiative," her father bantered back. "No . . . Second Company will be working in Viencet, and Jeraxylt needs to see what life is like away from Tempre."

"Viencet?" asked Mykella.

"It's a lazy little town half a day's ride southwest, where the high roads split, the one west toward Salcer and the one southwest to Zalt and Southgate." Feranyt chuckled. "Do you know where its name came from?"

Mykella had no idea.

"The story is that it was named after Mykel the Great's younger brother, because Mykel said the people there were even more indolent than Viencet."

"I didn't know he had a brother."

"The legend is that Mykel threw him out because he wouldn't work."

"That's awful," said Rachylana.

"Was Mykel really that cruel?" asked Salyna.

Feranyt shrugged. "It's only a story. Most of them aren't true, you know. Not the old ones or the humorous ones. People make them up to show things, and what really happened is usually changed or lost." He paused for a moment. "There might be some truth in that one, though. Mykel actually exiled one of his sons. They didn't call it that, but he sent him south to bring Soupat and the southlands into Lanachrona. After he did, Mykel then left him there as his personal representative. The son died there, even before Mykel did."

"Why would he do that?" asked Rachylana.

Mykella could easily see how that might happen. If Berenyt were a brother, rather than a cousin, the most sensible thing to do would be to send him far, far away.

"It was a harder time," Feranyt temporized, then took refuge in the omelet that appeared on his platter.

"Do you know when Jeraxylt will be back?" Mykella finally asked.

"Not for several days," mumbled her father.

Several days? Mykella wanted to shake her head. Her brother's absence couldn't have come at a more inopportune time, but there was no help for that.

Her omelet appeared next, and she ate methodically. That was the best she could do, because the omelet was warm but had the texture of almost-congealed glue, if a better taste. The apricot preserves on the cool toast helped.

She wasn't happy about waiting, but how could a few days matter when the thefts had been going on for seasons, if not longer?

15

The remainder of Londi didn't bring any more surprises, but neither did anything occur to reassure Mykella. She had learned that everyone had one of the threads, even Eranya, whose thread was such a light brown that it was more like tan. That amused her, because to Mykella, that suggested that her father's mistress was not exactly the most mentally gifted. Still, from what she had observed, she'd decided that the strands were some form of life-thread. That did not reassure her, either, and by the time she left the dinner table, her stomach was churning because she knew what she had to do, and she was not looking forward to it in the slightest.

Especially since she didn't know when Jeraxylt might return, Mykella knew she needed to follow the soarer's advice about the darkness beneath the Table. Despite her fears, she did need to learn more. So, after it seemed quiet in the family quarters that night, she slipped out of her room once more, using her Talent to conceal herself.

This time, she merely waited until the guard stationed near the staircase to the lower level moved before slipping behind him and quietly unlocking the door, then opening it and relocking it behind her.

The emptiness of the staircase and the long lower corridor reminded her, if in a different way, just how alone she was in what she was attempting. She pushed that thought aside as she entered the ancient chamber. The Table remained as it had been before, nearly quiescent, but the darkness beneath seemed stronger and closer. Given her father's lack of concern about Joramyl, she might indeed need to escape Tempre, but did she really want to do it by trying to travel those dark webs?

For a time, she just looked at the Table, feeling the unseen purpleness. Finally, she stepped up and onto the Table, seeking the green blackness once more. Nothing happened. She concentrated on becoming one with the green, and, this time, she once more found herself sinking through and beneath the Table and into the depths beneath. She could not move, and a chill filled her from her bones outward.

Chill? What was so cold?

She tried to reach for an even more distant greenish blackness. Slowly, she began to sense movement, but it was as though she remained suspended and frozen in place while the greenish darkness sweep by her. The motion ended. She willed herself to rise upward, and she found herself in a different darkness—a mere absence of light—and the biting cold of a raging winter. Somewhere above her, the wind howled. She exhaled, and she did not so much see as hear and feel it as ice crystals fell from the steam of her instantly frozen breath.

Her entire body was so cold, so tired . . .

She shook her head. Wherever she was, if she didn't leave, she would likely freeze to death in the darkness where she stood. Trying to reach the darkness beneath her was far harder than it had been before. Her eyes watered, and her tears began to freeze on her cheeks. Even sliding downward seemed to take forever. While she had thought the depths would be warmer, she remained cold, immobile, icy tears frozen in place on her cheeks in the silent depths.

Tempre! She had to reach Tempre. This time, she called up an image of the Table chamber, with her standing before the Table, its purple mist just faintly sensed.

At last, she felt movement, as though walls of blackness swept by and around her while she stood, frozen like a statue of ice, with tears on her cheeks, ice upon ice.

Later, how much later, she could not tell, she found herself standing on the Tempre Table for a long moment. She tried to make her
legs move, to carry her off the cold stone, but as her boots touched
the stone of the floor, her legs collapsed, and another darkness en-
folded her.

When she woke again, beside the Table, she knew it had to be
close to dawn. It took every bit of strength she had to hold the sight-
shield as she started the return to her chamber. Each step was an effort, and opening and closing the door to the lower staircase seemed
to take an entire glass in itself.

Her head felt as though it were floating away from her body as she
climbed the main staircase, slowly putting one boot in front of the
other, one step at a time.

Finally, she reached her chamber, where, once inside, she released
the sight-shield and slumped onto the bed, her entire body shuddering and shivering with the chill that remained from her attempt to
travel the Tables. Her last conscious effort was to drag the quilts
around her in an attempt to get warm.

16

Duadi morning came all too soon, and Mykella did
not even hear the mild *thrap* of Uleana's first knock on her door. The
second knock was louder, far louder.

"Mistress Mykella, it's almost time for breakfast."

"It can't be," Mykella muttered to herself before she slowly pulled
herself into a sitting position on the side of the bed. "It can't be."

She realized that she was still dressed, except for her boots. So she
pulled them on and tried as best she could with the brush to smooth
her unruly hair into place. Then she hurried out of her chamber to
the washroom, where she quickly did her face and smoothed her hair.

For all her rush, she reached the breakfast room just as Salyna did.
The two were seated when Rachylana arrived. The redhead wore a

deep blue day dress, not quite so form-fitting as one of her ball gowns, but a garment definitely designed to show her charms.

Mykella refrained from asking whether Rachylana intended to see Berenyt, but she did glance sideways to Salyna. The blonde, who wore trousers and a riding jacket, rolled her eyes for a moment. Mykella swallowed a grin.

"Good morning, daughters," announced Feranyt.

"Good morning," replied the three, not quite simultaneously.

"It's blustery out, but the clouds have yet to show," said the Lord-Protector as he seated himself. "It might be a few days more before we get snow."

"I hope not, or if it does snow, I hope it melts before the season-turn parade," said Rachylana. "What's the point of standing up there on the reviewing stand all wrapped in wool and nightsilk so that no one can see you when we're supposed to be seen."

"Rachylana," replied Feranyt firmly, "*that* is precisely the point. The Lord-Protector and his family are meant to be there, in fair weather and in foul. It matters little to the people whether we are in heavy cloaks or jackets or in finery, but it does matter that we are seen. A Lord-Protector cannot be seen only when times and weather are good."

Mykella had to agree with her father on that. She also wondered if being seen in finery regarded as too ostentatious might also be unwise, particularly when times were hard.

"Yes, sir," replied Rachylana demurely.

Even though Rachylana smiled, Mykella could sense her resentment at being corrected. That aspect of her Talent might be useful, if only to avoid upsetting people. For the remainder of breakfast, she ate quietly, finishing the egg toast and ham strips with two full mugs of strong tea.

Then she sat, waiting for her father to finish.

When he stood, he motioned to her. "You're finished, I see. I'd like a moment with you."

"Yes, sir." Mykella rose and followed him from the breakfast room and out into the main upstairs corridor. He was concerned about something, but she couldn't tell what.

Feranyt turned and waited until Mykella halted less than a yard from him. "I heard that you rejected an offer of a dress from Lady Cheleyza." The Lord-Protector's green eyes fixed on his daughter.

"It was most kind of her, Father, but the dress would not have suited me." That was true enough. "I attempted to convey that neither the colors nor the cut would reflect well on me or you."

"Rather too forcefully, I would judge," Feranyt said gently. "According to Joramyl, Cheleyza was rather upset."

Mykella could see the writing appearing on the slate. "I wouldn't want her to think that. Perhaps I should ride over to see her and to convey my apologies for any inadvertent misunderstanding."

"Perhaps you should. Today."

"I'll dress and leave immediately."

"It's best not to let unintended slights go unaddressed, especially with family." Feranyt smiled. "I'll let the duty guards know."

"Thank you." Mykella smiled as warmly as she could manage.

The expression seemed enough, because her father returned the smile, then nodded and turned toward his official study.

As Mykella walked back to her quarters, she considered matters. Riding over to tender what amounted to an apology to Joramyl's wife would take a good part of another day, or at least of the morning, but she might as well rebuild the stones in that wall because she really couldn't go any further in gathering proof about what Joramyl was doing until Jeraxylt returned. It also might deflect attention from what she was investigating, and, if she were careful, she might even learn something. For all that, she was worried. She definitely hadn't planned on Jeraxylt being away from the palace for so long.

She wasn't about to change into the split skirts used by Rachylana for riding. Trousers suited her far better, but she did wash up more thoroughly and changed into her best set of nightsilk blacks, along with her better nightsilk riding jacket. As a concession to her father and fashion, she searched until she found a brilliant green scarf that would soften the severity of her otherwise all black ensemble. Then she left her chamber and made her way down the main staircase, past the guards, and onto the main level. It was early enough that the lower level of the palace had not yet been opened to those who had business there,

She took the east door and crossed the courtyard to the stables.

There she groomed and then saddled the gray gelding. Just as she was about to lead him from the stall and out into the courtyard, she paused. She sensed that even the gelding had a form of life-thread, more grayish, and thinner. Did everything?

For a moment, she felt as though her entire world had turned somehow under her and that while it all looked the same, nothing was quite as it had been. She forced her thoughts back to dealing with Cheleyza and led the gray out of the stable and into the courtyard, where six Southern Guards, already mounted, awaited her. At the front was an older squad leader. All of them had life-threads of various shades of brown.

"You'll be riding to Lord Joramyl's, Mistress Mykella?" asked the squad leader.

"I am," she replied, searching for the guard's name amid her momentary confusion at sensing so many threads and finally recalling it, "Jekardyn." She could sense a combination of satisfaction and concern when she pronounced his name, as if he were glad to be recognized, and yet worried about it as well.

She mounted quickly, then nodded to Jekardyn.

"Forward!" ordered the squad leader.

Mykella rode in the middle, with a pair of guards before her, Jekardyn beside her, and the other three behind her. The iron gates on the south side of the courtyard swung wide as the first guards neared. Once past the gates, the guards and Mykella rode down the paved entry road and then turned eastward onto the avenue that led to the main compound for the Southern Guards.

With the chill gusts of wind that came and went, but were always out of the north, Mykella was glad for the nightsilk riding jacket and trousers, since the white light of the winter sun coming out of the silver-green sky of the east afforded little warmth.

Mykella had always been vaguely amused that the Southern Guard building had been built exactly 2,000 yards—one vingt precisely—from the center entrance to the Lord-Protector's Palace. Had the Alectors even used the same measurements? Or had people just kept using them? She supposed it was the latter, but no one had ever really said, and there was nothing about that in the histories.

The gray stone structure—a square building a good two hundred yards on a side with a huge paved center courtyard—was even more massive than the palace. Behind it, separated by a good fifty yards of ancient gray pavement, were the stables for the Southern Guards.

As they rode past the Guard building, Mykella couldn't help but hear the low words from the trio riding behind her.

". . . younger and older ones ride better than his heirness . . ."

". . . redhead does, too, for all her airs . . ."

". . . this one . . . different . . ."

She glanced at the squad leader, but he was scanning the avenue ahead. Couldn't he hear what she did? She didn't sense any concern from him, and a squad leader should have been concerned about what his men were saying, even if he said nothing to them until later. Or was the acute hearing part of her Talent, something she hadn't fully recognized before?

Another half-glass passed as they followed the eternastone avenue, which was also the high road that eventually ran south out of Tempre. Then, on the east side of the road appeared Joramyl's estate. The dwelling itself, standing back a good three hundred yards from the road at the end of a paved drive that curved through low gardens, was not exactly either a mansion or a villa, Mykella decided, but something of each, a two-story structure constructed as a V, with the open area between the two wings forming the entry courtyard. But the entry portico was on the north wing, and a walled garden filled the innermost section of the vertex of the V. At one time, it had been a family dwelling for Feranyt's grandfather, but Feranyt had allowed Joramyl to use it as his own, although it did belong to the Lord-Protector.

As she rode up the drive toward the entry portico, Mykella straightened in the saddle. She was not looking forward to seeing Cheleyza. Joramyl's first wife had died almost a year after Berenyt had been born, but most believed that she'd never really recovered from the lengthy labor. His second wife had not borne any children, and then had died after a lengthy illness following a miscarriage some three years earlier. Joramyl had married Cheleyza—the youngest daughter of the Prince of Northcoast—almost two years ago. In fact, it would be two years on year-turn day.

The two footmen stationed by the entry doors stiffened as they saw Mykella and the Southern Guards. Then one scurried inside for a moment, before returning to his post.

Mykella dismounted carefully. Even with a mounting block, it was hard to be graceful, short as she was.

"Mistress Mykella . . ." stammered the graying footman. "No one . . ."

"I'm here to see Lady Cheleyza. I believe she is here."

"Yes, Mistress, but she was not expecting . . ."

"I do understand, but convey to her that I will not require much of her time. I know she has much to do in supervising the house."

The footman bowed again. "Yes, Mistress Mykella. If you would not mind waiting in the receiving parlor while I inform her . . ."

Mykella followed him through the oiled and shining golden oak double doors—opened by the junior footman—and across the polished rose marble floor of the high-ceilinged entry hall. Slightly darker rose marble columns framed walls of white marble. Besides a pair of archways, situated on both sides of the hall, there were also two doors of dark oak, both closed.

The footman led her through another archway to a small parlor. There, he bowed again and backed away, before turning and heading across the high-ceilinged hall to the left side of the double staircase that led to the upper level of the mansion.

Mykella settled into a straight-backed armchair that faced the archway. From there, she studied the pictures on the wall of the parlor. One had been recently painted and hung, because it depicted Joramyl and Cheleyza standing on the upper rear balcony, the morning light bathing them and granting them a splendor Mykella hadn't seen in either. But then, she reflected, that was one purpose of portraits.

She forced herself to remain calm while she waited almost a quarter glass. She even managed to remain in the chair until Cheleyza descended the stairs, crossed the entry hall, and stepped into the receiving parlor. Then, and only then, did Mykella stand and step forward to greet her aunt.

Cheleyza was taller than Mykella, almost as tall as Salyna, but slender, with fine black hair that never seemed out of place, and an elegant long neck and an equally elegant, if narrow, face. She wore an ankle-length dress of gray shimmersilk, and a darker gray vest of the same material. Behind her gray eyes was a certain amused sense of satisfaction as she stepped forward. "Mykella . . . I did not expect you."

Mykella could sense a certain anger and resentment, in addition to Cheleyza's amusement, but she only smiled and inclined her head politely. "I did not have an opportunity to send a messenger, but I did so wish to convey my appreciation for the dress that you offered. It was in the best of taste, and most thoughtful, but . . ." Mykella offered a sigh, and tried to project a sense of regret. "You are so tall and beautifully proportioned, and I am not. I just could not do that garment justice, and I fear I will have to make do with something far less elegant. But I had to come to thank you for your kind gesture, and to tell you how much I appreciated it."

For the slightest instant, Cheleyza seemed taken aback. "Oh, you are *so* kind to come in person. I had heard that you had . . . chosen not to wear the dress, but at times one does not hear all of what might have been said."

"That is why I decided to come and tell you myself." Mykella managed another smile, a winning one, she hoped. "I would not wish there to be a misunderstanding about such a kind gesture, especially not with you. You have made my uncle's life so much more rewarding, when he has endured so much sadness, and I would not wish you to think that I, or my family, are not most grateful for that, and for your many kindnesses."

"It is so good of you to come and to share that with me, but Joramyl has always been most vocal about how kind your father is. I know you all take after him."

"You've changed some of the paintings and decorations," Mykella observed, after a moment. "The changes lighten the feeling." That much was certainly true, although, for Mykella, the lightness had a certain chill to it.

"Just in the receiving rooms and in the master chambers so far. It is a most tedious affair, dealing with workmen, and having to settle for the guest chambers."

"I'm certain that it must also have been rather tedious for Lord

Joramyl and Berenyt," suggested Mykella, "with so much chaos within. Still, it looks so much more elegant, more like one might envision a palace." She paused. "You were raised in one, as I recall."

"You are kind, but the Great Villa in Harmony was far less elegant than this. It was somewhat larger, but drafty, especially in winter." Cheleyza smiled. "In that, it was similar to the Lord-Protector's Palace. I doubt it was built to house a ruler."

"What do you think it was built for?" Mykella asked.

"I have no idea, but so many of the rooms are exactly the same size—or they were before the walls were altered. You can see where those changes were made by the difference in the stones."

Mykella waited.

"I would judge that many were studies, like Joramyl's Finance study. Perhaps the Alectors put many minions in the building doing things we can only guess about."

"There are still so many things we don't know," Mykella replied. "Is it that way in Harmony?"

Cheleyza laughed. "Mykella, dear, Tempre is so much more civilized than the Northcoast." She paused. "If those there, or in Midcoast, only knew, they would march their armies eastward to try to take what we have here. We will need a strong Lord-Protector for years to come."

"And a strong Southern Guard," suggested Mykella. "With leaders like Berenyt."

"Yes," agreed Cheleyza. "He is quite determined, and he is rather a dear."

"Dear" was definitely not a term that Mykella would have applied to Berenyt, but she could sense that Cheleyza regarded Berenyt almost with amusement, but a cool and detached amusement that chilled Mykella.

"You must stay and at least have some midmorning refreshments. I do insist," said Cheleyza, with a smile.

"I'd be delighted." Mykella offered her own smile in return.

It was likely to be a very long morning.

17

Mykella finally returned to the palace and her small table in the Finance study shortly after midday.

As she seated herself before the master ledger that Kiedryn had placed there and opened it to the most recent entries, the white-haired clerk looked up from his longer table, stacked with five different account ledgers. "Good afternoon, Mistress Mykella."

"Good afternoon, Kiedryn." She smiled crookedly. "I had some . . . obligations." How else could she explain where she had been without getting into messy details? But then, she was probably the only one in the family who even felt a need to explain much of anything.

"For the Lord-Protector and his family, there are always those." The chief clerk nodded.

"Some of them seem so useless. I'd rather be here."

Kiedryn offered a smile. "Here you can only determine what has been done and what in the way of golds remains to do what else must be done."

Mykella's laugh was rueful. "That's a very polite way of saying that keeping track of golds may give me some understanding, but that mere accounting changes nothing."

"People decide how golds are spent, people like your father and your uncle."

Certainly not mere daughters like Mykella and her sisters. While Mykella thought that, there was little point in saying so. "I can hope that studying the ledgers will teach me something about how to spend wisely and how to avoid foolish spending."

"The ledgers can teach more than that, if you look closely, Mistress," replied Kiedryn. "That is, if you understand who controls which ledger."

There was a click as the door to the outer corridor began to open. The clerk turned his eyes back to the ledger before him.

The outer door swung wide, thumping into the stone wall. Joramyl stepped into the chamber. He immediately addressed Kiedryn. "Did you make the transfer from the general tariff account to the Southern Guard procurement account?" His voice was deep and commanding, his pale green eyes hard under the bushy blond and silver eyebrows.

"Yes, sir. I took care of that yesterday."

Joramyl nodded and stepped past the senior clerk. He opened the door to his inner study and entered it without so much as looking at his niece.

Mykella looked down at the entries and the figures entered in the black iron-gall ink. Exactly what was Kiedryn suggesting? Joramyl was the Finance Minister, but he didn't actually control spending.

She turned her thoughts to what her uncle had said. Why was Joramyl transferring golds to the Southern Guards? The Guards actually were carrying a considerable surplus over the previous years, and it was near the end of the year, and there were more than enough golds to cover the likely outlays.

She went to the shelves, took out the ledger that held the record of Guard expenditures over the past two years, and carried it to her table. She opened it and began to check the entries. Almost a glass later, she closed it. There were no regular entries in the last week of the previous year that suggested a periodic significant expense. Was someone planning another large purchase of riding gear from Berjor? But why, when the number of Southern Guards was down from the level in previous years?

As she puzzled, Berenyt pushed his way through the door, nodded brusquely to Kiedryn, then, almost as an afterthought stopped, turned, and smiled at Mykella. She could sense the falsity.

"You're far too pretty to spend your time poring over account ledgers, Mykella." His wide smile accented his slightly-too-big white teeth.

"It makes me feel useful, and I'd like to think that it helps Father," she replied.

"You'd help him more with a match that would bring him allies and trade," suggested Berenyt winningly.

Much as she bristled inside, she matched his smile with one she hoped was more genuine-looking, even if it happened to be just as false. "Others have to make matches for daughters. Until they do, I can be helpful here."

"So you can. So you can." After flashing another smile, he turned and opened the door into his father's study.

While Berenyt was talking to his sire, Mykella replaced the Southern Guard ledger, then reseated herself at her table. "Are there many large expenses that come due near the end of the year, Kiedryn?"

The chief clerk tilted his head. "Not that many, Mistress Mykella. At other times, there are. There are always larger outlays for bridge and pier repairs in the spring, and the Southern Guards usually acquire mounts in summer . . ."

Mykella listened carefully, but Kiedryn's recitation of various expenditures only suggested that large expenditures near the turn of winter were not a common occurrence. She supposed she'd have to wait and see what the Guards ended up buying that required so many additional golds.

After his brief talk with his father, Berenyt hurried out, bestowing a quick smile on Mykella, an expression that faded even before he was past her. Before long, Joramyl also left, not really looking at either Kiedryn or Mykella.

For the rest of the afternoon, Mykella just reviewed the new entries, if at times pausing to try to think about why the Southern Guards might need more golds. Even though she couldn't find an answer that satisfied her, she was certain about one thing. It wasn't a good idea for either her or Kiedryn to ask Joramyl about the transfer.

Neither Feranyt nor Jeraxylt were at dinner on Duadi evening, and, of course, neither was Eranya. Even before the serving girls had brought the bread pudding that was often dessert when the men were not present, since both despised it, Rachylana had excused herself, leaving Salyna and Mykella.

"How was your day?" Mykella asked Salyna.

"I could only practice against the more junior guards, and they're really not good enough."

"With the saber, you mean?"

"With anything." Salyna snorted. "I practice left-handed against them, and they hardly notice."

"They're afraid they'll hurt you."

"They don't try that hard against each other, either. The real guards are the ones garrisoned in Indyor or in the border forts on the high roads. The companies guarding Tempre and the palace are mostly for show."

"We don't have any real Southern Guards here?"

"Oh . . . there are some. They rotate a few through Tempre to give them a rest or easier duty, and they rotate some out of Tempre to give them experience. That's if they show some true ability."

"Who told you that?"

"Most of the guards, in one way or another." Salyna looked at Mykella. "How did your meeting with Cheleyza go?"

"I told her I appreciated her kind gesture with the dress. She accepted my explanation and insisted I stay for midmorning refreshments. She knows I refused the dress because I didn't want to look like a sack of flour, and I know that was her intent, and we were both very polite."

"She's a scheming bitch." Salyna's voice was as casual as if she had said that it was dark outside.

"She also said that Berenyt was a dear."

"If I were Berenyt, I'd worry."

"I'm not about to worry over him. Rachylana can do that."

"She's so infatuated with him that she can't think to worry," replied Salyna.

"She'd best learn."

"Mykella . . . she is our sister."

Mykella sighed. "He can't marry her, not under normal conditions. Even if he could, he wouldn't."

"He might. I think he does care for her—as much as he can care for anyone."

"There's not much we can do. She won't listen." Mykella paused. "You're right. I'll try to be gentler. It's hard, though."

"You need to be matched to a ruler, Mykella. You're meant to do things."

Mykella smiled and shook her head. "That won't happen, either. Never in a thousand generations."

"Never say 'Never.'" Salyna took the last bite of her bread pudding and eased the dish away.

Mykella looked down at her empty bowl. She didn't even remember eating it.

Salyna rose, as did Mykella, but Mykella did not wait all that long after she returned to her chamber before she created her sight-shield and slipped out of the family quarters and down the main staircase, and then the smaller one to the lower level. She managed to be quiet enough that the sentries at the top and bottom of the main staircase heard nothing, nor did the guard near the door to the lower staircase.

The Table looked and felt the same—dark to her eyes and faintly glowing purple to her senses. The light-torches cast the same weary amber glow across the chamber, and she wondered, not for the first time, for how many generations they had continued to shine.

She stepped up to the Table, knowing she had to learn more. She just had to.

Then she looked down at the mirrorlike surface, concentrating on Joramyl, his blond hair and green eyes, and the coldness within him. The swirling mists appeared, then cleared to reveal Joramyl—seen from behind—embracing Cheleyza. Both were naked, but the one thing that transfixed Mykella was the lambent hardness of her aunt's gray eyes. Mykella pushed away the image, then concentrated on finding Berenyt through the Table.

Not surprisingly, the mists cleared to reveal her cousin and Rachylana seated side by side on a long settee in the sitting room adjoining the Lord-Protector's official study. They were not talking, unless it was lip-to-lip, but at least they were both fully clothed.

Mykella took a deep breath and released the image, letting the Table's surface return to its mirror finish. Now what?

She looked at the Table again, then forced herself to climb up onto it. She stood there for a time, then began to cast forth her thoughts toward the greenish-blackness beneath the purple. This time she dropped through the Table and into the darkness and chill beneath far more quickly. In the blackish green distance she could sense more clearly what seemed to be points of light. One was the black point she had "visited" before, but she had no idea how black could also be a point of light—except it was. There was also an amber point and one of sullen red that did not seem too distant.

As the chill began to seep through her nightsilk jacket, she focused on the sullen point of red. For a time nothing occurred. Then, slowly, the sullen red point grew larger, before rushing toward her with a wave of purpled miasma.

Chill and the purple shattered around her and vanished, replaced by far warmer air and a dry mustiness. The chamber was dark, and as she tried to turn, her head bumped into something with enough force that she staggered and her eyes watered. As she turned, carefully, she could see nothing, but she could sense the chamber around her, what of it that remained intact. Two stone supports crossed above the Table, the lower of which had banged her head when she had tried to straighten up. Sand and dust filled much of the space around the Table, and the door lintels had collapsed into each other, blocking access to the still-solid door behind them. Some sort of chest had been crushed into a flat and splintered mass by another massive stone pillar that rose through the mass of stones seemingly held in place by the two columns that intersected above the Table.

Mykella could tell that there was no escape from the chamber, but she couldn't help wondering what had brought down the building above with such force. Did Tempre hold the only Table chamber that was not damaged or otherwise inaccessible?

As she moved her feet, dust sifted upward, and she sneezed. Her head struck the stone pillar, if not so hard as the first time. There was no question. Once more, she needed to return to Tempre.

She concentrated on dropping into the greenish black darkness. Even as she did, her nose continued to itch, an itch frozen by the chill of the darkness. As the blueness that seemed to be associated with the Tempre Table (at least from a distance) rushed toward her, she began to feel another kind of chill, one purplish and almost slimy.

The Ifrit was searching for her!

Once she was standing on the Tempre Table, she jumped off, her boots hitting hard on the stone floor, then glanced back at the Table.

Purplish mists began to rise from the mirrored surface. It had to be the Ifrit. Did she want to deal with him?

Not when she was as tired and as fretful as she found herself.

She hurried out the door, quickly closing it behind her. She hurried toward the staircase up to the main level, almost running down the long corridor, trying to ignore the voice inside her that kept telling her that she would have to face the Ifrit sooner or later.

Later . . . when she was rested and knew more. Later.

18

Mykella didn't lie awake on Duadi night, but neither did she sleep all that well. Again, her dreams were far from pleasant, especially the one in which the Ifrit appeared and purple arms rose from the Table and captured her, time after time. Despite the chill in her chamber, she awoke damp with sweat that smelled of fear, and it took her longer than usual to wash up and dress. Part of that slowness was because she was still thinking, distractedly, about how little she had been able to learn or accomplish through the Table and how long it was taking her to learn much of anything about either the Table or the tariff situation.

When Mykella stepped into the breakfast room on Tridi morning, she was surprised to see Jeraxylt sitting in his place, wearing a clean Southern Guards uniform. "When did you get back from your maneuvers?"

"Early evening," he replied with a smile.

"You weren't at dinner."

"I had other plans." His smile was broader.

Mykella managed not to flush or to make a cutting remark. She just nodded as she settled into her place just before her father stepped into the breakfast room.

"Good morning," offered Feranyt cheerfully.

"Good morning."

"It's good to see you all so cheerful."

Both Muergya and Akilsa served breakfast, beginning with Feranyt—crispy bacon, cheese omelets that were warm enough that Mykella could see the heat rising, and mixed berry biscuits.

"What did you do on your maneuvers in Viencet?" asked Salyna.

"Maneuvers," replied Jeraxylt after swallowing a bite of omelet.

"I know *that*," replied Salyna. "What kind of maneuvers? Charges? By squad or by full company? Open terrain pursuit?"

"Pretty much everything. They have a special area there where they train . . ." Jeraxylt let his words die off as he took a swallow of spiced tea.

"All the replacement troopers before they're sent to the border posts?" pressed Salyna.

"Salyna," interjected Feranyt, "you might let your brother eat his breakfast."

"Yes, Father."

Mykella could tell that Salyna was irritated, despite the sweetness in her voice.

After that Salyna didn't say much, and neither did Mykella nor Rachylana.

Before long, Feranyt finished his second mug of spiced tea, then rose from the table with a nod at his offspring and strode off.

Mykella followed immediately, but waited outside the family breakfast room for Jeraxylt because she definitely didn't want Rachylana to hear the conversation that would follow, whether Jeraxylt agreed with her plan or not. As he stepped into the hall, she cornered him. "Have some of the guards left or been stipended off?"

"How would I know?" Jeraxylt looked past her down the corridor toward the staircase to the main level of the palace.

"You know everything about the Guards," Mykella said gently. "You've told me how many companies and battalions there are . . ."

"The numbers change every week, and every season. There might be a few less now. Some of the companies are under strength." Jeraxylt paused. "I wouldn't know about stipends to ranker guards. I do know that Majer Querlyt petitioned for an early stipend because of deaths in his family. The Arms-Commander granted it. Commander

Demyl said that there were reasons to grant it, but they only gave him a half stipend, and if he'd served two more years, it would have been full."

"Was he a good commander?"

"One of the best. He and Undercommander Areyst were the ones who turned back the Ongelyan nomads three years ago, and he hardly lost any men at all. Neither did Areyst. Oh, Majer Choalt was there, too, but he was a captain then. Good man, though."

"Jeraxylt? How would you like to help me?" Mykella tried to make her voice confidentially winning.

"Mykella . . . I am rather . . . involved in my training."

"What I have in mind will certainly not interfere with your training." She offered her most persuasive smile.

"Whom do you want to meet?" He grinned broadly.

"It's not that kind of help." She didn't need Jeraxylt's assistance in meeting men, not that she'd seen any in the Southern Guards or around the palace who appealed to her. "I need to follow up on some of the tariff collections, and I need an escort."

"Mykella . . ." His voice expressed extreme doubt.

"Of course, I could make it known that you've been bedding Majer Allahyr's younger daughter."

"So?"

"Father wouldn't be pleased that you're taking your pleasures with the younger sister of his mistress, nor would he like it known. Besides, if you help me, you'll get to ride through Tempre in that uniform, and everyone will know who you are and admire you."

"Why don't you ask Arms-Commander Nephryt?"

"My asking him might make matters . . . difficult, because, well . . . I hope you understand. Anyway, the collections don't match up. You don't want to see Father cheated, do you?"

"I don't know . . ."

"Would you like to be cheated when you become Lord-Protector?" she asked. "Would you like to see the cheating continue until you do, and then have to be the one to tell everyone that they can't keep doing what they've done for years?"

Jeraxylt thought about that for a moment. "How do you

know . . ." He shook his head. "You and your ledgers and figures." Then he cocked his head and smiled.

Mykella could sense what he was feeling—the mix of wanting to show initiative, the appeal of being seen in uniform, and the idea of wanting to call in a future favor from Mykella, as well as a certain doubt.

"I can get some of my squad to do it tomorrow afternoon, the first glass of the afternoon," he said after a moment. "I'll make it a squad exercise. They'll think it's all an excuse, but it's the sort of thing they'd think I'd want to do." Another smile followed. "You do realize . . ."

"That I'll owe you a favor? Yes. But it has to be the same kind— nothing that's improper."

Jeraxylt nodded. "I'll expect the same diligence from you when I'm Lord-Protector."

"You'll have it." That, she could promise, and he would certainly need it . . . assuming she hadn't been packed off to Dereka or some other awful place.

When he stepped away and headed for the main staircase, she realized that she could sense that her brother also had one of the unseen threads that ran from him into the ground—but his thread was more of a golden brown, and it trailed into the distance, while hers seemed to plunge into the depths beneath the palace. Everyone had such a thread, but what did the colors and the direction in which the thread stretched mean? What did it mean?

After she washed up and left the family quarters, Mykella headed toward the Finance chambers for another day of looking at figures and trying not to appear concerned, while she waited to see what she could learn from visiting various factors on Quattri. If Jeraxylt would keep his promise. If . . .

19

The remainder of Tridi dragged out, while Mykella sat at her table and reviewed and refigured, then calculated some more. Usually, working with the ledgers and tracking the numbers calmed her, but not on Tridi, because the more she figured, the more different places she thought she was finding where golds had been diverted in differing ways. But in all of those instances, she had no proof, only a sense based on the patterns of the figures themselves.

At dinner she said little, leaving the conversation to Eranya and Rachylana, who talked about the forthcoming year-turn ball. Once her father and Eranya had left, and then Jeraxylt, she thought about visiting the Table once more, then decided against it, even as a small voice in her thoughts insisted that she would regret not doing so. Yet . . . knowing that the Ifrit was waiting . . . lurking, she just could not bring herself to descend into the depths.

Breakfast on Quattri didn't begin all that more auspiciously.

"You didn't spend all that much time on maneuvers," Salyna said to Jeraxylt. "Will you be doing more before long?"

"Maneuvers and exercises are scheduled regularly," he replied. "We have to be prepared for whatever might happen."

"Berenyt says that the Prince of Northcoast and the Prince of Midcoast are developing an alliance and will attack us in the spring." The redhead smiled brightly.

"On what basis did he make that pronouncement?" asked Feranyt, his tone skeptical.

"He just said it," replied Rachylana.

"Words without backing are just words. So are numbers," Feranyt said dryly.

"I'll ask him," replied Rachylana. Her face tightened slightly, but she did not say more.

Mykella was not about to dismiss Berenyt's words as casually as her father had appeared to, especially since Berenyt's stepmother just happened to be the daughter of the Prince of Northcoast.

After that, conversation was rather limited, and Jeraxylt hurried away immediately after Feranyt rose.

"Berenyt, always Berenyt," Mykella said quietly.

Before Mykella could say more, Rachylana snapped back, "He's more interesting than all those ledgers you bury yourself in. You can't wed a ledger, you know." Then she turned to Salyna. "Nor a saber, either." She pushed back her chair, stood, and walked out of the breakfast room.

Salyna and Mykella exchanged glances.

"You can't tell her anything," Salyna said quietly, "not if it's the slightest bit critical of Berenyt."

"He's using her so much, and it's so hard not to say anything," Mykella replied.

"We all make our own mistakes." Salyna stood. "I might get to spar with Dulfuss this morning. He's good. I always learn when I work out with him."

"That's good." Mykella swallowed the last drops of her tea, then rose.

After washing up, she made her way to the Finance study, where her eyes kept skipping over the pages in the ledger while she waited for the time when she could leave and saddle the gray and meet Jeraxylt. She just hoped he had remembered and had been able to arrange everything.

A good quarter glass before Jeraxylt and his squad were to meet her, Mykella was already mounted, her ledger in the saddlebag, waiting in the cold winter air of early afternoon. She was vaguely surprised at how warm the nightsilk riding jacket was, but she was most comfortable as she studied the rear courtyard of the palace.

Finally, Jeraxylt rode in and reined up beside her. "The squad's waiting in front."

"Thank you." She smiled and urged the gelding forward beside her brother's chestnut.

Neither said anything until they were at the head of the column.

"Where do you want to start?" he asked. "At the barge-piers or the Great Piers?"

"Actually, the first place is that of Seltyr Almardyn."

"You said we were visiting tariff collectors," Jeraxylt murmured, his tone cool.

"No," replied Mykella softly, "I said we needed to check on the tariff collections, and that means visiting those bargemasters and trade factors who paid them."

"They'll just say that they paid . . ."

"They have to have receipts . . . and I'll *know* if they're accurate, once I compare them all."

"You would." The words were under his breath. "Column! Forward!"

The faint chill breeze stiffened into a colder wind as they rode westward from the palace and then turned south. Seltyr and High Factor Almardyn's warehouse was less than a block to the south of the Great Piers, an ancient amber stone structure of two stories with a series of loading docks on the west side.

Jeraxylt had the squad rein up in front of the front entrance, a simple doorway, if with an ornate marble arch above it. He accompanied Mykella to the door. "You would start with a Seltyr."

"He's first on the list."

Clearly, the sound of a squad of Southern Guards had alerted someone, because Almardyn himself opened the door. His eyes widened as he looked from Jeraxylt to Mykella, and back to Jeraxylt, but he barely paused before saying, "Please come in."

Mykella noted that his life-thread was more of a deeper brown, and somehow . . . frayed.

The two followed him to the study, a small white-plastered chamber with a table-desk, and wooden file boxes stacked neatly to the right. There, Almardyn turned. "Both the Lord-Protector's heir and daughter at my door . . . I am indeed honored. Might I ask why?"

"It's a bit . . . unusual," Mykella said. "You might know that I oversee the accounts of the Finance Ministry for my father . . ."

"I did not know, but would that all daughters were so dutiful . . ."

Mykella could sense the doubts, but she just smiled before speaking. "And I discovered that some figures had been entered incorrectly. It might be that an entire column was one set of numbers off, but since several of the payment receipts were spoiled, it seemed that the easiest thing to do was to check with those who paid the last tariffs." Mykella did her best to project absolute conviction and assurance, along with a hint of embarrassment about Lord Joramyl.

"What would you like of me?"

"Just a quick look at your receipt for your fall tariff," Mykella said. "I may not have to visit every factor, but since the lists are in alphabetical order . . ."

"I'm the fortunate one. Just a moment." Almardyn turned and lifted one box, then another, opening the third. "Should be on top here. Yes." He turned and extended a heavy oblong card, bordered in the blue of the Lord-Protector. "Here you have it. The seal is quite clear."

"I'm certain it is," Mykella replied. "The fault lies not with you or the tariff collector." She copied the number into the new ledger she carried, one she had designed to show the discrepancies. Almardyn had paid a good ten golds more than had been entered in the collection ledger. She straightened. "Thank you very much, Seltyr and High Factor. Your diligence and cooperation are much appreciated."

"I'm certain your sire appreciates yours as well," replied Almardyn.

"We do thank you," Mykella said, inclining her head slightly, before turning to depart.

Little more was said, until Mykella and Jeraxylt had left the factor's building.

"For all your fine words, he'll still think you're checking to see if he's a thief," murmured Jeraxylt as they walked out and to their waiting mounts and Jeraxylt's squad.

"Not after word gets around that everyone's been visited," replied Mykella. "Besides, is anyone going to fault a Lord-Protector for checking on tariff collections once in a while during his reign?"

"It's going to cause problems," predicted her brother.

"I'm sure it will, but it will create more problems if we don't verify that it's happening and how much Father is losing."

"That's the only reason I can see for this."

Mykella had to jump to mount the gelding, since there was no mounting block nearby and she wasn't about to ask for a leg up. Besides, she had done that for years, and managed it relatively gracefully, she thought.

Once mounted, she turned in the saddle. "We'll see High Factor Rhavyl next. He's just two blocks down."

"That's not in alphabetical order . . ." began Jeraxylt.

"I know, but I wanted to disarm Almardyn as much as I could. I did arrange the order so that it's the shortest to ride."

Jeraxylt shook his head.

Out of the twenty-three bargemasters and High Factors Mykella visited, she managed to meet eighteen. With the exception of Hasenyt—the sole factor whom the Lord-Protector and Mykella knew personally—every single one had a receipt for paying more golds than had been entered in the ledger as having been received, a fact Mykella did not reveal even to Jeraxylt.

Finally, he leaned over in the saddle. "You haven't told me what you've found, and I've gone out of my way . . ."

"I don't know for sure, yet," she temporized. "Now I have to compare the numbers to the tariff ledgers. I used a fresh ledger, because I didn't want to take the one with the receipts from the palace."

She had to work hard to keep a pleasant expression as they rode back toward the palace. She had no more than reined up outside the gates to the courtyard, about to take her leave of Jeraxylt, when another officer rode toward them. He was blond, of medium height, and muscular. While his face was calm, she could sense the anger.

"Oh, frig . . ." muttered Jeraxylt. "I knew this might be trouble. That's Undercommander Areyst."

The undercommander reined up and looked directly at Jeraxylt. His green eyes conveyed a chill that was not reflected in the tone of the words that followed. "I don't recall authorizing any sort of patrol in Tempre."

Mykella eased her gray gelding forward, cutting between Jeraxylt and the senior officer. She smiled politely. "Undercommander? Does the Finance Ministry serve the Lord-Protector?"

Areyst turned to her, not that he had a choice. "I beg your pardon, Mistress Mykella?" His tone remained cool.

"I asked you if the Finance Ministry served the Lord-Protector."

Areyst's thin lips turned up slightly at the corners. "How could I possibly contest that, Mistress?"

"On behalf of the Ministry, I requested an escort to check some tariff records. Perhaps I should have contacted you directly, but was there any harm done by Jeraxylt's arranging the escort for me?" Mykella extended the ledger she carried. "I was cross-checking the entries in this ledger. Would you care to see them?"

"I think not, Mistress. Your word, as is your sire's, is more than enough."

Mykella thought she sensed a grudging admiration from the undercommander, the man third in line of command for the Southern Guards, although his anger had not totally abated. "Thank you, Undercommander. I apologize if I've caused any difficulty, but, as always, I have only the best interests of the Lord-Protector and the people of Tempre at heart, as I know you do." Mykella tried to project true concern, which she felt, because she could sense the basic honesty of Areyst, whom she had only seen previously from a distance, or in passing. She added, "If there is any fault, it must be mine, for I was the one who requested the service of my brother. If you find that a fault, please tell the Lord-Protector directly, and let him know that it was my doing. Jeraxylt was only trying to accommodate me."

Areyst smiled faintly, an expression now devoid of bitterness or anger and holding barely veiled amusement. "It might be best if it were logged as a commercial verification patrol." He turned to Jeraxylt. "I would appreciate it if you would do that." Then he looked back to Mykella, still appraising her. "I would also request, if further such patrols are needed, Mistress Mykella, that you contact me."

"I would doubt the need anytime in the immediate future, Undercommander, but I will indeed follow your advice." And she would, because she could sense that honesty and loyalty ran all the way through him . . . and through a life-thread that held a faint green amid a golden brown.

Areyst eased his mount forward slightly and nodded to Jeraxylt. "Your squad will be doing arms practice on foot tomorrow. Riding the stones all afternoon is hard on mounts."

"Yes, sir."

Only after Areyst had ridden off, eastward, in the direction of the Southern Guard compound, did Jeraxylt turn to Mykella. "You owe me double for this."

"I do," she acknowledged demurely. *And you owe me far more than you realize.*

By the time she had unsaddled and groomed the gelding, then returned to the Finance study, only Kiedryn remained, and he was replacing the ledgers on the shelves.

"Mistress Mykella." He nodded.

"I'm going to take several of the ledgers to my chambers, Kiedryn. I'll have them back in the morning. They won't leave this level of the palace."

"I'm certain they won't, Mistress."

Mykella gathered the tariff collection ledger, as well as the current account master ledger for the Southern Guards, then left Kiedryn to close and lock the study.

After the evening meal, at which Feranyt made no mention of patrols, thankfully, Mykella retired to her chambers to study the ledgers. That required going through the collections, line by line, season by season, and then comparing the entries to the figures she had recorded from the stamped and sealed receipts she had observed.

It was a good two glasses later when she leaned back and looked over her calculations.

What she had suspected was in fact true. The total discrepancy for the fall tariffs was close to two hundred golds. If the same had been true for the other four seasons, and her estimates suggested that it had been, Joramyl—or someone—had diverted close to a thousand golds from just seventeen factors and bargemasters. Her calculations suggested that other diversions were also taking place, but she was not about to try further excursions without presenting what she had verified to her father. Nor, after his remarks that morning, was she about to suggest those other diversions, not until she had a similar level of proof.

She still had some misgivings about presenting her findings to her father, but to whom else could she turn? Jeraxylt knew nothing about figures and ledgers, and her Uncle Joramyl was either part of the diversion or unable to discern what was happening.

She knew she would not sleep well.

20

Mykella had hoped to be in the Finance chambers before Kiedryn or Joramyl on Quinti morning, but she'd been so tired that she'd nearly slept through breakfast. As she had feared, her sleep had been anything but peaceful, with nightmares about struggling through a blinding blizzard of black snow, trying to reach . . . something. She'd awakened after that one, and settled herself, only to fall asleep and find herself in a second nightmare, one in which her father disregarded her figures and confined her to her chambers because her ledger had vanished, and none of the Seltyrs or High Factors dared to tell the truth.

Her stomach was roiling when she finally got up, washed, and struggled into her garments. She knew she couldn't face the day and what she had to do without something to eat. Everyone but Rachylana had already eaten and left when Mykella got to the breakfast room, and Rachylana immediately rose and departed without a word or even a glance at Mykella. Mykella could sense the smoldering anger. All because Mykella didn't like Berenyt's scheming and his using Rachylana?

By the time Mykella had eaten cold egg toast and gulped down lukewarm tea, then hurried to the Finance study, Kiedryn was already at his table-desk. Fortunately, as she had hoped, Joramyl was nowhere to be seen.

"Good morning, Kiedryn."

"Good morning, Mistress Mykella."

Mykella gathered the ledgers she needed, then wrapped the sight-shield around them, not that Kiedryn more than glanced in her direction as she paused by the door. "I need to get something. I'll be back in a while." She almost said that she'd be back before long, but she realized she had no idea how long what she planned would take—and even if her father was available at the moment.

The chief clerk merely nodded as Mykella left.

With the concealed ledgers under her arm, Mykella walked past the main staircase and then along the corridor until she reached the front of the building, where she nodded to the two guards stationed beside the double doors. Neither said a word as she opened the door and stepped into the outer study.

"Mistress Mykella," offered Chalmyr, the calm-faced man who had been her father's private scrivener and assistant ever since Mykella could recall. "How might I help you?"

"I need to see him. It's important, and it's about . . . it's not personal."

Chalmyr nodded. "He'll have time after he finishes with Seltyr Porofyr. There's almost a glass before Arms-Commander Nephryt will be here. If you'd care to sit . . ." He gestured to the armchair across from and to the left of the writing desk he occupied.

"Thank you." Mykella seated herself. The chair was positioned so that anyone opening the door and looking in would not immediately or easily see her, and that was fine with Mykella. Absently, when Chalmyr was not looking, she dropped the concealment shield around the ledgers.

She had to wait for nearly half a glass before the Seltyr departed— with scarcely a glance in Mykella's direction.

Chalmyr nodded at her.

Mykella stepped through the single door, closing it behind her, then sliding the bolt into place. The last thing she wanted was Joramyl arriving, unlikely as it might be.

"We wouldn't be interrupted, anyway, daughter." Feranyt paused, then leaned forward from where he sat behind the wide black oak desk. "Since you're not asking me anything at meals, this must have something to do with finances."

For a moment, Mykella stood there, studying her sire with her senses, more than with her eyes. His life-thread was almost the same as Jeraxylt's—golden brown—and for the first time she noticed that there was a knot of sorts in the thread, as if tiny threads from all over his body merged into that nexus that connected him to the life-thread.

"Perhaps we wouldn't be interrupted, sir," replied Mykella after a pause, "but it's best that there's no chance of that." She laid the ledgers on the corner of the Lord-Protector's desk. "Father . . . I've been worried about your accounts. Receipts have been going down, yet everyone has been saying that times are good. I couldn't track everything, but I did track the fall tariffs of the bargemasters and the High Factors . . ." She went on to explain how she had cross-checked by visiting most of those on the lists and how their sealed receipts uniformly showed greater payments than those shown as having been received. She used each ledger to point out the exact differences. ". . . and since we don't use tariff farmers the way they do in some places, the numbers should agree, but they don't. Someone has diverted or pocketed nearly a thousand golds this year—"

"You only know about two hundred for certain."

"I can only prove two hundred at the moment. The ledgers suggest a thousand."

"We can only go with proof, daughter."

Why couldn't her father see? Why wouldn't he?

"Mykella . . . you've been diligent and thoughtful, and I appreciate what you've let me know. Corruption is always a problem, because there aren't enough golds to sate all men's appetites." He looked at his daughter more closely. "You're exhausted. You have black circles under your eyes. You shouldn't have pushed yourself so hard."

"Father . . . I don't see how this could have happened without Lord Joramyl knowing something about it."

Feranyt laughed ironically. "Just how often does he even come into the Finance chambers? I suspect that you and Kiedryn do most of the work, after the entry clerks take in the papers and order the entries."

Mykella *was* tired, if not for the reasons her father had suggested, and she had no real answer to his statement, not at that moment.

"Dear child . . . I am the Lord-Protector, and you'll have to trust me to handle it. It's not something that can be rushed."

"You are the Lord-Protector, Father, and I am your daughter. But please don't think I'm overstating matters. It's not just a matter of two hundred golds. And two hundred golds are hardly insignificant."

"Mykella, I understand your concerns for me, but if I rush and handle matters wrong, things will only be worse." He paused. "I will look into it and do what is necessary."

She could sense that, if she pressed her father, it would do no good, and he would only resist. "That's all I wanted, sir. Do you need the ledgers?"

"Not right now, but keep them safe."

"I can do that." Mykella straightened and stepped back. Within her father, she could feel a combination of worry and resignation, as well as doubt. The doubt bothered her, but more words would do nothing. Should she have tracked down more examples?

For better or worse, she had not.

"I'll see you at dinner." Feranyt offered an affectionate smile.

For all his doubt, he was touched by her efforts.

She returned the smile, hard as it was to do. "At dinner."

21

Kiedryn wasn't even in the Finance study when Mykella returned and replaced the tariff ledger. When he stepped through the door some half a glass later, he nodded to her and said, "I had to go down and deal with the new accounts clerk. That's Wasdahl. Some of his entries aren't clear enough and could be misread."

"That's not good," Mykella agreed.

"One can never be too careful with accounts and entries." Kiedryn settled himself behind the long table and opened a ledger. "Shenyl does an excellent job with the Southern Guard accounts, and Vyahm is almost as good with the transportation and highway accounts. Wasdahl needs to follow their example."

For the rest of the day, Mykella forced herself to look into another area of the accounts—the tariffs collected on the wine and spirits from the vintners in the Vyanhills. The entries were all consistent, unlike those she'd seen with the shipping tariffs, but that only meant that the bookkeeping was better, not that the tariff revenues were necessarily correct.

Was she getting cynical about everyone?

She frowned, then shook her head. Was there any doubt about it?

The day dragged on, and Mykella slipped away a half glass early, then waited near the dining room . . . and waited, hoping to catch her father. She couldn't very well just barge into his study and ask what he had found out, but if she did encounter him—accidentally—he might reveal something.

Just after the soft bells announced dinner, Mykella caught sight of her father and Eranya stepping out of his private quarters and walking toward her. She waited.

Feranyt slowed as he neared his daughter.

Mykella merely raised her eyebrows.

The Lord-Protector shook his head. "I've done what I can do for now, and I'll let you know." Feranyt's voice was calm and reasonable.

Despite the chill of apprehension that ran through her, Mykella smiled. "I've been concerned, and thought you should know."

"I know, dear daughter, and I appreciate it. Now . . . might we enjoy dinner?"

Her father might appreciate her concern, Mykella thought, but he didn't seem to understand the gravity of the situation. Enjoy dinner when thousands of golds were being diverted? After but a momentary pause, she replied, "I'm certain we should."

"Good food is always worth enjoying," added Eranya. "Sometimes, the simple pleasures are the best."

"True." Feranyt glanced at his mistress.

That look and the feelings behind it caused Mykella to turn her eyes away, toward the door to the family dining room. She hurried ahead and opened the door, as much to avoid revealing the way she had flushed as to be polite. Her increasing ability to sense what others felt was going to be a considerable drawback unless she learned to maintain a pleasant demeanor and expression—no matter what she sensed.

Once she followed her father and Eranya into the dining room, where her other siblings were already seated and waiting, she quickly sat down.

Immediately, Muergya began serving. Each diner got a small browned game hen, accompanied by cheese-laced potatoes and apricot-walnut beans. Mykella knew the beans would be cool, the potatoes warm, and the game hen as warm as it should be.

Ice pellets rattled against the windows, hard and fast, then died away as the wind subsided, before resuming their clicking against the glass.

"A bit of an ice-storm," mused Feranyt.

"Winter has been so chill this year." Eranya shivered, then looked at her platter. "This is a good meal for a cold night."

Rachylana and Salyna exchanged glances. Mykella maintained a pleasant smile. They all knew the winter had been mild. Two years before, snow had fallen week after week, tenday after tenday, until it filled the streets of Tempre, and all but the main channel of the River Vedra had frozen over.

"You must have grown up in Syan or Soupat," suggested Rachylana.

"There aren't any Southern Guard posts in Syan," said Jeraxylt.

"We spent more time in Hyalt," replied Eranya. "Father was the detachment commander there before he was stipended off."

Mykella just hoped that Rachylana didn't press. Majer Allahyr had died, just the year before, from some sort of lingering illness he'd picked up patrolling the eastern side of the Coastal Range in the high hills west of Hyalt. That was why he'd been given a stipend. It was also probably why Eranya had been receptive to the Lord-Protector's advances, because stipends went only to wives when a guard died, and Eranya's mother had died years earlier.

"Is Hyalt that warm?" Salyna asked quickly.

"In the summer, it can be as hot as Soupat, but the winters are cooler." Eranya smiled. "I do like the seasons in Tempre . . . and the people." She smiled fondly at Feranyt.

Mykella actually sensed warmth from the young woman when she looked at Feranyt. He was so much older than Eranya, but her father was kind, and generous, and Mykella knew that Majer Allahyr had worked his way up through the ranks of the Southern Guards. So Eranya's early life could not have been that easy, especially after her mother's death.

"Oh . . . did I mention that we received a communiqué from the Landarch?" asked Feranyt, glancing toward Rachylana. "His envoy will be arriving shortly, certainly within the week. He's likely to stay through the season-turn."

"Envoy for matching?" Rachylana raised a single eyebrow.

"And to work out more effective terms for sharing the patrols of the passes between Lanachrona and Deforya along the northern high road. The brigands have gotten worse this winter." Feranyt took a small swallow of the amber wine.

Of course they had. Mykella wanted to snort. Without nearly so much snow, and without the bitter winds, there were more traders and more opportunities for the brigands.

"Has the Landarch expressed . . . any preferences?" Rachylana's tone was polite.

Mykella could sense intense interest—and worry—emanating from her sister.

"I believe any preference will be reflected in what the envoy reports." Feranyt smiled. "That is usually how it works. That was how I found your mother."

"Wasn't Uncle Joramyl your envoy?" asked Salyna.

"He was indeed, and for that I'm most thankful. The years we had together, short as they were, were far better than for many who spend a lifetime in hidden strife."

Mykella nodded at that. Certainly, she could recall just how happy her parents had been, even given her mother's often fragile health. Her eyes flicked to Eranya, but the dark-haired beauty didn't radiate either jealousy or resentment, but a vague sadness. Mykella could understand that.

She said little more at dinner, and then slipped away quickly, avoiding the family parlor. When she was sure she was unobserved, she created a sight-shield and slipped past the guards on both levels and down to the lowest level of the palace—and the Table chamber.

Like it or not, Ifrit or not, she *had* to learn more about the Table.

Once she had closed the door and made her way to the Table itself, she studied it for a moment. Then, given what her father had said before dinner, Mykella concentrated on having the Table find him. Immediately, the mists appeared in the silver surface, then vanished, revealing her father, now in a silver-trimmed blue dressing gown, leaning forward in his favorite armchair in the sitting room off his bedchamber and looking at Eranya, who also wore a robe, wrapped tightly enough around her to reveal her rather curved figure. Feranyt's face was intent as he talked, then shook his head.

Was he telling Eranya about what Mykella had revealed? Or was he concerned about something else? Mykella couldn't make out his lips well enough to guess at his words. She only wished the Table conveyed words.

What about Joramyl?

The mists swirled and then vanished, revealing Joramyl in the darkness. He was riding, and Mykella could catch glimpses of men in dark cloaks riding with him. She did not recognize the street or lane from what she could see, but it had narrow houses, set wall to wall, not the meanest of streets, but definitely not a street holding the dwellings of those of means. What was Joramyl doing there?

For a time, she concentrated on following Joramyl in the Table, but even with the better vision afforded by her Talent and the Table, she could see little but the riders and houses and intermittent lamps. Finally, she released the image and tried to get a sense of the Table— and to check if she could sense any hint of the Ifrit's possible reappearance.

Since she didn't feel any hint of the increased slimy purple that had heralded the Ifrit before, she half-vaulted, half-climbed onto the Table itself and concentrated on the blackness below. As she dropped through the Table and into the chill darkness beneath it, she tried not to think about the seeming impossibility of her being surrounded by solid stone and tried to seek out the points of light that she had felt before. Neither the black nor the sullen red had been useful, and she sought other light-points.

Finally, as the chill seeped deeper into her, she could make out two brighter points of light—one silver and one crimson and gold—and one fainter point of amber. Although the amber was not so bright, she felt it was somehow closer. So she focused on it. As before, for what seemed an endless time, nothing occurred. Then the diffuse amber point rushed toward her, and, abruptly, Mykella found herself standing, not upon a Table, but in an oblong depression filled perhaps a third deep with fine sand. A single light-torch, hanging askew from a wall bracket, provided the faintest of amber light, as if it were close to failing. The walls of the chamber were smooth and certainly as ancient as those in Tempre. The air was cool, but not so cool as in Tempre, and dry, yet musty. After a moment, she climbed out of the depression, careful to avoid slipping on the fine sand that intermittently coated the polished stone floor.

How had she gotten to where she was . . . when there was no Table here?

Beside the light-torch bracket was a square archway and a dark corridor beyond. Mykella could sense that the corridor was empty, and the dusty mustiness suggested that it had been empty for a long, long time. She stepped through the archway. Should she go on?

She took one step, then another, but before long the corridor ended at another passageway. Mykella looked to the right, then left. There didn't seem to be much difference, and she followed the right branch of the stone-walled corridor. Less than a handful of yards farther the passage ended at a wooden door. Mykella pulled the handle. The door opened, revealing an empty storage room, the far side of which was blocked with a jumble of heavy stones. After several moments, Mykella stepped back, closed the door, and returned to the branch in the corridor. After something like fifteen yards, she could sense the corridor beginning to curve, and in the distance a faint glow. After she had walked another ten yards or so, her boots crunching on the scattered sand covering the polished stone, she could make out a pair of ancient light-torches mounted in antique brackets high on the wall, one on each side of the corridor.

Another door appeared ahead. It opened easily, and Mykella found herself in an empty room, four yards wide and three deep, also lit by a pair of ancient light-torches. She could sense the absolute emptiness of the place, even beyond the open archway opposite the door. Abruptly, she realized that the door she had opened was stone-faced on the reverse, so that anyone looking at it would not even see it as a door.

After a moment of hesitation, Mykella slipped toward the archway, bounded by maroon ceramic tiles, only to discover a screen wall looming out of the darkness before her. The wall was less than three yards high and three wide, and she stepped around it.

There, she stood on a stone platform or dais, and beyond that was a soaring cavern or chamber. The platform held nothing, and there was no one in the cavern. Yet . . . something . . . something about the cavern nagged at her.

She took another step, and the darkness vanished. Light-torches she had not seen or noticed—behind her on the cavern side of the screen wall—flared into brightness. Then a roaring wave of sound crashed around her—except that it was not sound at all, but something inside her own head.

"What is . . ." She broke off her words as she sensed the echo and as the roaring subsided to a murmur.

The light-torches revealed the cavern to consist of tiered platforms that rose away from the one on which she stood, almost like an underground and far larger version of the reviewing stand in Tempre near the Great Piers. But who would build an underground reviewing stand—and for what? From what she could see and sense, there was no exit, although two archways filled with broken stones suggested that there once had been.

Finally, she turned and started walking back toward the Table chamber—or what had once been one. She did close the stone-faced door behind her, although she could not have said why she did.

Once she stepped through the archway into the chamber where she had begun, Mykella turned, reached up, and touched the half-hanging light-torch bracket. It turned slightly. As it did, a grinding followed. Her mouth opened as a smooth stone wall slid into place, so well fitted that there was no sign at all that there had been an entry to the corridor behind it. Then a *sizzle* issued from the light-torch, and the amber light vanished, leaving Mykella in darkness. The patter of falling pieces followed.

She could sense that the light-torch and bracket had fallen . . . and disintegrated into nothing. Just because she had touched them? Or had they been about to fail anyway, and had her touch merely hastened the process?

She took a deep breath. Had all her recent exploration of the corridors and the strange cavern just been so that she didn't have to confront the question before her? With no Table, how was she supposed to return to Tempre?

She forced herself to consider her situation. When she had arrived, there hadn't been a Table, and that suggested that she didn't need a Table, that she could reach places just through the greenish black below the Table, or below where the Table had been. The fainter points of light—were they where Tables had been? She wished she knew what locations the colors represented.

She concentrated on the greenish blackness in the stone beneath her. Time passed more slowly, and the effort clearly took more energy, but she began to drift down through the sand and stone and into the chill beneath, although the greenish black did not seem quite so cold as the purple of the Table in Tempre. Locating the blue point that was Tempre was far easier, and before long she stood on the Table from which she had departed.

Mist billowed off her nightsilk jacket—ice-mist.

She did not sense the purple of the Ifrit, and she vaulted down from the Table, then turned to see if she could determine what Joramyl might be doing. The mists swirled and then vanished, showing her uncle still riding. This time, he was in a more lighted place, and coming down the main avenue past the public gardens and toward the palace. He was accompanied by the same men in black and another figure, hooded, but in brown, so that she could not make out either his hair or face.

Her entire body began to shiver, and her legs to tremble.

Why did using the Table leave her so exhausted? It didn't seem to take that much effort, and the effort was all in her head, wasn't it?

She released the image shown by the Table and stepped back, then turned. Slow step by slow step she made her way from the chamber, along the corridor and up the narrow lower staircase. Only just before she unlocked the staircase door did she create a concealment shield. Immediately, she began to shiver. Yet she dared not be discovered.

How she made it along the west main level corridor and then up the main staircase undetected, she wasn't certain, but once she stepped into her own chamber, she released the shield . . . and swallowed.

"Where have you been?" asked Salyna crossly, looking up from the old armchair by the window, blinking, as if she'd dozed off. "Rachylana's upset and furious, and I couldn't find you anywhere."

Mykella sank onto the bed. "I was out . . . on the narrows . . ." That was the only explanation that came to mind.

"In an ice-storm? You were outside on those slippery stones? You could have fallen right into the courtyard." Salyna shook her head, half-sleepily. "It's stupid to risk getting yourself killed when you don't even know whether the Deforyan envoy might ask for your hand for the Landarch's heir."

"I had to think," Mykella evaded.

"That wasn't very thoughtful."

"I won't do it again." Not that she'd actually done it, but she certainly didn't want to reveal what she had been doing. "Rachylana's really upset?"

"Wouldn't you be? Father looked right at her when he said it."

"She's interested in Berenyt, but Father wouldn't allow that," said Mykella.

"Do we know that? He's never really said so."

"That would cause problems for Jeraxylt in the future, especially if he marries and only has daughters. Father wouldn't do that."

Salyna nodded, then stood. "I'm going to bed. Stay off the balconies in this weather." She walked toward the chamber door.

"I'm tired, too," replied Mykella. "And I won't climb out the window to any balconies. Not until we have better weather, anyway."

"Good night."

After Salyna finally left, Mykella undressed and climbed under the quilts on her bed. The shivering did not subside for close to half a glass, she thought. For all her exhaustion, she found she was not sleepy. She couldn't help but wonder what Joramyl had been doing, but what worried her most was her recollection of the almost puzzled and unbelieving air behind her father's acceptance of her findings about the missing tariffs.

Still . . . eventually sleep did claim her.

22

After all her worries, which had not only been increased by her father's words and certainly not helped by her efforts with the Table, Mykella slept poorly and restlessly, but found herself struggling to get out of bed long after Uleana had rapped on her door. She finally managed to struggle up and get to the washroom, then back to her chambers, where she quickly dressed. She paused and glanced out the window. The sun had risen, and white light shimmered everywhere. The ice-storm and its dark clouds had passed, although her windows were frozen shut, and lines of ice ran across the sills. She was more than glad to be wearing nightsilk when she finally left her chambers and headed for what would be a late and quick breakfast.

Even from down the corridor, she could see her father waiting outside the breakfast room. He turned, as if waiting for her. His face was stern, and she could sense concern . . . and sadness. He motioned to her.

"What is it?" Mykella asked as she stopped before him.

"I said that I would look into what you found out," Feranyt began. Mykella waited.

"There was a great deal of validity to your findings. So much so that . . . well . . . Kiedryn is dead. He took poison last night, right here in the palace. Can you believe that? Joramyl found him this morning. He left a note, saying that he'd stolen far too many golds. He said he was sorry, but he didn't want to disgrace his family. The note pleaded not to make matters public . . ."

Mykella managed not to gape. Kiedryn? He had likely been the only honest one there, besides Mykella herself. And Joramyl had found him?

"His family will have to accept exile, of course, but there's no reason to make it public."

"Kiedryn couldn't have . . ." Mykella protested.

Feranyt shrugged sadly. "I know you thought he was honest, but at times appearances are deceiving. I saw the note. Joramyl showed it to me, and we even compared the writing to his. He wrote it, without a doubt."

Under what sort of duress? Mykella swallowed. She'd even seen Joramyl in the Table mirror, doubtless bringing Kiedryn back to the palace, but . . . how could she explain that? Even if she could get her father to see objects in the Table, it would still be her word against Joramyl's, and there was no way her father would take her word over his brother's. That, she knew, and speaking against Joramyl would only result in her being unable to do anything . . . not that what she had done had gone as planned.

"I know this is hard for you, daughter, but that sort of hard truth comes with ruling. Those you trust most are often those who betray that trust."

"But . . . Joramyl?"

"He's been as solid as a rock."

"He's never been in the Finance study before midmorning." Mykella managed to keep her voice level. "It seems a little strange that he was the one to find Kiedryn."

"I asked him to look into it. He wanted to be there early to confront Kiedryn before anyone else was around."

Mykella managed to nod.

"There's just no help for it. Joramyl's assistant steward will take over until we determine a permanent replacement for Kiedryn. I'm counting on you to help him."

"Yes, sir." Mykella felt that her voice was coming from someone else. Why couldn't her father see what was happening? Yet she could sense that trying to convince him that his own brother was behind it all was futile.

Feranyt patted her on the shoulder. "I'm counting on you. I already ate. I need to get ready to meet with that envoy now."

Envoy? What envoy? Mykella just stood there as her father turned.

After Feranyt continued toward his official study, Mykella began to walk toward the breakfast room, only to find Jeraxylt standing outside the service pantry, also waiting for her.

"Father was pleased, you know," offered Jeraxylt. "He said you handled things the way a smart woman should . . . finding out what was happening, you know, and letting him know."

A smart woman? How smart had she been? Poor honest Kiedryn had been poisoned and set up as the guilty party, when Joramyl was the one who'd been diverting the golds—and now matters were even worse, because both her brother and her father believed Joramyl, and she had no proof at all who had diverted the golds . . . and no way to obtain it now that Kiedryn, who might have been able to help, was dead, and now that everyone was convinced of Kiedryn's guilt.

Mykella walked into the breakfast room and sat down. Now what could she do?

"Mykella, that Deforyan envoy is already here." Rachylana's eyes were red. "Father said . . ." She stopped, as if she could say no more.

"He said that the Landarch's heir is partial to redheads," added Salyna, "especially beautiful ones like Rachylana."

"You have to do something," Rachylana said. "You have to."

Mykella could feel the despair and desperation behind her sister's words. For a moment she said nothing. Finally, she said, "These days . . . these days, Father isn't listening to me, either."

"He just said something about your saving thousands of golds. He'll listen to you. He will."

"He'll listen about golds, but not about matching us. I'll try, but . . ." Mykella paused. "He and Uncle Joramyl just talk about what good consorts we'll make."

"Please. I don't want to go to Dereka," pleaded Rachylana.

"You're the only one Father will listen to," added Salyna.

Me? He doesn't listen to any of us, not really. "I'll see what I can do, but I'm not sure any of us have a choice about to whom we're matched or where we'll be sent." *More like shipped like prized breeding cows.*

"We should have some choice," Salyna declared.

"We should, but we don't," Mykella said, picking up the mug of tea and taking a sip. *Why can't you see that?*

She barely ate any breakfast, but she did manage to finish the mug of tea, and that helped settle her stomach . . . mostly.

Then, girding herself up, she made her way to the Finance chambers.

The man who rose when Mykella entered the outer chamber was barely a span taller than she was, and squat, like a human toad, she thought. Although his hair was sandy brown and curly, Mykella felt that greasy black would have suited him far better. He smiled, and from behind the white teeth and sincere expression flooded insincerity. Even his life-thread seemed snakelike, holding a sickly yellow-brown. "Maxymt, at the service of the Lord-Protector."

"I'm pleased to meet you, Maxymt. The Lord-Protector has asked me to make sure you're familiar with the ledgers and accounts."

"Once I've had a chance to become familiar with these, you really won't have to check the ledgers, Mistress. The Lord-Protector's daughter shouldn't be doing a clerk's work." Oiliness coated the insincerity of every word.

"How well do you know the accounts?" she asked. "Could you tell me which ledger holds the receipts from the smallholders? Or the one from the vintners? Or the distinctions between common factors and crafters?"

Maxymt smiled, again showing brilliant white teeth. "I'm certain that won't be hard to determine . . . assuming that Kiedryn was not too . . . creative."

"I'm sure that you will be able to learn," Mykella replied, "but while you are, I'm certain my father would wish me to continue as I have."

"As you wish, Mistress Mykella."

She could sense a most palpable dislike behind the honeyed words. Now what could she do, except try to strengthen those abilities awakened by the Ancient and her growing, but growing all too slowly, Talent? "We might as well get started. First, I'll show you the summary ledgers, and then the individual account ledgers, and you can go through each one to gain some familiarity."

"Yes, Mistress Mykella."

Almost a glass later, Joramyl hurried into his Finance study, smiling at Maxymt, who was still studying the master ledger, and at Mykella for a moment. Berenyt followed his father, and he did not look at Mykella.

Mykella *had* to know what they were saying. The moment Maxymt turned his head, she gathered her sight-shield around her and tiptoed to the study door, where she stood, her ear against the crack between door and jamb, trying to make out what the two said.

". . . don't talk about it here . . ."

". . . just wanted you to know . . . Mykella's sharper than she looks . . . don't think she'll accept . . . knew Kiedryn too well . . ."

". . . and what could she do, Berenyt? The Lord-Protector saw the confession . . . she's just a woman, barely more than a girl. If my brother weren't so sentimental, he'd have long since sent her to Dereka or Southgate and gotten a pile of golds for her as well . . . what women are for . . . golds and heirs . . . At least, he doesn't listen to her the way he did to her mother. Good thing Aelya died when she did."

Mykella stiffened. There had been something more there, behind the words, and she missed the next phrases.

". . . besides, Feranyt's offspring's meddling served us well . . . not have to worry about Kiedryn any longer . . . now . . . don't come see me here more than once a week . . . Off with you."

"Yes, sir."

Mykella slipped back to her table and, once the acting head clerk was looking in the other direction, released the sight-shield.

Maxymt turned with a start. Then he stared at Mykella. "Where did you come from?"

"Come from? I've been here all along."

"You weren't there a moment ago."

Mykella shook her head. "I haven't left the chamber. You would have heard my boots. Everyone's always said that I walk heavier than some of the guards. I did drop my figuring paper and had to bend down to get it."

"That must be it." Maxymt shook his head.

Mykella could tell that he wasn't totally convinced, but she hadn't dared to hold the sight-shield any longer, in case someone else had walked in, or Berenyt walked out.

That fear was confirmed, because the door to the inner study opened, but, once again, Berenyt didn't look in her direction when he hurried out of his father's study.

23

Even though she had to keep explaining matters to Maxymt intermittently through the afternoon, to Mykella, the remainder of the day felt never-ending, and she accomplished little beyond that instruction and keeping herself outwardly calm and composed. Joramyl left by midafternoon, with only a statement to Maxymt that he would be back by midday on Septi . . . and without a glance at Mykella. She did feel, all too clearly, his more than palpable dislike of her.

When the time came to close the Finance study for the day, Mykella explained the details to the acting chief clerk and watched.

As he stepped out into the corridor and locked the door, Maxymt smiled politely and said, "I'm certain it will be a relief to you when I can take over all these duties."

"My father and I will be gratified when everything is as it should be." Mykella smiled. "Good afternoon, Maxymt."

"Good afternoon, Mistress Mykella."

Maxymt was graceful enough in his movements as he walked to the main staircase that Mykella revised her initial assessment of the man. He wasn't a toad, but a lizard, with the ugliness of a toad, and the sinister aspect of a snake.

She immediately walked to the washroom adjoining her chamber in the family quarters, because she felt she had to wash up after spending most of the day with the man. The wash water was like ice, but she still felt cleaner when she finished and dried her hands and face. Then she slipped into the family parlor. She needed less revolting company.

Salyna was already there, working on her needlepoint, and wearing a heavy sweater. Frost coated the inside of the windows, and Mykella noted that the hearth held but embers. There was no coal in the brass scuttle to the side of the fire screen.

Salyna looked up. "You must have had a difficult day. I heard that you discovered the finance clerk was diverting golds? Is that true?"

How could Mykella answer that without lying and disclosing more than she wanted, but without blaming Kiedryn? After a moment, she spoke. "I did discover that someone was diverting golds. Jeraxylt helped me get the information. I showed the figures and the ledgers to Father. He told Lord Joramyl. That was yesterday afternoon. This morning, Lord Joramyl found Kiedryn dead of poison and a note in Kiedryn's hand confessing that he had taken thousands in golds."

Salyna looked at Mykella. "You don't believe Kiedryn did it, do you?"

"What I believe doesn't matter, Father pointed out. Only what can be proved does. The only proof points to Kiedryn."

"He couldn't have done it," Salyna said quietly. "The chief clerk doesn't actually handle the golds, does he? It's more likely the head tariff collector or someone like that. They'd have enough golds to pay for and arrange Kiedryn's death to cover their tracks."

"Father believes it was Kiedryn."

"Father is too trusting. He doesn't talk to enough people outside the palace."

Mykella agreed with that, but she only said, "We don't, either. Well . . . maybe you do, because you talk to a lot of the guards." She paused, then added, "What do they say?"

"All of them knew by midday, but they aren't saying much."

"That's not good."

"I worry about Arms-Commander Nephryt," said Salyna. "I've never liked him."

"Do you think he might have been in league with whoever did take the golds?"

"I don't know. He's capable of it." Salyna set the needlework frame down beside her on the settee. "But so is Commander Demyl. So are some of the other ministers."

"Father must know that," Mykella said. "That's why he wanted Uncle Joramyl as Finance Minister. He trusts him." Mykella kept a pleasant expression, but tried to catch whatever reaction Salyna might have.

"They are brothers." Salyna paused. "Joramyl saw the figures, and he didn't catch what you did. Is that because he doesn't spend the time you have?"

From what Mykella could tell, Salyna didn't show any repugnance or any other feelings besides curiosity. After a moment, Mykella replied, "He only spends a few glasses a day in the Finance study. Still, he's anything but stupid."

"I imagine his thoughts were elsewhere. Most people don't love numbers the way you do. Jeraxylt was right; Father was fortunate that you caught the problem." Salyna glanced toward the window and the setting sun. "Do you have any idea who was really behind it?"

"Ideas?" Mykella offered a rueful laugh. "Ideas are easy. Proving them is something else, and without proof . . ." She shrugged.

"Men like proof," Salyna said dryly. "Sometimes, it's a joy to provide it, especially with a saber, even a practice blade."

"More about blades?" asked Rachylana as she stepped into the parlor.

"And men," replied Salyna.

"Berenyt is good with a blade."

Salyna and Mykella exchanged glances.

Rachylana glanced from one sister to the other, then flushed. "Not that way. You two . . . You're terrible."

"We didn't say anything," Mykella said. "Not a word."

"You didn't have to." Rachylana shook her head. "Besides . . . Father wants to get me away from Tempre as quickly as he can. You know that."

"He's teased you," Salyna pointed out, "but that's not the same thing."

"It is too." Rachylana eased the needlework frame back toward

Salyna and sat on the other end of the settee. "Mykella has her numbers and ledgers and isn't interested in anyone here in Tempre. You'd rather practice with sabers—the sharp kind. That leaves me."

"It's not entirely up to Father," Mykella pointed out. "He can't really make an envoy choose someone who the envoy doesn't think is right."

"Maybe not the Landarch's envoy, or a Seltyr from Southgate, but any prince-heir from the coast will take whoever's offered. So would one of the Illegean horde leaders. You wouldn't like that, would you?" Rachylana looked at Mykella. "They don't even know what ledgers are."

"Don't be cruel because you're angry," said Salyna softly.

Rachylana shivered, opened her mouth, then closed it, pulling the heavy blue woolen shawl around her. She looked to Mykella. "Aren't you cold in just that tunic?"

"It's nightsilk, and I'm wearing a nightsilk camisole under it."

"So am I, and I'm still freezing. You don't ever seem to get cold anymore."

Mykella hadn't noticed that, but both her sisters were bundled up—and there was ice gathered on the inside of the parlor windows. The palace wasn't exactly the warmest of buildings, and most chambers were without hearths.

The chimes announcing dinner echoed outside the parlor, and Mykella rose. "I wonder what's for dinner."

"You don't want to know," said Salyna. "It's one of Father's favorites—overcooked, fried, and pounded river trout, doused in cheese and buried in rice."

Salyna was right. Mykella hated river trout. To her, the fish tasted like river mud, and nothing disguised that. "We might as well face it," she said resignedly.

Feranyt and Eranya were already in the family dining room when the three sisters arrived, followed in moments by Jeraxylt.

The Lord-Protector seated himself, as did Jeraxylt, then the four women.

Akilsa immediately began to fill the wine goblets with a clear vintage, and Muergya began serving.

"Ah . . . hot river trout," offered Feranyt, "just the thing for a cold winter evening."

"It is warm," agreed Rachylana.

"That it is, and tasty, too," agreed the Lord-Protector.

Mykella refrained from disputing that, and instead had Muergya serve her the smallest morsel of trout possible, and as much rice and cheese as possible that hadn't been close to the fish.

After eating several mouthfuls, and taking a swallow of wine, Feranyt looked up. "On Octdi night, we'll be having a reception and a formal dinner with the Deforyan envoy. I expect each of you young women to talk to him."

Although Rachylana smiled politely, Mykella could feel her anger . . . and a certain despair.

"Who else will be there?" inquired Salyna.

"All of us"—Feranyt nodded toward Eranya—"and Joramyl and Lady Cheleyza, and several other ministers and their wives, including Seltyr Porofyr and Arms-Commander Nephryt."

Why Porofyr? wondered Mykella. Was that because he was the minister for highways and rivers, and part of the talks between Deforya and Lanachrona involved more than the guarding of the highways against brigands?

"And . . . Jeraxylt," Feranyt added, "the envoy was kind enough to bring a miniature of the Landarch's young cousin."

"How old is she? Twelve?" A certain scorn lay behind Jeraxylt's words.

"Young compared to the Landarch. She is actually about a year older than you are, but she looks to be rather pretty."

"Rather pretty?"

"Enough," said Feranyt firmly. "Because of who we are, all our choices are limited, and that includes yours in the matter of marriage. Your sisters understand that, and so should you. A suitable match is vital for the Lord-Protector."

"Yes, sir." Jeraxylt nodded, politely.

Behind his pleasant expression Mykella sensed anger close to fury. Why hadn't she seen that before?

"Many would give everything for an attractive, well-connected, and wealthy spouse," Eranya said cheerfully.

No one but Mykella seemed to sense the contempt behind her words, and certainly not Jeraxylt.

"Exactly," murmured Feranyt. "Exactly."

"There wasn't any coal in the scuttle in the parlor," offered Rachylana.

"You could have gotten some from the coal bin in the courtyard," suggested Feranyt.

"There wasn't any there, either," said Salyna. "Not in mid-afternoon, anyway."

"Then bring it up with the steward. That's Jodhar's job, to make sure we're supplied with what's necessary."

Salyna nodded, but Mykella caught the sense that she was both less than satisfied, yet pleased.

After dinner, Mykella drew Salyna aside. "What about the coal?"

"Oh . . . Jodhar wouldn't talk to me about it. That's why I asked Father. Tomorrow, after I work out, I'll suggest that he take steps to replenish the palace's coal supply—and I'll still have my saber with me. But, this time, I'll have Father's express backing."

"You could have said that anyway."

"No. Unless he'd actually said it, Father wouldn't back me up. You know that. He's very particular."

"He'll know you tricked him into saying that."

"He will, but he always stands by his word, no matter what."

That, reflected Mykella, could be a strength . . . and a terrible weakness, if one had been deceived. "Then we should have a warm parlor before long."

"We will, indeed." Salyna smiled.

By the time she finally slipped away from her sister and, under her concealment shield, down the two sets of stairs to the Table chamber, Mykella had already decided that she needed to use the Table to track not only Joramyl, but Berenyt and Nephryt.

Once she opened the door to the chamber, she tried to sense if the Ifrit might be trying to use the Table, but all she felt was the faint purple glow that was always present. She stepped up to the Table and began to concentrate on seeking Joramyl.

The mists cleared to reveal her uncle seated at a heavy round table. To his left was Arms-Commander Nephryt. The two were talking. Heavy goblets were set before each man, and a third goblet was set before one of the two empty chairs. There was something . . . something about the chamber in which the two were seated. Mykella frowned, looking at the image.

The door opened, and another man stepped through. For that moment, Mykella caught a glimpse of the outer hall, with the stone walls and rose columns . . . and belatedly recognized the entry hall of Joramyl's grand mansion. The private study lay behind one of the doors she'd seen, with easy access off the entry. Only then did she concentrate on the latest arrival, Commander Demyl, second in command of the Southern Guards.

The very presence of the three together, meeting in Joramyl's mansion, confirmed for Mykella her feeling that her uncle was the one behind the diversion of golds—and that the diversion was more than mere greed on his part. Since she could not make out their words as they sat around the table and talked, she had no idea to what degree the three were plotting.

Yet . . . with her limited knowledge and lack of what her father regarded as proof, not to mention his inflexibility, how could she tell him?

She continued to watch the three for close to a glass, yet outside of a number of gestures, the most revealing of which was when Nephryt said something with great vehemence, and Joramyl clearly calmed him with what looked to be soothing words, Mykella could make out nothing, although she did get the impression that Joramyl was cautioning patience.

Finally, she let that image lapse, and concentrated on trying to find Berenyt next. The Table obligingly revealed him in a bed—not alone, and not with Rachylana, thankfully, but with a slender, if shapely, brunette whom Mykella did not recognize. She let the image fade immediately. She was neither a voyeur nor able to deceive herself into thinking that watching would reveal anything she didn't already know about her cousin.

There was no point in telling Rachylana about Berenyt, either, because Mykella didn't know who the woman was and couldn't have explained plausibly how she knew what Berenyt was doing. But . . . perhaps . . . perhaps, Salyna might know . . . if Mykella broached it in the right way.

That might offer a possible way to alert Rachylana about how Berenyt viewed women . . . and how little respect he would have for Rachylana were they ever matched.

Unfortunately, trying to warn her father about his brother was going to be far harder.

She turned from the Table and walked slowly from the underground chamber, her boots scuffing on the stone floor as she headed for the narrow staircase.

24

Mykella did not sleep all that much better on Sexdi night than she had the nights before, but she'd been so tired that, when she woke to Uleana's knocking on Septi, she did not remember her nightmares, but only the vague uneasiness that told her she had indeed had them. When she opened the window hangings, she almost wanted to pull them shut again because a gray fog enshrouded the palace in a chill gloom.

Instead, she pulled on a robe and left her chambers to wash up.

Salyna, smiling cheerfully as most early risers did, was leaving the washroom, and Mykella gestured for her to stop.

"You have that look," Salyna said, if pleasantly. "What is it?"

Mykella glanced in the direction of Rachylana's chambers, then said in a low voice, "Do you know who the brunette is that Berenyt's seeing? The one he's keeping from Rachylana?"

"How do you know that?"

"I've overheard a few things, too many to be mistaken."

Salyna frowned. "Have you told Rachylana?"

For all Rachylana's airs, Mykella didn't want to see her sister used and hurt, and neither did Salyna. That was clear.

Mykella shook her head. "I thought you might know. You're around the Southern Guards more."

"No. I've seen looks, and I wondered."

"Can you find out without letting her know?"

Salyna smiled wryly. "I can try, but . . . we'll see, won't we?"

"I don't want her hurt . . ."

"Neither do I, but what she wants is going to end up hurting her one way or another." With another smile, a sadder one, Salyna turned toward her chambers.

Mykella hurried through her morning efforts and managed to make it to the breakfast room just behind her younger sister. She had barely seated herself when Rachylana and Jeraxylt arrived, followed by Feranyt.

Beyond his cheerful "good morning," Feranyt said nothing until he had taken several healthy swallows of his spiced tea. "I'd hoped the envoy from Southgate would be here by the end of the week, but the latest dispatch indicates he will not arrive until Duadi at the earliest."

"An envoy from Southgate?" asked Salyna.

"The Seltyrs do have a preference for blondes, I hear." Feranyt grinned at his blond and youngest daughter.

Salyna grinned back, but Mykella sensed the anger behind the grin.

Rachylana maintained a pleasant expression, behind which, all too obviously to Mykella, simmered irritation. "Have you met with the Deforyan envoy?"

"Only briefly, when he presented his credentials," replied Feranyt. "He has been meeting with various ministers, including your Uncle Joramyl. It's less than wise to appear too eager to meet and negotiate personally with an envoy."

And even less wise to let Joramyl and Nephryt negotiate for you. But Mykella concealed her thoughts behind a pleasant smile, instead saying, "I thought you had not requested an envoy from Southgate."

"I didn't, but when one requests to come and meet, it's not wise to refuse. There's little sense in antagonizing a neighboring land over something like that. Besides, at some time before long, you all will have to be matched and married."

"We are still young," offered Salyna.

"*You* are, but your sisters are the right ages, and matching can take time." Feranyt offered a nod that signified that he would not discuss that issue any longer, then began to cut the ham strips beside the cooling omelet on his plate.

Mykella did the same.

After breakfast, Mykella followed her father out into the corridor.

"You have something on your mind, daughter?"

"I do. I was thinking about Kiedryn . . ."

"He betrayed his trust. He paid for it, and suffered little." Feranyt's voice was hard.

"Not about that part of it . . . about what it means, about being Lord-Protector . . ."

"Trust is everything to a ruler."

"Father . . . do you think all those you command are loyal?"

"What sort of question is that?" The firmness was supplanted by anger, although not all of it showed in the Lord-Protector's voice.

"I thought Kiedryn was loyal. Before this happened, you did also. How can a Lord-Protector tell? You rely on those around you. Anyone might betray you. Arms-Commander Nephryt . . . even Lord Joramyl, were he so inclined . . ."

"Mykella . . . I will not hear even the slightest suggestions that men of such honor and loyalty—"

"Father, I did not say that," Mykella interjected quickly. "I only meant to ask how one knows, when you must trust so many, and when those you trust the most could harm you the most. I worked with Kiedryn. I trusted him. So did you. How do you know who is honest and who to trust? How can you tell?"

Feranyt looked at his daughter.

Mykella looked back, trying to project earnestness and honesty.

"If you cannot tell, you will not long remain a ruler."

Mykella managed to keep looking interested, much as she wanted to point out that what he had said was obvious. "You must have ways, things you look for."

"Most times, you can trust those you have known for a long time and who have not betrayed you in ways large or small. Likewise, you can trust those who would have much to lose if anything happened to you. Those who appear too eager to please must be watched, as must those who cultivate indifference, for no one is truly indifferent to a ruler."

At her father's last words, Mykella nodded. She had not thought in those terms.

"Beyond that, dear daughter, it is a matter of learning and experience."

"Thank you, Father. I will keep your words in my thoughts."

Mykella managed to keep a thoughtful expression on her face until she reached the Finance study, where she tried to greet Maxymt pleasantly, before getting on with instructing him and checking recent entries.

About a half glass before midday, Joramyl strode into the upper level Finance study, ignoring Mykella and beckoning to Maxymt. The acting chief finance clerk stood and followed Joramyl into the inner study, closing the door behind him.

With no one else in the outer study, Mykella raised her concealment shield, then walked over to the inner study door, trying to use her Talent to overhear what Joramyl said to Maxymt.

". . . state of accounts?"

"All are perfect. Not even the daughter can find fault with them. She has searched diligently."

"She . . . Keep watching her. . ."

"That is not difficult. She thinks that everything is in the ledgers."

Mykella decided to offer an opportunity. She walked toward the door leading to the corridor, letting her boots hit the stone floor heavily. Then she opened the outer door and closed it, before quietly easing back into position beside the door to the inner study. There, she stood, listening once more.

Abruptly, Mykella straightened as Maxymt opened the door and peered out, then closed the door again.

"She's left . . . for the moment. She'll doubtless be back. She watches like a hawk," said Maxymt quietly.

"What about Shenyl?"

"That's been taken care of."

Shenyl? What about the entry clerk? What had they done to him? Mykella feared she knew. But why Shenyl? He hadn't been involved with the tariffs. He handled the accounts of the Southern Guards. Except. . . . her use of the Table had revealed Nephryt plotting with Joramyl.

"For now . . . do nothing to cause her alarm."

Mykella could hear footsteps. She walked to the outer door, opened it slightly, then closed it firmly and released the concealment shield before walking back to her work table and seating herself.

Only a few moments after she had begun to look at the ledger before her did Maxymt leave the inner study. She could sense his eyes on her, but she did not look up.

Mykella wanted to hurry right down to the main level and the narrow interior room where the clerks transferred entries and expenditures to the main account ledgers. She did not. Instead, she began to study the expenditures for repairs of roads and bridges within Tempre. She checked page after page of the detailed ledger. Nothing seemed unusual, and that bothered her. Or was she coming to trust no one?

Late in the afternoon, less than a glass before time to close, Mykella rose from the table. "I'll be back shortly, Maxymt."

"As you wish, Mistress Mykella."

She smiled pleasantly as she departed. At a measured pace, she walked to the main staircase, past the guards stationed at the upper landing, and down to the main level of the palace. Then she turned left and walked eastward for almost a hundred yards before stopping at an unmarked oak door. She opened the door and stepped into the long and narrow accounting chamber. One of the tables was empty— the one usually occupied by Shenyl.

The young clerk closest to the door was the only one she did not know by sight, and that meant he was Wasdahl. He glanced up, then stiffened. "Mistress Mykella."

"Wasdahl, have you seen Shenyl?"

The youth swallowed. "No, Mistress. He hasn't been in today. He must be ill. He never misses a day."

Haelyt, the older and graying clerk in charge of the clerks, cleared his throat.

Wasdahl closed his mouth.

"Mistress Mykella," Haelyt said firmly, "he is absent today. No one knows why. He has been most diligent in the years he has been here. Might I help you?"

"I am most certain that you could, Haelyt, but it is a small matter and would require your searching for an entry that Shenyl would know easily. I will see if Shenyl is well tomorrow. Thank you." Before the older clerk could protest, Mykella smiled, then turned and slipped back out through the door.

Her thoughts churning, she forced herself into a deliberate pace back along the lower corridor, avoiding those few functionaries and factors in the corridor, then nodded to the guards at the base of the main staircase as she passed to make her way back to the upper Finance study.

25

After an uneventful dinner, where Eranya chattered about how wonderful the formal dinner would be on Octdi, and how she loved meeting people from all across Corus, Mykella and her sisters retired to the parlor. Because Mykella did not wish to talk, she claimed a history she had not read before. Salyna addressed her needlework.

Rachylana talked. ". . . you'd think we'd made Father miserable. He seems determined to have us all matched and married off in the next year . . . and who in her right mind would want to go to Dereka? At least in Southgate, you wouldn't freeze, Salyna."

"I'd rather not go either place at the moment."

"You can't stay here."

"Why not? We all don't have to marry rulers or heirs, do we? I'm certain there must be a Seltyr or High Factor's son who might actually be intelligent and able to converse and who might feel gratified to have me, rather than obligated."

"Father won't allow it. You know that."

"He's never said that."

"He doesn't have to. That's the way things are."

Mykella's eyes had been flicking across the words of the history, as she half-read, half-listened, when she stopped and re-read the section in the middle of the page.

> . . . of all the thousands who strove on that battlefield, when the Ancient appeared to Mykel, few indeed saw her, for their eyes could not encompass her. A larger group, two score or so, beheld Mykel surrounded by an unworldly green glow. The others saw nothing. . . .

Mykella nodded to herself. Even back in the times of Mykel the Great, few could see the soarers. That didn't help her any, but it made her feel a bit better.

"Where would you rather go, Mykella?" asked Rachylana, turning to her older sister, "Dereka or Southgate?"

"There's no point in expressing a desire," replied Mykella. "We won't be allowed to choose anyway. Father and the envoys will work it all out, and we'll be told that it's our duty and destiny, and to make a good household wherever we're matched."

"They say that the Northcoast women can have lovers besides their husbands," ventured Rachylana.

"I'm certain they can," replied Salyna. "Many of them are trained in arms. That happened because they needed women as well as men to hold off the Squawts and the Reillies after the Great Plague. The women there were smart enough to keep training their daughters in skills with weapons."

"You would know that. Is that where you want to go, then?"

"It won't happen. Lady Cheleyza is from there, and Father will want to make ties elsewhere." Salyna looked down at her needlework.

"You handle the needle as if it were a dagger," prodded Rachylana.

"You need finesse with both."

Mykella went back to concentrating on her book.

Before long, Rachylana slipped away.

Mykella extended her Talent senses, but Rachylana had left and was not standing outside the parlor door, listening. No one else was, either.

After several moments, Salyna lowered the needlework frame. "What's the matter?" she asked Mykella quietly. "You're avoiding talking to everyone again. Is it Kiedryn? Are you still worried about the missing golds?"

"I can't help but worry. I think it's more than the golds, but I don't know what, and I can't seem to find out what it might be." Before Salyna could say more, Mykella asked, "Did you find out anything about Berenyt?"

"Her name is Clyena, and she's the sister of one of the Southern Guards in Berenyt's company. She's a maid for Lady Cheleyza."

That didn't surprise Mykella. "Cheleyza probably introduced them, or made sure Berenyt noticed her. I'd wager Clyena is overpaid as a maid."

Salyna nodded. "Or she gets clothes or food for her family or something like that. But isn't it safer and better that way?"

"I suppose so, but do you think Berenyt will stop seeing others after he's matched and married?"

The blonde shook her head. "Is there anything I can do?"

"Not now."

"I'm going to bed. I'll see you in the morning."

"In the morning." Mykella smiled. "Thank you."

Salyna returned the smile, then turned and left.

Mykella forced herself to read another full page of the ancient, and generally boring, history before standing and making her way from the parlor back to her chamber. There she waited until the corridors seemed quiet before raising her concealment shield and slipping out her door. She took care to walk as quietly as possible down the main staircase, taking her time.

Once she reached the Table chamber, she opened the door gingerly, ready for anything, but all she saw and sensed was the lambent purple glow. Her first effort was to see if she could find Shenyl.

While the mists swirled across the silvered finish of the Table, they did not part to reveal anything. Mykella frowned. In the past, the Table had either remained silvered or shown the mists followed by an image. Was there something wrong, either with her or the Table?

She concentrated on seeking Joramyl, but the mists appeared and vanished nearly instantly, displaying an image of her uncle with another man, again in the entryway study of Joramyl's mansion. The other man was not dressed as a Derekan, but in the white shimmer-silk tunic and trousers of a Seltyr of Southgate.

Her father had said that the envoy from Southgate would not be arriving in Tempre for several days more. Admittedly, Joramyl's mansion was just outside Tempre, but . . . or was the man just a Seltyr who had traveled to Tempre for trading purposes?

Again, Mykella felt hamstrung. By next week, she would know whether the man she now saw was the envoy, but she couldn't very well risk telling her father that the envoy was already meeting with Joramyl because she didn't know if the Seltyr were the envoy, and she couldn't explain how she knew . . . and if she tried, most likely Joramyl would lie, and her father would believe his brother over her.

An ornate silver and crystal wine decanter sat on the polished wood table, and before each man was a matching silver and crystal goblet. Both smiled a great deal as Mykella watched the conversation, but even without hearing their words or being able to sense their feelings, she doubted that either set of smiles was anything but a facade.

Finally, she let the image fade.

Now what?

She looked at the Table. Did any of the other Tables offer a place from which she could escape? She could only try. She tightened her lips, then vaulted up onto the Table, concentrating on the greenish blackness below.

This time, her descent into the bitter cold below was swifter, and she immediately tried to sense one of the light-beacons that she had not tried before, trying to determine which might be closest. In some fashion, although it was muted, the crimson and gold seemed closer than the brilliant gray-silver. She focused on the crimson and gold. As before, for a time nothing seemed to happen. Then the beacon rushed toward her and surrounded her.

Mykella staggered as she rose out of the greenish blackness, taking several steps on uneven sand before her hip slammed into a low stone wall—the edge of another stone depression. She glanced around hurriedly, but she saw and sensed no one. She stood in an empty chamber, in the kind of square pit that had once held a Table, she judged. The air around her was far colder than in Tempre, and much thinner. Again . . . she felt that she was belowground. A single ancient lighttorch on the wall illuminated the chamber, if faintly, and she faced an ancient door with a lever handle.

Mykella clambered out of the pit and studied the chamber around her more closely. As with the Table chamber in Tempre, there were no furnishings, just bare stone walls. At that moment, she realized that the walls themselves held the faintest illumination, and that sense of light was neither green nor purple, but gold, a gold that she sensed, not saw. The walls, ancient as they seemed to be, bore not a single mark. They reminded her of something else. After a moment, she nodded. They were gold eternastone. But . . . the only place in all Corus where there was gold eternastone, or so she had read, was in Dereka.

Had she finally gotten somewhere that might be useful? She looked at the door, then walked toward it, almost afraid to depress the lever, to find it locked or blocked beyond by stone. Finally, she pressed the lever, and pulled on the door. It creaked, but it opened toward her, revealing a narrow set of stone steps leading upward.

Mykella slipped through the doorway and began to climb. Each step she took raised a cloud of dust, and her nose began to itch. She stifled a sneeze with the back of her hand, because, if someone waited above, she certainly didn't want to alert them. At the top of the stairs was a small foyer, with another ancient door. She gently depressed the lever, easing the door away from her. She heard nothing and sensed nothing, nothing except rows of . . . something.

Immediately, she raised her concealment shield before stepping into what looked to be a large room, filled with rows and rows of barrels. A warehouse of some sort? Ahead of her, down an aisle between the barrels stacked three deep, was a faint glow. She eased toward it, finally coming to a low and wide window. The glass and sill were dusty, as if no one had cleaned either in years, yet there were no spiderwebs or signs of insects.

Mykella rubbed a patch of the glass as clear as she could and then peered out into the darkness, lit but by the pearly glow of Selena and scattered lamps. Below the building itself ran a paved yellow road, with shadowed grooves carved into the stone by years of wagon wheels. To her right, to the north, she thought, she could see something outlined vaguely in the full light of Selena—a structure that held the gold glow of ancient eternastone.

She wanted to laugh, but she knew she wouldn't be able to stop. She was trying to stop plots, and she didn't want to be matched and married to the Landarch's heir and live in Dereka . . . and where was she? In an ancient gold eternastone warehouse in Dereka.

She turned and walked back to the stone steps and down to the Table chamber that no longer held a Table, and then into the sandy depression. She concentrated on the darkness beneath.

Nothing happened. It was as though a barrier lay between her and the greenish darkness beneath where the Table had once been.

How could there be a barrier? Was she trapped in Dereka?

She swallowed. There had to be some reason, something different, didn't there?

She tried again, but all that happened was that her boots slipped on the sand and she had to steady herself by reaching out to the stone edge of the Table pit. Even that felt clumsy, as though something blocked her from touching the stone.

What was happening? She had to think. Something had to be different.

Then . . . she shook her head . . . and dropped her concealment shield.

Almost immediately, she could sense and reach out to the greenish black below. Gratefully, she let herself sink into the depths. As the blue beacon of Tempre hurtled toward her, she sensed the slimy purpleness she associated with the Ifrit. But she had to return. Who knew what would happen if she tried to stop her travel?

When she emerged on the Table in Tempre, a heavy coat of frost covered her nightsilk tunic, and an icy fog appeared around her. She couldn't help shivering as she eased herself off the Table. A wisp of purple drifted upward.

Mykella fumbled mentally, but began to erect the kind of barriers she had used before. The purple wisp retreated, and the image of the distant Ifrit appeared in the mirrored surface of the Table.

You have returned. A harsh smile appeared on the white face. *You have learned much, it appears, but there is so much more you could learn . . . with the proper instruction.*

"You were not interested in instructing me before." Mykella remained a good step back from the Table, and that made it difficult to see the Ifrit, given the height of the Table and her own less than impressive stature.

The language is no longer as it once was, and I did not realize that you were a descendant of one of the changed ones.

"It took me a while to understand your words."

The white-faced Ifrit nodded. *Most here had thought that those who could use the Tables had perished, but there were some who argued that if your ancestors had had the foresight to merge with the world lifethread, they would survive, if not . . . precisely . . . in the form they had had before.*

"My ancestors looked like you?" Mykella shuddered inside.

Not all of them, most likely, but some must have, or you would not be able to use the Table. Nor would you have learned so much so quickly.

"You are not here on Corus."

No.

"Where, then?"

On Efra.

Efra? She'd never heard of a land or a city called Efra. Then she thought of exactly what he had said—*On Efra.* She swallowed. He was on another world. How . . . how could that be? She just stood there for a long time before replying. "Is that where my . . . ancestors like you came from?"

No. They came from Ifryn. Some used the Tables to come to your world, and some to Efra. There was a great battle on your world, and

contact was lost. Because some Tables still functioned, we knew life
remained, and we have tried to reach you over the years.

Mykella had the feeling that he was not telling the entire truth, not
that she could sense it through the Table, but something was not
quite right.

"I need to think about this." Mykella stepped back farther from
the Table, still holding the shields she had raised earlier.

Think carefully. We will talk later.

Slowly, Mykella backed away, watching the Table with eyes and
senses until she was out of the chamber. Then she closed the door
and moved quickly down the corridor, climbing the stone steps to the
main level of the palace.

She had no more than returned to her chambers and settled onto
her bed to pull off her boots when she sat up straight. She could
sense a green miasma seeping out of the stones of the outer wall.
Then the ancient soarer appeared.

"What is it?" asked Mykella.

The Ifrit will ensnare you with partial truths. None of your ancestors
were as he is.

"I didn't think so. I couldn't believe that."

Others like you, across Corus, did have ancestors such as he, and
they are not as their ancestors were. They are like you, and their chil-
dren and their children's children will remain so.

"He mentioned a battle. Was that the Great Cataclysm? Who was
fighting?"

There was a battle. It was between the evil Ifrits and those who had
come to understand that what had been occurring would kill the world.
We helped those who would save the world, but most of us and most of
those we helped perished. All those who would have destroyed the
world perished. It was indeed a Great Cataclysm. Those few of the
good Ifrits who lived became as you, as they always should have been.
That is why you must oppose the one who wants you to help him. He
would again bring evil into this world, no matter what else he tells you.

With those words, the soarer began to fade, then slipped into the
stones and down toward the greenish blackness beneath the palace.

Mykella watched, or sensed, what the soarer had done.

Could she do that? Just slip down through the stones?

Her entire body shivered, reminding her just how exhausted she was.

Another time, she decided, as she finished disrobing for bed. As she drifted into sleep, a vagrant thought crossed her mind . . . something about not being able to shield herself in the depths or when traveling through the darkness.

26

The soarer's presence might have been comforting, or Mykella just might have been totally exhausted. Whatever the reason, she slept soundly and without nightmares and awoke refreshed on Octdi morning. She remained cheerful until after breakfast, when she made her way down to the lower level of the palace and to the accounting chamber.

Haelyt immediately turned and bowed as Mykella entered. "Mistress."

"I don't see Shenyl. Have you heard from him?"

"Haven't you heard, Mistress?" asked Haelyt. "He was attacked and murdered by brigands the night before last, apparently on his way home. We just got word this morning."

"Oh . . ." Mykella shook her head. She'd feared just that, but having it confirmed still upset her. "Oh . . ." She did not speak for a moment. "Was he married?"

"His wife was the one who told me. She was carrying their youngest." Haelyt's eyes were bright.

Mykella could sense that the older clerk had been taken by surprise and that he was truly disturbed. That both reassured and concerned her. "We need . . . to do something for her."

"Shenyl had been here ten years, Mistress. She will get a widow's stipend. It's not much, but . . ."

"You'll make sure she gets it? If you have trouble, let me know."

"Thank you, Mistress Mykella." Haelyt swallowed. "He was a good man."

"Thank you." Mykella inclined her head, then turned.

". . . wish she were Finance Minister . . ."

The murmur had come from Wasdahl, Mykella thought. Much as she believed she could do a far better job than Joramyl, *that* would never happen.

She walked down the corridor, then up the main staircase and to the right to the Finance study.

As she closed the outer door behind her, Maxymt looked up from the pile of ledgers stacked beside him. "We have had an unfortunate occurrence, Mistress Mykella . . ."

"Yes?"

"You may know that the Southern Guard accounts and ledgers were kept by Shenyl. He was most accurate and dependable."

Mykella wanted to scream—or slip a dagger between the lizard-like clerk's ribs. Two weeks before, Maxymt hadn't even known who Shenyl was.

"Unhappily, he was assaulted and murdered the other night, and we will need to find another entry clerk."

"I'm very, very sorry to hear that. He was among the best." Mykella paused. "What about his family?"

"He had a wife. Of course, we'll have to pay a widow's stipend."

"That's only right," Mykella said as she moved to her table. "He served loyally for more than ten years."

"In the future, it might be better to require a fifteen-year service . . ."

"That is something that the Lord-Protector must address."

"Of course . . . of course."

"From where do you plan to obtain a replacement?" asked Mykella, trying to keep her voice idle.

"I have not talked to Lord Joramyl about it. He will have to make that decision. He hasn't come in."

"They have clerks in the Southern Guards," observed Mykella. "Some of them might know enough about the accounts."

"That is possible."

From the feelings behind the acting chief clerk's words, Mykella knew he had someone in mind, someone who wasn't in the Southern Guards. That didn't surprise her, but she just nodded as she adjusted the high-backed stool.

Even by late afternoon—after Mykella had made her weekly trip to the Great Piers, earlier in the day than usual, as much to get away from Maxymt as anything—when Mykella and Maxymt were finishing for the day, Joramyl had not appeared, not even during the time she had been gone. Mykella made no observations about his absence. For the moment, she didn't want to deal with her uncle's snide observations and insinuations. She'd have enough of those to face during the reception and formal dinner to come.

She'd barely reached her chamber when Rachylana hurried up, followed by a harried-looking Zestela. Behind Zestela was Wyandra, the assistant dresser.

"What are you wearing?" asked Rachylana.

"The green dress isn't ready, I'm told," Mykella replied. "So it will have to be one of the blue ones, an older one most likely." The Derekan envoy wouldn't have seen it, and whether the others at the dinner had wouldn't matter. "And you?"

"Something red-maroon."

Mykella nodded. The red-maroon didn't really suit her redheaded sister, but that was doubtless exactly what Rachylana had in mind, something not totally tasteless, but just off enough so that she looked less striking and less poised . . . and perhaps not able to handle appearances before the entourage that would surround the Landarch-to-be. That approach also held risks, because, in the end, Rachylana could end up being matched to some secondary cousin in someplace worse than Deforya.

"Mistress Mykella," offered Zestela, "Wyandra can help you . . ."

"Thank you. That would be fine." In more ways than one, reflected Mykella, since it would keep Wyandra away from Rachylana and her touchiness, and Rachylana away from Mykella.

Mykella gestured for the assistant to follow her toward the narrow chamber that held formal gowns. In the end, Mykella ended up wearing a deep blue dress, with an ankle-length skirt that allowed her to wear the special formal boots she'd had made a year earlier. She would have preferred a formal jacket and trousers or even an elegant split riding skirt, but trying to wear those would have risked her father's anger and his insistence on some lower-cut dress that would have been even worse, not that her figure wasn't adequate for such, but she would avoid being paraded as a broodmare or cow as much as she could. Some women, like Rachylana, when she wanted to, could use their sexuality as a weapon. That approach bothered Mykella.

Once she was dressed, she walked to the family parlor to wait until she was summoned. Salyna was already in the parlor, dressed in a pale green dress that made her fair complexion look slightly washed out.

"Quietly tasteful, I see," offered Salyna.

"Tastefully pallid, I notice," returned Mykella with a smile. "Not enough for it to be that obvious to Father or Eranya, I'd wager."

"I'd rather not go to Dereka."

"Who would?" asked Rachylana, entering the parlor and closing the door behind her. She studied Mykella. "You'll do. The envoy will choose you."

"Did that make you feel good?" Mykella asked mildly.

Rachylana stiffened, then laughed. "It's not about feeling good. You could survive Dereka. I couldn't, and Salyna would end up murdering her consort."

Before Mykella could think of an appropriate rejoinder, Uleana opened the parlor door. "The Lord-Protector wishes to know if you ladies are ready."

Salyna and Mykella nodded, and Mykella led the way out into the corridor and to the top of the main staircase.

There Jeraxylt stood waiting, arrayed in the dress uniform of an officer of the Southern Guards. His eyes raked over his older sister. "Rather plain, don't you think?"

"It suits me."

"You've always been understated. That's not a virtue when you're looking to be matched."

"Perhaps not." *That assumes I want to be matched and shipped off to Dereka.*

Rachylana and Salyna halted behind their brother and sister. Then Feranyt and Eranya walked from the Lord-Protector's private apartments and took their places behind the two youngest daughters.

A short trumpet fanfare echoed from the entry foyer below, and Jeraxylt escorted Mykella down the steps, past the Southern Guards stationed at the top and bottom in their dress uniforms of cream and dark blue. Once clear of the stairs and the three trumpeters, Jeraxylt and Mykella turned right until they reached the doors on the west side of the wide corridor.

The two then stepped through the open double doors of the small receiving room off the grand dining hall. The reception before the dinner was small, and less than thirty people had gathered there, but all turned to watch the Lord-Protector's family enter. Jeraxylt escorted his sister toward the right side of the room, but well short of the table behind which servers clad in blue stood, waiting to resume offering various vintages to the Lord-Protector's family and guests.

Among those waiting, Mykella noted Joramyl and Cheleyza, as well as Arms-Commander Nephryt and Seltyr Porofyr. Several others had to be ministers. She thought she recognized both the chief High Factor and the First Seltyr of Tempre before she and Jeraxylt turned to watch their sisters—and then their father—enter the receiving room.

As soon as Feranyt and Eranya reached the center of the room, another short trumpet fanfare echoed from the corridor outside, then died away.

"Welcome to all of you," called out Feranyt. "You can certainly resume what you were doing."

Jeraxylt nodded to Mykella. "I'm going to get something to drink. Father's headed toward you anyway."

"Enjoy yourself," she said, turning as her father approached with a slender, angular, and gray-haired man, with an equally gray square-cut beard, attired in dark green trimmed in silver.

"Mykella," said the Lord-Protector cheerfully, "this is Sheorak of Aelta. Not only is he the Envoy of Landarch Fialdak, but he is also the Landarch's cousin and trusted confidant."

"I'm pleased to meet you, Envoy Sheorak," offered Mykella pleasantly, noting that her father had stepped back and eased away.

"Not so pleased as I am to meet you." Sheorak bowed slightly.

Mykella had to concentrate to understand his words, because his pronunciation and word cadence were so different from what she was used to. "Then we are both pleased." She finished her words with a smile. She knew, once she ran through the pleasantries, that she could never play someone simpering and compliant, and beyond that, there was always the danger that the Landarch was looking for a consort for his heir who was just that.

"Indeed," replied the envoy.

"What is the Landarch-heir's name?" asked Mykella.

"Only his closest acquaintances call him by name . . . but he is Aldakyr, Heir of Light."

"Aldakyr . . ." mused Mykella. "That does sound distinguished. Is that a family name?"

"It is indeed." The Most Honorable Sheorak smiled politely.

Mykella could sense that he resented being questioned, and while she needed to learn more, it would be easier without too much hostility. "Are all Deforyans as distinguished as you?"

Sheorak laughed politely, and the sense of resentment diminished. "I would like to think so, Mistress Mykella. Certainly, Aldakyr is much more distinguished. He is also rather younger than I."

"That is doubtless why you are here, and he is not. You would not have been chosen to come here, I think, were you not distinguished and your judgment not respected."

"How can I dispute that?" Sheorak shrugged broadly.

"You should not." Mykella smiled, trying to project warmth. "What can you tell me about the Heir of Light?"

"There is much to tell, but I will try to be brief. He is accomplished in all the manly arts, and he has completed many studies. This is possible because there is a fine library in the Landarch's Palace, and many of the volumes date from before the Great Cataclysm. He is of moderate height, and possesses great discernment . . ."

Nodding politely, Mykella encouraged the envoy for close to a quarter glass before she smiled once more and said, "You have obviously put much thought into everything that you do, and, with such fore-thought, you must have also consulted with many about Tempre and when best to arrive . . . and doubtless many missives were exchanged, which must have created much work for you."

"Oh, indeed. There was much correspondence."

"Someone must have told you that winter-turn is a time when we are more festive. We are, you know."

"That, I had not heard."

"You will see, then. And I suppose various ministers all offered ad-vice and pleasant comments?"

"Not so many. Your uncle the Finance Minister was most helpful."

"Yes. Uncle Joramyl can be very helpful. He understands a great deal."

"Your father is fortunate to have such an able brother."

"Yes, Uncle Joramyl is most able." *If not in ways for Father's best interests.* "You seem to know him well."

"Not so well, I think, as I would like. He was the one who sug-gested that your father might be amenable to . . . my arrival." Sheo-rak studied Mykella casually.

She could sense more than casual interest—more like intense scrutiny of her possible reaction. "Father has been most clear that it is time that we consider appropriate matches." That was true enough. "And he and Uncle Joramyl are quite close, as brothers should be."

Sheorak nodded.

Mykella could sense that the envoy was pleased about something, but what she could not tell. She could also see her father approaching with Salyna. "It has been most enlightening and enjoyable talking to you, Envoy Sheorak, but I see my father and sister approaching."

"Most enlightening for me as well." Sheorak bowed slightly, and his eyes raked over her appraisingly.

Mykella smiled pleasantly and stepped back. *He's looking for an intelligent broodmare for the heir.*

"Ah . . . I wanted you to meet my youngest daughter, Salyna," said Feranyt.

Mykella slipped over to the sideboard, hoping for a moment alone, where she wasn't sensing the feelings that swirled around the receiving room like smoke from a fire burning too-green wood.

"Mistress?" asked the server. Even his apprehension jabbed at her.

"The amber Vyan Grande, please."

After she received the goblet, Mykella stepped away, only to see Cheleyza angling toward her. She smiled. "Good evening."

"Good evening, Mykella. You talked a great deal and rather animatedly with Sheorak. Don't you think he is distinguished and charming?"

"He is . . . but aren't envoys supposed to be?" asked Mykella lightly, trying to ignore the insistent curiosity bubbling out of Cheleyza.

"Not all of them are. There was one from Southgate who came to Harmony . . ." Cheleyza shook her head. "And the Reillies . . ."

Mykella sipped her wine and listened, trying to ignore the barrage of feelings emanating from her aunt, feelings as scattered as the words they accompanied.

". . . think that some of them had never seen a wash basin or a tub . . . and those awful plaid coats . . . women wear them, too . . . Squawts might be worse, from all that I've heard . . . Joramyl says that the nightsheep herders wear black all the time . . . the way you . . . well, it looks good on you . . . and what's the point of the white shimmersilk the Southgate Seltyrs affect, and it really is an affectation . . ." After a time, Cheleyza stopped and sipped her wine, then asked, "Do you think that Rachylana's wearing red-maroon will matter in the slightest to the envoy? Joramyl says he's one of those men who doesn't see colors."

Mykella couldn't help smiling slightly. "Even men who can discern colors often don't seem to notice."

"You're so right, there. My brother was far more interested in what was in the dress than what color and shade it might have been."

"Isn't that true of all young men? Even Jeraxylt and Berenyt?"

Cheleyza laughed softly. "They're bright enough to say kind words. . . ."

Before all that much longer, the sounds of a set of chimes echoed through the receiving room, and the doors on the north end opened, revealing the grand dining room and the long table, set with crystal and silver, all illuminated by the soft light reflected from wall lamps and the shining brass mirrors behind them.

Mykella slipped toward her place at the long table, marked not by anything obvious, but by the blue crystal goblet with her initial upon it.

Once everyone was seated, the Lord-Protector turned to the envoy, seated to his right. "Would you like to offer a blessing, Envoy Sheorak?"

"I would offer our traditional prayer, Honored Lord-Protector." Sheorak paused, then spoke. "To the Time Eternal, to the One Who Is and to the Unknown, as all three are and have been forever."

Mykella hoped, vainly, she knew, that the dinner would not be so long and tedious as the reception that had preceded it.

27

Although she had been more than careful to limit herself to three glasses of wine over the entire evening, Mykella's head was pounding when she dragged herself out of bed on Novdi morning. But then, it had been pounding before she went to sleep. Why? she asked herself as she sat on the edge of her bed. Had it been the wine? Or the food?

Or the bombardment of feelings swirling around her?

Her Talent encompassed more than one ability—but she felt as though none of those abilities were what would help her most. Even traveling the Tables had led her to dead ends . . . and to Dereka, where she might well end up anyway. More and more, she could sense what people felt, but the only way to use that ability, so far as she could see, was to lie and scheme in order to play on people's feelings. She could move unseen, but that appeared useful for stealth— eavesdropping and theft. All of those abilities could easily push her into being the sort of person she really didn't want to be—more like

Rachylana or Cheleyza. When she'd tried to use them to bring matters to light, she had only caused death to innocents.

Her eyes burned.

Then she swallowed, blotted her eyes. She would find a way out of the situation in which she found herself. She *would*, and feeling sorry for herself wouldn't help anything. With that resolve, she washed up, and dressed in her normal black nightsilk garb. Then she hurried toward the breakfast room.

Not surprisingly, since it was an end-day, she was the first there, although Salyna appeared moments after Mykella seated herself.

"You made quite an impression on the envoy," offered Salyna.

"Oh?" Mykella took a sip of the tea Akilsa had poured into her mug.

"He kept looking at you while he was talking to me." Salyna smiled wryly.

"I asked him too many questions. I don't think young women are allowed to question men in Dereka, especially older and distinguished men."

"That might be . . . but he still kept looking at you."

"Well . . . that's good for you, I suppose."

Salyna glanced to the door, as if in warning, and Mykella turned to see her father walk into the breakfast room. She sensed a certain lack of color in her father, not to her eyes, but to her senses. Should she say anything?

"Good morning, daughters. It was a good dinner, wasn't it? I thought the boar was tasty, and no one seemed uncomfortable." Feranyt settled into his chair at the head of the table.

Akilsa hurried in and filled the Lord-Protector's mug with hot spiced tea. Mykella could see the steam rising—unlike her own tea, which was barely more than lukewarm.

"Good morning, Rachylana," Feranyt added as the redhead slid into her chair.

"Good morning, Father."

"I haven't seen Jeraxylt this morning." Salyna's words were slightly flat.

"Oh . . . Joramyl organized a hunting party for today—out in the wilder part of the Preserve to the east. Jeraxylt has already left with them." Feranyt took a swallow of spiced tea.

"You didn't go?" asked Rachylana.

"I felt a bit tired. Yesterday was a long day."

Had she not sensed the grayness in her father, Mykella would have thought his words a transparent excuse, since they all knew that their father only believed in hunting for game that would be used and disliked large hunts intensely.

"I'm sure a quiet day won't hurt you," Mykella said, "and Jeraxylt will be most happy to tell you everything that happened."

"I'm certain he will." Salyna's words were chill.

Feranyt looked to his youngest daughter. "You can hunt with family, Salyna, but it would not be seemly to do so with a foreign envoy in the party. Nor would it help your chances of obtaining a good match."

"I'm not made of fine porcelain."

"Salyna, dear daughter, I have allowed you the freedom to learn skills most women do not. Please do not make me regret my indulgences with you."

Salyna sighed. "Yes, Father."

"There won't be a dinner tonight, will there?" asked Rachylana.

"Not for you or the women in the palace. There will be a hunters' supper after they return, a rough thing. I will join them, of course."

"Of course . . ." murmured Salyna, but so quietly that no one but Mykella heard her words, or the bitterness in them.

"Tomorrow afternoon, Cheleyza will be holding an afternoon gathering for you and some of the Seltyrs' wives and daughters. Did I mention that?"

"No," replied Rachylana, "but Berenyt did."

"I trust you will all have an enjoyable afternoon." Feranyt smiled and began to eat.

Mykella did as well, although she was not that hungry. The egg toast did seem to help in relieving her headache.

By the time Feranyt had drunk a second mug of spiced tea, the unseen grayness in his face had almost entirely departed, and he clearly felt better. Mykella didn't sigh in relief, but she wanted to.

After breakfast, she walked out of the breakfast room with him.

Feranyt continued without speaking until they were a good ten yards away from the door to the breakfast room. Then he asked, "How did you find Sheorak?"

"He's very shrewd, I would guess. He appraised my conversation, probably my intelligence, and looked me over like a broodmare." Mykella kept her tone light. "I'm certain he's looking for the best match for his cousin."

"You or Salyna could do far worse."

Much as she knew that to be true, Mykella didn't like the idea of marrying someone because the other alternatives were far worse. She wasn't about to say that. "I'm certain it will have to be discussed with the Landarch and his son."

"Yes . . . these things take time, but Sheorak was most impressed with your demeanor. I'm very pleased with the way you handled yourself. Your mother would have been proud of you."

Mykella hoped so, if not in the way her father meant it. "Thank you." She paused, then said, "Father . . . I've been thinking about the Table in the lower level . . ."

"What about it?"

"Do you think that Mykel the Great actually could travel to other places using it?"

"Who knows?" Feranyt's words were close to dismissive.

"Or see things in it?"

"Mykella, there are always stories, and I heard the stories when I was younger than you are now." Feranyt's voice took on a patient, paternal, and tired tone. "Both Joramyl and I prowled around the lower levels of the palace. We poked and prodded the Table. We stood on it and imagined that we could travel to other lands. We even tried to use it as a mirror or a window that showed other places. I asked my father the same questions you have, and he told me that he'd done as I had done, and that whatever the Table might have once been, it was that no longer." He paused. "Anyone who sees anything in polished stone is only seeing what he imagines, and not anything real."

"Then . . . why is it still there?"

Feranyt snorted. "It's a solid stone cube that must extend a good yard or more down. It's like the eternastone of the high roads, and that makes it impossible to chip apart. To remove it would require taking apart the foundations and rebuilding a whole section of the palace, and we've got better things to do with the golds we collect in tariffs."

"Thank you." Mykella had her answers, not just to the questions she'd asked, but to the ones she had not. There was no way that her father would believe anything she told him she'd seen in the Table, and from his reactions, she had strong doubts that even if she called up images that he would believe they were anything but visions she had created—and that assumed he could even see what she saw. "I hope you feel better before long."

"I already do." Feranyt smiled, then reached out and patted her shoulder. "Enjoy a day without worrying about the ledgers."

Mykella watched as he walked toward his private study.

28

Novdi evening found the three sisters eating alone in the family dining room. Mykella looked down at the remnants of the rather dry fowl that the cooks had attempted to disguise with a cream sauce, then took a last bite and set her knife aside. The sauce had helped with the overcooked potatoes, but not the fowl.

"It's probably better than what they're eating," said Salyna.

"They aren't eating much, I'd wager," returned Mykella, thinking of the men gathered in the long chamber at the end of the stables— the informal "hunting lodge." "They're drinking their supper, or a lot of it."

"You two are terrible." Rachylana straightened in her chair. "They've been riding all day, and they're hungry."

"They're also thirsty," rejoined Salyna, "and they'll drink all night and either complain about it all tomorrow or look stoic, as if they've suffered some terrible illness that they're too proud to complain about, when it was just stupidity."

"No, they won't. Berenyt's not like that. Besides, there's another hunt tomorrow," Rachylana declared.

"Another one?" Salyna's words dripped ice. "They'll tear up the Preserve . . ." She shook her head.

"You're just mad because they won't let you hunt with them," added Rachylana.

"No . . . she's mad because she's better than most of them, and they're not about to let her prove it," replied Mykella.

"Better than many of them," corrected Salyna. "Uncle Joramyl's very good. So is Lord Gharyk."

Mykella pushed back her chair. "I can't eat any more." She stood. "I'm going to get something to read. I'll be in the parlor." With that, she turned.

". . . she's not a hunter like you. Why is she so upset?" The words Rachylana murmured to Salyna as Mykella left the dining room stayed with Mykella as she strode to her chamber.

Why *was* she so touchy?

Because Salyna was hurt and upset? Or because it was just another example of what she and her sisters had to look forward to? Although . . . Mykella paused in her thought. Rachylana seemed to anticipate that life, at least if she could have it with Berenyt.

Once she reached her chamber, Mykella had to search her room for the history she had gotten from her father's library, finally locating it on the bottom of the short stack of books on the corner of her writing desk. She was certain it had been on the top, and Uleana would never have changed the order. Maids didn't do that.

At that, she looked over her chamber even more carefully, but she did not see anything else amiss.

Finally, she walked to the parlor. Rachylana had settled into one of the armchairs with something she was embroidering, while Salyna was on the settee with her needlework.

"You really should practice some skill with a needle or yarn," suggested Rachylana. "It does settle touchiness."

Mykella settled into the armchair she preferred for reading, the one with a slight incline to the back. "I've tried, you might recall. I don't have any skill that way. So there's no point in practicing it." She deliberately refrained from commenting on touchiness as she opened the history and turned to the section that dealt with Southgate's secession from Dramur two centuries earlier.

After less than ten pages, she glanced up, but neither sister looked in her direction. The way the history read, the only reason the Seltyrs of Southgate declared their independence from Dramur was because the Seltyrs in Dramur refused to acknowledge any debt to or heritage from the vanished great Alectors. Mykella had the feeling it was far more likely that the Seltyrs in Southgate didn't like the tariff over-rides that had flowed back from Southgate's trade across Corus to Dramuria.

Hadn't Mykel's wife Rachyla originally come from Dramur? Mykella had read that somewhere. Might that have been another reason why he'd been so successful?

As she sat in the family parlor, the history in her lap, Mykella's thoughts continued to spin in all directions. In the end, she couldn't help but think about her Talent, and all the things she couldn't do, as she had on and off all day. Yet the soarer had insisted that she had the ability to save her land. At the thought of saving the world, she laughed silently. She wasn't even having much success in avoiding a match that would send her somewhere she didn't want to go to bear children for a man she'd never met.

Have you met anyone whose children you'd want? She pushed away that thought with another. *How many suitable men have you been allowed to meet?* How could she even tell who was suitable? She shook her head. She could tell, and there weren't that many in Tempre, or not in and around the palace, at least.

She wasn't getting anywhere with reading, and she didn't want to talk.

After several moments more, she decided that it wouldn't hurt to be able to observe the Deforyan envoy and listen when he didn't think she was anywhere around. Mykella glanced toward the parlor door. She supposed she could use her concealment skills and avoid the guards to go to the Table. But for what purpose? Anyone she wanted to observe in the Table would be at the hunting lodge, and the Table didn't reveal what people said, not so far as she'd been able to discover. If she wanted to risk it, she could walk the entire way to the lodge room with a concealment shield and stand in a corner and listen. But . . . if anyone suspected, she'd be trapped, and trying to explain would not be pleasant at all. If she were only like the soarer, able to slip through stone walls. . . .

She sat up straight, wanting to beat her head against the outer stone wall of the parlor. What had she been doing every time she'd used the Table? Why had she assumed that she could only do it near the Table? The soarer hadn't been limited in that way.

Mykella closed the unread history and, holding it in her left hand, stood.

"What is it?" asked Salyna.

Mykella offered a smile. "I've just been thinking. It's too hard to explain. When I get it all sorted out, I'll let you know."

"What are you sorting out?" Rachylana looked almost predatory.

"Life," replied Mykella. "Or as much of it as I can." She slipped the history under her arm and walked to the door.

"Are you all right?" Concern colored both Salyna's words . . . and her being.

"I'm fine." Mykella smiled, then hurried from the family parlor.

When she returned to her chamber, she slid the door bolt locked, then walked to her writing table, where she rearranged the books in a different order and slipped a longer loose hair from her brush between the covers of the history and the one below. If the books were moved, she could ask Uleana if she'd touched them. If the maid hadn't . . .

She smiled wryly. And then what could she do? Make wild accusations that people were spying on her or moving her things?

For a time, Mykella stood in her chamber, just beyond the foot of her bed, trying to recall exactly what the Ancient had done. There had been a greenish glow from the stone . . . and a darkness, and then the soarer had appeared. When she had left, she had seemed to slip into the gray granite.

But . . . how did one start?

With the darkness below? Mykella concentrated on reaching the green darkness that lay below the palace.

Nothing happened. She remained standing in her chamber.

After several moments, she walked over to the window and pressed her hand against the stone next to the casement, reaching with her thoughts, her Talent, toward the greenish blackness beneath the palace. For a time, she could sense, could almost reach, but not quite connect with the green. Then it seemed to extend upward, as if recognizing her, and she could feel it rising to her. In moments, she could feel that she was enshrouded in the green that could not be seen, but only felt. She willed herself into the stone and downward toward the Table. In moments, she was within the Table chamber.

Grinning idiotically, she just stood there, less than a yard from the Table. Her eyes and senses traversed the Table, but there was no sign of the Ifrit's presence in the Table, for which she was grateful.

Could she use the same technique to travel elsewhere around the palace? Or across the courtyard to the stable's hunting lodge? She frowned. She'd have to be careful where she emerged, because she couldn't use the concealment shield until after she was clear of the stone or ground. Still . . . she might as well try.

She let herself merge with the green and black and slide into the gray foundation walls and then northward, trying to gauge her depth belowground—by a vague sense, because she could not see. The main corridor from the auxiliary kitchen seemed to have people standing there. In the end, she had to emerge from the ground in the stables themselves, so close to a pile of hay that, once she stood in the dimness, she had to use her left hand to stifle the sneezes that racked her.

When she finally gained control of the sneezing, she created her concealment shield. She was just grateful that none of the stableboys and ostlers had been near enough to hear or see her, because she hadn't managed to raise the concealment shield while her body was convulsing with sneezes, muffled as she had tried to keep them.

Mykella walked carefully to the end door of the stable, slightly ajar, and stepped into the courtyard, then along the wall and past the kitchen to the archway between the kitchen and the lodge hall. She waited until one of the servers hurried toward the double doors with a large pitcher, then followed unseen in his wake.

Once inside the rough hall with its single long table, Mykella moved slowly and quietly along the inside north wall of the lodge, toward where her father sat with his back to the wall, with two guards behind him. Feranyt sat, not at one end of the long table, but in the middle, with Sheorak to his right and Joramyl to his left. Across from Feranyt sat Jeraxylt, with Seltyr Porofyr to Jeraxylt's right. Berenyt sat two seats to Jeraxylt's left, with a man between them whom Mykella did not recognize, save that he was wearing much the same hunting garb as was Sheorak, suggesting that he was an assistant to the envoy.

She settled on standing against the wall behind Arms-Commander Nephryt, who sat to Sheorak's right, and to the left of Lord Gharyk, the Minister of Justice. As she stood watching, her back firmly against the wall, just a fraction of a yard from one of the guards behind her father, Mykella noticed several things. Nephryt and Berenyt hardly spoke to each other, even though they were seated across from each other, and Berenyt conversed almost entirely with the Deforyan seated between himself and Jeraxylt, while Jeraxylt spent most of his efforts on Sheorak and Porofyr. Also, Lhanyr, the chief High Factor of Tempre, was seated to Berenyt's left and as far from the Lord-Protector as physically possible, while Joramyl sat between Feranyt and Khanasyl, the First Seltyr.

She just tried to take in the various conversations.

". . . quite a large buck . . ."

". . . say that you have antelopes that can outrun the fastest mounts in Deforya . . ."

". . . some of the does are bigger than the smaller bucks . . . have to wonder how they manage . . ."

A raucous laugh followed that comment.

". . . large women have their charms . . ."

". . . small ones, too . . ."

After a quarter of a glass of such comments, Mykella began to wonder if she'd hear anything of import or interest. She had learned something from the positions of those at the table, and that had bothered her, because that positioning had been Joramyl's doing. Still . . . she kept listening.

"...keep poachers at bay...string them up with their own guts..."

"...let commoners hunt everywhere, and you end up with ruffians like the Reillies...Squawts...might be worse..."

"...times have shown that Lanachrona...must always have a strong Lord-Protector..."

Mykella focused on those words from Berenyt, clearly addressed to Envoy Sheorak and his aide.

"...of Midcoast and Northcoast respect only strength..."

"There are many kinds of strength, young Berenyt," Feranyt interjected firmly. "Not all problems need be solved with blades and rifles."

"Of course not, sir, but wouldn't you agree that other measures work better when princes know that the blades and rifles are there to be used?"

Mykella didn't like the way Berenyt had phrased that.

"One can have so many blades and rifles that one can have trouble paying the stipends of those who use them or too few men to grow the food to feed them. Everything in a land must balance."

"Strength must balance strength—that is so," added Sheorak.

At that moment, something heavy and sharp jabbed into Mykella's right leg, throwing her into the wall. A wave of pain shot up her leg, and her eyes blurred as her head slammed into the stone wall. The server who had rammed Mykella with the end of a small cask of something staggered back into Gharyk's chair.

From where he sat across the table, the Deforyan assistant's mouth opened, and he gaped at Mykella, while she struggled with the pain and tried to regain control of her concealment shield. Her eyes still watered, but she managed to raise the shield and take two unsteady steps past the server and Justice Minister Gharyk.

"Sir," stammered the server, trying to hold the heavy cask and stepping back, "I don't know..."

"Someone there," murmured the Deforyan.

"Where?" snapped Nephryt, who was already out of his chair with a deadly grace, a short blade in his right hand, one that had appeared seemingly from nowhere. The blade swung through where Mykella had been an instant before, yet she could sense that Nephryt had no idea that she had been there. He'd just reacted to the eye motions and expressions of the Deforyan.

The Deforyan shook his head. "Nothing. I must have been mistaken." Under his breath, he murmured something. ". . . Ancients . . . here?"

At least, those were the words Mykella thought she heard, but she had kept moving, painful as it was, sliding around two more servitors and out into the archway, and then into the courtyard. She kept walking, or, more accurately, limping, until she reached a shadowed and empty niche near where the secondary kitchen and stable connected.

Then she released the concealment shield and immediately sought the darkness beneath.

She didn't even try to go to the Table chamber but followed the stone and granite walls until she was back in her own chambers, where she gratefully dropped into a sitting position on the edge of the bed. The cold of using the darkness seemed to help, but her thigh still throbbed with pain.

She glanced toward the night table beside her bed, and the pitcher of boiled and cooled water and the accompanying glass, then shook her head. The boiled water was safer than water from the wells, but it was flat. Even to her senses, it somehow felt that way.

She'd learned more than a few things on her little night excursion, most of which were things not to do and circumstances to avoid. As usual, she hadn't discovered anything that she could have explained to her father—or to anyone else—even though she was more worried than ever.

And the outside of her thigh was so sore that she was going to have a massive bruise.

29

Just after noon on Decdi morning, a glass or so after finishing a skimpy brunch with her sisters, Mykella walked to her chamber door, answering the knock she had expected.

Wyandra stood there. "Good day, Mistress."

"Good day, Wyandra. We might as well get on with this."

"Yes, Mistress," replied the assistant dresser.

"See if you can find a plain green dress with a black jacket or vest, and the longer the skirt the better." Mykella knew full well that shorter skirts only made her short legs appear stumpy. Slender-cut trousers or long skirts were better for her, unlike Salyna or Rachylana, who looked good in any length, and for whom color was a greater challenge.

Wyandra inclined her head and hurried off.

As Mykella waited for the dresser to return, she couldn't help but think about all the small matters that she had observed, from the positions where the important advisors to her father had been seated the evening before to the strange grayness she had seen in her father's countenance the morning before. When she added in Kiedryn's death, she had no doubts that Joramyl was behind it all. Yet her father would not believe her, and she had no proof that he would not dismiss instantly.

Before long, Wyandra returned with three dresses and two jackets. "I brought these, Mistress. There are others, but these looked to be the closest to what you requested."

"Thank you."

Mykella already had donned the form-fitting nightsilk undergarments, and she couldn't help but wish she'd worn the undertrousers the night before. The looser-fitting outer trousers didn't help much against wine casks. The outside of her thigh had not only bruised, but was tender to the touch, and the soreness that accompanied every step reminded her of her carelessness the night before.

When Wyandra straightened the second dress, even with the protection of the nightsilk, Mykella twitched.

"You're bruised, Mistress?"

"I ran into the writing desk in the dark last night. I bruise easily." So had her mother, Mykella recalled. Why did she have to be so physically fragile? Salyna could spar with blunt sabers and not show a sign of a bruise—even when she'd been struck hard—and Mykella could bump into a table or get thrown into a wall without that much force and immediately bruise.

"Do you like this one, or do you want to try the third one?" asked the dresser.

"This one is fine." Mykella could tell that the third dress was too full in the mid-section and would just make her look dumpy. "Thank you."

"My pleasure, Mistress." Wyandra inclined her head, then turned and departed.

Mykella could sense that the "pleasure" was perfunctory, but that Wyandra wasn't unhappy or displeased, only relieved that it had taken so little time to find a dress that Mykella would accept.

Shortly before half-past the first glass of the afternoon, Mykella made her way to the parlor, where her sisters were already waiting. Both Salyna and Rachylana were more festively attired than their older sister, with Salyna in a deep purple dress, with a white-trimmed matching jacket and Rachylana in a rich green with a gray jacket.

"That green is becoming," offered Salyna.

"You do wear the darker greens well," said Rachylana.

"You both put me to shame," replied Mykella.

"I just threw this on," Salyna said. "I was going over the menus for the season-turn dinners with Auralya. She's been working to make sure that everything for the celebrations will be perfect. She says that no matter how hard you try, something always goes wrong."

"She just says that." Rachylana's tone was dismissive.

"She doesn't. There was a problem last night with the hunting dinner. Father was furious. One of the servers hit the wall or something with a cask of a good vintage, and stumbled over Lord Gharyk. Arms-Commander Nephryt thought someone was attacking Father, and he almost cut the man down. The Deforyan was muttering something about the Ancients . . . and Lord Gharyk got a gash from the cask across his neck."

"That sounds awful. What happened then?" asked Mykella.

"Oh . . . the server got whipped and dismissed. He shouldn't have been so clumsy," said Salyna. "He should have known that he had to be especially careful when they're drinking like that."

Rachylana nodded.

Mykella managed to maintain an even expression. "That does sound terrible."

"It sounds like he got off too easily," added Rachylana.

"No matter what, things like that happen, Auralya says."

"They shouldn't," replied Rachylana. "Not in a well-run house or palace."

"We should go down to the carriage portico," suggested Mykella, hoping to change the subject.

"We should," agreed Salyna.

Mykella and Salyna led the way out of the family parlor and down the main staircase, then along the front corridor and around to the east side entrance. The Lord-Protector's coach was waiting, as were the six mounted Southern Guards who would escort them.

Mykella entered the coach last and ended up on the forward seat, facing her sisters. She'd rather have seen where they were going than where they'd been, but she also liked having the seat to herself.

The coach pulled away from the portico and out into the white light of the midday sun. Once clear of the gates, the driver turned east onto the avenue.

"It's good weather for a hunt. There's almost no wind, and it's clear," Rachylana observed, peering to her left in the direction of the Preserve.

"I hope they get everything they kill properly dressed out," Salyna said. "Several of the carcasses from yesterday's hunt went to the dogs and some of the retainers for their animals."

"That's what the retainers are for," Rachylana replied. "That's their job."

Salyna glanced out the carriage window.

"I didn't mean to upset you," Rachylana said quietly to Salyna.

"I don't think it was you," lied Mykella. "I imagine that Salyna would rather be hunting than going to an afternoon gathering at Lady Cheleyza's." Mykella knew she would have rather been on the hunt herself, not for the kill, but for the ride.

"Women don't hunt in Deforya or Southgate," Rachylana pointed out. "That's what Berenyt says."

"What else does he say?" Salyna did not quite snap.

"He says that they have the most elegant balls and dinners in Southgate, but that the musicians in Deforya—in Dereka, anyway—are quite good."

"I wonder if things have changed since the time of Mykel the Great," mused Mykella.

"Why?" asked Rachylana.

"What do you mean?" added Salyna.

"There isn't much about it, but the history I've been reading—"

"Histories again?" Rachylana shook her head.

"—said something about how Rachyla came to Tempre in order to escape the confines of Southgate," Mykella concluded firmly.

"That was more than three hundred years ago," Rachylana said. "Times have changed. Berenyt would know. Besides, Southgate's not ruled from Dramuria anymore."

Salyna rolled her eyes, and Mykella managed to keep her expression pleasant.

Before all that long, the coach came to a stop under the main portico of Lord Joramyl's mansion—that still belonged her father, Mykella pointed out to herself. She let her sisters step from the coach first.

"Lady Cheleyza awaits you in the upstairs withdrawing room," announced the graying footman in his blue uniform.

Inside, a young maid, also in blue, bowed. "Ladies, if you would follow me . . ."

The three followed the dark-haired girl up the grand staircase and then to the left of the upper landing and through an open set of double doors.

Close to ten other women, all at least Mykella's age and most a good decade or more older, except for Cheleyza, were seated in chairs or upon settees around the withdrawing room, a chamber with white oak wainscoting, above which were walls covered in pale blue damask. All eyes turned toward the three sisters, and Mykella could feel a seething mixture of emotions that ranged from jealousy and anger to admiration and pity.

Cheleyza immediately stood and stepped forward. "The Lord-Protector's daughters, all charming and beautiful. We're all so glad that you could join us."

"We're glad that you offered the invitation, Aunt Cheleyza," replied Rachylana, smiling warmly.

Salyna smiled and inclined her head.

Buffeted as she felt by the cascade of emotions that filled the withdrawing room, Mykella managed a smile and a slight inclination of her head.

A slightly plump woman in fuchsia and gray, with iron-gray hair, had followed Cheleyza and stepped up beside her.

"Lady Gharyk," offered Rachylana.

"Jylara, please. I'm so glad to see you all."

Mykella had always thought that titles were a public necessity, but, like overcoats in winter, to be discarded inside with warm company. She wasn't so certain that she wanted to part with formality around Cheleyza.

Jylara looked toward Salyna. "You look much like your mother, except you're a bit taller." Then she looked at Mykella, slowly nodding.

Mykella wanted to ask why she nodded, but refrained, hoping the woman would explain.

"You're the one with the skills in numbers and accounts, the one who actually understands what ledgers say. You don't look so much like your parents," Jylara went on, her eyes on Mykella, "but like one of the old paintings of Rachyla, except you're not quite so tall, but your face and hair and eyes are so alike you could have been sisters, were you living in the same time, of course."

Mykella could sense Jylara believed totally what she had said, and that was somehow chilling. "I didn't know that. I don't believe I've seen a painting of Rachyla."

"There's one in Gharyk's study in the palace. I'm certain he wouldn't mind your coming to see it." Jylara turned back to Rachylana. "You're the only redhead in the Lord-Protector's family in a long time, and you carry it well. Once I was a redhead, but, unhappily, it didn't last."

Another woman appeared from Mykella's left. "You're Mykella, the eldest, aren't you? I'm Elyasa, and my older sister knew your mother . . ."

After that, Mykella felt that all she did was smile and nod and murmur pleasantries. She couldn't help but notice that not a single word was about anything except who knew or had known whom, how someone looked or didn't, or who was related to whom.

Close to a glass later, Mykella slipped back toward Cheleyza. "If you will excuse me . . ."

"To the right, across the landing," said Cheleyza with an understanding smile.

Mykella smiled in return, then walked across the landing. The door was ajar, and Mykella stepped inside, into a wash chamber with rose marble walls and an adjoining smaller chamber for other functions. Standing alone there, she took a deep breath, then raised her concealment shield.

She turned and eased the door open slowly, trying to give the impression that it had not been closed and had swung open. Then she walked out, trying to keep her steps quiet on the stone floor and steps as she made her way down the grand staircase to the entry hall. She definitely wanted to investigate the nearly hidden study there.

When she tried the door it was locked. So she crossed into the receiving room where she had waited for Cheleyza the last time she had come and stepped into a corner where the footmen could not see her and dropped the concealment shield. Then she began to search for the darkness beneath.

It wasn't there. Or rather, it was so far away that she could not reach it.

Why had she supposed it was everywhere? She shook her head

and raised the concealment shield, then made her way back up the steps and into the marble-walled ladies' wash chamber, still empty.

She dropped the shield.

After a time, she returned to the withdrawing room.

Cheleyza turned and stepped toward her. "I'm glad you're all right. I thought you might have used the facilities, but, as we're about to have refreshments, I grew worried and checked. You weren't there."

"I was in the courtyard. I needed some air."

"Sometimes the cool does help." Cheleyza's smile did not conceal the disbelief within, but she said nothing more.

"I'm certain the refreshments will as well," returned Mykella with a smile she did not feel.

Mykella had no doubts that Joramyl would hear that Mykella had been roaming through the mansion. That wouldn't help matters, but it was getting so that she wondered if everything she did was wrong. She'd told her father about the stolen golds, and poor innocent Kiedryn had been killed. She'd tried to overhear what the men were discussing, and a poor server had ended up getting whipped and dismissed. She would do something about that, but any help for the man would have to wait.

In the meantime, she would endure the rest of the afternoon.

30

After a small and cold supper, the three sisters had repaired to the family parlor, where Salyna attacked her needlework and Rachylana worked on crocheting something. Mykella had picked up the ancient history and begun to read.

. . . Mykel never set forth any reason for creating the Lord-Protector's Preserve, particularly since he never hunted, for all the time that he devoted to the Preserve. After his death, which fol-

lowed Rachyla's by but a few days, his eldest son, Olent, re-affirmed
the status of the Preserve by proclamation . . .

Mykella looked up. "Did you know that Mykel the Great never
hunted?"

"Not animals, anyway," replied Salyna.

Rachylana lifted her head abruptly, then lowered it quickly, as if
she were dizzy.

"Are you feeling ill?" asked Salyna.

"I'll be all right. I'm just tired. I think I need to go to bed." The
redhead stood and took two unsteady steps before suddenly collapsing into a heap.

Instantly, Mykella set aside the history and rushed to her fallen sister, kneeling on the floor and turning her over. Rachylana's head
lolled back on her older sister's arm. Mykella's mouth opened as
she sensed both a grayness about Rachylana's head and a bluish
greenness centered under her ribs. "Salyna! Go find Treghyt! She's
very ill."

Salyna jumped to her feet, looking at Mykella.

"Go!" snapped Mykella.

Salyna ran from the parlor.

Mykella eased open Rachylana's mouth. Rachylana's tongue looked
normal, and Mykella could feel her sister's breath . . . but the breaths
were short and shallow. Rachylana was also hot, as if she were burning up inside. For a moment, Mykella just looked down at her sister,
helplessly.

What could she do? Could she do something with her Talent?

Gingerly, she reached out to the greenish black below, and then
tried to press a tendril of that against the ugly blue-green—almost
spiderlike in shape—within Rachylana.

Something flared back, and blue-green and blackness swirled
around her.

When she opened her eyes again, she was looking up at the parlor
ceiling.

Mykella eased herself into a sitting position. She and Rachylana
were still alone in the parlor, but Rachylana felt warm, though not so

hot as before, and the bluish green within her had subsided to a faint grayish blue. She moaned, if barely.

The door burst open, and Salyna rushed in, followed by Treghyt, the white-haired healer Mykella had known for years.

"She's better," Mykella said. "For a moment, she was hot enough to burn my hands. It seemed that way."

"Let me see." Treghyt dropped to his knees on the other side of Rachylana from Mykella. He touched her forehead, then ran his fingers along her jaw and then lower along her neck. "Not swollen there . . ." His fingers rested on her wrist. "Pulse . . . not as strong . . . but steady . . ."

Rachylana moaned again. Her eyes fluttered. Then she slumped.

Mykella started. "No!"

"It's not that," said Treghyt quickly. "She's sleeping . . . or something like it. That sometimes happens." He looked to Mykella. "Did she eat something that you two didn't?"

"We all ate brunch here, and had refreshments this afternoon at Aunt Cheleyza's, and dinner here. We served ourselves . . ." Mykella shook her head.

"She didn't eat anything but that," added Salyna.

"It could be that she had some bad food," said the healer. "Sometimes, only parts of things are tainted. Neither of you feels unwell, do you?"

"No," said Salyna immediately.

"No," added Mykella.

"Let me know if you do." The healer's eyes went back to Rachylana. "She'll need to rest, and someone should watch her."

"We'll take her to her chamber," Mykella said.

"No," Salyna said. "My bed is big enough for two. We'll take her there. I can watch her."

"Are you—" began Mykella.

"That would be best," suggested Treghyt.

The two lifted their limp sister and carried her out of the parlor and down the corridor to Salyna's chamber. Once they had laid Rachylana on the bed, Treghyt again examined her.

After a short time, he straightened. "Her pulse is a little stronger, and the fever feels less intense. She shouldn't have anything to eat, and only boiled tea or boiled water until I'm certain that it isn't some sort of flux . . . or something worse."

Mykella knew exactly what he meant by "something worse," but she only nodded. So did Salyna.

Salyna asked, "Isn't there something you can do . . . ?"

Treghyt shook his head. "The way these . . . things work, unless I know the cause, or unless it's clear that the person will die unless something is done, it's better to do nothing. That's because the remedy for one cause will make matters worse if it's actually caused by something else. If she were close to dying . . . then I'd try . . . and I'd hope that it would be right."

"But . . . what . . ." Salyna looked to the sleeping Rachylana.

"She might sleep through the night, or she could wake up at any time. If she gets hotter, come get me immediately. I'll be ready if she takes a turn for the worse, but she seems to be getting better, and usually when something is this severe so quickly, if people start to get better, they keep getting better."

"That's . . . good," said Salyna.

Mykella nodded.

After Treghyt left, Salyna looked to Mykella. "It wasn't food. We all ate the same things."

"But what else could it be?"

"Something she drank," Salyna declared.

"But why? Rachylana's not perfect, but she's no danger to anyone. None of us are."

"There's Berenyt. I'd wager one of the women at Cheleyza's has a daughter they want to marry him. No one but us would suspect, and there were so many people there, how could we even tell who it might be?"

"And it might not have been one of them . . . or there." Mykella walked over to the bed and let her Talent range over Rachylana again. The last trace of blue had vanished, but a faint pall of gray still clouded the redhead's midsection. "I think she is getting better." *I just hope it continues.*

"It makes me feel better to hear you say that," said Salyna.

"When I say that?"

"About that sort of thing, you've always been right." Salyna shook her head. "You didn't say anything, but I could tell. You knew Mother wouldn't recover, and you tried not to let anyone know you knew."

Mykella didn't want to relive that. "Will you be all right? To-night?"

"I'll be fine, and if I'm not, I know where to find you."

After Mykella left Rachylana and Salyna, she slipped into Rachylana's room, where she let her Talent range over everything, but she could sense nothing like the blue-green that had struck her sister.

Although Treghyt had suggested that Rachylana suffered from a bout of bad food, he'd really been worried about poison, and Mykella shared his concerns.

Still . . . why would anyone want to poison Rachylana? Mykella could think of reasons to poison her father, or even Jeraxylt or Joramyl, but Rachylana? For all that Salyna had said, why would any mother risk the displeasure of the Lord-Protector over a marriage that likely wouldn't occur? Their father had as much as indicated that another envoy was being sent to negotiate a match for Rachylana.

Mykella closed Rachylana's door and walked slowly back to her own chamber.

31

On Decdi night, sleep was a long time coming to Mykella, not only because of her worries about Rachylana, but also because the bruise on her thigh seemed to hurt more when she wasn't doing something and because her mind kept spinning through question after question. What exactly had caused Rachylana's collapse? Was it really some sort of bad food, as Treghyt had said? Or something more deliberate, as the healer had hinted? But, if it were, why would anyone wish to poison Rachylana? That made little sense to Mykella.

Then there were other questions. Why exactly had Cheleyza held a gathering of mostly older women and then invited the Lord-Protector's daughters? Why was the greenish darkness only in some places beneath the ground? Was that why the palace had been built where it had been? And the suggestion by Jylara that Mykella visit Lord Gharyk's study to see the painting of Mykel the Great's wife—that had also been strange, because Mykella hadn't sensed anything untoward or malicious behind the words. But then, she hadn't really been looking for that, caught unaware as she had been.

She was the first at breakfast on Londi morning, and she drank half a mug of tea before Salyna and Rachylana appeared. Mykella immediately studied Rachylana, noting a trace of the gray mist around her middle, but it appeared patchy, as if it were dissipating, like fog in the sunlight. Mykella certainly hoped so. "How are you feeling?" Mykella's voice held concern.

Rachylana smiled, if faintly. "Much better, but Treghyt says that I'm to have only tea this morning."

"That's all you will have," added Salyna. "I'm here to see to that."

"And have your own breakfast," added Mykella lightly.

Just after Muergya poured Salyna's tea, Jeraxylt stumbled into the breakfast room, slumping into his chair.

"You had a late night, it appears," offered Salyna to her brother.

Mykella could sense Jeraxylt's headache, even before he replied, "I'm not used to drinking the way some of them do."

"Then, I suggest you don't," said Feranyt dryly as he stepped into the breakfast room. "No one will notice how much you drink so long as you lift your goblet as many times as they do. They only notice if you don't lift it. Laugh, whether you think what they say is humorous or not. Laugh and appear to drink and enjoy it, and no one will notice."

Except those who are watching closely, thought Mykella. She studied her father. Did he have a faint tinge of gray about him? She wasn't certain, but she was certain of something else—that many little unseen threads that spun out from his body into a knot—a node—did carry a gray tinge, although that vanished beyond the node where they fused into the single life-thread that arched away from him. Mykella turned her senses toward her sisters, and the same pattern existed with them as well—but without the gray. Rachylana still had the faintest trace of the gray mist around her mid-section, but none around the node, which Mykella thought was good, although she couldn't have said why.

"It's . . . rather late for that advice, sir." Jeraxylt winced as he lifted his mug of spiced tea.

"I offered it before dinner both on Novdi and Decdi. You either didn't hear or didn't listen. When one doesn't listen, one usually pays double. You are." He turned to Rachylana. "Treghyt said you had a bout with bad food. Are you feeling better?"

"Yes, Father, but I'm to be careful with what I eat."

"You do that." Feranyt paused, then added, "Good morning to you, Salyna and Mykella."

"Good morning," the two replied quietly, if scarcely in unison.

"And we will hope that it will be a good morning." Feranyt smiled, then picked up his mug and took a long swallow. As soon as Muergya served him his omelet, he began to eat heartily.

Mykella found that she was far hungrier than she had realized because she left nothing on her platter. She was eating a second piece of too-brown toast when her father began to speak again.

"Tomorrow night we will have a formal dinner with the envoy from Southgate. Your uncle informs me that he will arrive sometime today, possibly this morning."

"What about Envoy Sheorak?" asked Rachylana quietly.

"Both envoys will remain through the season-turn events and celebrations. That way they can observe both Tempre and you three. One cannot be too careful, and I would like them to know you all better. It certainly was most helpful that your uncle was given time to learn more about your mother when he was envoy in Dramuria."

"What was her sister like?" asked Salyna. "You've never said."

"I've never said because I don't know." Feranyt laughed. "Joramyl only said that your mother was far better suited to me, and time proved that to be so."

Her father's words bothered Mykella—not because they were false, but because they bore the ring of truth. If Joramyl had wanted the best consort for his older bother, why was he now plotting against him? Or was he merely trying to feather his own nest without the Lord-Protector finding out? That didn't seem right, either.

"You're all young and good-looking," Feranyt went on. "You're truly good matches for anyone of power and ability, and you can make good households anywhere, just so long as you realize that your role is to be supporting. If you see something, or if you have advice, always give it to your husband quietly, and when no one else is around. That way, the people always believe in his strength." He shook his head. "Too many women don't understand that when they appear strong and capable, it undermines their husband. That's a pity in many ways, but that is how the world works."

Mykella could see that her father believed that. She could even see how such a practice might work. She didn't have to like it . . . and she didn't. She thought about asking whether the same would apply to a husband if the wife were the ruler, then decided against it. Her father would only say that she was asking a question about something that could never happen.

"Are there times when a wife can speak for her husband?" Salyna asked.

"Very few. If he is away on a military campaign, I suppose, but only if she repeats what he would have said, and only before small groups of his strongest supporters." Feranyt took another long swallow of his tea. When he finished, he pushed back his chair. "That should hold me."

As he stood, Mykella studied him. If there had been any gray around or within her father, it had certainly vanished, and that, she felt, was all for the good.

When she finished her own tea, she hurried off to wash up, then made a quick stop before the mirror in her own chamber. After studying herself in the mirror, she added a green shimmersilk scarf to the nightsilk tunic—since she had decided to visit Lord Gharyk before going to the Finance study.

She walked deliberately down the main staircase and along the front corridor, heading east. Her steps conveyed purpose, but not haste, as she made her way nearly to the east end of the palace, before stepping into the antechamber of Lord Gharyk's study.

The clerk who sat at the table inside the door looked at Mykella for a moment, his face wrinkling as if his thoughts were conflicted between questioning what an unaccompanied young woman was doing coming into the study of the Minister of Justice and trying to recognize who she might be.

"Mykella," she said, adding the words she hated to use, "the Lord-Protector's daughter. I'm here to see Lord Gharyk."

The clerk bolted to his feet, his eyes taking in and abruptly recognizing the nightsilk garments that only the wealthiest in Tempre could afford. "Oh . . . yes, Mistress Mykella . . . he's here. Let me announce you."

Before Mykella could have said a word, the clerk turned, took three steps to the door behind and to his right, opened it, and stepped inside, leaving it barely ajar. "Sir . . . it's the Lord-Protector's daughter, the dark-haired one, to see you."

"Show her in, Nealtyr. Show her in." Even through the crack between the door and its frame, Gharyk's hearty voice filled the outer chamber.

Nealtyr scurried back out, holding the door open and bowing, then gesturing for Mykella to enter the study.

She would have closed the door behind her, but Nealtyr did so before she could.

Lord Gharyk had risen from his desk and stepped out before it, but Mykella's eyes skipped past him to the full-sized portrait that hung on the wall behind the Justice Minister's desk. The woman portrayed at the bottom of the grand staircase of the palace had shimmering black hair, shoulder-length, with piercing green eyes that dominated her face. She wore a high-necked dress of a green so dark it was close to black, with a brighter green scarf and matching belt. Her forehead was neither too high nor too low, although her eyebrows were strong and dark. She also had high cheekbones, and a strong nose, but not one that could be called overlarge. The hand that rested on the balustrade showed long fingers—the only trait besides height, Mykella realized, that she did not share with the image of Rachyla.

Gharyk—a slender, short, and balding man barely half a head

taller than Mykella—offered a faint smile and inclined his head slightly, but did not speak.

"I do hope that I'm not intruding, Lord Gharyk, but yesterday your wife mentioned that you had a painting of Rachyla here in your study and that she thought there was a certain family resemblance. She suggested that I should visit you at my earliest convenience."

Gharyk stepped back and gestured to the painting that hung on the paneled wall behind his desk. "I knew you resembled the portrait, but not how much. As you see, you could be sisters, so close are your likenesses."

"I did not know," Mykella admitted. "I've never seen the portrait."

"I imagine not." Gharyk smiled warmly.

Unlike so many of those with whom Mykella had conversed lately, Gharyk's expression and inner feelings seemed to match, although there was a concern behind that warmth, Mykella sensed. "I would have thought it might have hung in the receiving hall or . . . somewhere else."

"Somewhere of greater prominence?" Gharyk nodded, then asked, "Do you know why this painting remains with the Minister of Justice? Or has for the last hundred years or so?"

"I cannot say that I do."

"Mykel the Great is reputed to have said that justice must always be tempered with practicality and that he had learned that in the hardest way possible from Rachyla. According to the stories, her portrait was placed where she could look down at the Minister of Justice and remind him of that." Gharyk laughed softly.

"Does she?" asked Mykella lightly.

"She reminds me. I can't speak for most of those who preceded me, but my immediate predecessor thought so as well."

Mykella looked up at the portrait again. The image conveyed strength and purpose, so much so that the woman's beauty faded behind the intensity of that strength. And yet Mykel the Great had won her? A mere Cadmian majer? Or had she inspired him to become Lord-Protector of Tempre so that he could win her?

"She had to have been most impressive," Gharyk said.

"I can see that." Mykella waited to see what else the Minister of Justice had to say.

"Did you know that Mykel never called himself the Lord-Protector? He only claimed the title of 'Protector of Tempre.' His great-grandson was the first Lord-Protector. That might have been because Mykel understood from the beginning that justice depends not only on strength of arms and a consensus among the powerful, but also upon standards that apply to rich and poor, high and low alike. That understanding is rare, and a ruler who applies that principle is even rarer. In our day, all across Corus, all too often blood is stronger than the water of justice, and all suffer when that becomes the law and supercedes equal standards applied equally to all. Did you know that Mykel threw out his own brother because Viencet didn't understand that the law of fairness applied to everyone, even the brother of the Protector of Tempre?"

"No, I didn't."

"He knew that entrusting his brother with any kind of power would only lead to great trouble. Few men or women, fair and just as they may be in other areas, can look beyond blood to do what is best. Some are so besotted with power that they destroy those close to them for fear of rivalry. Others fail to see the lust for power in those close to them, and still others see and ignore it. Rachyla shared that understanding with Mykel and was the one to insist that her cousin, a High Seltyr who had been her guardian, be forced to return to Southgate." Gharyk smiled warmly again. "You came to see a portrait, and you get a lecture in history. I do apologize. At times, I forget myself."

Mykella understood that he had forgotten nothing. "Your stories are fascinating. I'd never heard any of that, and none of it is in any of the histories I've read."

He shook his head. "I still cannot believe how closely you resemble Rachyla, even in deeds. You are overseeing the accounting of the master ledgers, I hear."

"Reviewing them and reporting to my father. That is more accurate, I fear. He will do whatever he thinks best with what I report."

"I'm sure that he will. He is a good man, and kind."

Mykella could almost sense the unspoken words—*too kind, especially to his brother.*

"And you are most kind, Mistress Mykella, to indulge my wife's whim and come and visit me and the portrait."

"You're the one who is kind," she returned. "I would never have learned what I have this morning from anyone else, and I do thank you."

"I only wish to serve Tempre and those who would safeguard and protect it, and you are certainly one who would understand that." The Minister of Justice inclined his head once more. "I should not keep you further." He stepped toward the study door.

"I'm the one keeping you," she replied warmly. "Please convey my thanks to your wife. I do appreciate her suggestion." Mykella turned and moved to the door, opening it easily.

Nealtyr was seated at his table-desk. He also bowed his head as Mykella departed.

As she stepped out of the antechamber into the main lower corridor, Mykella understood two things. First, others saw what she saw, and at least some of them wanted her to know. Second, unfortunately, they also had neither proof nor the ability to bring matters before her father . . . or they feared the consequences of doing so.

Much as she dreaded going up to the Finance study, Mykella turned toward the main staircase to the upper level of the palace. The accounts would be in perfect shape, of course, but they would remain that way only so long as she was able to keep reviewing them.

Mykella made her way up to the upper level of the palace and then to the Finance study. When she closed the door behind her, Maxymt looked up. "Good morning, Mistress Mykella."

"Good morning, Maxymt." Mykella glanced to the long table where Maxymt was reviewing another set of ledgers. "Those look to be the accounts of the Minister of Highways and Rivers."

"Indeed they are, and very well kept."

"Lord Porofyr's clerks have always been most assiduous." She paused. "How is the search coming for a replacement for Shenyl?"

"Lord Joramyl has been involved in other matters, as you may know, but he assures me that he will look into that in the weeks ahead."

In short, Joramyl hadn't done anything and didn't plan to anytime soon. "If he has said so, then I'm most certain it will happen."

Mykella slipped the master ledger off the end of the long table. "While you're checking those, I'll be going over this."

The acting chief clerk looked up and offered an oily smile. "Before long there will be no need for you to review these, and that is well, I would think."

"Oh?"

"I am close to mastering all of the accounts, and Lord Joramyl and I will no longer need your assistance. In turn, that will leave you free to pursue what is proper for a Lord-Protector's daughter."

"And what might that be?" Mykella kept her tone light.

"A most proper marriage. It is said that you may be matched to one of the highest in all of Corus."

"I don't believe that's been decided yet." For all the humor and lightness in her voice, Mykella felt heavy-hearted within herself. Maxymt's words confirmed that she had made a favorable impression on the Landarch's envoy . . . or the least unfavorable impression of her father's three daughters. Or . . . Joramyl had prevailed on the envoy in order to assure that Mykella would be removed from overseeing the Lord-Protector's accounts.

At the moment, Mykella told herself, there was little she could do. At the moment.

32

After a long day, during which she had found no obvious additional diversions of golds or questionable bookkeeping entries, Mykella sat through a quiet dinner with her father, Eranya, Jeraxylt, and her sisters, during which no further mention, thankfully, was made of envoys or matching. Rachylana looked tired by day's end, but the grayness had vanished from her, or from Mykella's ability to sense it. Mykella excused herself from joining Salyna and Rachylana in the family parlor by saying she was tired. Then she retreated to her chamber.

Once there, she did not slide the door bolt closed, because, if her sisters knocked and no one answered, they might well force the door, and that would lead to questions she could not answer. If they opened the door and did not see her, Mykella could always claim she had slipped away to be by herself. While they might wonder about it, she had done just that long before she had discovered her Talent.

She drew the window hangings, then stepped up to the window and its stone casement, where she concentrated on the stone and the greenish blackness beneath. This time she was able to reach the blackness almost instantly. She slipped into the stone and then let herself slide downward. When she emerged from the stones of the palace foundation, Mykella inadvertently looked down, and found her feet a good third of a yard above the stone floor. Was that how Mykel had "walked on air"? Had he only been able to do so in places where there was the darkness beneath? How could she discover where those places were?

Abruptly, she realized she had no shields—and raised them even before she checked the Table for the presence of the Ifrit. But there was no sign of his purple-pink presence in or through the Table. She took a deep breath, then let herself settle and her boots touch the stone beside the Table.

Immediately, she concentrated on the Table, seeking out Joramyl. When the mists cleared, she found her uncle sitting with her father in separate armchairs in front of the hearth in the Lord-Protector's personal and private study in the palace. Both men held goblets half full of what looked to be a red wine. Joramyl said something, then laughed.

Feranyt smiled and nodded.

Joramyl began to speak again, and even through the Table's mirror, his falsity leapt out at Mykella. Yet what could she do? Anything that she might say would be immediately rejected by her father.

After a time watching a conversation she could not decipher, she decided to see what Berenyt might be doing. The mists cleared to reveal her cousin seated at the table in the small study in Joramyl's mansion. Across from him were Arms-Commander Nephryt and Commander Demyl. Although the two were in fact Berenyt's superiors—at least in terms of the Southern Guards—seeing the three of them together left her feeling even more uneasy.

Her last attempt was to see what Lord Gharyk was doing.

She was relieved to find him and his wife in a small sitting room, also before a hearth, although the coals were red and low, as if the two had been talking for a time. Both Gharyk and Jylara looked concerned. At one point, Jylara said something emphatically, to which Gharyk nodded, then replied. He finished his statement with a shrug that suggested he was helpless in whatever circumstance she had brought up. His wife nodded, then offered a few words and a sad smile.

Mykella wished, not for the first time, that she could hear as well as see through the Table.

She stood there, letting the image fade from the Table and thinking about what Mykel the Great had been reputed to do, such as walking on air and water, and appearing from nowhere. Could she do the same, or at least what she'd seen the Ancient do? Could she follow the blackness through the depths for a distance around Tempre? How far?

Once more she slipped into the greenish darkness, trying to sense her way, trying to go westward. She thought she could sense the avenue to her left, and she eased herself through the dark depths that way until she felt that she was directly beneath the eternastone pavement that led to the Great Piers. Then, before long, not only did the chill creep through her nightsilks, but she could feel, before her and above her, a grayish purpleness, a long block of something that reminded her of the Table, if not exactly. She decided to let herself rise out of the depths, and in only moments she was hovering above the avenue just short of the Great Piers, surrounded by a cold and icy mist.

She immediately raised her concealment shield and tried to move herself above and across the piers toward the River Vedra, although she sensed that the ice-mist followed her. Soon she was moving over the stone, which lay less than a full yard beneath her boots.

Did she want to try "walking on water," really try? Mykella smiled and eased herself westward along one of the short river piers. Once she was clear of the stone, she felt herself sinking toward the water, slowly, but inexorably. She dropped the concealment shield, and her descent halted, a mere yard or so above the water. Something about the water weakened her hold on the blackness. She directed herself back over the eternastone of the Great Piers. Once she was over stone and not water, she raised the concealment shield. She had the feeling that the deeper the water, the more it would have weakened her Talent, at least for holding her above the water. So much for walking on water.

Another thought occurred to her. She really needed to find out just how wide the swath of greenish blackness was. It certainly hadn't extended as far to the southeast as Joramyl's mansion. She didn't want to try to use it in places where it wasn't, and it would be helpful to discover from what distance she could link and draw upon its power.

She let herself drop to the ground. Still concealed, she held her link to the blackness but began to walk southward along the avenue. She kept walking, ignoring the residual soreness in her upper leg. She had walked almost a vingt when she became aware that the blackness was no longer beneath her, but behind her. She attempted to strengthen that link and lift herself above the avenue. For a moment, she succeeded. Then she could feel herself—or the link—weakening, and she released the concealment shield so that she didn't fall heavily to the pavement.

Even so, her boots hit with a thud, and she winced at the pain in her injured leg. She stood there for a moment before she heard voices.

"Do you see that?"

". . . woman out of nowhere . . ."

". . . green moon is out . . ."

". . . wouldn't have believed . . . Asterta . . ."

Mykella raised her concealment shield. Only then did she see the two Southern Guards riding southward in her direction. She stepped to the side of the avenue and began to walk quickly back northward.

". . . gone . . ."

"She was there . . . saw her and so did you . . ."

". . . curse of Asterta . . ."

She couldn't help but wonder why the lesser green moon was associated with the Ancients and the unexplained, but it always had been. That she knew.

Once she was certain that she stood clearly above the greenish blackness, she extended a link, then dropped into the darkness and reached for the Table . . . and the palace. She did not enter the Table chamber, chilled and tired as she was, but emerged from the stone in her own chamber.

Mykella found herself tottering beside her bed, surrounded by an icy mist, her legs shaking and her eyes blurring. Her entire body was racked with shivers. She dropped into a sitting position on the edge of the bed and pulled the comforter around her.

For a long time she just sat there, huddled in the comforter. Slowly, she warmed, and the shivers lessened until they were no more. After a while, how long she could not tell, she glanced toward the bedside table. Uleana or Wyandra had put a fresh pitcher of water and a glass on the bedside table. She frowned. A tiny touch of something greenish blue was on the curved handle of the pitcher. She squinted, and the color vanished, then reappeared, clearly a dab of something she could only sense with her Talent, rather than actually see.

She eased herself to her feet and walked around the bed, the sound of her boots muffled by the old blue rug at the foot of her bed. She suspected it had once graced the family parlor, what with the crest in the center, but it was still thick in most places. When she reached the bedside table, she looked down at the pitcher, then bent over. Even with her eyes almost touching the handle, all she could see was the faintest smudge.

After a moment, she straightened, then concentrated on the water in the pitcher. She sensed nothing. Still . . . she decided against drinking it.

A long and involuntary yawn convinced her that she needed sleep, but she did force herself to walk back to the door and slide the bolt into place before she began to disrobe.

33

During the day on Duadi, Mykella went through her usual routine, except that she was careful to be polite at breakfast and quiet in reviewing finance ledgers for most of the remainder of the day, after which she returned to her chambers to dress for the formal dinner with the envoy from Southgate. She did not even ask whether the new green dress was ready, but instead chose to wear the same deep blue dress she had worn to the dinner with Envoy Sheorak. She did add a cream-colored shimmersilk shawl.

Then she made her way to the family parlor, where Salyna was already waiting, attired in a pale pink gown with a gauzy white scarf. Mykella studied her blond sister before smiling. "It might work."

"What else can I do? I'd rather go anywhere besides Southgate, even to those semi-barbarians of Northcoast."

"Our dearest aunt Cheleyza is from there."

"Ah, yes . . . dear Cheleyza." Salyna glanced toward the parlor door—still closed. "She won't let Berenyt marry Rachylana, not while there's the slightest chance she might bear an heir. You know that."

"What we know doesn't appear to matter much," Mykella pointed out.

At that moment, the parlor door opened, and Rachylana entered, wearing a high-necked dress of a deep rose that not only disguised her figure to a degree but, combined with a darker face powder, managed to create the illusion that her skin and complexion were darker than they were. "What doesn't matter?"

"What we think," replied Salyna. "We're just women."

"It's not that bad," said Rachylana.

"You don't think so? If it had been Jeraxylt who had suffered from bad food, both Father and Treghyt would have stood by his bed all night." Salyna's voice was flat.

"We can't change that." Rachylana raised her eyebrows and looked directly at Mykella. "The same dress as last week?"

"I wouldn't want to give one envoy an advantage over another," Mykella replied dryly.

"The shawl changes it enough that the men who were at the last dinner won't notice," Salyna added, turning to Rachylana, "unless you happen to mention it. Of course, that might enhance your chances of going to Southgate."

"They also like redheads there," Mykella commented blandly.

"I wouldn't think of saying a word." Rachylana drew herself up, if ever so slightly.

"That would be good." Salyna's words were syrupy.

A long moment of silence ensued. Then Wyandra eased the parlor door open. "The Lord-Protector awaits you, Mistresses."

Mykella immediately stepped out into the corridor and strode to the top of the main staircase, coming to a halt beside Jeraxylt in his dress uniform.

"If you had a saber, you could run it through someone."

Mykella offered a charming smile. "You do look superb this evening, dear brother. It's too bad that you aren't the one being inspected for a match." Her tone was as sickeningly sweet as she could make it, except that she couldn't put nearly as much false syrup into her words as could either of her sisters.

"That much confectionery in speech always disguises poison," he replied. "Good poisoners are those who don't change the taste or the flavor."

"I'll never be a good poisoner. Not in speech or anything." *Nor do I wish to be.* She paused. *Why did he mention poison?* Yet his feelings held nothing but affection and humor. *You're too touchy,* she told herself. But how could she not be?

". . . could have fooled me . . ." murmured Rachylana under her breath as she and Salyna halted behind their older siblings.

The four waited for a time until Feranyt and Eranya strolled down the upper level corridor to stand behind them. The trumpet fanfare provided the signal for the entry procession, and Mykella matched her steps to those of Jeraxylt, down the stairs past the Southern Guards and the trumpeters, along the lower corridor and through the open double doors of the small receiving room.

From what Mykella could see, for the most part, those waiting were the same thirty or so functionaries that had been at the last reception, except for the two men in the white shimmersilks of Southgate. Joramyl and Cheleyza stood well back, as did Arms-Commander Nephryt and Seltyr Porofyr. Berenyt was also present, but close to the serving table, as if he were waiting to obtain a goblet of wine as soon as possible.

Once Feranyt and Eranya completed their entry, another trumpet fanfare echoed from the corridor outside, then died away.

"Welcome," called out Feranyt. "Please return to what you were doing."

Jeraxylt inclined his head to Mykella. "Try to be polite to the envoy."

"I'll be most polite," she said quietly.

Jeraxylt slipped away, toward the servers and his cousin.

Mykella turned toward her father and the heavy-set and round-faced older man in white, noting that his golden belt seemed tarnished in places.

"Envoy Malaryk, this is my eldest daughter, Mykella," said the Lord-Protector heartily.

Mykella could sense that her father was far less enthused with the envoy from Southgate, at least compared to Sheorak, but she inclined her head. "I'm pleased to meet you, Envoy Malaryk." Mykella kept her words coolly formal, but polite. If she had to make any choice, it would be Dereka over Southgate.

As had occurred at the last reception, her father eased away to leave her momentarily alone with Malaryk.

"Ah . . . you are the one who knows the coins and the accounts, a most useful trait for the consort and chatelaine of a High Seltyr . . ." Malaryk's words were gentle, but his black eyes were hard as he studied Mykella.

"I had heard, Most Honorable Envoy, that the High Seltyrs have little need to count their coins. All the riches of Corus are said to flow through Southgate."

"Not all, Mistress, not all."

The lilting accent of Malaryk's words was both true and false to Mykella, and she disliked the hint of sibilance they held. "But many, do they not?"

"Ah, yes, but we are traders, and we always have been. Even the best of your traders can trace their heritage back to Southgate."

"And Dramuria," Mykella added with a smile.

"Ah, yes. That is indeed so."

Mykella could sense a certain displeasure behind the honeyed words. "Please tell me about the Seltyr for whom I am being considered as a match, if you would?"

"Gheortyn is a Seltyr, not a High Seltyr, and he will not be one for many years, as his father is close in age to your sire, but he is handsome, most intelligent, and a horseman without peer."

That's what any envoy would say. "A few particulars about him would be nice, if you might indulge me."

"But, of course." Malaryk smiled insincerely. "His hair is shining black, as black as that of the Alectors from whom sprang the forebears of Southgate, and his eyes are equally so. He is long of limb, yet sinewy, and strong, and a quarter head taller than your brother, I would judge. His eyesight is that of a hawk, and he can ride any mount."

Mykella concealed a wince at the overtones and feelings behind the envoy's last phrase. "You said that he was most intelligent. In what fashion?"

"He knows all the verses of Elharyd, and most of those of Sheidahk. He has also studied the works of the great military strategist Gebyet."

A poetry-spouting stud whose father is looking for an intelligent woman so that his grandchildren won't be complete idiots. And who hopes to rule until those grandchildren are old enough to succeed him. Wonderful. "He sounds most handsome and athletic."

"That he is, Mistress. That he is." Malaryk looked slightly past Mykella.

She smiled and stepped away, letting her father escort an appropriately pallid Salyna to meet Malaryk. She had taken but three steps before Lady Jylara appeared, inclining her head respectfully.

"Mistress Mykella . . ."

"Mykella, please, Jylara." Mykella had no trouble being pleasant, especially as she sensed the friendliness and concern behind the words of the older woman. She also had no doubt that Jylara had more to convey.

"Gharyk said that you visited him and that you had a chance to see the portrait of Rachyla that hangs in his Justice study. He was quite amazed at the resemblance when you stood before it. Quite amazed indeed."

"I was surprised myself," Mykella replied. "I'd never seen that painting before. In fact, no one had ever mentioned it to me. It is quite striking."

Jylara laughed. "Some men just don't think of those things, especially when they think about rulers and ruling. To them, it's just a painting of a beautiful consort or a wife on a wall, and she was beautiful indeed. But from what Gharyk told me, Rachyla was such a force that Mykel the Great always listened to her. Her father didn't, alas, and that might be why he was killed . . ."

Mykella managed to keep smiling, even as she understood the meaning behind the words, even as she kept listening.

"He was a High Seltyr of Dramur, you know, and once he was killed, the lands went to one of her cousins, and she was sent to live with another. It would have been better for Dramur had the lands gone to her, but the way things turned out, it was better for her and for us that they didn't."

"That's true. It's a pity that more men aren't as perceptive as Mykel." Mykella paused, then added, "But Lord Gharyk seems most perceptive, I must say. I imagine you two have many interesting conversations."

"That we do, indeed. Of course, he tells me that I see things that aren't even there, and he nods when I insist that they are, as if he must humor me. He does, but I do appreciate that." Jylara smiled broadly and warmly. "I won't take any more of your time, but it was a pleasure to see you again."

No sooner had Jylara slipped away than Rachylana appeared, slipping close to her older sister and commenting in a low voice, "She's rather loud, isn't she? Everyone in yards could hear what she had to say. A history lesson to you, no less."

"She's very cheerful, and, at a time like this, that's helpful."

"I see that the envoy is still talking to Salyna. He seems taken with her."

"Your turn will come," Mykella pointed out.

"I simply cannot wait."

Mykella smiled and eased away. She really wanted a goblet of wine, but she kept smiling, exchanging pleasantries as she crossed the few yards between her and the nearest sideboard and server.

"The Vyan Grande, please."

The server poured a goblet, and Mykella let her senses range over the wine and the goblet, but she sensed no sign of the bluish green she had felt on her pitcher or within Rachylana, and nothing seemed amiss.

Then, with the goblet of Vyan Grande in hand, she took tiny sips and continued to make light conversation until the chimes sounded. Once everyone was seated at the long dining table, Feranyt nodded to the envoy seated to his right.

"In the name of the One Who Shall Never Perish, we offer praise and thanks for the poetry of life, for the beauty of sunrises and sunsets, for lands filled with handsome men and fair maids, for the bounty of love and the children that bounty brings, and for all the blessings that cannot be named but should never be forgotten, in the name of the Eternal and Imperishable."

Mykella was less than impressed with the idea of children as the bounty of love, at least after having listened to Envoy Malaryk wax on about Seltyr Gheortyn. Still, throughout the dinner, Mykella smiled, offered more than a few pleasantries, and listened, using her Talent to concentrate on what the envoy said. One exchange particularly intrigued and concerned her.

". . . We of Southgate have always had a great interest in the strength and good will of Lanachrona. We welcome strong leadership in Tempre. Once more the nomads of Illegea and Ongelya are rallying their clans. Unless they are crushed, trade all across Corus will suffer . . ."

And Southgate wants the Southern Guards to take the casualties so that Southgate's traders can continue to prosper at our expense. Mykella stifled a snort of disgust, keeping a pleasant smile upon her face.

". . . and there have been secret meetings between the advisors of the princes of Midcoast and Northcoast. Should they unite in an effort to increase their territory and power, that would not be in the best interests of either Southgate or Lanachrona." Malaryk offered a smile meant to be supportive and friendly.

Mykella noted that the smile was directed at Joramyl, who nodded politely, the expression masking intense interest. Yet her father seemed not to notice. At least Mykella could sense nothing other than polite boredom, and the words of Lady Jylara echoed in her thoughts, only reinforcing her own feelings.

34

On Quattri, Feranyt was smiling broadly as he took his place at the breakfast table. "Matters are looking promising indeed."

Mykella could sense his satisfaction, but what bothered her far more than that was that the node in his life-thread held a shade of bluish gray. "Promising, Father?"

"Joramyl tells me that the envoys from Dereka and Southgate both seem pleased and that they plan to return to their lands with recommendations for the Landarch-heir and the heir of the High Seltyr of Southgate, and their choices do not conflict."

Across the table from Mykella, Jeraxylt nodded knowingly.

But which of us gets bartered to whom . . . and for what? Mykella feared she knew all too well who was likely destined to go where. Strangely, she worried more for Salyna than for herself. Was that because she could escape? Yet, what sort of life would that be, fleeing from everything she knew? And for what? Still. . . .

"Are you going to tell us?" she finally asked.

"You probably already know, daughters, but until an actual offer of a match is made, no one will say anything. Nor will I."

Salyna and Mykella exchanged glances. Salyna was pale. Rachylana was trying to conceal a smile of satisfaction.

"Next week we are expecting an envoy from the Prince of Midcoast," Feranyt added.

Rachylana's half-smile vanished.

"Is there anything else we should know?" Salyna's voice trembled slightly.

Mykella sensed that the emotion behind the unsteadiness was neither sorrow nor despair, but fury barely held in check.

"Not for now." Feranyt continued to smile.

Jeraxylt spoke quickly. "I did hear something interesting yesterday."

"Oh?" asked Rachylana.

"Some of the Southern Guards on patrol saw a ghost of Rachyla the other night."

"A ghost? That's absurd," snapped Salyna. "She's been dead for centuries."

"They say they saw her. They swore it. Two of them." Jeraxylt nodded seriously. "Good solid men, too. They said that she was floating in the air, or walking on it."

"Maybe it was a soarer," suggested Mykella.

"That's ridiculous. Soarers are just as dead . . . and they have been for longer," added Rachylana.

"The pier watch saw her, too," added Jeraxylt, "but the woman he saw floated over the water, and she was partly shrouded in mist."

"That had to be fog," Mykella said. "There are always patches of mist or fog over the river in winter."

"A ghost is more interesting, though." Jeraxylt laughed, then paused and looked at Mykella. "Duadi night, at the reception, someone was talking to you about Rachyla, weren't they?"

"Oh, that was Lady Gharyk," Mykella replied. "She was telling me that there was a portrait of Rachyla in Lord Gharyk's study on the lower level of the palace."

"I'd forgotten about that," mused the Lord-Protector. "It's been there for years. There's some story about it . . ." He paused, then shook his head. "I don't remember, but it's another one of those legends that don't make much sense. I recall looking for something in the archives to verify it, but there wasn't anything to it at all. No proof at all, and what's the point of talking on and on about something that you can't prove?"

Lord Gharyk thought there was. But Mykella did not speak that thought, though she trusted Lord Gharyk's words about the portrait far more than her father's, and that was somehow sad.

"Do you have any other news . . . that is more . . . substantial?" asked Feranyt, looking at his son.

"Majer Choalt will be leaving on Octdi to take command of all of the Southern Guards' operations out of Soupat," Jeraxylt replied.

"You said he was a good man, didn't you?" asked Mykella.

"Very good," replied Jeraxylt, "and he was effective in dealing with the nomads. He learned a lot from Undercommander Areyst." Jeraxylt paused. "There's some talk about Areyst being dispatched to the east once the terms of the border-guarding agreement with Deforya are worked out—"

"This isn't the place for discussing that," Feranyt said.

"I didn't know that brigands were a problem in Soupat," offered Salyna, clearly obeying the letter of their father's prohibition, but not the spirit.

Jeraxylt looked to Feranyt, who nodded, before replying. "Commander Demyl says that the winter has been cold and that with the coming of spring they'll be especially dangerous this year."

"They'll be planting crops, like everyone else," replied Salyna. "Brigands never attack places like Soupat in the spring. It's not on the main trade routes, and those are the only places where there's much in the way of booty early in the year."

Soupat was on the way to nowhere, Mykella reflected, except for the copper mines immediately to the south of the town. She didn't like the idea that both Choalt and Areyst were being posted away from Tempre—not at this time and not when both were characterized as "good men."

"If Undercommander Areyst is likely to be posted to the east,"

Mykella said, "perhaps that posting should be delayed until matters of matching are determined. Then he could accompany . . . whoever . . . It would be good to have someone of experience . . ." She smiled as winningly as she could, hating herself for stooping to that.

Feranyt frowned for a moment, then nodded. "That might be for the best. It might indeed. I'll so inform Arms-Commander Nephryt."

Mykella could sense the puzzlement from all of her siblings, especially from Salyna, and she wasn't surprised when her younger sister cornered her in the corridor after breakfast.

"Why did you do that?" Salyna's voice was low, if intense. "You don't even know the undercommander. You're not serious about going to Dereka, are you?"

"I didn't say I was." Mykella smiled. "It hasn't even been formally proposed, for either of us, but Undercommander Areyst is supposedly a good and solid officer, and if a match is made and accepted . . . I'd certainly feel better, the way things are happening, with someone like that commanding the escort party."

"They could still . . ." Salyna broke off her words. "Yes . . . I can see where that might be for the best."

"It's all I can think of right now."

Salyna nodded.

After that, Mykella quickly washed up, then checked how she looked in her chamber mirror. Just as she stepped out and closed her door behind her, heading for the Finance study, Rachylana appeared.

"A mere undercommander, Mykella? What's come over you?"

"I don't even know the man," Mykella pointed out. "I just want protection." And that was true, so far as it went.

Rachylana smiled widely. "How do you know you're going to Dereka?"

"I have black hair. Salyna's blond. You darkened your face when you met the Southgate envoy."

"That's hardly—"

"Would you like to wager against it?" Mykella forced a smile.

Rachylana could only keep looking at Mykella for a moment before she glanced away. "You think you're so smart."

"I know I'm not. I just do what I can." *If I were really smart, I'd have figured out what to do about things, and I still haven't.*

Rachylana's voice dropped into almost a whisper. "Be careful, Mykella. Please."

The concern in her words—and behind them—touched Mykella, and she swallowed, but only said, "Thank you."

"Nothing's quite right, but there's so little we can do," added Rachylana. "You and Salyna always think you can do something, but you can't, and . . . I don't want you hurt or angry."

Salyna's furious, and I'm not that much less angry. "I understand, but we're all different."

This time, Rachylana was the one to nod, before offering a sad smile, and then turning away.

As she watched Rachylana walk away, Mykella couldn't help but wonder what her sister knew or suspected. She also knew Rachylana had said all that she would. After a moment, Mykella began to stride down the corridor toward the Finance study.

When she entered, she merely nodded to the acting chief clerk.

"Good day, Mistress Mykella," offered Maxymt.

"It is, if you like cold rain and fog," Mykella replied dryly. "I'd rather have snow."

"They'll both pass before long, and travel to other places will be far more pleasant." The clerk proffered his oily smile.

"Only if one stays on the high roads or waits until the mud is gone, and that will be a while." Mykella walked to the shelf that held the Southern Guard accounts and slipped the ledgers out, then carried them to her table. "Has Lord Joramyl made a decision on Shenyl's replacement?"

"Not yet, but it will not be too long, I understand."

"That puts extra work on the others, especially Haelyt."

"They do not appear to be overstrained . . . as of yet."

Mykella merely nodded. She'd said enough, and talking to Maxymt was like trying to carry water in a sieve. She ended up frustrated and never accomplishing anything.

Less than a glass past midday, scarcely half a glass after he'd arrived and closeted himself in his study, Joramyl opened the inner door and beckoned. "Maxymt, we need to talk over some things."

"Yes, Lord Joramyl." The acting chief Finance clerk immediately rose and walked quickly from his table, closing the inner study door behind him.

Although the heavy-set clerk was not that large or ponderous, his walk was a scurrying, swaying waddle, reminding her of a lizard in a hurry.

Mykella glanced to the closed outer door, then raised a concealment shield and tiptoed up to the inner door, where she focused her Talent beyond the door into the study, trying to make out the conversation. Even so, she could only hear parts of the low-voiced interchange.

". . . keeping the ledgers as you ordered, sir . . ."

". . . any hope of squeezing out some golds?"

". . . she knows where every gold goes . . . no way to divert anything . . ."

". . . no matter . . . for now . . . pay for it myself . . . won't be long before she's matched and gone . . . won't matter then . . . better head back to your ledgers . . ."

After she slipped back to her own smaller table and the Southern Guard accounts she had been reviewing, Mykella dropped the concealment shield. Sitting there looking down at the entries, she couldn't help wondering about Joramyl's last words, because she had sensed a falseness about them. Yet he'd made no secret about wanting her matched and away from Tempre.

35

Quinti passed. So did Sexdi, Septi, and Octdi—and her weekly trip to the Great Piers—and then came Novdi afternoon, when Mykella stood in the reviewing stand for the traditional parade to mark the end of winter and the turn of spring, although, formally, that did not occur until Decdi evening. For the past four days, Mykella had watched and listened, and worked with her Talents, and used the Table to observe others. Yet she had learned absolutely nothing she had not suspected or known already, and she had no more proof about anything, or not the kind of proof her father would have accepted. Joramyl and Arms-Commander Nephryt continued to meet, as did Joramyl and the Lord-Protector. The Finance ledgers remained scrupulously kept, and Rachylana talked far too much in far too great detail about what she would wear to the ball on Novdi night.

Only one thing, so far as Mykella could tell, had changed. She continued to observe herself and others with her life-senses, if that happened to be what they were, and from what she could tell, only her life-thread held that strange combination of black and green. Everyone else's seemed to be some shade of brown, although a few held traces of yellow. She had the feeling that with each day that passed the green in her thread was becoming more brilliant, and the black was shrinking away bit by bit. But was she just imagining that? Was she imagining everything?

As she stood in the reviewing stand, the wind gusting around her, grateful for the nightsilk jacket she wore, Mykella forced her concentration back to the avenue below the stand and waited for the companies of the Southern Guards stationed in Tempre to ride past. The small reviewing stand was set at the base of the Great Piers, equidistant from the green towers at each end. The mounted guard companies rode northward toward the Piers along the great eternastone highway that split farther to the south, heading west to Hafin and southwest to Southgate, due south to Hyalt and east to Krost and the wine country of Syan. Once the guards reached the reviewing stand, they would turn onto the Palace Road and head due east past the palace itself, and then back to their compound.

When she'd been little, Mykella had once asked her mother why the reviewing stand wasn't before the palace, but Aelya had just smiled and said, "It's tradition. Tradition is very important. Some day you'll understand how important."

Tradition might well be important, but the day was raw and damp under heavy gray clouds, and a chill wind blew out of the northeast with such vigor that Mykella wouldn't have been surprised to see snow by the next morning, whether spring was supposedly on the way or not.

Mykella stood to her father's left. Had Jeraxylt not been riding with the Southern Guards, he would have stood to his father's right. Instead, Lord Joramyl did. To Mykella's left was Cheleyza, while Salyna and Rachylana stood below them. Mykella still found it hard to believe that she was only five years younger than Cheleyza.

Four Southern Guards bearing trumpets rode toward the stand, raising their instruments to their lips. A crisp but lengthy fanfare echoed into the chill air. A good fifty yards back rode the standard bearers of Third Company, followed by the company officer and his squad leaders, and then the company rankers.

"I don't ever get tired of watching the guards," offered Cheleyza. "They ride so proudly and so well."

And they're all so handsome. That thought was as clear to Mykella as though Cheleyza had shouted it. There was something else about Cheleyza . . . a faint thread in addition to her own life-thread, so faint that Mykella had almost missed it. But no one else had two. Mykella almost nodded. Her aunt was pregnant. Why hadn't she noticed earlier? Or did a life-thread develop as the child grew within its mother?

"They do ride well, all of them," replied Mykella, after grasping to come up with a response.

Just before Third Company passed the Lord-Protector, the standard bearer lowered the company ensign in a salute, holding it at a forty-five-degree angle all the way past the stand before snapping it back erect.

"Joramyl rides so very well," Cheleyza said, with obvious pride. "Far better than the guards."

"I'm certain he does," Mykella agreed, quickly adding, "Here comes Second Company, and you can see Berenyt there, at the front."

"He rides well, too, like his father." Cheleyza paused.

Mykella caught an impression of something about Berenyt . . . less than favorable, but so fleeting that she could not determine what it might be. "He doubtless takes after his father in many ways." *As in plotting and treachery.*

"What are you wearing to the ball tonight?" asked Cheleyza.

"Something green . . . I think. And you?"

"Blue and silver, with a special shimmersilk scarf from Dramur. Joramyl wants me to look my best."

"I'm certain he does." Mykella kept the sarcasm she felt out of her voice. Even so, she could sense Salyna's amusement from below her.

Rachylana seemed oblivious to the conversation, her eyes following Berenyt as Second Company neared and then passed the reviewing stand. Berenyt, like all the guards, did not turn his head toward the stand.

"Joramyl is very particular about the way I look."

"Many husbands are, I've heard."

"You'll find out, dear, and before all that long, from what I hear."

"It may be a time. Neither Southgate nor Dereka is that close, and the envoys will not leave until tomorrow or Londi at the earliest," Mykella pointed out.

"That time will pass quickly, and you had best make plans for what you wish to take with you."

"Did you find that difficult?" asked Mykella politely.

"Not at all, but then, Joramyl did arrange for an extra baggage wagon."

"That was thoughtful of him."

"He is most thoughtful and very wise in how he thinks ahead."

After Second Company came First Company, and Mykella was happy to change the subject by noting, "Oh, there's Jeraxylt, leading his squad." She could also see a well-endowed redheaded girl at the end of the reviewing stand, taking a special interest in her brother. Her brother did not look to the reviewing stand, nor did he smile as he and his squad rode past.

Following First Company were the senior officers of the Southern Guards, followed in turn by the headquarters group. First came Undercommander Areyst, and Mykella sensed both respect and sadness as he bowed his head to the Lord-Protector.

Sadness? Does he suspect or know something? Mykella wanted to ask him, but she couldn't very well corner him and blurt out a question.

Behind Areyst was Commander Demyl, but while the commander looked toward the reviewing stand and bowed his head to the Lord-Protector, Mykella could sense Demyl's contempt. Arms-Commander Nephryt merely radiated arrogance, despite his formal nod to Feranyt.

Mykella glanced sideways toward her father and uncle. Her father had nodded in satisfaction once the guards had passed. So had Joramyl, but her uncle's smile concealed another sort of satisfaction. Exactly what that meant, Mykella could not tell, except that it made her even more uneasy.

What could she do? She *knew* what others were thinking and feeling, and yet she had no proof of anything beyond what she had shown her father, and now, even that proof had been reduced to uselessness by Kiedryn's supposed suicide and her father's unthinking trust in his brother. And before long, unless she could do something, she wouldn't even be able to watch the treasury and his land's finances.

In the meantime, once they returned to the palace, she'd have to ready herself for the evening ahead . . . and attending a ball where, once more, she'd be scrutinized like breeding stock by one or both of the envoys and where every word would be weighed and analyzed.

She kept smiling as she prepared to leave the reviewing stand with the others.

36

"It's . . . different, Mistress," allowed Wyandra, after fastening the last button of Mykella's new ball gown and stepping back.

Mykella surveyed herself in the mirror on her chamber wall. The brilliant green gown was both conservative and daring, as she had specified, with a high neck and sleeves that tapered to almost skin-tight at her wrists. Above the waist, the green shimmersilk was close to form-fitting as well. The skirt was but a quarter full, just enough to allow easy movement, and did not quite touch the floor, but was a shade longer than ankle-length, allowing her to wear the formal boots she preferred. Because her shoulders were covered, she did not need a shawl, and that also gave her greater freedom.

"I like it." Mykella picked up the green gloves from the dressing table. They did not match perfectly, but would have to do. White gloves would have made her look like a doll, and black were reserved for older and married women—or women who intended not to marry at all.

Wyandra remained silent as Mykella left her chambers and walked to the family parlor. Before she even closed the door, Rachylana was examining her gown.

"That's not really a ball gown," observed Rachylana. "The skirt's not full enough, and the top . . ."

"It looks good on you," Salyna said. "I couldn't wear anything like that." Her square-necked gown was a muted but rich blue that brought out the color in her face, and was not cut low enough to reveal too much of her pale skin.

"You could wear anything so long as it isn't white or pale." Mykella closed the door and laughed, then looked at Rachylana, who wore a scoop-necked gown of a paler but bright blue that highlighted her mahogany hair, with a shawl of the same material. "That shade is most becoming on you. You'll show us both up."

Rachylana smiled. "I hope so."

"Berenyt should definitely notice."

"That is the idea, I presume," added Salyna.

It won't help, though, if she shows up Cheleyza, thought Mykella. *Not at all.*

The door opened, and Jeraxylt stepped into the parlor. He wore the full dress dark blue and cream uniform of a Southern Guard officer. "It's time for us to go down and receive our guests, few of them as there are that we're truly pleased to see." He bowed, then extended a hand to Mykella. "Eldest sister?"

"My pleasure, younger brother."

Jeraxylt and Mykella led the way down the main staircase and along the back corridors of the palace—those cordoned off by the guards—to the north entry to the ballroom. Slightly behind Rachylana and Salyna followed the Lord-Protector and Eranya.

The ballroom itself was just north of the southeast corner of the main level of the palace and had been created centuries before by merging a series of chambers, so that it was long and comparatively narrow, with windows only on the eastern and southern walls. A parquet floor, now ancient, if polished and shining, had been laid over the stone floor tiles, and the wall hangings were of dark blue and cream—the Lord-Protector's colors.

The Lord-Protector's family formed the receiving line, with the youngest, Salyna, at the front, and the oldest—and the males—at the back. That put Mykella right in the middle, after her sisters, but before Jeraxylt and her father.

Invitations to the ball were limited to those of import in Tempre, such as her father's ministers and the High Factors and Seltyrs. Among the first that Mykella actually knew by sight were Lord Gharyk and Jylara.

"Mistress Mykella," offered Gharyk, his tone and entire body suggesting that the receiving line was to be absolutely formal.

"Lord Gharyk, Lady Jylara, how nice to see you."

Gharyk offered a pleasant smile, as did Jylara.

Perhaps fifteen people later a Southern Guard officer stepped past Rachylana and bowed his head politely to Mykella. It took her a moment to recognize Undercommander Areyst, mainly because she had not expected him.

"Mistress Mykella."

"Undercommander, welcome to the palace and the ball."

"Thank you." For just a moment, his eyes lingered on her, but on her face, actually looking at her, sizing up far more than her figure.

She looked back at him directly, but she neither saw nor sensed anything that contradicted her earlier impression of his basic honesty. She almost froze as she took in his life-thread, because it held the tiniest fragment of green. She'd noted that before, but now she *knew* that his life-thread had the only green she had sensed in anyone except the soarer and herself. She wanted to ask where he had been born, but he had already stepped past her to pay his respects to Jeraxylt.

Envoy Sheorak was not far behind, and he made no pretenses at dissembling as he ran his eyes over her. "Mistress Mykella, you look most beautiful tonight." *Best of the three . . . pretty enough . . . bright.* So clear were his thoughts and feelings that he might as well have spoken them.

"Thank you, Envoy Sheorak."

Envoy Malaryk was polite, but his attentions were definitely on Salyna.

Somewhat later among those entering were High Factor Hasenyt and his wife, and even later Seltyr Almardyn and his wife. Seltyr Porofyr said only Mykella's name, almost dismissively, as if to question why she was unmatched and even at the ball.

Finally, the ordeal was over, and Mykella and Salyna followed their father and Joramyl toward the orchestra, where Eranya and Cheleyza stood waiting as music began to fill the ballroom. The four began to converse—although the women seemed to be saying the most, while Feranyt nodded, and Joramyl smiled and smiled.

Neither Arms-Commander Nephryt nor Commander Demyl had gone through the receiving line, Mykella noted, as she caught sight of them across the ballroom. She and Salyna stopped near the wall beside the low dais on which the orchestra players were seated, a permanent platform set against the midpoint of the long inner wall of the ballroom.

Rachylana was already off dancing, and Mykella wished that she were, not that she cared that much for dancing, but the smiling hypocrisy of Joramyl's apparent concern for his brother, the Lord-Protector, was making Mykella more than a little uncomfortable.

At that moment, a man perhaps ten years older than Mykella approached her. He wore what looked to be a Deforyan uniform, and he bowed deeply. "Mistress Mykella, Majer Smoltak at your service. Might I have this dance?"

"Of course, Majer." Mykella wasn't about to antagonize the Deforyan.

Smoltak took her right hand in his left and barely touched her back with his right, deftly guiding her into the flow of those dancing. "You may have guessed that I'm Envoy Sheorak's principal aide."

"I thought that was likely. I must confess that I don't recognize the uniform, except that it's Deforyan." Mykella noted his heavy accent, but it didn't bother her as Sheorak's had when she had first spoken to the envoy. Familiarity? Or her Talent? Both, perhaps?

"The Landarch's Lancers. I've actually been assigned to the Heir of Light for the past year as an aide-de-camp of sorts."

"What is Lord Aldakyr like?" Mykella asked.

Smoltak laughed softly. "The envoy doubtless told you that he is handsome beyond words, talented beyond description, and educated above all others. There is a grain of truth in each of those. He is pleasant-looking, certainly not unpleasant to behold, and he has a warm smile that goes with an equally warm disposition. He is a good but not outstanding rider and marksman and knows how to defend himself with a saber—but he would fall to your youngest sister."

"How do you know that?"

"I watched her spar against some of the guards. She did not see me. Many of your guards are quite skilled with blades. We tend to emphasize marksmanship more."

"What else about Aldakyr?" pressed Mykella.

"He is moderately intelligent, but very well read, and has enough sense to understand what he does not know."

"That is a most valuable quality," suggested Mykella. "Since you are so observant about the Heir of Light and my sister, what did you observe unseen of me?"

"Alas, very little." He laughed again. "That is one reason why I asked you to dance."

"What are you learning?"

"You are more athletic than you appear, and that Aldakyr would be well-advised to press for your hand and to listen to whatever advice you have to offer."

While Mykella bristled inside at the implication that she would just accept the offer of a match, she was also impressed by the majer's acuity.

Smoltak lowered his voice. "I also see that matters in Tempre are not entirely as they might seem and that you and your sisters might be better served elsewhere."

"You see a great deal, it appears," Mykella said lightly. Was what she had learned through the ledgers and her Talent so obvious, even to someone without Talent? "Don't you fear that I might pass on what you said? Or that I might think that you're attempting to deceive me so that I might agree more readily to a match with the Heir of Light?"

Smoltak's laugh was low and wry. "You have the eyes of the Ancients. In Deforya, we have lived where they once lived, and women with your eyes cannot be deceived. I know that you know every word I have spoken is as true as I know it to be. You would know before I spoke if I intended to deceive."

With his words, Mykella almost lost her footing, and tightened her grip on his left hand for a moment.

"I have surprised you with truth." The majer smiled. "That is the only way to surprise one like you."

"You have," she admitted. "And you're not afraid I'll reveal you?"

He shook his head. "Who can you tell? Those you trust will not believe you, and those who would believe you are the ones you cannot trust."

Mykella forced a soft laugh. "You are a great credit to Deforya and to the Heir of Light."

"When one has no rivers or oceans and little enough to trade, one must nurture observation and wisdom."

As the music of the dance died away, Smoltak escorted her back to a point close to where they had begun. "My thanks for the pleasure of your company, Mistress Mykella."

"And mine for your insights."

Smoltak inclined his head politely, then took two steps backward before turning.

"That was a long dance," observed Salyna. "Who is he?"

"An assistant to Envoy Sheorak. They will ask for my hand," Mykella said quietly. "He as much as said so."

Salyna's eyes brightened. "Oh . . ."

"That doesn't mean it will happen," Mykella said in an even lower voice.

"What . . . can . . . you do?"

Mykella honestly didn't know, only that, persuasive and honest as Majer Smoltak had been, going to Dereka didn't feel right. Yet Salyna's question gnawed at her. Exactly what could she do?

As the orchestra began to play another melody, Undercommander Areyst eased across the space before the platform toward Mykella. He bowed politely. "Might I have this dance, Mistress Mykella?"

"You might." Mykella inclined her head and smiled.

Areyst took her right hand in his left, and positioned his right hand at waist level on her back, guiding her gently into the flow of dancers. His touch was even more deft than that of the Deforyan majer.

"After our last meeting, Mistress Mykella, I've discovered that you're quite good with numbers and ledgers. That is an unusual pre-occupation for the daughter of the Lord-Protector."

"Not so unusual as one might think," replied Mykella. "A Lord-Protector's daughter should know her heritage, yet she cannot mingle so freely as a son. From where golds are collected, and in what amounts, and where they are spent and at what frequency can tell a great deal . . . if one knows where and how to look."

"Pray tell, what do they say to you?"

"The Southern Guards are currently under strength. The Guard lacks as many experienced officers as it once had. Supplies such as tack for mounts are more costly than in the past, possibly because of the depredations of the Ongelyan nomads several years back—"

"That was several years ago, though." Areyst guided her past another couple.

"Tack requires leather. Calves take several years to become steers," Mykella pointed out.

"Tell me more."

"Ammunition supplies are down, most probably because gunpowder costs are up, and that is because brimstone has become more costly. I wouldn't be surprised if you or the Commander had considered ordering great care in rifle practice."

"Considered? That is an odd way of putting it."

"If you had actually done so, Jeraxylt would have let it slip. Since you have not, and since you are a prudent officer, I would wager that you have considered it, but possibly did not because that might have made the Seltyrs of Southgate and the plains nomads more bold. It might also have encouraged the Landarch to request a concession or two."

Areyst laughed. "Would that some of my officers understood so well."

Mykella forbore to comment on that, instead asking, "What can you tell me about a saddlemaker or leatherworker named Berjor?"

"Nothing, I fear. Hemylcor and his sons currently supply the Southern Guards." He paused. "There might be a few small items bought by the outposts on the borders, but that name is unfamiliar. Why do you ask?"

"I had run across the name, and it was associated with tack."

Areyst nodded politely, but Mykella could sense he would remember the name.

"What else might you tell me from your ledgers?" asked the undercommander. "About something other than the Guard?"

She could tell he was interested, and not merely patronizing her. "The vineyards in Vyan had a bumper crop last year, and that reduced tariffs . . ."

"Reduced?"

"There were so many grapes that the prices went down, and tariffs are leveled on prices. Not so much as if the crop had failed, but the slight increase in tariffs on raisins showed that the cause was a surplus of grapes."

Areyst looked directly at her. "You could unsettle any man, Mistress Mykella."

"I don't usually speak so, especially to men, Undercommander, but you did ask, and you were interested, and since you were most kind to my brother, I thought you deserved an explanation of sorts."

"Your golds will tell what *has* occurred. Can they tell what *will* happen?"

"Can you?" she countered. "What do you think of what lies ahead for Tempre and Lanachrona?"

Areyst forced a soft laugh, and Mykella could sense his unease.

"You are uneasy with my question," she prompted.

"I said that you could unsettle any man, Mistress Mykella." He paused. "I am concerned, although I cannot say why. I fear that we face harder times than most would wish." He shrugged.

"And what do you think of my father?" she asked.

"That is most . . ." He shook his head. "He is a kind and just man who has always done what he believed to be right. I would hope that his rule will be long."

Because she had expected his answer, Mykella managed not to be startled by what she sensed—that Areyst truly hoped for Feranyt's long rule, yet feared that it would not be.

"As do I," she replied lightly. "As it should be."

"You never answered my question, Mistress, about whether golds will tell the future," he prompted gently, swinging her around another couple.

"No more than good judgment and observation," she replied. "Some things are obvious. If tariff collections are lower than in the past, that will mean that expenses must be reduced, or tariffs must be raised. If times are hard, raising tariffs will create unrest and discontent. Yet, if one reduces expenditures, say, for the Southern Guards, that can create another kind of discontent." She smiled. "Would you not agree?"

"That is true if the Guard is required to do as much as before, or more," Areyst acknowledged.

"But when times are hard, there are always more challenges to the Lord-Protector and the Guard."

At the end of that dance, when Areyst escorted her back to her sisters, Mykella could tell that her comments had not so much upset Areyst as put him in a far more thoughtful mood than when he had asked her to dance. Strangely, she found that thoughtfulness far more attractive and appealing than a smile or pleasant and meaningless banter would have been.

"You left the undercommander with a most serious expression on his face," observed Salyna. "That's not what you wish to do with a man who has no wife. You want to put him at ease."

"He asked some most serious questions," replied Mykella, "and I made the mistake of replying seriously." She doubted that it had been a mistake, but it was wisest to say so. Her eyes went to the dancers and to where Rachylana danced with Berenyt.

They both looked to be enjoying the dance.

"Mistress Salyna, might I have a dance?"

Mykella turned to see Envoy Malaryk bowing to her younger sister. She had no doubts that the remainder of the evening would be long for both her and Salyna, but especially for Salyna, for whom the attentions of Malaryk confirmed the possibility of a match that would take her to Southgate, a match Salyna feared more than any other.

37

In thinking over the ball as she lay awake on Novdi night, several things struck Mykella as odd. For all his candor, the Deforyan majer had only asked for a single dance, yet it had been clear that he would press Aldakyr to ask for her as a match. She had not seen Undercommander Areyst except for the single dance he had requested. On the other hand, as she had expected, Arms-Commander Nephryt had carefully avoided Joramyl, and Salyna had been asked to dance several times by Malaryk. Those dances—and the probable match they represented—had left her younger sister close to tears, as much fueled by anger as despair, by the end of the ball. And, of course, Rachylana had danced often and happily with Berenyt, who had been most attentive.

When Mykella woke on Decdi, it was early and gray, and she knew she wouldn't be able to sleep any longer, although brunch would not be served until a glass before midday. So she dressed in her nightsilks and riding gear and went to the serving pantry off the breakfast room. There was little enough there except bread and cheese, and some cold sausage. There was some ale in a covered pitcher, and while she didn't care much for it, it was better than water. The crumbs on the cutting board suggested someone else had been there as well, and her suspicions were confirmed when she carried her cold meal into the breakfast room.

Salyna was sitting at the table eating bread and slices of sausage. She'd never liked cheese all that much.

"Good morning," offered Mykella.

Salyna did not reply, and Mykella did not press her sister, but seated herself and began to eat. The ale was flat, but wet enough to get down the bread, cheese, and sausage.

Salyna continued to eat. She also did not look in Mykella's direction.

Finally, Mykella said, "If I had a choice, it wouldn't be to go to either Dereka or Southgate."

After a pause, her younger sister said, "What would your choice be, then?"

"I don't know," Mykella admitted. "Those don't feel right."

"Nothing feels right," Salyna said.

"You're worried that you'll have to go to Southgate, aren't you?" Mykella was stating the obvious, she knew, and she wished that she could promise Salyna that such would not happen, but how could she?

"Wouldn't you worry? You know how they treat their women. Dramur is even worse." Salyna shuddered. "Why do you think Mother consented to marry Father so easily?"

"It wasn't just that—"

"It was in the beginning. She told me so."

Why had her mother told Salyna that and not her? "She never said anything to me."

"She didn't have to. You were different. That's what she said."

"Different?"

"She said she couldn't explain, just that you were."

Mykella didn't understand that, but what could she say? She took another swallow of ale before she spoke again. "What are you going to do today?"

"Try to avoid everyone." Salyna's words were tart.

"Let's take a ride. If we leave now, no one can say anything."

"That's true." The hint of a smile appeared on Salyna's lips, although it vanished immediately.

After finishing the last crumbs of her breakfast, Mykella stood. "I'll see you in the stable. I'll tell the guard detail." She strode from the breakfast room, retrieved her riding jacket and gloves from her chamber, and hurried down to the courtyard, stopping at the duty box of the Southern Guards.

"Salyna and I will be taking a ride through the Preserve as soon as we finish saddling up our mounts."

The duty guard's eyes widened. Then he swallowed.

"I thought you'd like to know," Mykella added, before turning and heading from the duty box to the northwest door to the courtyard less than five yards away.

"Ah . . . yes . . . Mistress . . ." The Southern Guard's words drifted after Mykella.

Mykella crossed the courtyard to the stables, where she began to saddle her gray gelding, not hurrying, but not dawdling. A few moments later, Salyna entered the stable and began to saddle the big bay she always rode.

When they finished and led their mounts into the courtyard, eleven Southern Guards rode across the stone payment to join them—half a squad and a squad leader.

Mykella mounted, then eased the gray toward the squad leader, reining up short of him. "Usually we only need four or six Guards to accompany us," Mykella observed. "Why do we need half a squad today?"

"Undercommander Areyst's orders, Mistress," replied Sancaryt, the graying squad leader. "He didn't say why."

What did Areyst know that Mykella should . . . and clearly didn't? Was it just that she and Salyna were even more valuable now that the envoys were interested in them as matches? Or did the undercommander's worries about her father extend to her and her sisters?

Mykella nodded politely. "We'll be riding for a while." She turned the gray toward the northeast courtyard gate—the one that opened onto the trail through the Lord-Protector's Preserve. Immediately five of the Guards urged their mounts into a fast trot and rode past Mykella and Salyna before the sisters reached the gate. One opened the iron gate, and the others continued into the Preserve, but at a walk.

Sancaryt and the remaining Southern Guards formed a rear guard.

Once she had ridden through the gate and into the Preserve, Mykella extended her Talent toward and below the ground, checking to see if she could make and maintain a link with the greenish blackness that lay below the palace and the courtyard. Touching the greenish black was certainly no more difficult than from the Table chamber and easier than from her own room, and she let the link subside to a thin line. That was how she sensed it, at least.

The wind was light, broken by the trees, leafless though they were, but chill. Mykella had no doubt that it was far colder on any exposed hill crest, since the tops of the taller oaks and firs were swaying in the wind. "It's brisk out here."

"I'd still rather be here," replied Salyna.

Mykella noted that her sister not only wore her saber, but that she'd added a rifle in a Southern Guard holder. "Where did you get the rifle?"

"From Majer Choalt, before he left. He said he'd let me have a spare if I could score better at the range than half of the squad there. He didn't think I could."

"How did you do?"

"I only shot better than twelve of them. That was enough to get the rifle. He didn't want to keep his word, but the undercommander said he had to."

"You never told me."

"You didn't ask." Salyna turned in the saddle and grinned at her older sister.

Mykella grinned back.

After they had ridden almost a vingt, to where the trail split in three directions, Mykella took the left fork, the one that led almost due north. Before long, patches of fog and mist began to appear in spots along the trail, drifting south from the River Vedra, up over the ridge that ran north from behind the palace and then eastward through the middle of the Preserve. The fog drifted unevenly through the trees, filling the lower sections of the trail, but seldom coming to more than shoulder height on their mounts. Even the heaviest fog was light enough that Mykella could discern outlines with her eyes, but her Talent sense was more reliable.

For another vingt or so, they rode without saying much. All the time, Mykella couldn't help but wonder about the undercommander's decision to make sure Salyna got the rifle. Finally, she turned in the saddle. "Give us some space, if you would." She tried to project pure authority along with her words.

"Yes, Mistress." Squad leader Sancaryt reined back his mount.

One of the guards flanking Sancaryt swallowed.

Mykella eased her mount closer to Salyna, but she couldn't help but Talent-hear some of the exchange behind them.

". . . scary . . . way she did that . . ."

". . . like a senior captain . . ."

". . . rather have the captain . . ."

Salyna looked from her mount to Mykella. "What was that all about?"

"I wanted to know if Undercommander Areyst said anything special to you about why he wanted you to have the rifle."

The blonde brushed back a strand of hair, looking at the trail ahead, before replying. "He just said that it was best for me to be able to defend myself, and that even the most devoted of the Southern Guards couldn't always prevent everything." She paused. "Oh . . . he did say that I might point that out to you."

"To me?"

"He actually said, 'to your sister,' but I don't think he meant Rachylana."

"Probably not," Mykella agreed.

"Why did you want to know? You're worried about something, and you have been for weeks. What is it?"

"I told you about the golds. I don't know anything more, but things still don't feel right. Yet . . . there's nothing solid that I can tell Father . . . or anyone."

"What about the ghost . . . or the soarer? When Jeraxylt told us about that, you weren't all that surprised. You tried to act that way, but I know you."

Mykella managed a shrug. "I saw a soarer. I've seen her twice. No one would believe me. That's why I never said anything. I feel she's trying to warn me, but . . . you know how Father is. If there's no proof . . . imagine what he'd say if I told him what I just told you."

"He'd probably have Treghyt examine you for brain fever." Salyna's voice was dry. "You really saw a soarer?"

"Yes. I suppose you don't believe me, either."

Salyna shook her head. "If you saw her, you saw her. If Rachylana said that, I wouldn't be so certain, but you see what is." After a moment, she added, "I don't think that's good."

"Neither do I, but what can I do? It's all so uncertain and vague." Absently, Mykella tried to strengthen the dark link to the greenish black below.

"Mykella! What are you doing?"

The combination of edginess and concern in Salyna's voice brought Mykella up short. She turned. "I wasn't doing anything. I was just thinking."

"You were, too. There was this . . . this green mist . . . and it was all around you."

Mykella could sense a combination of fear and concern. "Maybe the soarer's nearby. There was a green mist around her when I saw her."

Salyna shivered.

Mykella almost missed that, but managed to ask, "What's the matter?"

"You . . . everything . . . Mother was right. You are different." Salyna gestured around her. "It all seems so unreal, and so dangerous, and everyone acts as if nothing is wrong. Except you, and even you've changed."

"What do you mean?"

"You always did see things, but it's as though you see everything now, and that you know what everyone is feeling, maybe what they're thinking."

"I'm just guessing," Mykella lied.

"You're guessing well enough to scare me."

"What do you want me to do?" Mykella asked.

"I don't know. I know you can't make it all go away, but I wish you could."

"So do I," Mykella replied. "But I can't. So we might as well just try to enjoy the ride."

"I'll try."

So far as Mykella could tell, although she dared not try too hard, the greenish blackness remained close enough for her to maintain at least a tenuous link throughout the entire ride. Yet she knew that she had not been able to do that south of the palace. Was the greenish blackness somehow connected to the ridge that passed immediately north of the palace and then extended to the northeast?

After more than a glass, the mist began to turn into a light rain, almost icy in its chill, and the sisters turned their mounts back toward the palace.

Undercommander Areyst was waiting—mounted—at the crossroads where all the trails rejoined.

"Undercommander!" called Mykella. "What are you doing out here?"

"Your father was concerned when he discovered you had gone riding." Areyst eased his mount around so that he rode beside Mykella on the wider trail leading back southward to the palace.

"I notice that you did not travel all that far, Undercommander," Mykella said quietly.

"I had few doubts that you would be safe. I picked the guards to accompany you, and your sister is as good as most men with her blade and the rifle."

"I heard you made certain she had the rifle."

"I thought it was for the best, Mistress Mykella." Areyst smiled pleasantly.

Beneath the smile, Mykella felt his concerns, but she could not sense exactly what they were, except that, despite his words, he was clearly relieved to see her and Salyna. Especially her, and that unsettled her just a bit.

Once they reentered the courtyard, Areyst inclined his head, then mustered their escort into a formation outside the stable.

Although Mykella was not slow in grooming and rubbing down the gray, she did not rush. Nor did Salyna, yet, when they left the stable to cross the courtyard to the palace, the Southern Guards who had accompanied them—and the undercommander—still remained mounted and ready.

Areyst inclined his head to them, but did not speak.

38

On Tridi morning at breakfast, Feranyt looked up from his tea at Mykella. "Have you been prowling around the lower levels of the palace again?"

"Sir?" Mykella didn't have to counterfeit confusion. She could go anywhere she wished in the palace unseen. "No, Father. I haven't been prowling anywhere. I have more than enough to do teaching Maxymt about the accounts. Why?"

"There have been reports, strange things, doors opening with no one around, silvers lying on the stones, door locks clicking when no one was there. . . ." He kept looking at her.

Mykella was surprised—and more than a little worried. Not that there were reports, but that such reports had been brought to her father weeks after the events had occurred. Was that just another indication of how out of touch he really was?

Feranyt chuckled. "I can see you're as surprised as I am. Good. I wouldn't want you to make a habit of nocturnal prowling."

Not like Jeraxylt, she thought, without voicing the thought.

After breakfast, she made her way to the Finance chambers, thinking about both her father's questions and Undercommander Areyst. She'd been concerned about the undercommander ever since they had danced that single waltz at the ball because he had come across as direct and honest. After what had happened to Kiedryn and what she had sensed from both Nephryt and Demyl, the thought that something might happen to Areyst was disturbing. Yet how could she even warn Areyst without putting him in danger? And what could she say—that he was the only honest senior officer left in the Southern Guards and that he was in danger because he was? Who could possibly believe that? Equally problematical was that there was little way for her to see him anytime soon in a setting where she could convey her concerns. To create any public opportunity would be noted, and jeopardize him, while any use of the sight-shield to reach him might well create questions better left unraised. Then, too, there was the problem that, she realized, she found him attractive . . . and, if anyone discovered that, she'd be on her way to Dereka even sooner than would otherwise be the case—or she'd be confined under observation. That would leave her with few choices, and none of them enviable.

Once in the Finance chambers she gave Maxymt a polite but perfunctory, "Good morning."

"Good morning, Mistress Mykella."

Mykella went to her table, where she began with the highway and river ledgers, reviewing the entry clerks' work. Then she compared those entries and summations to Maxymt's entries in the master ledger. She had to admit that Maxymt had learned quickly and that he was probably sharper with figures than Kiedryn had been—and that worried her as well.

She forced herself to concentrate on the columns of figures in the ledgers before her. Slowly, slowly, the figures began to absorb her, and she was beginning to see yet another pattern. . . .

"Mykella!" Salyna burst through the door to the Finance study.

Mykella looked up from the ledger, biting off the words of annoyance she had almost voiced when she sensed the grief and fear radiating from her sister. "What's the trouble?"

"Jeraxylt . . ." Salyna opened her mouth, then closed it. Her body shook with silent sobs.

Mykella bolted to her feet. "What about Jeraxylt?"

"He . . . there was an accident . . . they were practicing with blunted sabers . . . and his broke. So did the other guard's, but . . ."

Mykella glanced to Maxymt, then back to Salyna. Somehow, Maxymt was surprised . . . yet not surprised.

"I'll be back when I can," Mykella said, moving toward Salyna.

Mykella did not say anything more until they were outside in the corridor. "He's dead, isn't he?"

Salyna, still shuddering, nodded. Then, she straightened. "They sent a messenger to Father. Eranya told me."

"Where's Father?"

"In his study, Eranya said. He wanted to be alone."

He can be alone, but not until I've talked to him. Mykella increased her stride until she was almost running.

"You can't . . ." protested Salyna from behind her.

Mykella hurried to the front of the building, barely looking at the two guards stationed beside the double doors before she stepped into the outer study, leaving the door open for Salyna, if her younger sister chose to follow.

Chalmyr stood by the inner study door. "He said—"

"I know." Mykella summoned her Talent, projecting all the authority she could muster. "I will see him. Now."

Chalmyr looked at her, then stepped aside.

Mykella did open the door gently, closing it softly as well.

Feranyt sat behind the wide desk, looking almost blankly into space, his face ashen, although Mykella did not sense any of the unseen grayness she had discerned around his frame from time to time.

"Father . . . what happened?"

Feranyt shook his head. "He's dead . . ."

"Do you know how it happened?"

"It doesn't matter . . ."

She could sense that she'd get no real answers from him, not at the moment. "Thank you. I'll be back later." She turned and started to head out of her father's study.

"Mykella . . . don't . . ."

She ignored his words and kept moving, through the door and past Chalmyr and Salyna, both of whom just looked as she swept past them, hurrying out into the corridor and then down the steps and out into the courtyard.

Once out in the chill, she glanced around, but there were no mounted guards anywhere in sight. So she hurried across to the stable, where she saddled the gray as deftly and quickly as she could. She thought she heard horses, but when she led the gelding out of the stable, the section of the courtyard she could see held neither Southern Guards nor mounts. So she jump-mounted and rode toward the avenue gates.

One of the two guards stepped out of the sentry box. "Mistress . . . wait . . . you need an escort . . ."

"If I have to wait for an escort, you'll be hung by morning." Her voice blazed with fury . . . and the power of her Talent. Her words filled the courtyard, so much that the gate vibrated and rattled.

The other guard scrambled out and began to open the gate, murmuring to the first, "There's a squad beyond the stables . . . the ones who brought . . . let her go . . . tell them . . ."

As soon as the gate was wide enough, Mykella urged the gelding through.

She didn't urge her mount into a full gallop; it was more like an easy canter for the vingt eastward to the square stone building with the enormous center courtyard. She swept past the duty guards and into the courtyard, reining up before the bronze posts with the hitching rings for the senior officers.

The ranker stationed there gaped as Mykella vaulted down and handed him the gelding's reins. "Tie him up. I need to see the Arms-Commander." With that she rushed through the outer doors and then to the left, and down the corridor to the headquarters section. There she pushed her way through the double doors to the Arms-Commander's outer study.

The single ranker bolted to attention. "Mistress Mykella . . ."

"Where's the Arms-Commander?"

"He's not here, Mistress."

"Commander Demyl?"

"Ah . . ."

"Where?" snapped Mykella.

The ranker's eyes flicked to the left, toward a golden oak door.

"Thank you." Mykella went through the door.

By the time she'd closed the door, Commander Demyl had risen. "Mistress Mykella—"

"What happened?" Her voice was like ice.

"I'm so sorry for you," Demyl's voice oozed sympathy, but beneath it was cold calculation. "It was an accident, Mistress Mykella. We really don't know how it occurred."

Despite his soothing tone and sympathetic demeanor, Mykella knew the commander was lying. "You must know something, and I'd like to hear it."

"Your brother and a junior guard were sparring. The blades were unedged practice weapons. Somehow the other guard's blade shattered, and a fragment went through your brother's eye and into his brain. There was nothing anyone could have done."

"I'd like to hear about it from the other guard."

"Alas, that's not possible, either. He was so distraught at wounding the Lord-Protector's heir that he slit his wrists with his dagger, then fell on his saber. The duty ranker discovered him, but he was too far gone and died in the exercise yard."

"And no one saw any of this?" asked Mykella.

Demyl shook his head. "The Arms-Commander needed some of the hay moved in the stables, and asked Captain Vealdyn to detail the First Company rankers who were practicing in the yard. He couldn't very well ask the heir to the Lord-Protector or the guard with whom he was sparring. At that time, no one else was there."

How terribly convenient. It was all totally untrue, and yet Mykella could sense that there was no way that she could disprove the Commander's story. Jeraxylt would have died from a steel splinter from a shattered blade, and the practice blade would match, and the only known witness had died from his wounds, although Mykella doubted that any had been self-inflicted.

"No one?" she temporized, hoping to draw him out.

"No one was near enough to see anything, and if the other guard called out, no one heard him. Terribly tragic . . . just terrible . . . I'm so sorry for you and your family, Mistress."

Mykella forced herself to say, "Thank you." But she dared not look directly up at the Commander, knowing her glance would tell him that she knew everything. He might guess . . . but that was something else.

"I . . . need to get . . . back to the palace." She turned and hurried out of the study, leaving him standing there. Even so, as she departed, she could sense his concern and worry—and it certainly wasn't about her brother or Mykella herself.

The ranker still held the reins, but four Southern Guards had pulled up behind her mount. She didn't know whether they had been summoned from the headquarters barracks or whether they had followed her from the palace. She also didn't care.

She mounted and began the ride back to the palace.

None of the Southern Guards said a word on her return.

When she finally reached the palace, after a far slower ride on the way back, she turned the gelding over to the ostler's assistant, something she normally wouldn't have done, and made her way back to her father's official study.

There were four guards out in the corridor, and both Chalmyr and Joramyl were in the antechamber.

"He's not seeing anyone, Mykella," said Joramyl.

"He'll see me."

"He said no one. Not you, not your sisters, not Eranya, not even me."

Mykella could sense the absolute truth of Joramyl's words. While she could have used her Talent to slip through the stones of the palace itself, she knew her father well enough to understand that, at that moment, he would hear nothing of what she might say. Her eyes burned with unshed tears, tears of grief, but also of frustration.

After a moment, she turned away, and walked slowly back toward her chamber.

At that instant, she didn't want to see anyone, especially Salyna, who might see all too much about what Mykella knew and felt.

39

Mykella did not feel ready to deal with her sisters for a time, and almost two glasses passed before she made her way to the parlor. Rachylana and Salyna sat opposite each other, Salyna on the settee, Rachylana on the edge of an armchair. Both looked up and toward Mykella, but Mykella said nothing, just closed the parlor door and walked toward her usual chair.

"Where did you go?" Salyna sniffed after she spoke.

Mykella stopped. She knew her younger sister was still upset, but Salyna's eyes bore only a trace of redness at the corners.

"I talked to Father and then rode over to the Southern Guard headquarters. I wanted to know what really happened," Mykella replied. "Arms-Commander Nephryt wasn't there, but I talked to Commander Demyl."

"What did he say?" asked a red-eyed Rachylana.

"Not much more than you heard. He gave some details. He said the guard whose blade shattered and killed Jeraxylt slit his own wrists and fell on his saber. They couldn't save him."

"It was easier on him that way," Rachylana said. "How could he have been so careless and stupid? How?"

"Stupid things happen because people are stupid." Salyna looked to Mykella, then asked, "Didn't anyone else see it?"

"All the others in the practice area had been conscripted to unload hay for the mounts. No one heard anything until it was too late."

"Did you talk to Father?" asked Salyna.

"I did before I left. I tried to when I got back. Uncle Joramyl wouldn't let me. He said Father didn't want to see anyone. I could tell that was what Father told him."

"He's like that when he gets upset." Salyna shook her head. "Remember what he was like after Mother—"

"I don't want to," snapped Rachylana. "You two are being so

rational. So logical. Jeraxylt's dead! Dead! Doesn't that mean any-thing at all?"

For a moment, neither Mykella nor Salyna spoke.

Finally, Mykella replied, "We're all different. It doesn't mean we care less. I had to do something. That's why I rode to the Southern Guard headquarters. I left my escort behind."

"It didn't do much good," Rachylana replied morosely.

"Sometimes, nothing does," Salyna said.

Mykella sank into the chair where she usually read, not that she had anything to read or that she even felt like it.

"Why did it have to happen to Jeraxylt?" asked Rachylana. "A broken practice blade . . . why not someone else?"

Because they weren't Jeraxylt. Mykella absently wondered how many blades Demyl or Nephryt had broken before they had gotten one to shatter in the right way. Would there be any pieces hidden somewhere? She shook her head.

In late afternoon, Mykella returned to her chamber, then stepped over to the stone wall, letting her fingers touch the bare gray granite. She reached out for the darkness, then let herself merge with the stone. Instead of sinking to the depths of the palace, she willed her-self to move sideways through the granite, following the heavy walls until she came to the Lord-Protector's chambers. She followed sev-eral walls that did not lead where she wanted—it was different trying to find her way through feel from inside the stone—until she reached her father's private study, but no one was there.

She finally located him in his sitting room. When she slipped out of the granite wall, Feranyt didn't even look up from where he sat in his chair, his eyes on the low coals in the hearth. She took several quiet steps sideways until she could slide the door bolt into the unlocked position before she moved forward. She was almost to his chair, when he started.

"Eranya! Leave me alone. I told you . . ." Feranyt looked up, sur-prised. "How did you get in here, Mykella?"

"The door was unlocked, Father. I wanted to talk to you, but Uncle Joramyl wouldn't let me see you earlier."

"That's because I told him I wanted to be alone." He sighed. "What do you want?"

Mykella took the armchair adjoining his, but she sat on the edge, turned so that she could look at him in the dim light. "After I left you, I went to see Commander Demyl . . ." She went on to tell him exactly what the Commander had said, as closely as she could recall. Then she girded herself up and concluded, "The death of the other guard seems very strange to me."

"It doesn't to me. He knew he was as good as dead, accident or no accident."

"He didn't try to run. He didn't try to escape. He just slit his wrists and fell on his saber. Young men don't do that." *Especially not young guards. They all think they can outrun and outfight anyone.*

"Mykella . . . it was an accident. I sent Joramyl to look into it immediately. He talked to everyone."

"Except the guard sparring with Jeraxylt."

"What could you expect? I told you. I would have ordered him killed anyway." Feranyt looked at her with sunken and bloodshot eyes, then shook his head.

Mykella could again sense the faint grayness pervading his frame. *Why can't he see?*

"It wasn't an accident," she said firmly.

"You can't think that," countered her father. "Joramyl has investigated thoroughly. He talked to everyone. While you were gone, Arms-Commander Nephryt came here to tender his resignation."

"You accepted it, I hope." Mykella did the best she could to keep the frustration and fury out of her voice, but she could still hear a trace of it.

"What good would that do? I've lost a son and an heir, and I should lose a trusted Arms-Commander as well? I can't blame a senior officer for a bad practice blade, carelessness by a junior guard, and ill chance."

All that she could say, Mykella realized, was, "I'm so sorry."

Then she just sat there, silently, with her father, for almost a glass.

In the end, she let herself out of the sitting room and walked slowly back to her chamber. How could she do anything at all when her father refused to see what was happening around him?

40

Just before midday on Quinti, Mykella and her sisters led the family procession, including Joramyl, Berenyt, and Cheleyza, to the family's hillside mausoleum behind and slightly to the northwest of the palace, beyond the private gardens. Waiting for them were an honor guard and the three senior officers of the Southern Guards—Nephryt, Demyl, and Areyst. Once there, everyone took their positions, the mourners facing the mausoleum, the honor guard in front and to the right, and the three officers to the left, opposite the honor guard.

Under a clear silver-green sky, her head lowered, Mykella studied the mourners standing in the sunlight facing the gray stone arches of the open stone structure, in the middle of which stood the narrow granite memorial table on which rested an ornate gold-trimmed urn that held Jeraxylt's ashes. Her father radiated sadness in a distant way, and Salyna had trouble holding in sobs. Silent tears ran from the corners of Rachylana's eyes, as Berenyt stood beside her. Neither of Mykella's sisters looked directly at the urn.

To the right of Feranyt stood Joramyl, his head bowed. Within him, Mykella could detect, not so much a sense of triumph or gloating, but a feeling of acceptance and inevitability. Arms-Commander Nephryt actually seemed saddened, but Commander Demyl held within himself a sense of righteousness and duty.

A mournful trumpet fanfare echoed through the cool air, and Feranyt stepped forward from the mourners facing the mausoleum, then turned to face them. "We acknowledge that Jeraxylt, beloved son and heir to the Lord-Protector of Lanachrona, has died, and that he has left a legacy of love shared by his family. We are here to mourn the loss of what might have been and to offer our last formal farewell in celebration of his life." While sadness tinged every word, his voice did not falter or break. After a moment of silence, he stepped back, rejoining his family, and nodded to Arms-Commander Nephryt.

The Arms-Commander stepped forward, and half-turned to face the family. "Jeraxylt was a young officer of noble character and warmth of personality. Even had he not been the heir of the Lord-Protector, he would have distinguished himself by his honor and his devotion to duty. All who knew him respected and liked him. His death is a loss beyond words and beyond measure."

Mykella sensed regret, of a sort, behind Nephryt's words, as he bowed his head, then stepped to the side to rejoin the other two officers.

Another moment of silence followed before Undercommander Areyst stepped forward to deliver the final blessing. "In the name of the One and the Wholeness That Is, and Always Will Be, in the great harmony of the world and its lifeforce, may the blessing of life, of which death is but a small portion, always remain with Jeraxylt, son and heir of the Lord-Protector. And blessed be the lives of all those who have loved him and those he loved. Also, blessed be both the deserving and the undeserving, that all may strive to do good in the world and beyond, in celebration and recognition of what is and will be, world without end."

His words had been offered with dignity and a clear sense of sadness and mourning, for which Mykella was grateful. She didn't know if she could have concealed her rage if either Nephryt, Demyl, or Joramyl had offered the blessing.

Then one of the honor guard raised his trumpet and played the haunting "Farewell to Arms."

In the moment of silence that followed, Mykella eased over to the undercommander. "Thank you for the blessing. You offered it well, and in a spirit of honesty that reflects the past heritage of the Southern Guards."

She could sense him stiffen inside.

"I know you embody that spirit, and that made the blessing meaningful. Thank you." She inclined her head as if in respect, and murmured, "Take great care of yourself."

From his internal reaction, she could sense he had heard.

Areyst inclined his head in response, then straightened. "I could do no less in serving Tempre and the Lord-Protector."

"It was still appreciated, Undercommander." Mykella eased back toward her father.

"Mykella?" inquired Feranyt, his voice betraying an irritation at her breach of formality before the procession back to the palace.

"I just thanked him for the blessing. He offered it well, and he meant it." She stepped back and waited for the honor guard to begin the long walk back to the palace.

41

That night, unsurprisingly, Mykella knew she would not get to sleep soon, nor sleep well. Had her actions led to Jeraxylt's death? Would the "accident" have occurred had he not accompanied her on her visits to the factors? She had the clear feeling that, although she had not intended it that way, at the very least her inquiries had been indirectly responsible.

Standing there in the darkness of her unlighted chamber—with the night-sight conveyed by her Talent, she now seldom lit the lamps unless she wanted to read—she felt torn between a near-uncontrollable urge to sob and a desire to rip and smash everything she could see or sense.

She didn't even have a single thing by which to remember her brother. Fool that she'd been, she'd thought that mementos were only for those far older than she was. A grim smile crossed her lips. Although Jeraxylt's chambers were sealed—for the moment—that presented no problem for her.

She reached out to the darkness beneath and then used the granite walls as her pathway into her brother's chambers, for as heir he had possessed two, a study and a bedchamber.

In the end, she returned to her chamber with but two items—the brilliant blue vest he had worn at various ceremonial events to signify that he was the heir of the Lord-Protector, and an oval medallion of gold, bearing a Dramurian crest, that he had received from their mother when he had turned ten. The medallion went into the hidden back of the jewelry box whose contents she almost never wore, and the vest into the bottom of her armoire, under several sweaters she also never wore, one of which had been her mother's.

While her theft—or reclamation in the case of the medallion—helped reduce some of her anger, it wasn't enough. She had to do *something*.

Again, she touched the cold granite, but this time, she did sink into the depths of the palace, emerging before the Table. There, she stepped closer and looked down, concentrating on trying to see Joramyl in the mirrored surface. When the swirling mists cleared, she found herself looking at the image of the Ifrit. At least, she thought it was the same Ifrit.

You have returned once more. Most excellent. The violet eyes burned, and immediately, she could sense the misty purple arms rising out of the Table, out of a Table that held an aura more pinkish than she recalled.

Mykella only took one step back, throwing up her shields against the arms, yet those arms did not move toward her as they swelled with purplish power and malevolence, but toward her life-thread where it passed through the solid stone floor toward the greenish blackness below.

Instinctively she extended her shields to protect it, and the arms lunged toward her midsection and that node where the fine lines of her being joined to form her life-thread. The arms still pressed, and she could feel her shields buckling.

She managed a second set of shields, behind the first, but she found herself being pressed back by the expanding force of the arms. The Table itself was glowing an ever-brighter purple, so bright that she wanted to close her eyes, although she understood closing them would do nothing because the glare was in her senses, not in her eyes.

Did the arms have a node, something similar to what the Ifrit sought to attack in her? She made a probe, like a saber, extending from her shields, angling it toward a thickness in the leftmost of the arms facing her.

Just as suddenly, one of the arms hurled something at her. Her shields held as the object shattered against them, but Mykella found herself being thrown back against the stone wall of the chamber. Her boot skidded on something, and she went to one knee. She put out a hand to steady herself, and found the stone floor wet, with fragments of ice chips.

Ice? The arms had thrown that icicle with enough force to disembowel her, had it not been for her shields.

I will not be defeated by something attacking me from inside a stone Table. I will not! She forced herself erect and called on the darkness, and the greenish depths to which her life-thread was somehow attached.

A purplish firebolt sprayed against her shields, and she staggered, but moved forward, calling . . . drawing on the greenish blackness of the depths, the green that recalled the Ancient.

The entire chamber flared greenish gold, and under that flood of fully-sensed but unseen light, the purplish arms evaporated into mist and haze, and then vanished.

The Ancients . . . still there . . .

There was a sudden emptiness around the Table, as it subsided to the faintest of purplish sheens. Then, that too, vanished.

Mykella realized, belatedly, as it vanished, that there had been an undercurrent of pinkish purple around the Table for weeks, if not longer. Had the Ifrit been watching, scouting out her weaknesses, and preparing for the attack he had just made?

Mykella felt a smile appear on her face. Exhausted as she was, she had learned two things. Her shields were proof against weapons, some of them, at least, and she could stand up to the distant Alector. And if she could stand against an Ifrit, surely she could hold her own against Joramyl and his scheming supporters, could she not? Could she not?

42

On Quattri, Mykella was nearing the Finance chambers in late afternoon, after returning from carrying a summary of recent expenditures to her father in his study. She'd taken to doing that after she had realized that Joramyl had only been verbally briefing her father and that Maxymt had not continued Kiedryn's practice of providing such weekly summaries.

Feranyt had seemed tired, almost gray, and had taken the sheets from her with a weary expression. "Thank you, Mykella."

While he had not actually dismissed her, he might as well have, for his eyes had dropped to the papers on the table-desk before him. Mykella had slipped out, nodding to Chalmyr as she left, once more asking herself what she could do. Sooner or later, she feared, either Joramyl or Berenyt would become Lord-Protector, and with the weariness she saw in her sire, she feared it would be sooner, and that was her fault.

With Jeraxylt's death, her father had become quieter, more withdrawn, as well. Why was it that everything she tried to do had made matters worse? She'd tried to warn her father and only succeeded in warning Joramyl. She'd let Jeraxylt know, and that had made him a danger to Joramyl, and now her brother was dead; and then her going to see Commander Nephryt had surely alerted both Nephryt and Joramyl to her suspicions about their plotting. Would she be next?

She shook her head. They would marry her off and be rid of her.

Her thoughts were interrupted by the sight of an officer in a Southern Guard uniform standing outside the Finance door, waiting. It was Berenyt.

She forced a smile as she neared. "Good afternoon."

"Good afternoon, Mykella. You're looking well."

"After all that's happened, you mean?"

"It's been a difficult time for everyone," he replied.

What bothered her immediately was that he clearly believed that. Why had times been difficult for Berenyt? He hadn't been all that close to Jeraxylt, and he certainly hadn't cared anything about Kiedryn.

"It has, but we'll manage. Life does go on."

"It does," he nodded, "often for the best, although we don't always see it that way. You know, Mykel the Great lost his entire family in the Cataclysm? You have to wonder if he'd been so good a Lord-Protector without suffering that loss."

"I'm sure he wouldn't have wished that." Mykella barely kept her voice pleasant. Rachyla had lost her entire immediate family as well, but Berenyt wouldn't have cared about that in the slightest.

"You know, Mykella, it's too bad that Jeraxylt had that accident."

Mykella had doubted that Berenyt's words were ever anything but carefully chosen, and this was no exception. "It was a surprise to all of us. He was always so careful in arms practice."

"He wasn't always as careful in other matters. He could have been a great Southern Guard and Lord-Protector, if he had concentrated on arms. That was his strength."

Mykella managed to keep her expression puzzled. "Jeraxylt was always careful, and he certainly did concentrate on arms."

"He should have. He should have concentrated on those more, rather than using you as a front for his calculations."

Mykella wasn't sure from the swirl of feelings within Berenyt whether he actually believed that Jeraxylt had been the one to discover the diversions of golds and bring them to the Lord-Protector's attention or whether Berenyt was not so indirectly offering her a way to disavow what she had discovered. Although she felt frozen inside, she managed to offer a sad smile. "We all have different talents."

"With all of your abilities, Mykella, it's too bad we're cousins," said Berenyt, not quite jokingly.

"I like you, too," Mykella replied politely. "And so does Rachylana." Always implying, never saying, that was Berenyt's style. He never really used words that committed to anything, even as he was implying the unthinkable.

"It really is too bad you and your sisters and I are related," insisted Berenyt.

Even though his eyes remained fixed on her face, Mykella could sense the physical appraisal . . . and the muted lust. She barely managed not to swallow or show her disgust. "We are cousins. Nothing will change that."

"You might wish otherwise." Berenyt smiled brightly.

"What I might wish, Berenyt, has seldom changed what is."

"That's true, Mykella, but often what I've wished has." With a pleasant smile, he nodded, then turned and walked down the corridor.

Within herself, she shuddered.

Then, for a time, she stood outside the Finance door before reaching out and opening it. Had Berenyt decided that she'd be a better consort than Rachylana? Or was he merely feeling her out? Whatever he might have been doing, for whatever reason, it only reinforced her opinion of him.

43

Early on Quinti morning, immediately after breakfast, Mykella donned black, from nightsilk all the way outward to boots, tunic, and trousers, as well as a black scarf that could double as a head-covering, if necessary. The events of the past week, especially Berenyt's words and her last encounter with the Ifrit, had convinced her that anything she could do as a woman—anything that would be seen as acceptable for a woman, she corrected herself—would not save her or her father, or her sisters, from Joramyl and his schemes.

She'd finally had a little time to think over her encounter with the Ifrit. He'd attempted to misdirect her initially, but his attack on her had been aimed at the node of her life-thread. Three things had come together in her thoughts. First was the fact that everyone had a node. Second was the Ifrit's attack. Third was her recollection of what Kiedryn had said before he'd been murdered—that Mykel the Great had been able to kill men without touching them. That suggested something she could master—and use, if she had to.

She had a sickening feeling that it would be necessary.

Under cover of her sight-shield, she made her way from the upper level of the palace, down the steps and across the western courtyard, past the low extension that held the kitchens, to the small building behind the kitchens that served as the slaughterhouse. She waited until no one was looking, then opened the door and closed it behind her, walking as quietly as she could toward the open-roofed but walled slaughtering area in the back.

Three lambs, close to being yearlings and mutton, were confined in a pen—an overlarge wooden crate. Several fowl were in the next crate. Mykella could sense the grayish life-threads of the lambs, thinner than that of her gelding, but definite life-threads. From where she stood, she could not sense those of the fowl, though she had no doubt that they also had life-threads.

Two men—or an older bearded man and a youth—stood beside the pen.

Nelmak, the head butcher, looked to the rangy youth. "We need to get on with it. The first one."

As the young man folded down the front of the crate and lifted a blunt stunning hammer, Mykella reached out with what she could only call her Talent and grasped the node of the lamb's life-thread, a thread that felt both thinner and yet coarser, or stronger, than her own seemed to be. But no matter how she tried, she could not break the node or the thread.

The hammer came down, and the life-thread remained. Then the youth dragged the stunned animal out of the pen and over to the iron hook and chain. Only after he slit the animal's throat did the life-thread break—spraying apart at the node, as if all the tiny threads unraveled at once.

Mykella thought she had sensed a point, a tiny knot within the node, that might be where she could strike. She readied herself as the assistant stunned the second lamb, but it took more time than she thought, trying to work a sharp Talent probe into that tiny knot. Just before her probe reached the knot, the assistant completed the kill.

She struggled to work more quickly on the last animal, using her Talent almost like a knife-edged crochet hook—and she succeeded in stabbing the key knot, and then twisting, unraveling, and cutting the threads. The lamb died before the assistant even raised his bloody knife.

"It's dead."

"Never seen the like of that before," wondered the butcher.

"Nelmak, sir, you just scared it to death."

"It was you. You hit too hard with the hammer. You don't pound them to death. You stun them. Otherwise it's a bitch to get all the blood out."

Mykella just stood there, shuddering behind her concealment shield. A cold chill ran through her. She'd never killed anything before—except spiders and flies and the like. And it had been terrifyingly easy once she had discovered how.

She swallowed, telling herself that the lamb would have died one way or the other. And Jeraxylt and Kiedryn had both been killed by Joramyl's plots . . . and most likely so had an innocent Southern Guard, not to mention Shenyl.

She had to remember that. She had to.

After several moments, she stiffened and then eased her way back through the slaughterhouse. Once outside, still holding the concealment shield, she took a deep breath before walking back across the rear courtyard toward the palace. She'd discovered that her Talent was more than just a tool for observation—much more.

She shivered again, this time at the thought that she could no longer claim she was powerless. She kept walking.

44

True early spring had finally arrived in Tempre—or at least several days and afternoons warm enough to enjoy the private gardens to the northwest of the palace, and on Decdi afternoon Mykella slipped away from the palace to the gardens and their budding foliage to be alone. She was edgy and still had trouble sleeping, even though the ledgers showed no more diversions, and the actual receipts continued to match the ledger entries. There were no more tack entries assigned to "Berjor" for the Southern Guards, either. For all the brighter and warmer weather, her father remained withdrawn, spending even more time with his brother, and drinking more wine than he should have.

One of Mykella's favorite places was the small fountain in the northwest corner of the extensive walled garden. There, water trickled down what resembled a section of an ancient wall, and tiny ferns circled the shallow pool below. In summer and fall, miniature redbells bloomed.

She was halfway across the garden on the side path when she heard a feminine laugh from behind one of the boxwood hedges forming the central maze. The laugh was Rachylana's, and Mykella could sense that her sister was not alone. She moved closer, drawing her sight-shield around her.

"You're much more beautiful than Mykella." That voice was Berenyt's.

"Mykella has her points."

"But so many of them are sharp . . ."

Mykella snorted. Time to put a stop to this particular scene. "Rachylana! Where are you?" As if she didn't know.

There was absolute silence from the hidden bower, but Mykella dropped the sight-shield and moved toward it, making sure her boots echoed on the stones of the curving pathway. When she came around the last corner of the boxwood hedge before the bower, Berenyt stood.

"Mykella." His tone was pleasant.

Mykella could sense the unvoiced condescension and the irritation. "Good day, Berenyt," Mykella said politely. "I didn't realize you were here."

"It was a most pleasant end-day, and I happened to encounter your sister, and she suggested we enjoy the garden. It has been such a long and gray winter."

"It has indeed," Mykella agreed, "some days being even grayer than others."

Berenyt bowed. "I will not intrude further. Good afternoon, ladies." His smile was clearly for Rachylana. He stepped gracefully past the sisters and made his way down the hedge-lined path that would lead him out of the maze.

Mykella waited for the outburst that was certain to follow once Berenyt was out of earshot.

"You came out here looking for us, didn't you?" accused Rachylana.

"No. I came out here to be alone, but you were giggling and making over him. He's your cousin."

"He's going to be Lord-Protector some day. Father won't wed again."

Mykella had tried to avoid thinking about that. "If Lady Cheleyza doesn't have a son, and if nothing happens to Berenyt." She almost said that Cheleyza was expecting, but realized that she'd have to explain.

"He'll still be first in line."

So long as Cheleyza doesn't poison him. Mykella managed not to swallow at the implications of that thought. Had Cheleyza tried to poison Rachylana because a marriage between Berenyt and Rachlyana would have reduced, if not eliminated, the chance for her child to become Lord-Protector?

"Mykella?" pressed Rachylana.

"He's your cousin," Mykella repeated, almost lamely.

"So?"

"Berenyt's just using you," Mykella said, regaining her composure and not concealing the exasperation in her voice. "You're behaving like every other silly woman, even like a tavern trollop. You think that he cares for you. All he wants is information and power. He really doesn't even want to bed you, except to make his position as heir apparent to his father more secure."

"That's not Berenyt."

"That's very much Berenyt. While you're thinking he's appreciating you, he keeps asking you questions, doesn't he? He flirts, but never says anything." Mykella's words were edged with honey more bitter than vinegar. "He hints, but never actually says anything."

Rachylana lunged toward Mykella.

Mykella stepped aside, but also called up the unseen webs of greenish energy.

Rachylana reeled away from the unseen barrier and staggered back, nearly toppling over the stone bench. "You hit me!"

"I never touched you, but I certainly should have." By using her Talent to avoid a physical confrontation, Mykella realized, she'd only made matters worse. "You were so ready to lash out at me that you tripped over your own feet, and you'll trip over more than that if you're not careful."

"You and your pride. You and Salyna. The two of you seem to think that you can do anything a man can, and you can't," snapped Rachylana. "You're the one who'll trip." She straightened herself and smiled. "You seem to forget, Mykella, that you're a woman, and women need to carry themselves with care if they're to acquire what they wish."

Mykella had never forgotten that she was a woman. How could she, reminded as she was at every turn about what women couldn't do, shouldn't do, or ought not to do? She said nothing more as Rachylana turned and stalked down the garden path.

Only after Rachylana had left did Mykella walk to the far corner of the garden. How could she make people pay attention to her—truly pay attention to her? She was half a head shorter than her sisters, and she was a woman. Her voice and perhaps her posture were the only commanding aspects she possessed.

Could she use her Talents . . . ? Could she summon the Ancient?

Standing in the shadows of late afternoon, she concentrated on the soarer. Nothing happened. How could she reach the Ancient? Through the blackness below? This time, she reached downward toward the greenish black darkness. Surprisingly, touching that underground web was far easier immediately away from the Table. Did the Table make it harder?

The Table interferes with many things. The soarer hovered to Mykella's right, in the deeper shadows. *You have called me.* A sense of amusement radiated from the soarer. *What do you wish?*

"Some assistance with a few small things," Mykella said.

Why should I offer such?

"You wanted me to deal with the Ifrit, didn't you? I did. Now, I may need to deal with others."

Mykella gained the sense of a laugh.

You need little from me. You have repulsed the Ifrit. So long as you guard the Table, your world will be safe from him and those like him. You can already tap the lifeweb of Corus.

"Outside of the shields and the sight-shield, and seeing the lifeweb, I don't know much," Mykella confessed.

You can kill and travel through stone near the web, reminded the soarer.

Mykella winced. Did the Ancient know everything?

Only what you have done when you are close to the lifeweb. You can do much. If you link to the web itself, and do not just draw upon it, all that you do will be strengthened. A sense of somberness radiated from the hovering soarer. *Anything of value and of power gained through the lifeweb bears a cost. Those with great power—and you will be one of them, if you follow your destiny—can often avoid bearing those costs themselves. But there is a price, because those costs will not be denied, and they will fall twofold on others linked to you who have no Talent.*

"Twofold?"

The soarer vanished.

"Who are you talking to, Mykella?"

At the sound of Salyna's voice, Mykella whirled. "Salyna?"

"I thought you were talking to someone, but there wasn't . . . there isn't anyone here." Salyna frowned.

Hadn't Salyna seen the soarer? Did one have to have some vestige of Talent to see the Ancients? Was that another reason why the soarer had contacted Mykella?

"Mykella?"

"Sometimes . . . sometimes I just have to talk things out to myself," Mykella temporized.

"What's a lifeweb?"

"Oh . . . that's something I learned in the archives. Everything in the world that is living is tied together. That's what the Alectors thought." Mykella hoped that her hasty explanation would be enough. "I was trying to work out . . . about why some things happen. Sometimes, it helps to put it in words."

"I thought I was the only one who did that," offered her younger sister, pausing, and then adding, "You know . . . you really made Rachylana mad."

"I'm certain I did, but she shouldn't be sneaking off and flirting with Berenyt. They're cousins."

"He can be nice."

"He can. Of that, I'm most certain, but I'm also certain that he's selfish and that he'll bed any pretty woman he can, and that, if Rachylana and he are matched, she'll be miserable within seasons, if not sooner." Mykella smiled. "Not that she will listen to either of us. We might as well head back so that we won't be late for supper."

"She won't . . . but that makes it sad. She can't see that we worry. All she can see is Berenyt." Salyna shook her head, clearly unhappy about Rachylana and Berenyt, but knowing the truth of Mykella's words.

After Rachylana's reaction, and her father's withdrawal, Mykella knew she had much to practice—and learn—in the days ahead.

45

Mykella had waited a glass before trying to find Rachylana, hoping that her sister had calmed down, but Rachylana was nowhere to be found, and when she returned late that evening, she immediately locked herself in her room.

Disturbing dreams and thoughts had kept Mykella from sleeping well or long. When she woke on Londi morning, the warmth and sunshine of Novdi and Decdi had vanished. Outside was dark and gloomy under heavy gray clouds. After she washed up and as she dressed, the soarer's words about others bearing the cost of her Talent kept running

through her mind. Why should she or others have to pay for gaining
an ability or power? But had Jeraxylt's death really come from her Talent? Her discoveries of the golds stolen from the Lord-Protector's accounts had begun even before the soarer had appeared to her, and
that meant Joramyl's plotting had as well.

So why had the Ancient warned her about the cost of Talent? Was
the growing distance between her and Rachylana because Mykella's
Talent allowed her to see more? But wouldn't that have been true as
well if she'd been perceptive in the ways in which her mother had
been? If this . . . if that . . . and what about that over there?

She wanted to scream.

Instead, she waited several moments to let herself settle, then
walked calmly—outwardly, at least—from her chamber to the family
breakfast room. Salyna was already there.

No sooner had Mykella seated herself than Rachylana appeared
and sat down. "Good morning, Salyna."

"Good morning," replied Salyna.

"Good morning, Rachylana," Mykella said warmly.

"I don't know that I'm speaking to you," Rachylana said, archly.

"You might as well. There aren't too many others around. Besides,
whatever I've said has been because I love you. I also care what happens to you. You can fault me for saying what I believe, but it isn't
because I don't care, and I've said nothing to anyone but Salyna, and
I won't."

"I know that." Rachylana paused as Muergya appeared with a
large teapot, from which she filled the three mugs.

"Good morning, daughters."

Even without Talent, Mykella could have told that the cheer of her
father's greeting was forced. With it, the pain behind it was almost
agonizing—and that bothered her. But she also knew that, had she or
one of her sisters died, their father's grief would not have been nearly
so deep.

How do you know that? she asked herself. But the answer was obvious, because Feranyt had not shown nearly as much grief when
their mother had died six years previous. He had grieved, and he had
refused to remarry, but he had not seemed so inconsolable. *Could it*

be the loss of both of them? Mykella didn't know, and she might never know, but she *knew* his grief over losing a daughter would not have been nearly so great.

Jeraxylt's place at the breakfast table remained vacant. Neither Rachylana nor Salyna wished to take it, and Feranyt had said nothing. His occasional looks to the empty chair had been more than enough to keep it vacant.

"I do have some good news." Feranyt forced a smile.

The three waited.

"Joramyl has informed me that we should expect an envoy from Midcoast later this week. He could arrive as soon as Quattri."

"An envoy?" pressed Mykella. While her father might be grieving, sending for another envoy or even agreeing to see one who had already set out from Hafin, so soon after Jeraxylt's death, was anything but caring, even though he knew nothing about Rachylana's feelings for Berenyt.

"To consider a match, of course." A faint irritation entered the Lord-Protector's voice. "I won't live forever, and you all need to be provided for."

Rachylana's face paled, and her smile was faint.

Salyna's hand reached out under the table, as if to Rachylana, but dropped away. The table was too wide.

Mykella wanted to ask exactly why one of them couldn't provide for the others . . . or even become Lady-Protector of Tempre, but she could sense the combination of anger and irritation behind her father's words. And if she brought up Mykel's proclamation, he'd claim it was a legend without substance—unless she could produce it . . . and she couldn't. There was only the one mention of it, so far as she could tell.

"Anyway . . . that's that," Feranyt announced.

"As usual . . ." murmured Rachylana.

"What did you say?"

Rachylana smiled brightly. "I said 'another formal dinner.' Isn't that so?"

"How else will the envoy know how you appear in such a setting?"

"Yes, Father."

Feranyt sighed, then pushed back his chair and stood. "I need to get ready to meet with Joramyl and Lord Porofyr."

Mykella glanced back at her father. He had eaten sparingly, leaving almost half the omelet on his plate, and he had not even finished his second mug of spiced tea. More important, Mykella had been so distracted and irritated that she hadn't noticed that the grayness had returned to her father's frame . . . and that breakfast had not reduced it, or not much.

Once Feranyt had left, Mykella turned to Rachylana. "I'm sorry . . . about everything."

"It's not your fault. We'll all be sent away. It's just who gets sent where." Rachylana's eyes were bright.

"Father's not himself," added Salyna. "You know that."

"Yes, he is. He's always wanted to send us away because we remind him of Mother."

Mykella frowned. None of them looked exactly like their mother.

"It's true," protested Rachylana. "He just couldn't do it until we were old enough. Now, he can say it's to protect us."

Could that be true? Mykella hadn't sensed that in her father, but Rachylana well might be right. Mykella would have to see what she could sense in the days ahead.

Salyna glanced to Mykella, then said quietly. "Father is only doing what he thinks best."

"I know." *What he thinks best . . . but what about what is best?* Mykella did not voice that thought, and, after swallowing the last of her tea, she rose and walked back to her own chambers.

Almost for reassurance that she could do what she'd been doing, she slipped the gold medallion that had been her mother's and Jeraxylt's from its hiding place in the back of her jewelry box. She looked at it for a long time, wondering what had happened to the chain. A rumble of thunder rolled over the palace, and she glanced toward the window, before realizing that she had never opened the hangings. As she turned back, her hand brushed the edge of the dresser, and the medallion went flying, clanking on the stone and vanishing.

She began to search for it, but it was nowhere visible, and her Talent senses were not precise enough, she discovered, to locate a small metal object.

Had it skittered under the bed?

With the dimness in the chamber and the darkness in the narrow space under the bed, she could see nothing. Finally, she took the striker and lit the small lamp, setting it on the floor by the bed, but the lamp flame was too high to cast light far enough under the bed.

Could she use her Talent to help focus the lamplight?

She almost shrugged. She could only try.

After close to a quarter glass, she managed to narrow the light into a beam that she could bend to search under the bed . . . and a golden glint rewarded her. Once she had replaced the medallion in its hiding place, she was about to blow out the lamp. Then she paused, and carried the lamp with her until she stood before the mirror.

In the end, she managed to concentrate or focus light around herself without making herself less visible. The effect was to heighten her presence, as if she were outlined in light. She smiled. That was another way to stand out, especially for someone who did not have imposing stature—like her. If she were the Lord-Protector, such a skill might be valuable, but for now, it was merely a curiosity.

She blew out the lamp and set it back on the bedside table, behind the water pitcher, then walked back to the mirror and studied her appearance, not that she looked any different from the way she did any other morning in her nightsilk tunic and trousers and black boots.

When she stepped out of her chamber and into the long main corridor, she looked toward the Finance study. At that moment, she saw Maxymt turn eastward from the main staircase and continue his lizardlike waddle-walk toward the Finance study. Even his posture was smug and condescending. She wanted to unsettle him. He deserved it . . . and more. But how?

Several moments later, she smiled.

When she had ridden from the palace to confront Demyl, she'd done something with her Talent and voice, because she'd felt a certain power. Even the gate had shaken at her Talent-amplified voice. Could she channel that, more subtly, in a more directed fashion, to unsettle Maxymt? Without rage?

She stepped back into one of the regularly spaced alcoves, then Talent-reached along the long corridor. She only clicked her tongue disapprovingly, since Maxymt would recognize her voice.

The clerk stopped and looked around. That Mykella could sense. He resumed walking toward the Finance study door.

She clicked her tongue again.

While Maxymt twitched, he did not look back, but deliberately made his way to the door and unlocked it.

Mykella waited for close to a glass, experimenting with projecting sounds up and down the corridors, before she finally walked to the Finance study and entered.

Maxymt smiled politely. "Good morning, Mistress."

"Good morning." Mykella took her place at her table, hoping the day ahead would not be so long as she knew it would be. Still, she was pleased about what else she had discovered about her Talent, even if she wasn't quite sure how she might use either ability.

46

On Duadi, Mykella woke to a day that promised to be brighter, with clear skies and early white light flowing across the palace courtyard below her window. Brighter or not outside, she was dreading going to work on the ledgers. That had become more and more of a chore, and yet Mykella felt that, if she did not keep overseeing the accounts, matters would revert to what they had been. She also had discovered traces of another problem, and she knew she needed to investigate, and she feared her father—or Joramyl—would find yet another excuse. In some ways, she wondered why she both-ered, because, if her father had his way, she'd end up in Dereka, certainly before the end of summer. Yet . . . part of her insisted that it was important.

So she washed and dressed and had breakfast with her father and sisters, and spoke little, but politely, and learned that the envoy from Midcoast would arrive on Quinti. At that point, Rachylana had excused herself, claiming she felt unwell.

After a more strained end to breakfast, Mykella had made her way to the Finance study, where she resumed her investigation. Late on Londi, she had discovered that the outlays and the paychests sent to the Southern Guard outpost in Syan over the winter had been a fifth larger than in the previous winter, but the number of guards stationed there had not varied, and the pay scales had not changed. But tracking down all the entries was a tedious business, and she needed to make sure that all her figures were correct before she brought them to her father. At least, when she did, he wouldn't be able to accuse Kiedryn.

In mid-afternoon, as she was completing her comparative listing of figures, the door to the Finance chambers slammed open, and Salyna rushed in. "It's Father! He's had a seizure. He's dying, Treghyt says, and he wants you!"

Mykella bolted from her table-desk, not even glancing at Maxymt. She dashed out of the study and down the long upper corridor toward the Lord-Protector's apartments, with Salyna running beside her.

They burst into the Lord-Protector's private quarters, past the pair of duty guards, then came to a stop at the door to the bedchamber. There stood Joramyl. His face wore a concerned look, and there was worry beneath the expression, although Mykella had the feeling that the internal worry was somehow . . . different.

"What happened?" Mykella asked.

"We were having an afternoon chat in his study, and he began to shake." Joramyl shook his head. "He tried to stand, and his legs gave out. I helped him here to his bed and summoned the healer . . ."

"Mykella . . . he needs you." Salyna pulled on Mykella's sleeve.

Mykella turned.

Treghyt, the white-haired healer Mykella had known for years, stood at the far side of the wide bed on which Feranyt lay, still in the brilliant blue working tunic of the Lord-Protector, although the neck of the tunic had been opened and loosened. Treghyt had just placed a cold compress on Feranyt's forehead, then had grasped his left wrist, as if checking his pulse.

Mykella stepped into the bedchamber and moved to the nearer side of the bed. She bent over the shuddering figure. "I'm here. I'm here, Father." She forced the tears back from her eyes.

Salyna stood beside Mykella, silent, but bending over and reaching down to touch her father.

"... Lord-Protector ..." gasped Feranyt.

"You're the Lord-Protector," Mykella insisted quietly, taking her father's hand in hers, aware that his fingers were like ice, even though she could feel the heat radiating from his forehead despite the cool compress there.

His life-thread was fraying as she sensed it. She tried to link with the greenish blackness below and to reinforce that disintegrating thread with her Talent, but the fraying accelerated faster than she could cope with it.

"Joramyl, and ... after him ... Berenyt ... they ... must ..."

"Berenyt?" blurted Mykella.

"... still of our blood, daughter." Feranyt took short shallow breaths, each one more labored than the one previous. "Promise me ... promise me. The Lord-Protector must ... must be of our blood."

"The ruler of Tempre must be of our blood," repeated Mykella. She could promise that ... somehow.

The faintest smile crossed Feranyt's lips before a last spasm convulsed him.

"He's gone," said the angular healer, looking toward Joramyl, who remained standing beside the doorway. "It happened so quickly. There was nothing ..." Treghyt shook his head. "Nothing."

Mykella's cheeks were wet, and she hadn't even realized that her tears were flowing.

The healer turned to Joramyl and bowed his head. While he did not say, "Lord-Protector," he might as well have.

Mykella wanted to protest those unspoken words. She did not, but straightened, looking down at the silent figure of her father. There was an ugly bluish green that suffused his form, fading slowly into gray as his body cooled. Poison? It had to be. She had no doubts about who had been behind it. Yet how could she prove it when the only evidence was what she could sense that no one else could? Treghyt doubtless suspected, but he would say nothing when the only heir was Joramyl.

And if she insisted it had been poison, too many questions would arise as to how and why she knew. Besides, her father was dead. So was Jeraxylt, and Joramyl was Lord-Protector. And . . . all of it had happened in spite of everything she had tried to do to stop it.

Salyna reached out and put her arms around Mykella, and the two clung to each other.

Joramyl, thankfully, said nothing.

47

The night of her father's death, Mykella was still numb all over. When Tridi dawned, she did not feel that much better, knowing that, at least overtly, she would have to go through the motions of being a dutiful daughter. She did not go to the Finance study. One way or another, what she had been doing with the accounts could have no effect, not any longer.

At the same time that she struggled with her grief, she knew that matters would not improve, not when both Treghyt and Joramyl had announced that her father had died of a brain seizure. She would have to act, but her actions would have to be dramatic and open, where they could not be hushed up or overlooked or excused as the efforts of an emotional and hysterical daughter.

So she planned . . . and forced herself to wait. Waiting was the hardest part, and that was the part of the role of a woman of Tempre that had always challenged her. The second hardest part was something that should have been easy for a "traditional" daughter, and that was altering the brilliant blue vest that had been her brother's. Mykella's needlework skills were not excessive, but the work in the seclusion of her own chamber—and practicing using her Talent to manipulate light and her voice—did pass the glasses on Tridi.

Then, late in the day, there was a knock on the door of Mykella's chamber. She walked to the door.

"Yes?"

"A missive for you, Mistress," said Uleana.

Mykella opened the door, if warily.

"It's from Lord Joramyl, the guards said." The maid handed Mykella a sheet of parchment, sealed shut in blue wax.

"Thank you." Mykella eased the door shut and walked back to the window, where she broke the seal and unfolded the single sheet.

The salutation read, "My dearest niece," and Mykella bridled at the words. "Dearest indeed," she murmured, but she forced herself to read the remainder of the words that followed.

In this time of your great sorrow, my thoughts, and those of Berenyt and Cheleyza, are with you and your sisters, for you have been asked to endure much in such a short time.

For all your sorrow, however, the last needs of your father must be met, as must those of Lanachrona, and I would like to request that you, as the eldest, gather your sisters to meet with me tomorrow after breakfast in the Lord-Protector's formal study.

The signature was that of Joramyl.

Instead of crumpling the parchment, as she would have liked to do, she folded it and walked from her chamber to the parlor, hoping to find both her sisters there. Only Salyna was present, her eyes on the window, looking blankly beyond the courtyard to the trees of the Preserve beyond the gardens and the rear walls of the courtyard.

"Salyna," Mykella began softly, "where's Rachylana?"

"She said she had to get out. She's somewhere being consoled by Berenyt, I'm sure. Why?"

Mykella held up the parchment. "Our dear Uncle Joramyl wants to meet with us tomorrow after breakfast."

"For what?"

"To go over the arrangements for Father's memorial, it appears, and other matters of import to Lanachrona."

"And those are how to get us out of Tempre as quickly as possible, and how soon he can officially take over as Lord-Protector, no doubt."

"I wouldn't be surprised," Mykella said.

"You sound so calm."

"I only *sound* calm," replied Mykella.

"Oh . . . Mykella . . . what can we do? I don't want to go to Southgate. Do you really want to go to Dereka?"

"No." Mykella sat down across from her younger sister. "We do have some time. It will be at least another week before the Seltyr's reply—or his envoy—returns."

"What about you?"

"There's no point in talking about it until something happens."

"You're thinking about something, aren't you?" said Salyna.

Mykella offered a wry smile. "I wonder what would have happened if Mykel had died before Rachyla."

Salyna frowned. "What does that have to do with anything?"

"Nothing. Except she was a strong woman, and no matter what they say, most men don't care for strength in women—except in childbirth."

"They do, too. Mother was strong, and Father loved her."

Mykella laughed, ironically. "I'll phrase it another way. Men like strong women, provided they're stronger than the woman they marry."

"That may be true, but that doesn't help us."

"Not now." Mykella glanced toward the window. "Will you tell Rachylana about the meeting with Joramyl?"

"I can. What are you doing?"

"I need to see if I can find something." Mykella turned and walked from the family parlor, making her way back to her own chambers.

While she could have walked down to the lower levels of the palace, she didn't know which of the guards were loyal to Joramyl, and she did not want him to know what she was doing. Instead, she stepped over to the outer stone wall of her chamber, touching it with her left hand, and reaching out to the darkness beneath and then guiding herself down to the basement chamber that held the oldest archives.

The old wooden steps were where Mykella had left them on her last visit, and the dust had settled, to reveal that no one else had been there since. She clambered to the top of the steps, and once more, she could barely reach the topmost box. Just as she eased it out, she sneezed, and almost dropped it.

Then, she balanced the wooden box on one of the middle steps and, forcing herself to be even more careful than she had been in her earlier and more cursory searches about Mykel and his Talent, she paged through the documents, one at a time. There were proclamations for this, and for that. In the third box, she found a complete set of summary budgets for all the years of Mykel's time as Protector of Tempre.

In the end, when she finished, close to midnight, she had found nothing new about Rachyla's possible succession as Protector of Lanachrona in the ten boxes of papers that were all that remained of the records of Mykel's years ruling Lanachrona. The only reference remained the notation to the documents proclaiming his son Olent as Protector of Tempre, in which there was a single line noting that the contingent succession proclamation naming Rachyla as Mykel's successor had been rendered moot because she had predeceased her husband.

She slipped that complete set of documents inside her tunic before she reached out to the greenish darkness in order to make her way back up through the cold granite to her own chambers.

48

On Quattri, the three sisters sat alone in the breakfast room, talking after they had eaten, not that any of them had partaken of all that much.

"Where were you last night?" Rachylana looked at Mykella. "We looked for you, but you weren't anywhere around."

"Outside . . . in the gardens," lied Mykella. "I wanted to think."

"It was damp out there." Rachylana shivered. "Why . . . ?"

Salyna offered the slightest frown, but said nothing for a moment, then asked, "Do you think Uncle Joramyl wants to talk about more than the memorial?"

"It can't be about matching," said Rachylana quickly. "The Midcoast envoy hasn't even arrived."

"He's supposed to arrive later today," Mykella pointed out.

"He wouldn't talk about matching," insisted Rachylana. "It has to be about Father."

"It might also be about his investiture as Lord-Protector," suggested Salyna.

Mykella wanted to ask why everyone just accepted that Joramyl would be Lord-Protector. She did not raise the question, saying only, "That's possible. He's not the kind to tarry when it's . . . something like that."

"That's unfair, Mykella," protested Rachylana. "Father was terribly close to Uncle Joramyl."

Unfortunately. "He was, but that doesn't change anything."

"Who else could be?" asked Rachylana. "The only men related to Father are Uncle Joramyl and Berenyt."

"That's true," Mykella said, "but Father's only been gone two days. Joramyl is already acting as Lord-Protector, and not one of us has been asked about anything."

"Why would he ask us?" questioned Rachylana.

"Mykella knows more about the finances than anyone," Salyna pointed out. "She knows more than Father or Uncle Joramyl did. She's the one who discovered the missing golds."

"He probably should have asked you about that." Rachylana's tone was grudging.

"We need to get ready to meet him." Mykella rose from the table.

Once they had washed up, Mykella led the way down the wide western corridor on the upper level, past Jeraxylt's quarters, still sealed, and the Lord-Protector's private apartments, also sealed.

When they walked past Chalmyr and into the formal study, Mykella could not have said that she was in the slightest surprised to find Joramyl behind her father's table-desk, at least the desk she had thought of as her father's. Nor was she particularly amazed to see Berenyt there, although he was standing beside the desk.

"If all of you would be seated." Joramyl gestured to the four chairs set in a semicircle before the desk.

Mykella recalled that there were usually only three chairs there.

After waiting until the four were seated, Joramyl went on. "Everything has been arranged for your father's funeral tomorrow. There will be a week of mourning following the ceremonies. The procession will be public, along the avenue and in front of the palace, the interment and final blessing private, in keeping with tradition. Do you have any questions?"

"Who will do the blessing?" asked Salyna.

"Would you like to, since you asked?" inquired Joramyl. "I had thought that Mykella might offer the statement of his life, since she is the eldest."

Salyna nodded.

"Is that acceptable to you, Rachylana?" asked Joramyl.

"Yes."

A silence descended on the study. Mykella waited, unwilling to be the one to speak and wanting Joramyl to be the one to commit himself.

Joramyl cleared his throat. "Now . . . uncomfortable as it may be, we need to talk about your future." The Lord-Protector-select's words were mild.

Mykella could sense the calculation and the disdain behind the politeness. "Now? We have not even had Father's funeral."

"By the end of the week after the funeral, of course, you will all retire to your father's hill villa for a half season of mourning. Before then, you will all have a chance to see and meet the envoy from Midcoast. If necessary, we can begin the negotiations for Rachylana's match and marriage. I understand that the Landarch's heir will be making an offer for your hand as well, Mykella, as will Seltyr Gheortyn for yours, Salyna."

"Salyna isn't old enough to be married to anyone," Mykella said quietly.

"She needs the protection of a strong consort, especially now," suggested Berenyt. "So do you and Rachylana."

"And you think that the princeling of Midcoast would be strong enough for Rachylana?" asked Mykella.

"There are other possibilities," ventured Berenyt.

"What else do you suggest?"

"Cousins have married," Berenyt said.

Joramyl merely offered the slightest of smiles.

"You and Rachylana?" asked Mykella, knowing full well that that was exactly what Berenyt had in mind.

"I would leave that decision to Rachylana, after she talks with you and Salyna." Berenyt smiled.

"You three should discuss such matters," added Joramyl, gazing pointedly at Mykella. "Your father did wish his successors to be of his blood."

Mykella looked blankly out the window toward the public gardens beyond the avenue before the palace. If Berenyt married Rachylana, no one would ever complain, not loudly, that Joramyl had succeeded her father, because both bloodlines would be united in their children. But . . . it was wrong.

Yet, if she challenged Joramyl and Berenyt, she would be acting against her own sister's desires. And what could she really do? Could what she had learned sustain her against Joramyl and the leaders of the Southern Guards?

Still . . . now was not the time and place for confrontation. If she had to fight, it would be on her terms.

After a moment, she inclined her head politely. "That is true. He did wish his successor to be of his blood, and his successor will be."

Berenyt relaxed ever so slightly. Joramyl did not, although he smiled broadly. "I'm sure he would have been glad to know that you intend to support his wishes."

"I have always been a dutiful daughter," Mykella replied, inclining her head, "and his wishes are and will be my command."

"After you three talk and agree on what you wish, and until matters are formalized, of course," Joramyl added, "we will entertain the envoy of Prince Skrelyn."

"Of course," Mykella said politely.

Joramyl stood. "You are all well-bred and most intelligent young women, and you know that I have your best interests at heart. As close as I was to your father, I want to see you all matched suitably and happily, and I know that you understand that." He smiled warmly.

Mykella rose and inclined her head to her uncle. "You are most kind, and, as you suggested, we will talk over these things. It is difficult to try to be practical when we have lost both a brother and a father in such a short time, but we know your advice is meant for the best, and we thank you."

"We do," murmured Salyna.

Rachylana merely nodded politely before the three sisters took their leave.

None of the three spoke until they returned to the parlor.

Once the door was closed, Rachylana glared at Mykella. "Do you want me to have to wed that barbarian from Midcoast?" asked Rachylana. "Is that what you two want?"

"No," Mykella said firmly. "What I want is for you not to be pushed into things. If we all agree right now, then Joramyl and Berenyt will push you around for the rest of your life. You have one thing they want, and that's the security of your being Father's daughter. You will write a note to Uncle Joramyl saying that you are extremely fond of Berenyt and that you know he is most fond of you, and that everyone has observed this. At the same time, you feel it is not seemly or respectful to make a commitment to marrying Berenyt until at least several weeks after Father's memorial." Mykella looked hard at the redhead. "You do not wish to do anything disrespectful to Father or his memory, and you are certain that Uncle Joramyl would not wish that either, but you look forward to the time when it is seemly to make such a commitment."

"That seems better," suggested Salyna.

"What if he presses me?" Rachylana looked from Salyna to Mykella. "Then what?"

"Tell him that's what you want," replied Mykella. "It is, isn't it?" After the briefest of pauses, she added, "But tell him that you just can't have it made public right now."

Rachylana looked helplessly toward the window, then the floor. "I don't want to lose Berenyt and get married off to some Midcoast barbarian."

"He won't press you, not until after he's invested formally as Lord-Protector," Mykella said. "If he does it could become public, and that might raise the question of why he pressed, and that might suggest that his claim to being Lord-Protector isn't that strong. After all, a brother has never inherited yet."

"That's because there have always been sons," Salyna pointed out.

"That's true," said Mykella, "but Uncle Joramyl wants things to go smoothly. He always has. But, if you want Berenyt to respect you, you have to hold fast on not making a commitment this moment."

"What if he insists?"

"Tell him that, if he won't respect your respecting your father, how can he expect you or anyone to respect him? You can say it more politely than that," Mykella said dryly.

"Mykella's right about that," Salyna said.

"You're not the one who has to face him," Rachylana said.

"No . . . we're the ones who'll end up in Dereka and Southgate," snapped Salyna.

Rachylana sighed. "I know that . . . but I worry."

Don't we all? But Mykella only nodded.

49

That evening, after a cold dinner, Salyna followed Mykella back to her chamber.

"What do you want, little sister?" asked Mykella gently.

"Rachylana's worried, Mykella," Salyna said quietly.

"Why should she be worried?" replied Mykella. "We went over this earlier today. Joramyl will allow Rachylana a little time before Berenyt asks formally for her hand, whether he loves her or not, and she'll become the wife of the future Lord-Protector of Tempre. That's what she wants more than anything, isn't it?"

"She thinks you'll do something stupid, like try to poison Joramyl, and that you'll be killed, and we'll be exiled."

Mykella laughed, a low and ironic sound. "You can tell her that I never once thought of poisoning anyone, not after I saw what it did to Father."

"Father? You think he was poisoned?"

"I can't prove it to anyone. But he was healthy. He had a glass of wine, and he had a seizure. He was dead in less than half a glass. That all happened less than half a season after Jeraxylt died in a sparring accident that probably wasn't an accident at all. Most convenient, don't you think?"

"I had wondered." Salyna's face crumpled, and her eyes brightened. "But what can we do? You can't . . . Either it was all the way Uncle Joramyl said it was . . . or . . ." She said nothing for a moment, before asking, "If you're right, who would believe it?"

Mykella nodded. "And if anyone poisoned anyone now . . . I'm most certain everyone would look at me. For all your swordplay, you're still seen as too sweet, and Rachylana has everything to lose. So you can tell Rachylana that I have no intention of poisoning anyone."

"And then they'll send you to Dereka and me to Southgate."

"That's possible." Mykella didn't want to let her sister know any-thing, for Salyna's own protection. "We'll probably be safer there than here. Rachylana will be safe enough." *At least until she has a son or two.*

"What . . . about you? How do you feel about going to Dereka?"

"I understand it's not too bad a place, except that it's cold and dry."

"Do you know what he's like?"

"He's supposed to be warm and kind, and caring. But that doesn't seem to matter, does it?" replied Mykella.

"But . . . Mother loved Father . . ."

"They were fortunate," Mykella pointed out.

"What will happen, Mykella?" Salyna's voice was small.

"We'll have to see, won't we? But there's no use in worrying right this moment." Mykella wrapped her arms around Salyna, all too con-scious that her younger sister was the taller.

Once Salyna had left, Mykella reached out to the green-blackness below and slipped through the stone down to the Table chamber.

There was not the slightest sign of the pinkish purple tinge that she associated with the Ifrit, for which she was thankful, as she stepped up to the Table.

First she sought out Berenyt. When the mists cleared, not surpris-ingly, the Table revealed that he was entertaining a redheaded young woman in his chambers. Mykella thought she was the one who had been eyeing Jeraxylt at the season-turn parade, although she couldn't be certain.

Mykella released the image, shaking her head, although she wasn't about to tell Rachylana about Berenyt's interests, for more than a few reasons.

Next, she sought out Joramyl, who was, surprisingly, exactly where he should have been, in a sitting room with Cheleyza. From what Mykella could determine, he was trying to reassure her about some-thing, although he was smiling warmly and confidently.

Arms-Commander Nephryt and Commander Demyl were in a small chamber, somewhere she did not recognize, talking intently and intensely. In turn, Mykella let that image lapse.

For a time, she looked down at the mirror surface of the Table. Then she swallowed, and concentrated on Undercommander Areyst. She could feel the relief when she saw the image. He was seated at a writing desk, with stacks of papers on both sides, studying them and making notations, as if comparing one set to another, and noting the differences . . . or the discrepancies.

She let the images in the Table lapse.

What else could she do? She'd practiced with using light and sound, and, as the soarer had said, she could move unseen, and even kill. But now . . . all she could do was wait for tomorrow and trust that what she had planned would indeed work.

50

Mykella rose early on Quinti. She prepared herself for the ordeal of the funeral procession and memorial service, in all the ways that she could, including her dress, severe dark green and high-necked, trimmed in black. Her headscarf was black, but of shimmersilk—and had been her mother's—and her cloak was black. Under the long skirt of the gown, she did wear her black formal boots, well polished.

She forced herself to eat at breakfast, but kept to herself, even as she stood near her sisters, until the time for the ceremony. She said little as the three joined Joramyl, Cheleyza, and Berenyt, before a small honor guard escorted them to the small reviewing stand set up on the north side of the boulevard, directly in front of the wall enclosing the palace. More than a thousand people lined the space on the south side of the boulevard, crowding the area between the low wall that marked the northern edge of the public gardens and the edge of the boulevard. The warm spring sun doubtless had swelled the crowd.

As the late Lord-Protector's eldest surviving child, Mykella stood on the uppermost level of the stand, under a clear green sky, with a cool breeze blowing out of the northwest. To her right was Joramyl, and beyond him, Berenyt. To Berenyt's right was Lady Cheleyza. To Mykella's left were her sisters. Below the family were the Seltyrs and High Factors of Tempre—in effect the councilors of the city and more—and their wives.

"I can see the Southern Guards are leaving the Great Piers now," Joramyl said conversationally.

"It won't be that long now." Berenyt concealed his impatience badly, so much so that Mykella could have read it clearly even without her Talent.

Her eyes and senses went to Cheleyza, whose second life-thread was more pronounced, if thin. Mykella couldn't help but worry about what might happen to Rachylana, should she actually wed Berenyt, given Cheleyza's prior attempt at poisoning Rachylana. Mykella had no doubts that Cheleyza wanted her yet unborn offspring to become the ruler of Lanachrona, and that did not bode well for Rachylana.

As Berenyt had predicted, it was not that long before the funeral procession appeared, led by two Southern Guards riding on each side of a riderless horse whose saddle was draped in the blue of the Lord-Protector. Behind them rode Second Company, and all the officers and men wore black-edged blue mourning sashes. Directly following them was the caisson carrying the ceremonial coffin that contained the urn holding her father's ashes, drawn by four black horses.

Just before the caisson carrying her father's coffin, also draped in the blue of the Lord-Protector, drew abreast of the reviewing stand, Mykella stepped forward slightly. She drew upon the lifeweb darkness beneath her and Tempre and focused light around her . . . and then around the coffin, not enough to be blinding, but just enough, she hoped, so that all who watched saw the faint link of light between her and the coffin of the late Lord-Protector. Then she projected respect and honor for her father, the Lord-Protector, easing it out across the area, but she let that projection center on her as the caisson passed. The riders of Second Company looked back and those of First Company, following the caisson, also fixed their eyes upon the

Lord-Protector's daughter. Mykella remained motionless, but she did not bother to try to control the tears that rolled down her face.

Then, once the last of the riders had passed, she stepped back.

"How . . . did that happen . . . ?" murmured someone.

"Don't say a word," murmured Joramyl.

Mykella let tears continue to roll down her face as she watched the caisson heading into the palace grounds and toward the mausoleum on the hillside behind the palace.

After the last horseman in the procession had entered the palace gates, as Mykella walked down the steps toward the honor guard that would escort them to the mausoleum, Salyna slipped beside her.

"What did you do?" whispered Salyna. "They all looked at you. Joramyl got that stern stone-faced look he gets when he's displeased."

"I didn't do anything," Mykella lied, "except step forward a bit to pay my respects to Father—publicly."

"But everyone looked at you . . ."

Mykella certainly hoped so.

Joramyl certainly had felt both anger and worry, but he had said nothing to Mykella. Even so, she maintained a Talent shield around herself as she let the honor guard escort them through the plaza in front of the palace and then through the rear courtyard and the rear gate to the memorial garden around the private mausoleum—to the north and uphill from the regular palace gardens.

Once the urn had been removed from the coffin and carried to the granite presentation table under the front arch of the mausoleum, and everyone had assembled facing the small outer rotunda, Joramyl began the ceremony.

"We acknowledge that the Lord-Protector of Lanachrona has died, and that he has left a legacy of love and goodness bestowed on his family and people throughout a long and prosperous life. We are here to mourn his loss and offer our last formal farewell in celebration of his life." With that, he stepped back and nodded to Mykella.

Mykella stepped forward. She waited several moments before she began to speak, letting silence fall across the mausoleum and the area beyond. Her eyes traversed the three Southern Guard officers present, but she did not look sideways at Joramyl, nor at her sisters.

"Our father was the Lord-Protector of Lanachrona, but he was more than that. He was a good man, a caring man, and a trusting man, who loved his wife, his children, his larger family, and his people. He believed most deeply that the principal goal of a Lord-Protector was to protect his people, both from those outside the borders of Lanachrona and from those within our borders, for there are enemies in both places. He spent his efforts as Lord-Protector to assure peace and prosperity for all his people, and not just a favored few. And . . . to the end of his days, he believed in the goodness of those around him. We will miss him, and so will Lanachrona."

While her words were brief, Mykella did not know that she could have said more, or that more needed to be said.

After another silence, Salyna delivered the blessing. "In the name of the One and the Wholeness That Is, and Always Will Be . . ."

Mykella listened intently, but while Salyna almost choked on the words near the end, her voice remained firm, steady, and loving.

During the entire brief ceremony, Mykella had barely glanced in the direction of Undercommander Areyst, except one time in passing, not because she had not wished to do so, but because she felt that any favor she might show him might jeopardize his very life.

The honor guard re-formed below the steps of the mausoleum.

Joramyl turned to Mykella, a pleasant, but thoughtful look upon his face, an expression belying a mixture of anger and worry within him. "You were very . . . impressive today. I trust you will be equally supportive of your father's successor."

"I intend to be, Lord Joramyl. Like you, I am beholden to my father's legacy." She paused. "I apologize if my words are brief, but it has been a trying time." She did her best to offer an apologetic smile.

51

Mykella wasn't certain exactly how she made it through the rest of the day, replying to all sorts of meaningless platitudes politely. She was just thankful when she could plead exhaustion after a light supper and retire to her chamber.

As she closed the door, she realized she was thirsty, and she walked toward the side table by the bed. The tumbler there was empty, but the pitcher beside it had been refilled by the staff, most likely by Uleana, and she reached for it. Her hand stopped short. A bluish green aura surrounded the pitcher—the exact shade she'd perceived shrouding her father just before he died.

She bent over the pitcher and sniffed, but she could smell nothing.

For the briefest of moments, she thought about using the sight-shield to place the pitcher where Joramyl would use it, but that was not a good idea for two reasons. First, he had not moved into the palace and would not until after he was formally installed as Lord-Protector at noon the next day—far too soon, Mykella thought, but no one had asked her. In fact, she had only found out late in the afternoon. Second, as Salyna had pointed out, Berenyt would make certain that Mykella was blamed, and Berenyt would just become Lord-Protector sooner— and then he probably wouldn't even have to marry Rachylana.

Mykella snorted. If she'd drunk the poison, doubtless Joramyl would have claimed a brain weakness ran in the family.

She did make sure that the door bolt was fastened before she put out the lamps and climbed into bed. She was more than tired; she was exhausted.

The faintest click awakened her from a restless sleep. She could sense someone outside her door, and she immediately reached for the greenish darkness deep beneath the palace, even as she slipped from beneath the covers and to her feet, waiting.

The door bolt slowly slid open, and then the door opened. Despite the near pitch-darkness of the room, Mykella could make out that the slender but muscular figure who entered her chamber was garbed entirely in black, with even a tight-fitting black hood. She waited until he closed the door and edged toward the bed, a loop of something in his hand.

Using her Talent, she reached out and slashed at his life-thread node. Tiny threads sprayed away from him, and he pitched forward onto the stone floor. The *thud* was muffled by the old rug at the foot of the bed.

After cloaking herself and the dead man with her sight-shield, Mykella eased open her door. As she half-suspected, none of the guards was anywhere in sight. Although she was no weakling, it did take her quite some time to drag the assassin's figure to the staircase, where she rolled the body off the top landing.

How far the dead assassin rolled down the steps she didn't know. Nor did she care.

She made her way back to her chamber where she rebolted the door, and then took the desk chair from before her writing table and propped it under the door handle lever. While it might not hold against a determined assailant, anyone who could break it to get inside would definitely make enough noise to wake her.

She smiled grimly.

Her dear uncle was obviously worried. The fact that he was suggested that his support among the Seltyrs and High Factors was not all that he might have liked. She hoped so.

She also hoped that she could get some sleep. She needed it.

52

Mykella was the first in the breakfast room—for what was to be her last meal there, at least according to her uncle. Salyna and Rachylana entered just behind her.

"Did you hear?" asked Salyna. "They found an assassin on the main staircase early this morning."

"How did they know he was an assassin?" asked Rachylana. "No one would claim that."

"He was dead," Salyna said. "That's what Pattyn said—he was the head of the guards on morning duty. The man was wearing assassin's black, and he had a dagger and a garrote."

"The guards killed him?" asked Mykella, sitting down at her place, all too conscious of the empty seat where her father had always seated himself. Her eyes burned, and she looked down for a moment, then swallowed before she raised her head.

"No one knows," Salyna replied. "Pattyn said he was dead, and there wasn't a mark on him." She poured herself cider.

The serving girl brought Mykella tea, but Mykella studied it for a moment, deciding it was safe, before taking a sip. The fact that the night guards had not found the body suggested in whose pay they were. It was going to be a very long day, and it had barely begun.

Rachylana glanced at Mykella. "There have been too many strange things happening, like the light that fell on you yesterday."

"It fell on Father's coffin," Mykella pointed out.

"And on you."

"She is the eldest, Rachylana," Salyna said. "What other heir does Father have?"

Mykella hoped her younger sister hadn't guessed too much.

"Daughters can't inherit."

"Can't . . . or haven't?" asked Mykella. "There's nothing in the charter or the archives that forbids it. In fact, Mykel made a proclamation that declared Rachyla his heir if he died first. She died before him, though."

"You've looked? I would have thought as much," sniffed Rachylana. "Even if Joramyl and Berenyt didn't exist, just how many of the Southern Guards would accept a woman? Old proclamation or no old proclamation?"

"Rachylana . . . that's . . ." Salyna shook her head.

"Who would know?" asked Mykella. "There's always been a male heir."

"I still say that too many strange things are happening," Rachylana finally said, after swallowing some cider.

"Like the doors that opened in the palace with no one around," added Salyna quickly, clearly thankful not to have to discuss the possibility of a woman as Lord- or Lady-Protector. "One of the guards even found a silver in the middle of the lower corridor. But that was weeks ago."

"Some factor probably dropped it. He wouldn't have missed it," Mykella pointed out. "Some people can't see what's before their faces."

Salyna gave the slightest of headshakes, and Mykella wished she could have taken the words back.

"What are you wearing today, Rachylana?" Mykella asked quickly.

"A new gown of light blue, I think . . ."

Mykella knew she would have to work not to reveal more than she already had until the time was right for her to act, and patience had never been her greatest virtue.

53

At just before a half glass before noon, Salyna and Mykella walked down to the rotunda inside the main entrance to the palace. Rachylana was already there, talking with Berenyt, who wore the full dress uniform of a Southern Guard.

Rachylana looked at Mykella. "That long black cloak makes it look like you're still at the funeral."

"I can wear mourning garb if I wish," Mykella replied. "It is appropriate. Father's memorial was only yesterday, and Joramyl said we were in mourning." Actually, under the cloak, Mykella had chosen what she wore with care—everything was black, except for the vest of brilliant blue she had retailored to fit her, if not as carefully as Wyandra would have. While she appeared to be wearing a full skirt, it was actually a formal split skirt for riding, not that the difference was noticeable under the cloak.

"Uncle Joramyl said mourning began after the investiture," replied Rachylana.

"I don't recall anything like that," Mykella replied politely.

Salyna glanced to Berenyt, as if to ask for an intercession.

"I heard about the assassin," said Berenyt. "You'll all be safer in the hill villa. I've asked Father to send two squads with you as guards."

More like gaolers, Mykella thought.

"You will visit, won't you?" asked Rachylana.

"I wouldn't think otherwise." Berenyt bowed. "I have to leave you now and meet up with Father. He wouldn't wish his heir apparent to be late."

"No . . . you should be with him," Mykella said politely, "especially today."

Salyna frowned for a moment, but said nothing.

Berenyt smiled and turned, then walked briskly along the corridor, the sound of his boots echoing in the near-empty hallway, a space that normally would have held at least a score of people doing business with the Lanachronan functionaries housed on the main level of the palace.

"He's most elegant," observed Rachylana.

"He does look very handsome," Salyna replied.

"There's an old saying about handsome is as handsome does," Mykella said blandly. She still couldn't forget that Berenyt had been with the plotters at all too many meetings. That made him as guilty as his father, whether or not Rachylana thought she loved him.

Rachylana sniffed, and Mykella could sense her thoughts—*You're just jealous.*

Mykella wouldn't have wanted Berenyt on a silver platter, even if he hadn't been her cousin. Nor did she want Rachylana to have him, because sooner or later, that would be the death of her sister. In any case, Berenyt wasn't anywhere close to the man her father had been, nor a fraction of the man Undercommander Areyst was. She pushed away that thought for the moment.

"Ladies?" An undercaptain of the Southern Guards appeared, with Lady Cheleyza behind him. "It's time for you to take your places."

Mykella followed the undercaptain and Cheleyza, with her sisters behind her, for the short distance beyond the rotunda to the main entrance. There, they took their positions on the fourth of the five low and wide stone steps that led up the main palace entry. The topmost step was empty, by tradition, because the Lord-Protector-select had to ascend that last step alone. Cheleyza stood on the left side of the open space that formed an aisle down the center of the steps, alone, and Mykella and her sisters stood on the right. The lower three steps held the various ministers and senior functionaries, and their families. Mykella caught sight of Lord Gharyk and Jylara. Both looked worried, as well they should be, thought Mykella, at least once Joramyl became Lord-Protector.

The public crowds on the avenue beyond the front wall to the palace grounds were modest, with possibly fewer spectators than had shown for Feranyt's funeral, but since the courtyard was not that large, and since two of the three Southern Guard companies assigned to the palace were drawn up in mounted formation, the area before the palace and along the avenue to the south appeared full enough. The green sky was slightly hazed over, giving it a silver cast, and a light and warm breeze blew out of the southeast. Asterta stood full just below its zenith, its greenish tinge barely visible in the bright daylight. Was that a favorable omen? Mykella hoped so.

She shifted her weight from one boot to the other, then strengthened her link to the greenish-black darkness below the palace, building up her shields, almost against her body. The last thing she needed was someone shooting her from the cover of the crowd, and she wouldn't have put that, or anything, past Joramyl.

The investiture was a simple ceremony. Joramyl would ride in from the east side, accompanied by Berenyt, dismount, and present himself to the three senior officers of the Southern Guards, waiting on the east side below the steps, and then to the Seltyrs and High Factors on the west. After offering the traditional question and bowing to each group, he would slowly ascend the steps. Once he reached the top step he would turn and offer the ritual statement. Then he would walk down, alone, mount, and ride off—if only to the rear courtyard.

Very simple, and very traditional. Too traditional. Mykella turned her attention to the courtyard before her.

A single trumpet heralded Joramyl's approach. Wearing the brilliant blue dress tunic of the Lord-Protector, he rode slowly down the open space between the arrayed Southern Guard companies and the palace. Behind him rode Berenyt in his formal dress uniform.

The two reined up short of the senior Southern Guard officers and the Seltyrs and High Factors, then dismounted and handed the reins of their mounts to two waiting guards. Joramyl stepped forward and nodded to Arms-Commander Nephryt before turning and walking several paces toward the Seltyrs and High Factors, to whom he offered the ritual question, "Will you accept me as Lord-Protector?"

Mykella sensed that the murmured approval was somewhere between perfunctory and grudging.

After inclining his head to the Seltyrs and High Factors, Joramyl slowly started up the stone steps toward the outer columns of the rotunda, columns clearly added later, because they had already become rounded and pitted in places, while the stone of the original structure looked as though it had been built within the past few years. The Lord-Protector-select was followed by Berenyt, as Joramyl's heir apparent.

Although Mykella had begun to draw even more upon the darkness deep beneath the palace as soon as Joramyl had ridden toward the steps, she waited until Joramyl reached the third step before dropping her cloak and stepping sideways and onto the topmost step, where she looked down upon Joramyl.

"What . . . don't be a fool, Mykella," said Joramyl, his tone dismissive and contemptuous.

Blazing light flared around the Lord-Protector's daughter as Mykella focused those energies with which she had practiced and practiced.

"You killed my brother, and you poisoned my father."

Joramyl's mouth opened as Mykella's voice carried across the steps toward the Southern Guards and the crowd beyond the low front wall of the palace courtyard, her words amplified by her Talent—amplified and carrying the utter conviction of truth. "All this was done in shadows and silence. You cannot bear to have the truth come out, and that truth will kill you here where you stand!"

Without touching Joramyl—except with her Talent—she severed his life-thread node, and he pitched backward down the stone steps.

Behind him, Berenyt's eyes widened.

"You, Berenyt, plotted with your father so that you might become Lord-Protector in turn. The truth will kill you as well."

Berenyt's mouth opened, his face ashen, before Mykella cut his life-thread node. Like his father, he toppled silently.

"No . . ." murmured Rachylana. "No . . ." She swayed, and Salyna grasped her to keep her from falling.

A muffled scream issued from Cheleyza, who crumpled where she stood.

Mykella ignored her, and, in the stunned silence that followed, took the four steps down the stone stairs, decreasing slightly the intensity of the light that surrounded her. Then she stopped and surveyed the three officers of the Southern Guards.

"Will you have a Lady-Protector of Tempre?" she asked more quietly. "Or will you try to hide treachery as well?"

"You? No woman will rule Tempre while I'm Arms-Commander." Nephryt's saber slashed toward Mykella's seemingly unprotected shoulder.

His face turned ashen as the blade shattered against her unseen Talent shield.

Mykella reached out with her knife-edged Talent probes and ripped the node of his life-thread apart.

Nephryt's mouth remained open as he fell face-first onto the stone pavement of the plaza, his body landing on one or two fragments of the shattered saber.

Mykella turned to the two remaining guard officers. She smiled. "I believe that takes care of Arms-Commander Nephryt's objections."

Commander Demyl looked from Nephryt's fallen form to Mykella, then back to the body. He swallowed.

"You may leave Tempre this moment," Mykella said to Demyl. "If you do not, you will never leave."

Demyl glanced at the body on the plaza before him once more. "Much good it will do you."

"Go, traitor!" This time Mykella's voice rang across the plaza. "Be not seen in Tempre again, nor in Lanachrona!"

Demyl turned and walked woodenly toward the Southern Guard who held his mount. The crowd beyond the low stone wall watched as he mounted and then spurred his mount out through the gates.

Mykella turned to the undercommander.

Areyst looked to Mykella. "There has never been a Lady-Protector of Tempre."

"There's a first time for everything. Before Mykel, there had never been a Lord-Protector," she replied. "Interestingly enough, Mykel named Rachyla as his heir, and even more interesting, that proclamation was removed from the archive." She paused momentarily. "If I name you as Arms-Commander, will you serve me and the people of Lanachrona honestly and with all your abilities?"

Areyst inclined his head. "I serve Lanachrona, and I can do no less, Lady-Protector."

Mykella sensed his feelings—both dismay and respect . . . and a grudging admiration.

Those would have to do. She doubted that Mykel the Great had gained any more at the beginning, either.

Then she turned and walked to the Seltyrs and High Factors, inclining her head to the group of twenty-odd. She could sense the absolute fear radiating from them. "Honored Seltyrs, High Factors, will you have an honest and true Lady-Protector of Tempre? One who will not divert your tariffs or plot in secret and silence? One who will not stoop to murdering his brother and his nephew? One who will hold your liberties as dear as her own?"

There was a moment of silence. Then Almardyn and Hasenyt exchanged glances. Hasenyt nodded to Almardyn.

Almardyn cleared his throat. "Your father stood for us, and we would be unwise indeed to refuse a Lady-Protector of your power and his honesty."

Scarcely a ringing endorsement, but an endorsement. "You will have the benefit of all my Talent and all the honesty my father prized so dearly, even at the cost of his own life."

"We accept you as Lady-Protector," replied the two.

After a long moment, a chorus followed. "We accept . . ."

Mykella inclined her head once more, then turned. Grudging as it was, they would honor it, and she would honor her pledge, but she still held her Talent shields tightly.

As she walked back toward the steps, she stopped before Areyst. As Lady-Protector her choices would always be limited, but in this, at least, she could choose the best. "If you would follow me, Arms-Commander."

"I am no heir, Lady-Protector."

"For now, I have no other heir, and Tempre and Lanachrona deserve the best."

Areyst lowered his head. "I did not . . ."

Mykella smiled. "I know. Follow me."

Mykella turned and walked up the steps, sensing the approval sweeping the crowd—and the Southern Guards—of her designation of Areyst as heir apparent.

Much as she might have liked to have designated Salyna as her heir, that would have been more than the factors and Seltyrs could have accepted . . . and she could allow Salyna and Rachylana better choices than her sisters would otherwise have possessed.

When Mykella stood on the topmost step and turned, she surveyed the courtyard and those below and beyond the wall on the avenue for a long moment. Perhaps, as the soarer had said, she had saved her world. That might have been, but there was no doubt that she had saved her land, whether any of those before her would ever fully understand or appreciate that.

Then, she spoke firmly and quietly, though her voice carried to all, as she offered the ancient and original pledge that had not been used in centuries—and now, she knew why.

"I swear and affirm that I will protect and preserve the lives and liberties of all citizens of Tempre and Lanachrona, and that I will employ all Talent and skills necessary to do so, at all times, and in all places, so that peace and prosperity may govern this land and her people."

Her eyes flicked to the Arms-Commander—heir apparent . . . who would be more, much more.